WITHOUT A WORD,
SQUIRE FIRED...

Stands Twice staggered back a few steps from the impact of the ball. He was stopped by other warriors standing behind him. He slumped against them, and they eased him gently down onto the frozen ground.

A wail arose from one of the lodges, and a woman burst forth, still howling her grief. She raced to her man and knelt over him, the caterwauling never ceasing.

"Squire!" Melton said in shock. "How could you . . ."

"Shut up!" Squire hissed. A few of the warriors were heading for their lodges—and their weapons. "Who be leadin' ye now?" Squire roared, making the others stop.

There was confusion. Then another man stepped forward. He wasn't tall, but his chest was broad and powerful. He had a bull neck and a thick scar that ran from the top center of his forehead down the left side of his nose.

"I am Kills-Many-Sioux, war leader."

"Ye saw what I did to that fool," he said, pointing his rifle at the Crow's body. "Bring up our horses. And get them women to quit that wailin'."

Berkley Books by John Legg

WINTER RAGE
BLACKFOOT DAWN

BLACKFOOT DAWN

John Legg

BERKLEY BOOKS, NEW YORK

BLACKFOOT DAWN

A Berkley Book / published by arrangement with
the author

PRINTING HISTORY
Berkley edition / February 1993

ISBN: 0-425-13647-7

A BERKLEY BOOK ® ™ 757,375
Berkley Books are published by The Berkley Publishing Group,
200 Madison Avenue, New York, New York 10016.
The name "BERKLEY" and the "B" logo
are trademarks belonging to Berkley Publishing Corporation.

PRINTED IN THE UNITED STATES OF AMERICA

10 9 8 7 6 5 4 3 2 1

For my mother,
Joan Meneely Legg,
without whom
none of this
would have been possible.
Thanks, Mom, I love you.

·1·

RENDEZVOUS

The massive black stallion thundered into rendezvous. People yelled and scattered as the giant atop the midnight horse bellowed a war cry and fired his rifle into the air.

Nathaniel Squire jammed his rifle into the scabbard and yelled again—a long, ululating shriek of joyous savagery. He slid off the left side of the horse, bounced once, then twice on moccasined feet and then swung his six-foot-eight-inch, two hundred seventy-five pound body to the other side, hopped, then flipped back into the heavy leather saddle.

Mountain men, Indians, and squaws began lining up, making a wide lane for him to roar down. Most shouted or cheered; many fired off their pistols or rifles, creating a raucous welcome.

Squire flipped off the right side, bounced once and over the saddle to the other side and back and over and back and then into the saddle, the horse still racing, its great head bobbing to the thundering rhythm of the iron-shod hooves, its flaxen tail and mane flowing in the rush of the wind.

By now Squire was through the main portion of the sprawling, haphazard camp of mountain men and Indians, and he slowed the horse. Finally, he stopped and turned back toward the camp. "Ye done well, *Noir Astre*," he said softly, patting the horse's long, glossy mane. He always called the horse by its French name, thinking it sounded better than Dark Star.

The horse was a perfect match for the man. Nathaniel Squire was a giant who cut a wide swath wherever he went. With his long, pale-colored hair, shaggy mustache, and tawny beard down to his chest and his ferocious visage, he was quite a sight. The faded, watery blue eyes did not soften his commanding presence any.

"*Allons,*" he said, kicking the horse softly on the sides. He didn't use the spurs favored by so many mountain men, nor the quirt preferred by most of the Indians. Instead he used his hard heels, covered by the soft leather of his moccasins.

The horse started slowly, gathering its stride. Soon he was racing, his long, powerful legs stretching, haunches bunching and exploding. As they charged into the camp again, Squire pulled the two huge horse pistols from the scabbards on each side of the saddlehorn. He bellowed once more—a long, pulsing, hair-raising war cry—as a tide of noise rose from the assembled throng.

A mountain man, jug in hand, staggered out into his path fifty yards ahead, arms held out in welcome, but a few friends pulled him out of the way as Squire roared past, firing one pistol, then the other. He jammed the weapons away, and yanked the horse to a halt so sharp the animal nearly sat on its haunches. *Noir Astre* reared, standing almost perpendicular to the dusty ground, pawing the air. Squire's war whoop breached the hot afternoon once more.

The horse's huge frame landed back on the turf, and Squire roared, "I be *L'on Farouche,* the meanest, drinkin'est, fightin'est, cussin'est, and ruttin'est chil' that e'er stalked these here goddamn Shinin' Mountains, and I be here to fight, fornicate, and raise the hair of any niggur, red or white, who stands in my way."

No one doubted him. "And," he pointed to the South where three riders were charging hell for leather toward them, "here be my own lads comin'."

Li'l Jim—no one knew him by anything else—and Hank Carpenter zigzagged and crisscrossed, weaving an intricate pattern, firing their rifles and pistols, yelling and roaring. Abner Train thundered after them in a straight line, his bulky man-boy body low, his face on the side of the horse's neck.

All three jarred to a stop near Squire, rearing their horses, Abner's big body still leaning forward, hugging the horse tightly, though the cocky bantam Li'l Jim and the slight, slender Carpenter held on easily, both waving their caps in the air. Squire whooped, grinning, as the three horses landed back on their feet, snuffling and shaking their shaggy, full manes.

Train was a big young man. Though not as large as Squire, he was tall and powerfully built. He had a broad, open face, and a wild thatch of light brown hair. Despite his size and age—just past nineteen—he could barely raise fluff on his face.

Li'l Jim was a short, wiry youth of seventeen. He was a cocky young man whose recklessness often got him into trouble. Still, he would back off from no one. His sharp-featured face was highlighted by soft brown eyes and long lashes. He hated those eyes and lashes, believing they gave him a girlish look.

Carpenter was about the same size as Li'l Jim, with the same slender build. More than one man had looked into the sixteen-year-old's frank green eyes, had seen the slim, almost delicate physique, and figured Carpenter for slim pickings. All had regretted it.

"Where is yer plews?" someone called out. "Couldn't the great Nathaniel Squire make any beaver come this year?" There were a few laughs and snorts, but not too many. Squire was not a man that many wanted to mess with in any circumstance. He was as mean as he was big. He had acquired his nickname—*L'on Farouche,* which meant wild man or crazy man—after he had slaughtered half a Blackfoot camp when some of those warriors had killed his mentor. Few were foolhardy enough to challenge him. The nickname and reputation were well-deserved.

He smiled now, though, after glaring at the crowd for a few seconds, teeth gleaming whitely through the thick tangle of mustache and beard. "My plews be comin', lad," he said. "And there be a heap of 'em, too. More'n any of ye buff'lo-humpin' peckerwoods e'er seen at one time."

He looked back to where the three young men had come from, watching, waiting. Within seconds all could hear the pounding of hundreds of hooves.

Then with a roaring, a firing of guns and much shouting came almost two dozen young mountain men, led by a burly, hard-edged old-timer in the mountains. The man, Slocum Peters, pulled to a wild stop near Squire. Behind them came the horses and mules, close to eighty of them all told, being pushed by a small knot of yelling, screaming, nervous camp helpers and cavvy handlers.

The horde tore into camp, the heavy packs of beaver plews and supplies bouncing wildly on the backs of the animals. Over the din Squire could hear the inventive profanity of Homer Bellows and his young helper, Cletus Ransom, cursing men and animals with equal fervor.

The horses passed by, Ransom and the others pushing them to a clear spot where they could have fresh grass after their run. Bellows stopped near Squire, as did several Indian women and the man who brought up the rear with quiet dignity.

Colonel Leander Melton was a big man, though not nearly so big as Squire. He had a broad, fleshy face with a generous mouth, bright, alert brown eyes, and a long, thin nose. Prominent teeth gave him a faintly horse-like appearance, but it did little to detract from his dignity or joviality.

Melton had organized this brigade of trappers back in St. Louis almost a year earlier. It was he who had hired Nathaniel Squire and who had enough sense to let the big man run the show. It had produced what likely would be a profitable season.

Homer Bellows, on the other hand, was of average height and thin as a rail. The faded blue eyes surrounded by a heavy lacework of wrinkles attested to his life in the open. His head, topped by a thatch of pale hair, sat on a long, scrawny neck dominated by a large, bulbous Adam's apple. The protuberance bobbled vigorously whenever he talked, which was often.

Slocum Peters was a tall, fierce-looking man with something of a potbelly. His full, red beard hid some scars and added to his savage countenance, counteracting the oddness of his big, jutting ears.

Except for Melton, all the men wore fringed buckskin pants and shirts. All were decorated with beads, quills, and bits of metal. Squire's outfit was the most elaborate. Melton stood out in his Eastern finery and tall, curled-brim D'Orsay-style top hat. He looked dignified, though rather out of place amid the rough, weathered mountain men.

Before any of them could say anything, three French-Canadians pushed forward out of the crowd. All three wore heavily fringed buckskin pants, brightly colored osnaburg shirts and wide, colorful sashes around their waists. Despite the day's warmth, they wore red knit caps, the tops curled over and held jauntily at the sides with silver crosses.

"Well, well, look at dis," one of the three said. Etienne Gravant grinned, showing yellowed teeth, with a few gaps from where others had been lost. He was a short, wizened man of about sixty years old. His face was full of wrinkles, his eyes were faded, and his hands gnarled from long, hard use. "De great *L'on Farouche* come ridin' here wit' a few plews and act de big man, eh?"

Melton looked horrified, thinking Squire would kill the man. But Squire just grinned and dismounted. "Ye ain't seen so many plews in all yer days in the mountains, ye little Frog fart," he said. Though he had chuckled, he seemed a little reserved. He grabbed Gravant in a bear hug, though that, too, seemed less enthusiastic than might have been expected.

The French-Canadian looked like a child in Squire's embrace. "How are ye, *mon ami?*"

"*Bien. Trés bien,*" Gravant replied, still grinning.

Squire greeted the others, each in turn. "Marcel, Pierre."

Marcel Ledoux was about Squire's age, 35 or so. He was a short, blocky man, with a big chest, powerful shoulders, and heavy, strong legs. A tangle of black beard covered most of his face. So thick was it that he had years ago stopped trying to keep it trimmed.

Pierre Dumoulin was the youngest of the three French-Canadians, about 30. He had trapped on and off with Gravant and Ledoux for years. He was of medium height and weight, though faintly pear-shaped in build. Squire didn't know him all that well, though he had met him several times.

"An' who are dese odders wit' you, *mon ami?*" Gravant asked.

Squire made introductions, and Gravant said, "You will stay wit' us, no?"

"*Non, mon ami.* Near ye, *oui.* But we be havin' too many people and too many animals for us to be settin' in your camp. But we'll be close to hand." He harbored a little resentment against Gravant from times long past. Not enough any longer to keep him from being friendly, but enough that he kept Gravant at a little distance.

"*Bon,*" Gravant said. He knew how Squire felt and saw his acceptance as something of a warming toward him by Squire. "Now, come wit' us, you an' your friends. We sit by de fire and talk, eh? Your friends, they come too, *non?*"

"*Non.*" Squire said. "Leastways not 'til we be gettin' our own camp set up."

Gravant nodded.

"Where be your camp?"

"Dere." Gravant pointed. "I will show you, eh. Dere is a place nearby you can use."

"A goddamn desert, I reckon." Squire growled.

"*Mais non, mon ami.* It is good. Dere is plenty of grass, close to de water."

"How come this paradise ain't been took up yet?" Squire asked, eyes twinkling with the beginnings of humor. "Ye and your *amis* stink so bad nobody'll be takin' up quarters near ye?"

Gravant laughed. "I t'ink dey're just afraid of us true *hommes.*" Gravant grabbed his crotch and laughed crudely.

"What a pile of buff'lo shit," Squire said, roaring with laughter. He decided suddenly that maybe he had been holding a grudge for too long. Maybe it was time to forget the past, he thought. "But it don't matter none. Lead on."

Squire, Gravant, Ledoux, Dumoulin, Melton, Train, Li'l Jim, Carpenter, and the Indian women walked east toward the Green River. Homer Bellows rode off to where the others had gathered with the horses and mules.

-2-

Nathaniel Squire waved at people as the group walked through the camp, stopped for a word or two of greeting, a quick clasp on the shoulder, or an exuberant handshake. The place was alive with sounds, smells, and colors. Rather than one big camp, it was actually a series of smaller camps—Crows here, Shoshonis there, Flatheads and Nez Perces nearby.

There were shooting contests in several spots, with the participants whooping and hollering, offering catcalls and shouts and curses. In a tree-shaded site along the Green River, a handful of half-drunk mountain men tossed tomahawks at a battered stump, alternately laughing and groaning as they won or lost.

Suddenly two horses roared past, one carrying an Indian rider, the other a white. The two men slapped at their ponies, racing, while Squire and his friends could see a pretty, young Indian girl standing nervously alone to one side waiting to see who would claim her.

Small groups of men sat around playing three-card monte, euchre, or the hand game. Jugs, cups, and bottles of whiskey were always nearby. Men, women, and children wandered in and out of the various camps.

Three fights broke out as the small procession crossed the camp, each drawing a small but vocal crowd, and some freewheeling wagering.

Squire greeted Bill Sublette's partner, Robert Campbell, who looked a little harried trying to keep track of all the plews

7

he was bringing in and all his store-bought goods going out.

Rough-hewn logs, made flat by hasty treatment with axes and adzes, were laid across barrels all through the camp, with shouting, sweating men selling jugs of watered-down whiskey at hugely inflated prices. The results could be seen all over, with drunken mountain men and Indians staggering through the cookfires, knocking over tipis and cooking tripods, saddles, and other equipment.

Finally Gravant stopped. "'Ere," he said simply, waving his arms about with a flourish.

The others looked around. It was, Squire had to admit, though not aloud, a decent looking spot. It was far enough away from the main rendezvous area to give them some peace. The grass had not been cropped down too much by the thousands of horses around, and the section of the Green River here, in a sharp turn of the river, was unsullied by man or animal.

Heavy stands of tall willows lined both banks of the Green, dwindling with the distance from the water. Straight ahead was a small crook in the river that was devoid of trees and brush, giving the brigade access to the water. It also seemed to be a good place to ford the river, so they could bring the horses and mules across for fresh graze.

Squire could see several lodges, smoke drifting up from them, to the northeast a short distance. "That be your camp, Etienne?" he asked.

"*Oui.* You will come to visit soon, eh?" He sounded anxious.

Squire nodded. "Soon's we be gettin' our camp set up. Ye mind if'n our women be comin' over to your camp?"

"*Mais non, mon ami. Nous faisons votres femmes bon accueil.* Your women are welcome. My wife is Nez Perce. She is quiet and knows her place. She will no' min'."

Gravant, Ledoux, and Dumoulin strolled off. Dumoulin belted out an old *voyageur* song, *La Jeune Sophie,* quite badly as the three French-Canadians left.

About the same time, Bellows and all the others arrived. Within moments, the camp was going up. After almost a year together, the men didn't need to be told what to do. Not that such a thing stopped Bellows from offering up an unending string of profane orders.

Soon the camp was up and fires prepared. Squire led his trappers and the Indian women toward Gravant's camp. The camp helpers stayed behind to watch over the camp and the animals.

In Gravant's camp, half a dozen half-breed children of varying ages played around the fire in the center of the circle of tipis. "*Vous enfants, allez,*" Gravant growled with more bark than bite. "You children, get." He grinned his gapped-tooth smile at Squire. "Sit, *mon ami.* You, and your *amis,* Suzette," Gravant called out. "*Nous sommes amusons l'invités. Amene les aliment et la boisson. Vite!* We have company. Bring food and drink. Quickly."

A pleasant-looking Indian woman, probably forty years younger than Gravant, had looked up, then hurried into her lodge. By the time the men had all sat near the fire, she was carrying out bowls for the stew. Three other young women helped, and the women from Squire's group also pitched in. Then the women, chattering like they were lifelong friends, disappeared.

They ate in silence for a while, then Suzette, a tag given her by Gravant because he didn't like her Nez Perce name, handed Gravant a fur-wrapped earthen jug, before slipping back to the lodge to work.

Star Path sat next to her. The two women fell to working over the buffalo robe, scraping the flesh from the fresh hide. Neither could speak the other's language, but with the little French and English each spoke, plus signs, they could converse.

"Now you tell me, my frien'," Gravant said, after a long gulp from the jug, " 'ow was your winter, eh?"

"*Comme çi, comme ça,*" Squire said with a shrug. He reached for the whiskey. "The weather was a mite bad. Nearabouts the worst I e'er seen. Snow hump high to a full-growed buff'lo." He pulled off the bobcat-fur hat and plopped it on the ground, running a hand through the long, thick, slightly graying hair. "But we made them beaver come, *mon ami,* didn't we, lads?"

Several heads bobbed up and down vigorously.

"You 'ave any trouble?"

Squire shrugged and stroked the heavy beard that flowed down onto his massive chest. "Some," he allowed quietly. He gazed levelly at Li'l Jim, who had snorted in amusement at the simple statement. Then he said, "Mostly it be Blackfeet that was settin' on us."

"Ah, de Blackfoots," Gravant spat. "Damned no-good, dirty bastards. *Immonde fils des garces.* I 'ate dem more den any other Injin. Dey 'ave no *testicules.* Dey are dirty an' dere women are *souillon.* I kill dem all whenever I see dem."

Squire laughed, as did his companions. "Waugh! I hate them niggurs even more after what they done to us over the winter," Squire said harshly. He ignored the harsh looks Train and Carpenter gave him. "Bastards stole my woman and all my plunder, as well as carryin' off young Hank there. They tried to crack my skull afore takin' my hair, too. That be something this chil' don't take a shine to."

"Why would dey take de young boy?" Gravant asked, raising his eyebrows. It made his weathered face look almost comical. He grabbed the jug.

"Who knows what be goin' on in the heads of those pestiferous niggurs? Mayhap they wanted to be makin' him a slave or be havin' some sport with him." His face darkened with remembrance.

"What 'appened, eh?" Gravant's eyes glittered with interest. He hauled the jug up on the crook of his arm, tilted it, and drank deeply. He passed it to Squire. He, too, had his memories.

The big mountain man slurped down a goodly portion. After smacking his lips, he said, "Well, we was ridin' up toward the Absarokas when two of the lads come along with us threw in with the Blackfeet. That were the startin' of it . . ."

He told of how Star Path and Hank had been taken, and how he, Li'l Jim, and Train had been taken, too. How he had escaped and then managed to free the two young men before they set out on the trail after the Blackfeet. What he did not tell Gravant and the other two French-Canadian trappers was that Hank Carpenter's real name was Hannah.

Hannah had been disguised as a boy when she had signed on with Colonel Melton's brigade. She had fooled everyone, until Train found out about her quite by accident. The two had fallen in love and tried to keep it a secret. They had been mostly successful in it—until the trouble started.

Squire eventually learned of it. A man named Zeb Willis, one of the trappers with the brigade, had overheard Train explaining it to Squire and had used the knowledge to create havoc. With the help of the ubiquitous American Fur Company and one of its employees, Willis and Melton's aide, Joseph Strapp, had set up a deal with the Blackfeet. The deal would allow them to set up a trading post in Blackfoot land that spring. That way, the Indians would not have to travel all the way to Fort Union or far into Canada to trade their furs. To seal the pact, Strapp and Willis brought Hannah, and Squire's Sioux woman, Star Path, to the chief, Elk Horn. The two had almost pulled the scheme off.

But Squire, Li'l Jim, and Train tracked the Blackfeet to their camp. With two old friends of Squire they had met on the trail, they attacked the village, bringing home Hannah and Star Path and killing both Strapp and Willis.

The three Frenchmen nodded, understanding what their friends had gone through. It was an experience all had shared, in some way.

"Did you kill any of de Blackfoots?" Ledoux asked.

"*Oui*. I ain't rightly sure just how many of they niggurs we rubbed out, but we made 'em come for goddamn certain."

"You 'ave any men *succombre*—go under?" Gravant asked.

Squire's eyes misted, and he stroked his beard quietly for a few moments before saying slowly, "LeGrande."

"*Mais non!*" Gravant whispered, as the others gasped. "*Il ne faut pas!* It can't be. *Je regrette, mon ami.* I 'ad not seen 'im in five winters. More maybe. 'E was a good man, *mon ami. Trés bon homme.*"

Squire shook his head sadly. It was hard to believe LeGrande was gone, even after half a year. The sparse, quick-cursing French-Canadian had been like a father to Squire, had held a special place in Squire's heart. It was a loss Squire thought he might never get over up in the pleasant valley along the Gros Ventre River, but the snow had come regularly and much more heavily than he had ever seen . . .

"What 'appened den?" Gravant asked softly, trying to ease the pain he saw on Squire's face.

-3-
WINTERIN'

Winter lay hard on the small valley between the Snake and the Gros Ventre Rivers. Squire had to push the men to get everything done fast, since he, Train, and Li'l Jim wanted to go after the Blackfeet. The men had been mostly boys or losers when he had signed on in St. Louis, but after several months of working together, they worked hard with a minimum of fuss. The men of Milton's brigade had matured on the way into the mountains, had fought Indians, dealt with the harsh, unforgiving weather, faced wild grizzlies and wolves, and trapped beaver. A few of them—Train, Li'l Jim, Ransom and Hannah—had turned out to be exceptional.

Still, many of the men were young and inexperienced. The work was hard and seemingly without limit. Forage for the animals and food for themselves were the biggest problems. With so many horses and mules, the men had to walk far and wide to peel the bark of cottonwoods or dig under the snow where it was not too deep for a handful of grass; anything to keep the animals alive.

Game was scarce, too, though the men had put up hundreds of pounds of pemmican and jerky. It might be barely enough to keep them alive if the winter didn't last too long, but fresh meat was always needed. They ate prodigiously, their bodies fighting off the cold and the sickness the winter brought— colds, flu, dysentery, the ague, and more. Still, fresh meat was mighty hard to come by.

The valley was along the Gros Ventre River; the Snake River lay a few miles west. Squire had thought of it because it usually was a little warmer than most of the others in the area; game usually was plentiful, too, and forage handy. So he had directed Bellows and the others to it just before he, Train, and Li'l Jim rode off. This year the weather was worse than he had ever seen it.

"Can't we go somewhere else, Nathaniel?" Melton had asked one night, not long after Squire and the others had returned.

"Nay, Colonel. This be the best place I know of, less'n we was to be travelin' a heap of miles."

"Would that be worth it?"

"Nay, Colonel. The cold'd be killin' men and animals off quick as we leave the protection of these here trees, bare as most of 'em be. There's no tellin' how deep the snow'd be out of this valley. We be some protected from the worst by bein' here."

"But you made it back from the Blackfoot country."

"Aye, but that be only me and a few of the lads. And we had a tough time of it, to be certain, Colonel. If we be takin' near thirty men or so and all these animals, we'd have most of both gone afore we was out three days."

Squire paused a moment, chawing on a wad of tobacco. He spit, then said, "'Sides, any spot better'n this'll be taken up by others—either Injins or other mountaineers."

Melton, a tall, usually chubby man, had become quite gaunt during the trip and the winter. But he had lost none of his humor—nor his determination. He nodded. "Then here we will stay, and make the best of it."

Squire shrugged. There could've been no other decision.

There was no trapping, since the streams and ponds, and even the creeks were frozen. There was still plenty of work, though. Firewood had to be gathered often and fires tended, hunting had to be done, animals cared for. Those who had no women with them had to make or repair clothes and prepare the skins of what animals they did take. It was a time for fixing weapons, panniers, saddles and other equipment that needed repairs. Some of the men built a simple press for making bundles of plews when spring came.

There was time for leisure, too, when the work was done. The men gambled and wrestled and smoked and yarned. Slocum Peters, an old mountain man friend of Squire's who had joined them in the fight against the Blackfoot village and come back with them to the brigade in the mountains, was a good storyteller, regaling the men with wild tales.

But it was to Squire that the men turned when they really wanted some storytelling. And they did so often. Occasionally he would comply, though it usually took the wheedling of Melton, Li'l Jim, Hannah, and Train.

"All right, lads," he would say in mock exasperation. "Gather 'round and I'll be tellin' ye a story." Then he would be off on some tale: "Like the time me 'n ol' LeGrande be trappin' up on Wolf Creek in the Big Belt Mountains. It were comin' on to winter, and we was a lookin' for a spot to be winterin' up at.

"Well, we found it, all right, just as this here big-ass blizzard was comin' on. It were snowin' and blowin' and howlin'. Aye, lads, 'twas a frightful thing, that storm. So I says to LeGrande, *'Mon ami,* I be glad we found us this here comfortin' place, for I am plumb tired of all this goddamn travelin' and I don't take a shine to this here weather that's come about.'

"Ol' LeGrande allowed as he agreed and pointed toward a yonder large cave in the side of a mountain. So he says, " *'Bon. Allons.* We will make it our 'ome for de winter.' 'But,' I says, 'what'll we be doin' if there be a griz or two in there?'

"LeGrande shrugged and says, 'You will kick their asses.' Then he trudged off on his snowshoes, holding the reins of his horse, whilst I be followin' with my own horse and some pack mules. When we get close on to the entrance way, who should appear but the biggest wolf this chil' e'er set eyes to. He had himself a big buff'lo leg bone in one paw and was chawin' away on it.

"Well, them damned mules set to brayin' and honkin' in fright like it was the end of their days comin', though I be knowin' better. But them fractious goddamn mules took off a runnin' across the snow and the ice. So I says to myself, 'Nathaniel, ol' chil', this here be most unpleasant doin's.' Then I says to the wolf, 'Now, lookee here, *Monsieur Loup,* ye done set our mules to runnin', and they are gonner be plumb hard to catch. Now what have ye to be sayin' for all this?'

"That ol' wolf, though, he just sets there gnawin' on that goddamn buff'lo leg like he was king of the whole goddamn world. So I steps right up into his face, with my fist all ready to give him a powerful thumpin', but LeGrande stops me. 'Go get de mules, *mon ami*. I will take care of dis.'

"I looks that wolf right in his eyes and says, 'I be goin' now, *Monsieur* Wolf, but I aim to be comin' back directly. Ye'd best be makin' certain no harm comes to this man here, or I'll commence to be makin' a fur coat of your miserable hide straight off.' With that, I turned and set off.

"It took me more'n six hours to find them goddamn mules. And once I did, they was in no humor to be abiding my wishes, so's I says to 'em, 'I be in poor spirits, mules, and I ain't ate in some days, or so it be seemin'. Now I ain't real favored of mule meat, but I'll be seein' to change my thoughts was ye to continue bein' so knobheaded.' They came along peaceable after that, but it was still some time afore I was back to that cave.

"When I got there, what do I see but ol' LeGrande, settin' up in the snow, a blanket spread out afore him, playin' euchre with that goddamn wolf. I tied down them mules and sat next to LeGrande to see this here wolf all a-frownin' and such. 'Ye be winnin'?' I ask LeGrande.

"'*Mais oui,*' he grins at me, makin' the anger rise in that wolf. It wasn't no pleasant sight, I be tellin' ye, with that wolf's fangs all yellow and salivatin', just lookin' for to make a meal outten us. Then LeGrande lays out his winnin' cards, and that wolf set to howlin' so loud it shook the trees in the mountains and set the snow on the hills overlookin' us to quiverin'. LeGrande just set there calm as could be, whilst I was holdin' my hands over my ears to shut out that goddamn noise.

"Finally the wolf slows down his howlin' and LeGrande says, 'You 'ave lost, *Monsieur Loup,* and so we will take over your cave.'

"That wolf started snarlin', with teeth big as my pistols, lookin' like he was about to commence chawin' on Ol' LeGrande. So's I jumped up and latched my chompers onto that ol' wolf's nose. That set up another round of goddamn howlin' that put the mules and horses to shakin' and his own bitch and young 'uns to shakin'. He flang me about this way and that, so's I was floppin' round like a fish just come on land. But I wasn't lettin' go of that critter's nose come hell or high water, no sir.

"After a while, he concluded his howlin' and stopped his flingin' me about, which was a pure relief. I let go his snout and spit the taste out of my mouth before sendin' him on his way with a few well placed kicks to his miserable ass."

The men laughed at both the tale and the justice of it. But Squire sighed.

"Didn't do us much good, though," he continued. "E'er goddamn animal in them mountains wanted to use that cave for winterin', and so's we was set upon regular. Finally we just give up and moved out and looked for more comfortin' accommodations."

Squire yawned then and stretched. "Now ye lads best be gettin' some sleep."

-4-

All was not well with the winter camp, however. The men were bored with the routine, the harsh climate, and the work, as well as the too frequent free time.

Having just a few Indian women in camp—and Hannah—made things worse. Fights broke out frequently over the women, gambling losses, the division of work, and anything else that came to mind on any one day.

Only three women in the camp were free, for the most part, from the men's advances—Hannah, Star Path, and Silver Necklace. Star Path was Squire's woman. No one would bother her, since they did not want to tangle with Squire, or with Star Path for that matter. As Bellows's woman, Silver Necklace enjoyed the protection of not only Bellows, but also Cletus Ransom and Squire. Hannah, of course, was a special case. Besides, she was protected by Train, Squire, and even Li'l Jim.

The short, slim, green-eyed girl could hold her own, too, as one man had found out soon after she and the others had arrived back in the brigade's winter camp. Most of the men left her alone, but the tension of knowing there was a white woman amidst them all and knowing they could not have her brought a heightened tension.

One of the men on whom the stress preyed decided to take his chances, though. Farley Walker was seventeen, a little taller than Hannah, and of medium build. He was a hard worker, but had a mean streak that slipped out on occasion. He was a handsome youth, mostly, with cold, gray eyes and a face hardened by his early years in the teeming slums near Philadelphia's waterfront, but he had adapted well to the wilds and had proven himself a good hand.

He took a liking to Hannah when she returned with the others from her ordeal with the Blackfeet. None of the men except Train and Squire had known about her until she had been captured. Walker thought himself smitten by her.

He kept his distance for several weeks after she returned, but finally he could contain himself no longer. He approached her quietly on a rare evening when she was alone. Train was off with Squire and Li'l Jim chopping wood for the fires. Hannah was outside the lodge she and Train shared, scraping a wolf hide.

"Uh, Miss Hannah," Walker said, trying to effect some modesty which he did not really feel. "I'd like a word with you."

She looked at him in surprise. "Yes?" She was a little nervous. She had not been back all that long, and this was the first time she had really been without Train.

"I've been watchin' you from far off, Miss Hannah, and to tell you the truth, I've liked what I've seen." His smile was oily.

"And?" The nervousness crept up into her throat, but she kept her face and voice calm.

"Well, the way I see it, Train ain't got a real claim to you. I mean, it ain't like you're married or nothin' like that."

"And what makes you think that, Mister Walker?"

"Well, I . . ."

"Don't well nothin', Farley Walker. We was gone a spell. We could've been married by someone, you know."

"Shoot. Who? There ain't no preachers within a thousand miles of here. And you ain't never talked about it that I heard."

"Doesn't matter none. We'll do so soon's we do find us a preacher. Now go on about your business, Mister Walker, and leave me to mine."

"But I ain't through yet."

"I think ya are."

"Just hear me out, girl," Walker snapped. He was an arrogant, bullying young man used to getting what he wanted by whatever method he found easiest at the time.

Hannah clamped her lips shut and narrowed her eyes suspiciously, but she listened.

"I aim to come courtin' ya, Miss Hannah . . ." The words flowed out as smoothly as a greased wheel turned, " . . . and win ya from Abner fair 'n' square. I learned some things early, and I've been a man longer'n he has, if ya know what I mean." He winked slyly, and Hannah fought back a shudder of fear and disgust. "It'd do ya a heap of good to learn 'at, and you could reap the benefit."

"You through?" Hannah asked, growing bolder.

"Not yet, Hannah girl."

She shrugged. "Don't matter none if ya ain't. Just make tracks, Farley. I got things to do. I got no time to set and listen to you babble on."

Walker's eyes narrowed, and the skin tightened on his face. Then he relaxed and said calmly, "I ain't lookin' to make ya angry. That ain't no way to start off with a future bride . . ." he smirked a bit at her shocked look " . . . and that's what I aim to make ya. I ain't like 'at ol' Zeb Willis was, from the way I heard it, just wanted you for a few days of pleasure. No, ma'am. I've had my eyes set on you since ya come back from your troublin' times with the Blackfeet."

"I've heard far more than enough from you, Walker," Hannah said stiffly. "Now I ain't gonna say anything about this here talk—for now. But you come botherin' me again, and I'll not only tell Abner, I'll tell Mister Squire, too. Then you'll be in a heap of trouble."

Walker was taken aback a little, but put on his most charming smile. "I wish ya wouldn't do that, Miss Hannah. There'd be trouble, and a heap of it, and somebody just might get hurt. You wouldn't want that, would you?" His eyes narrowed.

"No. But I don't want you, neither, and Abner can take care of himself. Now, goodbye, Mister Walker." She turned to walk away.

"Wait," he said urgently. He grabbed her shoulder and spun her around to face him. She was surprised to see that his smirk was gone, replaced by a look that was more plaintive than lustful. She realized he really did want her, was in love with her. Or at least he really believed he was.

"I don't want no trouble," he said again. "I just want to make you my wife. Take you outta these mountains, back east where you belong. Put you up in a house, instead of you livin' in a tipi like some damned red Injun."

"I like it here, Walker. I like livin' in a skin lodge with my man out here. I don't much like houses no more." She shuddered. Houses brought back memories of her family and the homestead in Illinois, of bodies and blood and fire . . .

"You'll learn. I know you will."

"I ain't tellin' ya again, Farley. Keep away from me or I'll see ya get into deep trouble." She turned and huffed inside, the thought of Farley Walker eating at her.

She was uncomfortable that night, turning a cold shoulder to Train when they were in their robes. He was upset by it, but said nothing. It left him wondering, though.

Hannah was first up in the morning, after her fitful night. Outside, lying on a scrap of buckskin by the flap of her lodge, was a set of hastily made badger-claw earrings. She knew who the foofaraw was from, and her heart sank. She picked the earrings up and tossed them away, far beyond the tipi.

She was on edge all the time, knowing Walker's eyes were always on her. Each morning there was another present left at the door of the lodge—one day a bow of trade cloth for her hair, another a necklace of braided horsehair, then something else. With growing disgust, she threw the things away each day.

But it was wearing on her. She was sleeping little, and her temper was short, especially with Train. She wished he would understand what was going on without her having to tell him. She wished he could just somehow see it.

But, of course, he couldn't. He only knew that his woman was drawing farther away from him each day, and it worried and sickened him.

Nearly two weeks after Walker had encountered Hannah, she was not the first out of the lodge in the morning. Train was. He came back in and shook her roughly, waking her. She was so exhausted from not having been able to sleep that finally it had overcome her, and she was groggy.

"What's this?" Train demanded, shoving a set of otter-fur hair ties under her nose.

She 'shook her head, trying to free her mind of the cobwebs of sleep. She wiped at her eyes, feeling the crustiness on the edges. "Hair ties," she mumbled, taking them. "Where'd ya get 'em?"

"Layin' outside the lodge."

She snapped awake, fear and anger squirming in her belly. "Somebody must've dropped them," she said evenly, though she was nervous.

"Didn't look like it." When she did not answer, he said angrily, but with a note of sadness, "I know I ain't the smartest man on God's earth, Hannah, but I got me enough sense to know when somethin' ain't right. And somethin' ain't right now. Ain't been for a couple weeks or so. Now if'n you don't want me no more, just say so, I'll leave ya be. If'n there's somebody else ya want better'n me, I'll understand and set ya on your own. I won't like it, but I'll do it. You know that." He looked hurt, confused, angry, and worried, all at the same time.

She looked down, ashamed to have him see her face.

"That's it, ain't it?" he asked. He felt as if his heart had been wrenched out. "You want to give your favors to someone else, don't ya?" His lower lip trembled, and he cursed silently. This woman was his whole life. To lose her would be to die. But he would not stand in her way. And he was too prideful to let her see him cry over it.

"No," she whispered.

"What?"

"I said no, you big, dumb dope," she said, snapping her head up. "That ain't it."

"Then what is it? Tell me, Hannah." He inwardly cursed the pleading tone in his voice.

"I can't."

"Yes, you can. I'll help you, darlin', whatever it is. I'll . . ." Suddenly it hit him, and he was flooded with anger. "It's somebody been pesterin' you, ain't it?" he demanded. "Somebody's been tryin' to force himself on you. That's it, ain't it?"

"Yes," she said, staring defiantly at him.

"Who?"

"I ain't gonna tell ya."

"You got to, Hannah. I can't go on livin' like this. We can't go on like this. I've got to fight him."

"I don't want ya gettin' hurt, Abner."

"There ain't nobody in camp I can't whup, 'cept Nathaniel. And," he added bravely, "I ain't afraid to take him on if'n he's the one that's botherin' you. It ain't him, is it?" Worry colored his voice a little.

"No, Abner. You know Mister Squire'd never do no such a thing."

"Then who is it, damnit? Tell me." His voice was rising with anger. He grabbed her arms and began shaking her. The buffalo robe which she had pulled up with her to cover herself began slipping, exposing her small, tight breasts and the flat stomach beneath.

"Stop," she yelled at him. "Stop shakin' me, you damned big fool. Stop!"

He ceased, shaking his head as if coming out of a trance. He hugged her hard, his rough, greasy buckskin shirt scraping her milky white rosy-tipped breasts. "I'm sorry, Hannah," he whispered. "I'm sorry. I don't know what come over me."

"It's all right, Abner, but let me go now," she said reasonably.

He did, and she stared hard into his dark eyes, not bothering to pull up the sleeping robe. "You promise you'll not fight him, Abner, if I tell you who it is?"

"No," he shook his head firmly. His voice was flat, angry. "I can't promise ya that. I'll talk to him, tell him to leave ya alone. But if'n he keeps on trackin' you, I'll have to set on him. I'll try not to fight with him—for you—but if'n he don't let ya alone, well . . ." He paused, then said, "It's the best I can do, Hannah." He was unapologetic.

Her green-tinged eyes searched his face, seeing the love etched deep there. "I can't ask no more of ya, then." She said earnestly. She paused, drew in a big breath, let it out, then said, "It was Farley Walker, and he's been mostly nice about it. He's been leavin' them little presents every day for almost two weeks now and . . ."

"What've you done with them?"

"Threw 'em away."

"Did he molest you any?" The veins stood out on Train's neck, and his shoulder muscles bunched.

"No. He just stopped me one evenin' and told me he loved me and wanted to marry me and was gonna try to win me over fair and square." She fought back a giggle. It all sounded so ludicrous now.

Anger coursed through Train, and his hands formed fists in his lap. Hannah rolled up off her buttocks until she was kneeling. The robe fell completely down, exposing the rest of her. She reached out her slim fingers and wrapped them around the back of Train's head. With a tug, she pulled his face down toward her as he bent at the waist where he was sitting, until his whiskered face was against her bosom.

Her heat and the smell of her and the feel of her naked flesh, forced the anger out of him. It was replaced by a rising desire. She released his head, and he moved it, nibbling the valley between her red-tipped mounds before moving to one breast and eventually the other. She moaned, and he lifted his head to kiss her hard. Gently he pushed her back. With haste, he skinned down his trousers and then entered her with her willing help and acceptance.

Afterward they laughed and played quietly, until Squire's booming voice at the flap told them there was work to be done.

-5-

When Train stepped out of the tent, Hannah right behind him, he saw Walker sitting across the camp watching the tipi. The pleasurable feeling in Train's insides fled before the sudden onslaught of anger. He stepped off, but Hannah grabbed his arm. "Remember what ya promised," she said sharply.

"I will," he answered tightly. He strode across the camp.

Walker saw him coming and stood hastily. He showed no fear, but he wanted to be ready to fight, for that's what he figured he would have to do.

"You best keep away from my woman, Walker," Train growled, without preliminary. When Walker said nothing, Train said sharply, "You hear me, boy?"

"Yeah, I did."

"Just mind what I said."

Walker shrugged.

"What be goin' on here, lads?" Squire asked from directly behind Train.

"This ain't none of your affair, Nathaniel," Train said.

"We've had us enough goddamn trouble for one winter, lad," Squire said, but not very forcibly. While what he said was true, he knew plenty more would occur before spring came.

"This here's between me and Farley. We'll settle it."

Squire looked at him skeptically, face hardening. "A couple of my lads standing 'round ready to commence poundin' the shit out of each other makes it my business," he said harsh-

24

ly. Squire liked Train considerably, and didn't want to see anything happen to the big youth. In addition, he didn't like having his orders questioned, not even by his young friend.

"Just butt out, Nathaniel," Train said evenly. But he cast a dark, defiant glance at the big man.

Squire's anger boiled up, but he managed to bottle it before it burst forth.

"Aye, lad, if'n that be the way ye want it," he growled.

"I do."

Squire stepped back, watching closely, but Train only said, "You just remember what I said, Farley." Then he stalked away.

An hour later, Train stomped up to where Squire was wrestling with a recalcitrant shoe on a balky mule. Despite the cold, Squire was sweating with the effort and annoyance.

"I want a word with you, Nathaniel," Train said sharply. He had been fighting his hot rage since he had learned about Walker's advances on Hannah.

"I be busy, lad," Squire said diffidently. He did not look up.

"Now, Nathaniel," Train's voice was flat and hard.

Train's tone made Squire glance up. He gave a final yank, and the shoe came free of the mule's foot. He tossed the old piece of iron aside and eased the animal's hoof down. He straightened. "Speak your piece, lad," he said.

"You been awful good to me, Nathaniel," Train said. The words sounded strained. "And I'm obliged for it. And for you pullin' my ass out of scrapes more times than I can count. But . . ." He paused.

"Don't stop now, lad." Squire stroked his beard in contemplation, waiting.

"But I don't want or need your help no more." Train stuck his chin out defiantly.

"Ye don't, eh?" Squire was torn between anger and amusement.

"No, sir. Leastways not with such doin's as I was in with Farley Walker."

"Just what was them doin's, lad?" Squire asked quietly. He pulled a twist of tobacco out of his belt possibles sack and tore off a chunk with his teeth.

"I told ye before, Nathaniel, it ain't none of your concern."

"Just what be stuck in yer craw, lad?" Squire asked, voice hardening a little. He knew there was more to all this than what Train had said.

Train thought for a moment, wanting to say this just right. "I ain't the boy I was when we left St. Louis, Nathaniel," he finally said. "I've growed considerable since then. Both in size, and experience. I can handle my own affairs now." His voice contained elements of regret, sadness, and pride.

Squire spit tobacco juice, letting the residue stain his long beard. "So ye be thinkin' ye don't need ol' *L'on Farouche* no more, eh, lad?"

"I don't mean to say that exactly," Train said earnestly, knowing he was explaining himself poorly. "It's just that I don't need ya watchin' over me every minute. I can take care of myself."

"That be so, lad?" Squire flexed his massive right fist.

"Yessir." He braced himself. Squire had once hit him with that sledgehammer-size fist and coldcocked him. Train had no desire to face Squire again, but he could not back down.

Suddenly Squire laughed. He unflexed the fist and clapped the hand on Train's shoulder. "I reckon I have been a might protective of ye, lad. Ye and Hannah both. But I be thinkin' now that mayhap ye can stand on yer own, ye two."

"I think we can."

Squire nodded again. "Well, then, lad, I'll not be helpin' ye out no more." It sounded final.

"I didn't say I wanted that, either," Train said hastily. He smiled, realizing how much he had come to depend on and like his giant mentor.

"Eh?"

"Them Blackfeet come after us again, I'll take all the protectin' you can give," Train said with a laugh. It was a sound of relief. "Just let me do the askin' before you come trompin' in with them big feet of yours."

"Aye, lad," Squire said, laughing some more. "I can be doin' that."

"Thanks, Nathaniel." Train headed off, a light feeling resting on him.

Later that day Squire pulled Hannah aside and asked her

what had happened. She was reluctant to tell him, but finally did.

Squire nodded when it was told, saying, "I ain't aimin' to be doin' nothing 'bout this. I just want to be knowin' the lay of it if'n somethin' happens."

The next morning, Train found an elk-teeth necklace in front of the lodge. Hannah heard his curse and boiled out of the tipi to see him flinging the necklace away.

"No, Abner," she said grabbing his arm as he moved away. "Don't do it."

"Let me go, goddamnit." He yanked his arm free, but she followed, still tugging at him. "Don't do it, Abner. He ain't worth it."

The commotion brought everyone out. They looked around in sleepy wonder. Walker met Train in the center of camp. Walker had a capote pulled tight around him against the bitter wind that blew from the north.

"I told ya yesterday to stay away from my woman, damnit," Train snarled.

Walker shrugged.

"Now, I'm of a mind to give you one more chance, though I can't figure out why. Don't you come 'round her again."

"Why don't you let her decide for herself?" Walker finally said. "Maybe she'll want somebody else."

"Hannah?" Train asked over his shoulder, confident in his woman and in their love.

"If'n Abner was to die someday, I'd go back to Elk Horn before I took up with the likes of you, Walker," she said with a vicious grin.

"I wager you would, Miss Hannah. You must've liked that Blackfoot buck real well, didn't you?"

There were some sniggers from the crowd, as Hannah's face flamed red. But before she could respond, Train smashed Walker to the ground. He pounded on Walker with both fists, sending up a blue stream of curses all the while.

Suddenly he felt a blow to the back of the head and he fell to the side. He looked up and saw a laughing Tom O'Neely standing there with a taunting smile.

O'Neely was an eighteen-year-old, freckled son of Irish immigrants. He had a sharp temper, though he most often kept it in check. He spoke with a little of the brogue his parents had brought with them from Ireland when they were youngsters. "How did ye like that, me lad?" he asked with a sneer.

Train rose slowly, brushing off ice and snow. Walker did the same, but the blood of several cuts smeared across his face.

Walker and O'Neely started moving toward Train, who stood, fists balled, ready. Suddenly Li'l Jim came flying out of nowhere. The wiry young man leaped at O'Neely. Both went down in a tangle. The two wrestled on the icy ground, trying to punch, kick, or gouge, none with much effect.

Train moved close to Walker, and both raised their fists, swinging tentatively, jabbing. Walker suddenly let fly a flurry of punches. Train backtracked, fending off the blows as best he could. His foot slipped on the snow, and he fell, but rolled immediately. Walker's fist just missed his cheek, hammering a pile of icy snow instead.

Train hopped up and swung hard as Walker turned toward him. His knuckles raked Walker's forehead, sending him sprawling. He moved forward to finish Walker off.

Squire stood in the way. He held Li'l Jim by the scruff in one great hand, and O'Neely in the other. "That be enough, lad," he growled.

"But Nathaniel . . ." Train was enraged, ready to explode.

"No buts, lad. Ye let him be now. And ye," he turned to Walker, "best be keepin' your distance from Hannah." He winked at Train. "Or I'll let Abner loose on ye again. I don't want no more trouble from ye, lad. Do ye understand?"

When Walker nodded tightly, Squire said, "Now the rest of ye lads best be gettin' on to your work."

Train stood up, still seething inside. Li'l Jim sidled up, grinning. "You all right?" he asked.

"Yep. What happened to you?"

"Not much," Li'l Jim shrugged. "I was going over O'Neely right well," he bragged, though it wasn't true. If anything, it was a standoff. "Then Nathaniel pulled us apart. Good thing, too," he chuckled.

Li'l Jim was young and cocky. He always walked with a swagger. But he was a loyal and true friend, especially to Train and Hannah. His bravado often got him into trouble, but he always took his lumps from it without complaint.

"Thanks for your help, Li'l Jim," Train said, clapping his friend on the shoulder.

"It's all right," Li'l Jim said, suddenly embarrassed.

Hannah walked up and kissed Li'l Jim lightly on a peach-fuzzed cheek, embarrassing him all the more. Then she grabbed Train's arm. "Come on, Abner," she said, pulling her man away.

Walker did not bother Hannah again, though more than once she thought she could feel his pale, deadly eyes boring in on her. She never caught him at it, though. With time, the feeling began to fade.

-6-

The stress and boredom of the winter camp made the men lax in their work sometimes, and one morning they awoke to find nearly a dozen horses, including Melton's favorite, gone.

"Where could they have gotten to?" Melton asked. Squire, with Bellows, Li'l Jim, Train, and Hannah had gone straight to the rough cabin Melton was living in. They sat around the fire in the crude fireplace in the southern wall, listening to the wind whistle through the cracks in the walls. Squire had tried to convince Melton to use a tipi, explaining that a skin lodge was more comfortable and practical, but Melton would have none of it. He wanted something that resembled, no matter how roughly, a house.

"Injins took 'em, Colonel," Squire said. "Them horses ain't gonna just be walkin' off by themselves." He was not pleased by this turn of events, but he figured it might be a good lesson for the men.

"But who? And where are they?"

"I ain't looked for sign yet, but there be a camp of Shoshonis a day or two ride south, and there be one of Crows about twenty mile or so to the northeast."

"How do you know this?"

"I seen both camps, Colonel."

"Why didn't you tell me?"

"No call to. They weren't botherin' us none. All it would've

30

done was set the lads to worryin'. We be havin' us enough trouble without this." His face was tight and hard. "If'n them goddamn horse guards was doin' their jobs, them horses would've never been took." His voice was full of accusation.

Bellows, who had ultimate responsibility for the animals, kept his mouth shut. Squire might like him, even consider him a friend, but to start yapping now would only increase the giant's anger.

"Well, they're gone now and there is little we can do about it, Nathaniel."

"Buff'lo shit. I aim to be gettin' them horses back, Colonel. Homer, have some of the pork eaters saddle *Noir Astre* and horses for Li'l Jim, Hannah, and Abner. We'll be needin' some powder, a few trade goods, and a little jerky and some coffee. Enough for two, three days."

"I can do it, yep. When ya need 'em?"

"Half-hour, maybe. I need to look for sign first."

"Yep. Will do it." He left the cabin, and the ones inside could hear him yelling, "Cletus! Get your orn'ry, worthless ass over here, boy. Yep. Do it now, goddamnit. Come on. Don't be all goddamn day about it, you mule-headed, buffler-humpin' young snot."

His voice faded as he walked away. Squire almost chuckled as he pictured in his mind Ransom walking slowly toward Bellows, unmindful of the oaths Bellows continued to shout. Then Squire turned serious again. "I hope it be the Shoshonis," he said softly.

"Why?" Melton asked.

"They be more tractable than Crows, generally. Most likely be more'n willin' to talk, maybe take a few presents for the return of the horses. Ye never can be certain with them Crows. They usually be peaceable toward mountaineers, but they can be hard-ass niggurs at times."

The three young people sighed with worry, and Squire looked at them with fondness.

Train had been right the other day, Squire realized. He had grown considerably in the six months or so since they had left St. Louis. He was big and blocky, maybe six-feet-four-inches, two hundred twenty pounds, or a little better, a powerfully built

young man with a broad, open face and a long mat of light
brown hair. What little facial hair he could raise was so light
as to be almost invisible. He had, indeed, become a man in size
and deed, though he still had the impetuousness of youth. He
was hard working, a steady hand, and caring. He could also
be hard as stone when it was needed.

Then there was Li'l Jim—James Ambrose Hawkesworthy.
Squire had managed to pull that out of him, though he was the
only one who knew. Not much taller or heavier than Hannah,
but with a wiry toughness that would carry him far and long.
He was still cocky and wild, given to bursts of temper, and
of tenderness. He had become fast friends with a youngster
of his own age named Benji when they had left St. Louis,
but Benji had died in a fight with the Arikaras. Li'l Jim had
transferred his allegiance to Train and Hannah and, of course,
Squire after that.

Each had his or her own talents, too, found along the long
trail that had been only six months really, though it had seemed
a lifetime. Li'l Jim had turned into a superb shot, better than
anyone with the brigade, except Squire. He was a good tracker,
too, though not nearly as good as Train, whose eyes and ears
seemed to take in everything. Combined with his unwillingness
to quit, it made the small young man formidable on the trail.
Hannah, who could best almost anyone her size or a little
larger in a fight, had learned to handle a knife as if it were
an extension of her arm. She had also proven to be one of
the best at trapping beaver, causing many of the men with the
brigade to grumble.

"Well, let's get goin'," Squire said.

They stood, pulling their heavy coats around them: Squire's
buffalo-fur coat, made by Star Path; Li'l Jim's of heavy bear
fur, made by one of the Indian women after he had seduced
her away from the trapper with whom she had left her Sioux
village. Later he had tired of her and threw her out, sending
her back to the one she had left. Train and Hannah opted for
thick, bright blanket coats, complete with tall, conical hoods
and long tassels hanging from them. Li'l Jim had given his
capote to Hannah, with Train's permission.

They searched the area around the horse herd, looking for
sign. Within minutes Train called out, and the others hurried

over. "Here," he said, pointing to a moccasin track that had broken through the snow. "I found two more, each from a different Injun. Other sign, too. They're headin' southeast, which is toward the Shoshonis, but I think they're Crows."

"If they're Crows," Li'l Jim asked in derision, "why are they headin' southeast?"

"They can't come through our camp, and they can't go too far west 'cause of the mountains. So I think they're headin' that way till they get clear of us. Then they'll circle around and haul ass north toward their own camp," Train said.

"*Trés bien,* lad," Squire said with a grin. "Ye've found the lay of it easy enough. Ye be knowin' how many there was?"

"I ain't sure, Nathaniel. At least three, from them different tracks I seen. But there could be more; I need to look around some more afore I know."

"Ain't necessary, lad. They'll be at their camp by the time we catch 'em anyway."

"How do you know . . . ?" Train started, then stopped, nodding his head. "Hmmm. Yep, the prints're at least four hours old, right?"

"Aye, lad. How can ye be tellin'?"

"The way the snow is. It's been melted and then refroze. Figuring time of daylight and how cold it's been, I figure about that long. Plus I seen some horse droppin's that ain't with the others. Looks different than what I been used to seein'. I figure it's from the Crows' horses. By the looks of it, them horses passed by here four hours ago."

"Aye, lad. That be makin' 'em come. Ye've learned well."

"I could've told you the same things." Li'l Jim said it with an elfish grin. He could not have, and he knew it. He also knew that the others knew.

Hannah snorted in friendly scorn. She liked Li'l Jim more than a little, despite his foolish arrogance. Indeed, Li'l Jim had offered to take her in when Train had shown a few minutes' reluctance to accept her back after rescuing her from the Blackfoot. Li'l Jim had made the offer to force Train into doing what Train wanted to do anyway, but Hannah appreciated the gesture. More than once Hannah had wondered what living with Li'l Jim would be like. It would be interesting, of that she was sure, but she doubted it would last. Besides, she loved Abner Train; she only liked Li'l Jim.

"Let's be goin', lads," Squire said harshly. "There ain't no time for foolishment."

Back at the camp, Colonel Melton sat mounted, waiting with the horses for the others. Squire looked at him in surprise. "Ye aim to be comin' along?"

"Yes, Nathaniel. I've sat in this camp until I can't sit any more. It's time I saw some action."

"Aye, Colonel. Abner, ye be leadin'. Just find them Crow tracks north of camp and be followin' 'em. Colonel, ye be goin' next, then Hannah, then me. Li'l Jim, ye be watchin' our backs."

"Sure, Nathaniel," Li'l Jim said, swollen with pride that he would be given such a responsibility.

They moved out slowly, giving Train time to pick up the tracks of the Indians. Finally he spotted them, and they became easier to follow. It was bitter cold, and the wind whipped and whistled through the trees, though the sun was trying to push its way past the slate gray clouds.

They stopped as the day's light began to fade and made camp in a tight bunch of pines, which cut the wind considerably. The sun had played peek-a-boo with the clouds all day, but the clouds were thickening again. The wind picked up once more as the temperature plummeted.

Each took his turn watching the horses that night, while the others slept. They were all stiff with the cold by morning. As they sat to a breakfast of warmed pemmican and hot, black coffee, Train asked, "What're them Crows doin' out stealin' horses this time of year?"

"Crows'll be takin' horses any chance they get, lad."

"I know that, Nathaniel. But it ain't like them to be raidin' during the winter, is it? I thought they wintered up like us."

"They do, mostly. I reckon three or four of 'em went huntin'. They knew we was there, just like I knew their camp was around. Most likely they drifted o'er this way just to see if we was bein' lax. When they saw that we was . . ." anger drifted across his face again. " . . . they made themselves some medicine and then took our horses."

"We gonna have to fight 'em?" Li'l Jim asked. He sounded more excited than scared.

Squire shrugged. "Ain't likely," he allowed. "But ye ne'er can be tellin' with those notional critters."

They hurriedly finished their meal and rode out. It was another three hours before they spotted the Crow camp through the gloom. They rode into the seemingly deserted camp unmolested. There were no racks of meat drying, no women working outside, no outside fires burning, no yelling children playing. The only signs of life were the streams of smoke coming from tipi smoke holes and a few stray dogs scavenging for whatever they could find. An infant wailed and some children shouted from inside the lodges.

It was snowing again as they rode in to the village of ten lodges. It had been snowing for more than an hour, though not much was accumulating. The wind had stopped, and the temperature was up a bit, maybe a little above zero.

"I be *L'on Farouche*," Squire bellowed, the clouds of steam from his mouth carrying the words. "Come on out, ye heathen cowards."

Crows began peeking from lodge flaps at the strange apparitions, then a few came out. Finally, most of the men were standing outside, bunching up near the rough center of the camp, waiting impassively, blankets or robes pulled around them against the cold.

"I be wantin' my goddamn horses," Squire said harshly, the words as biting as the wind.

"We have only our own horses," one Crow answered in broken English. He stepped forward.

"Who be ye?"

"I am Stands-Twice-Against-the-Enemy," he said in Crow. "I speak for my people."

"Ye be speakin' buff'lo shit, lad. I ain't aimin' to spend the rest of my days here jabberin' with ye over some horses. Now fetch up the goddamn animals ye took from our camp."

"Not have."

"Perhaps we have the wrong Indians, Nathaniel," Melton said. "Are you . . . ?"

"Shut up, Colonel. I can see 'em from here standin' with the Crow horses over yonder."

"I see. But . . ."

"Just set, Colonel." He paused. "Now, I ain't gonna be

tellin' ye but this one more time, Stands Twice. Bring up our horses."

"Not have."

"But I can see 'em."

"They ours. Not yours." A few of the Crows began sniggering. Most were unarmed, except for knives or maybe a war club buried under their robes, but they were unafraid.

The wind ruffled the rough fur of Squire's coat where it poked out at the collar and hat as he stared, stoney-faced at the Crows. Some of the warriors had begun laughing. Then Squire pulled one of his horse pistols from the saddle holster. Without a word, he fired.

Stands Twice staggered back a few steps from the impact of the ball. He was stopped by other warriors standing behind him. He slumped against them, and they eased him gently down onto the frozen ground.

An ululating wail arose from one of the lodges, and a woman burst forth, still howling her grief. She raced to her man and knelt over him, the caterwauling never ceasing. Other voices joined in as two other women, younger, and a few children left the tipi and joined the woman.

"Nathaniel!" Melton said in shock. "How could you . . ."

"Shut up!" Squire hissed. A few of the warriors were heading for their lodges—and their weapons. "Who be leadin' ye now?" Squire roared, making the others stop.

There was confusion. Then another man stepped forward. He wasn't tall, but his chest was broad and powerful. He had a bull neck and a thick scar that ran from the top center of his forehead down the left side of his nose, just missing the eye, then cutting across both lips off-centered down to the chin and curling underneath it.

"I am Kills-Many-Sioux, war leader."

"Ye heard what I said to that goddamn fool," he said, pointing his rifle at the Crow's body. "I aim to tell ye only once. And get them women to quit that wailin'."

Kills Many turned and spoke a few words to some women at the flap of another lodge. They came out and, with the help of three warriors, pulled the women away from Stands Twice's body.

"We may have what you ask," Kills Many said in good

English. "We sit, talk. Smoke pipe. You give presents, then we give horses."

"I ain't aimin' to parley with you, lad. I aim to be gettin' my horses back. I don't trust none of ye sneakin' thieves."

Kills Many's eyes narrowed, and he fought for control. Then he said calmly, "We talk. Smoke pipe. You give presents. I give horses." Without waiting for an answer, he said something in Crow over his shoulder, while never taking his eyes off Squire.

Several warriors and women hurried off. Within minutes a fire was burning out in the open. Kills Many and Squire still stared hard at each other. "We sit, talk," the Crow said.

Squire nodded and rode forward until he was close to the fire. He slid off his horse, as did the others. "Ye be holdin' the horses, Colonel," he said in a voice that would accept no arguments. He sat across the fire from Kills Many. The three others sat in a semicircle around him, their backs to his, keeping a wary eye on the Indians.

"What you give?" Kills Many asked after he and Squire had taken the pipe, offered it to the north, south, east, and west, the earth and sky.

"I'll give ye what I gave Stands Twice, if'n ye don't be handin' over my horses, ye fractious, shit-eatin' peckerwood."

"My men took the horses well. Your fault. You didn't protect the horses, so we took 'em." He was proud of the fact. The Crows took a lot of pride in being horse thieves. They were the best and looked upon it as your fault if you were so incompetent as to let them do it.

Squire grunted. He did not like to admit it, but the Crow was right; his horse guards should not have let it happen. "I got nothin' for ye, lad, 'cept a few bits of foofaraw."

"Then we keep the horses."

"I can't be lettin' ye do that, lad."

"They belong to Fox Spirit. He took 'em; he keeps 'em."

A warrior stood, holding himself tall. Fox Spirit was proud of his dark, handsome looks, extremely long hair, and his horse-stealing talents.

"Then I'll be fightin' ye for 'em, lad."

"No," Kills Many said sharply. "You *L'on Farouche*. I've heard of you. You're too big."

"Then I'll fight him," Train said. He looked from the leader to the warrior. "You ain't afraid of me, are you, Fox Spirit?"

The Crow spit. "Not afraid of anyone. I fight *L'on Farouche*. I kill him."

"No," Kills Many said again. "You will fight the other."

He had spoken in Crow, but Squire understood much of it.

The two Indians argued some more in their own language before Fox Spirit finally said, "I will fight younger white-eyes." He spit in contempt.

-7-

Train stood, handing Hannah his rifle and pistol. He shrugged off the capote, but left his fur mittens on. He slipped out his knife and tomahawk and dropped them. He stepped away from the fire a little, facing Fox Spirit. He swung his arms against the cold and to loosen up his muscles.

A warrior hurried up to Fox Spirit with a few small pots of paint. Fox Spirit swiped them onto his face in bold lines of red and black. Like Train, he wore a plain buckskin shirt. He tucked his waist-length hair down the back of the shirt.

The two men charged, slamming into each other with a thùd. They stood locked, each clawing for a handhold on the other, grunting with the effort, frosty breaths mingling in the freezing air.

Train was taller, but the Indian was nearly as heavy. He had a huge barrel chest and thick arms and legs. It was, as far as the others could see, a fair match.

Hannah sat nervously next to Squire, her rifle ready. She was fully disguised as a boy here in the Crow camp. Squire sat with one eye on the fight and the other on Kills Many. A tense Melton still stood with the horses, and Li'l Jim was ever alert.

Fox Spirit suddenly reared his head back and then snapped it forward, butting Train in the nose and mouth with his forehead. Train staggered back, releasing his hold on the Crow. He slipped on the icy snow and fell.

Fox Spirit pounced on him, thumbs scrabbling for the white

man's throat. Train grabbed the hands and slowly forced them away from his neck, out and to the sides.

With a roar, he shoved the Indian off and over to the side. Train was barely up when Fox Spirit charged at him again. Train sidestepped quickly and threw an uppercut as hard as he could, like Squire had once done to him. The Crow grunted with the impact and staggered off to the side. Train followed him, thankful for the heavy mittens. He thought he might have broken his hand had he not had them.

He swung again, snapping the Crow's head back. Once more, and Fox Spirit went down, stunned. Train howled in victory and turned toward Kills Many. "Now give us our horses . . ."

He grunted when Fox Spirit crashed into his back, smashing him face first into the snow. Train, the wind knocked out of him, tried hard to push himself up and to start breathing again. Both maneuvers were difficult and were made more so when Fox Spirit began pounding on the back of his head and his right cheek, which was exposed.

Finally he got his breath back, and he pushed himself up a little so his left cheek was off the ground. He pulled his knees up under him. Then he jerked himself straight up. Fox Spirit fell off him to the side. Train whirled and punched the Indian again, sending him reeling.

Train shook his head to clear it, and wiped the blood off his face. He stood, warily watching Fox Spirit, who did the same to him. Both were breathing heavily, the air stinging their mouths and noses with the cold. Both were sweating hard, and it chilled them to just stand there.

Fox Spirit spit a little blood and pulled his war club—the lower jawbone of a grizzly with one long fang curling at the end, attached to an oak staff covered with fur. Dried rawhide bonded head and staff.

As Fox Spirit advanced slowly, Squire glared with deadly eyes at Kills Many. His rifle moved to point at the Indian's chest.

"Should I take him down, Nathaniel?" Li'l Jim asked. He was kneeling, rifle aimed squarely at Fox Spirit's heart.

"Hold yer fire, lad," Squire said softly, still glowering at the Crow war leader across the fire.

Hate spread across Kills Many's face, but he turned away from Squire and shouted harshly at Fox Spirit. The warrior stopped his advance and argued in his guttural tongue. But finally he tossed the weapon aside.

Train breathed a sigh of relief and charged, smashing his shoulder into Fox Spirit's chest. They both went sprawling. Train scrabbled up and sprang onto the Crow and began beating him mercilessly with his fists.

The Indian grunted with each blow and fought to get free. Then he raked his long fingernails across Train's forehead, seeking out the eyes. The young man yanked his head back and fell off the Indian, hand reaching for his bleeding face. Blood stung his eyes a little, and he wiped at them wildly. Quickly he dropped and scooped up a handful of icy snow and swiped it across the wounds a few times.

As he did, Fox Spirit staggered up and half-crawled toward his war club. He grabbed the weapon and stood, swaying a little, dark eyes glittering at Train.

He heard a rifle cock behind him and knew it was Li'l Jim.

"Hold off," Train snapped. "I can handle this horse thievin' son of a bitch."

The hate boiled up into his face and his eyes were hard and unfeeling. "You just come at me with that thing, boy," he said to the Indian. "You ain't scarin' me none, you horse-shit bastard."

The Crow screamed a war cry and attacked, the deadly weapon raised high.

Train flung off his mittens and clasped his hands, then swung them as one. The fists plowed into Fox Spirit's arm, knocking the war club free. Then he swung them back the other way, fracturing the Crow's cheekbone.

The Indian groaned and fell to the side. But he pushed himself onto one knee and yanked out his knife. Grimacing, he threw it with all his strength at Train.

The mountain man dove. The knife stuck into his forearm briefly before falling to the ground.

"You shouldn't have done that, boy," Train said roughly as they both rose. The Indian stood, pain etched on the unsmashed side of his face.

Fox Spirit charged again, knowing he had lost. Train stood firm as the Indian crashed into his chest, then he swooped his arms around the Indian, pinning Fox Spirit's arms to his sides. The Crow tried vainly to knee the white man in the groin, but Train only grinned devilishly and squeezed. Fox Spirit gasped, then spit at Train.

"You dirty, stinkin' savage," Train roared and then he clamped his teeth onto Fox Spirit's nose. He chewed and chewed, as the Indian danced and jiggled in his arms, trying not to scream. Finally Train felt his teeth grind together and stepped back letting Fox Spirit fall. Then he spit the better part of the Crow's nose at the fallen Indian.

Fox Spirit lay moaning, sprawled loosely on the ground. Train stood, breathing hard, not quite sure what to do.

"Take his topknot, lad," Squire called. He sounded almost cheerful.

Train turned slowly, a little stunned as the hate drained gradually from him. "But he ain't dead yet, Nathaniel."

"That don't mean shit, lad," Squire said with a note of harshness. "Just do what I be tellin' ye."

Hannah walked up to him, smiling proudly, and handed Train his knife. He took it and turned stiffly, and saw that Fox Spirit was sitting up. Train walked slowly toward the Crow. As he reached the Indian, Fox Spirit looked up at him with unbridled hate in his eyes. He spit something in Crow that Train could not understand, but he did not think it was anything pleasant. "Stinkin' savage," he snarled and reached for the Indian's hair.

Fox Spirit flashed out a hand and weakly punched Train in the cheek.

Train's head snapped up, and he hissed, "You son of a bitch."

He backhanded the Indian as hard as he could, knocking him flat on his back. With a viciousness he had not known he possessed, he slid his knife brutally around the crown of Fox Spirit's head, then yanked off the scalp with a sickening pop.

He turned, hate still burning on his face, and held the grisly prize aloft for all to see. "I'm the Crow scalp taker," he shouted, unheedful of the cold air that was chilling him. He whooped.

"Quit your howlin' and get your coat back on, ya damn fool," Hannah snapped, carrying his coat toward him. He suddenly realized how frigid it was, and he slid on the thick coat, thankful for its comforting warmth.

Through it all, Squire had stared at Kills Many, who sat with back ramrod straight. Rage burned in the dark embers of the Crow's eyes.

Finally Squire said, "What'll it be, lad? Ol' Abner here won fair 'n' square, and ye be owin' us some horseflesh, lad."

"You . . ." a scratching and scrabbling stopped him, and he and Squire turned their eyes toward Fox Spirit, who had crawled to his knife. With great effort, he stood shakily.

"What in hell's he howlin' about?" Li'l Jim asked a few seconds later.

"I reckon that be his death song, lad. He be makin' himself ready to go under."

"He ain't gonna die, Nathaniel," Train said. "He ain't hurt that bad. Some poultices and some care and he'll be right as rain in no time." He felt sick at the sight of the once handsome Crow standing there with his face sagging, having no topknot to keep it up. Despite his statement, he wondered how anyone could live after losing his hair—and all that blood.

The chanting continued for some moments. Then Fox Spirit suddenly plunged the knife into his belly and ripped upward as best he could with his fast-waning strength. He sank to his knees and then his face flopped forward onto the ground, still bent at the waist, his hand still holding the knife. The gray day shined dully off the bloody, bare patch of skull from where Train had taken the scalp.

"What'd he go'n do that for?" Train asked, sounding a little exasperated. It was one thing to kill a man in battle, but to sit here and watch what was left of a warrior kill himself was entirely another.

"Reckon he couldn't be livin' with the shame of what ye done to him, lad. Beatin' him down, bitin' off his nose and then takin' his scalplock. That be worse'n death to an Injin, lad. Any Injin."

"I'm sorry. I didn't . . ."

"Stop your goddamn whinin', lad," Squire snapped angrily. "Killin' himself o'er it was his idea, I expect. I don't think such doin's be a matter of tradition with the Crows or any other Injins. But they all be notional—and independent. Reckon he figured it'd be best for him, not that he was required to do it." He grinned harshly. "Fox Spirit looked to me to be a lad what favored his looks more'n a little. Reckon he couldn't live with the shame of his newfound ugliness."

Squire turned back to Kills Many. Suddenly a warrior yelled and charged at the group, tomahawk and knife in his hands.

Li'l Jim did not hesitate. He just fired. The ball plowed into the Indian's forehead, and he flopped backward. As Li'l Jim hurriedly reloaded, Hannah and Train kept a wary eye on the other warriors. But none moved now.

"Finished reloading." Li'l Jim said, "Can I have his scalp, Nathaniel?" He sounded eager. He felt left out because Train had taken a scalp today and he had not.

"If'n ye be wantin' it."

"I do, that's certain. I ain't so shy about such shit as Abner here." He hurried over and quickly and cleanly sliced off the scalp.

"Now," Squire said with flint in his voice, "We be wantin' our animals, goddamnit, and we be wantin' 'em now."

"You will have them," Kills Many said in Crow, choking back his rage. Also in Crow, he said over his shoulder, "Bring the white-eyes' horses. Quickly. And see to Fox Spirit and Bent Arm." The war chief turned back to face Squire and the others. His face was bland, revealing nothing of the fury seething under his skin. He vowed that he would one day kill these white-eyes for what they did here. Especially the giant, bearded one who had brought about such a disaster for the Crow.

Kills Many was angry at himself, too, though. He had insisted on putting the winter camp here, instead of wintering up near the Bighorns with the rest of the bands. But he knew that many of the white trappers wintered within a day's ride or so of here. He had figured their horse herds would be easy pickings for his warriors. Like this bunch of horses had been. He had not foreseen, though, a wild man coming after his stolen horses. He sighed. His medicine had gone bad, and he would have to work to regain its power.

Already the wails of grief were growing again, and there

would be no stopping them now. Squire sat and waited patiently, never taking his eyes off Kills Many. Within minutes all twelve horses were there, ropes holding them.

"*Bon*," Squire said. "Colonel, mount up. Then ye, Hannah, then Li'l Jim, and then Abner. One at a time. Keep your rifles primed, lads, for these bastards just might think to be causin' more trouble. Once ye all be mounted, Colonel, ye be herdin' our horses out of here."

The men did as they were told.

Finally Squire settled into the saddle on *Noir Astre*. "It'd be best if'n ye was not to follow us, Kills Many. Such doin's wouldn't be settin' kindly with me. Nay, it wouldn't. I know ye ain't got much control over all these here young bucks, if'n they be of a mind to commence somethin', but I reckon they'll be heedin' your advice most times, so's I'd be advisin' 'em to keep their distance, was I ye." He paused a moment. "Now let's ride, lads."

Train led the way back, but it was Squire who brought up the rear this time, his keen, almost uncanny senses scanning the trail behind them. They were extra careful guarding the horses that night, but it was not necessary. Hannah gleefully shed her breast wrappings and breathed deeply with relief.

They made it back in early afternoon the next day with no one cutting their trail. It had been snowing heavily since before dawn, and the temperature had dropped again while the wind had picked up.

Bellows greeted them as they rode in. He was almost lost in the thick bearskin robe he wore. He shoved off the hood and said, "It's time you was back. Yep, it is. Now let me look at them horses. Probably was powerful abused, they was, yep. If'n not by them dirty, horse-stealin' Crows, then by the treatment you damn fools give 'em. Yep. Let me see 'em now. Come on, get out of my way."

Ransom joined him. The two men, the older babbling constantly, carefully checked the horses over. "These animals look plumb bushed, they do. Yep. Ya pushed 'em too hard, didn't ya? Bet ya did. I told ya, Cletus, boy, didn't I, that they was gonna treat 'em poorly? Yep. I did tell ya. Yep."

Squire shook his head and laughed silently. He liked Homer Bellows, despite the man's strange ways, and often was thankful he had asked the man to join the brigade to handle the cavvy. "Just go on about your goddamn business, lad," he said. "We ain't done nothin' to your goddamn horses, though I might take to abusin' ye, lad, if'n ye be continuin' this here beratin' of me and the other lads."

"You'll do no such thing, Nathaniel Squire. Nope. I know ya won't. But I got to tend these horses. Yep. Treat 'em right, I will. Not like you others. They're the most . . ." His voice was lost in the wind as he moved the horses away, still gabbing, Ransom at his side.

Bellows had also taken their horses and the small group slumped into Squire's lodge and sat wearily by the fire. Star Path dished them up some stew and cups of boiled coffee. After they had eaten some and polished off a few cups of steaming coffee, Squire said, "What ye be thinkin' of, Colonel?"

"Oh, it's nothing, Nathaniel," he mumbled, waving it away with his hand.

Slocum Peters called from outside the lodge and entered after Squire acknowledged him. Star Path spooned some food into a bowl for the new guest.

"How'd it go?" Peters asked around the slurping.

"Weren't bad. Shit, only had to put three of 'em under." He grinned nastily.

"It was brutal," Melton snapped. "Terrible."

"That be what's fillin' your craw, Colonel?" Squire fought back a laugh.

"Yes, Nathaniel. Most of it was uncalled for. All three killings. We could've parleyed with them; we had gifts to give them. They would've given us the horses."

Squire stroked his beard. He liked Melton. The man was straightforward and pushed himself as hard as he pushed any of his men. But Squire had had about enough of Melton's Eastern ways.

"Mayhap, Colonel," he said. "But I be doubtin' it. 'Sides, I don't take a shine to lettin' any Injins get away with such doin's."

"But does it pay to gain their enmity?" Melton asked. He was terribly upset by the incident. "The Crows've done nothing to us. At least, nothing compared to what the Blackfeet did."

"Shit, Colonel, ye let them bastards get away with it this

time, ye'll just be askin' for 'em to come back and do it again."

"But three killings over a few horses . . ."

"I don't plan to be explainin' myself to ye no more, Colonel," he said harshly. "Ye've been out here as long as these others now; it be time ye was learnin' the ways of things out here."

Melton sat, face red, fuming as he tried to control his temper. He knew Squire was right, but it went against his ideals. And it galled him to have the giant mountain man upbraid him in front of the others that way.

As the others began to talk, though, he slowly started to relax. It was, he finally thought, his own fault. He had brought it up, and so had done a good job of making a fool of himself in front of the others before Squire started in on him.

I had better learn, he thought ruefully.

-8-

Spring came earlier than they might have thought, considering how harsh the winter had been. But it arrived slowly. Squire was the first to notice its humble beginnings; it was mostly a feeling he had, something beneath his consciousness that quickened his pulse.

Three weeks after they had gotten back from the Crow camp with their recovered horses, Squire went around the camp, saying, "Ye lads best be gettin' some sleep this night, I'd be sayin'. For tomorrow we'll be settin' our traps."

The morning came clear and cold, but an excitement ran through the camp. The dozen or so trappers split into two-man teams. Squire chose Li'l Jim as his partner, while Hannah and Train could not be split up though they did head out with Squire and Li'l Jim. On this day, each partner would lay six traps, sticking close by each other and the camp in case of Indian or animal attack. On succeeding days, one partner would wade into the creek, stream or pond, fishing up the drowned beaver. He would toss the carcass to the person on the bank, where it would be quickly skinned. When the traps were empty and reset, the men would head back into camp.

The traps generally were checked twice a day. Each partner would check his own traps, sometimes having to follow where his stick floated when a beaver had pulled the trap free from the bottom. It was tough work. The beaver weighed maybe forty pounds this time of year, and the traps were hard to spring.

48

Then there was the stench of the medicine, castoreum, they used to attract the beaver.

Worst of all was the cold of the water. The mountain-fed streams and ponds were frigid, and the men had to be in them for long hours. First, one had to find a likely spot for beaver, usually where there was a dam. But one could not just wade in there and set a trap. The trapper had to come up stream against the current to lose some of the man smell. The freezing water made the legs and hands ache. A few of the smarter ones emulated Squire, using pants either made entirely of heavy blankets, or at least cutting buckskin pants off above the knees and sewing blanket legs on. The blankets dried faster and did not harden like buckskin. It made it much more bearable, but few of the men had blankets to use, so most suffered.

Squire and his three companions brought in the most furs, rivaled only by one team of youngsters—Josiah Maxwell and one of the two black youths hired on, Gideon Hook. The two young men kept mum about where they were trapping, as did Squire and his three companions, and they were good at evading the men who tried to follow them.

The camp sprouted willow hoops by the score. Each fresh beaver pelt was stretched over a wooden circle, where it was fleshed, dried and tanned. The few Indian women and the camp helpers were kept busy with the steady number of pelts coming in. And once they were fully tanned, they were marked CMCO—Colonel Melton Company. Then seventy or so of them were pressed into one pack weighing about a hundred pounds. These were stacked in one large tipi and covered with canvas to keep them from the elements.

"How much longer are we going to stay here?" Melton asked one night over the fire.

Squire puffed his pipe a few times and then said, "Till the beaver be playin' out. With this many lads, I'd say another three, four weeks. Mayhap a little more."

"Does it look like we'll have a good year?"

"Aye, Colonel. So far. We been takin' plews pretty handy here, and there be a heap of other places we can get to afore headin' for rendezvous."

"How much can we expect to make?"

"Can't be sayin' for certain, Colonel. Plews was bringin' about three dollars and fifty cents a pound down in St. Louis last spring. They'd be bringin' a bit less at rendezvous, I reckon. Leastways, they'd be doin' so was ye to trade them for goods. Those niggurs has a heap of markup on price."

"Do you usually trade at rendezvous?"

"Some. Usually just enough for a little *fandango*. But I be taking most of my plews to St. Louis, gettin' the best price for 'em. Those lads what be doin' all their sellin' to rendezvous mostly always be in someone's debt, Colonel. Aye, that they be. They nary can get out of it. They be workin' all the year long pullin' in plews, then trade them in for trumped-up prices on whiskey, women, and foofaraw down to rendezvous. Come time to be headin' out again, they got to be gettin' their supplies on credit if they be free trappers or hire onto one of the brigades with the big companies. That ain't the life for me. Nay, it ain't."

"Why don't we just head to St. Louis from here when the trapping's done, instead of going to the rendezvous, then? I doubt I'll sell my furs to that bunch of cutthroats."

"Best not be callin' 'em that to their faces, Colonel." Squire said with a chuckle. "Such shit won't shine with those niggurs." He paused. "But I aim to go, and I misdoubt ye'll be able to tell all these lads they got to be missin' it."

"I suppose you're right, Nathaniel."

Two weeks later, the furs were far fewer in number. Many of the traps were empty regularly. "How be the cavvy, Homer?" Squire asked Bellows.

"All right, I reckon." Bellows's Adam's apple bobbled up and down as he spoke. "Yep. I reckon. Why'd ya ask?"

"I aim to be movin' on. Beaver be gettin' mighty scarce in these parts. It be time to move on."

"Then they'll do, goddamnit. I'll see to it. Yep."

It took them a few days to prepare, but finally they were leaving their home of the past several months. None was sentimental about it. They rode northwest along the Gros Ventre and then north along the Snake. They finally crossed the big river, moving westward along the thin strip of land between two lakes, heading toward Pierre's Hole.

They moved slowly, not being in any rush. They stopped a day or two, sometimes three in one spot, the same in another, trapping beaver, hunting fresh meat—buffalo, elk, deer, moose.

It still snowed occasionally, but it was light and infrequent, more of a nuisance than worrisome.

By early May they had moved into Pierre's Hole. The men marveled at its beauty. Spring was going strong now. The aspens bloomed, and there was a profusion of the colorful Indian paintbrush, mountain laurel, aster, columbine, and other mountain flowers. The many streams and creeks were full of trout. Berries grew in abundance. Game was plentiful, though beaver was not. A perplexed Li'l Jim asked why.

"There was at least one group wintered here," Squire explained to him and the others. "More than likely there was two or three. It be a shinin' place to winter. Ye can be seein' the leavin's of them others all over: old fire spots, flattened grass where lodges were, pieces of equipment, other refuse. Them lads would've trapped this place out and moved on. They been gone near a month, I reckon."

The men were quiet around the fire, eating, smoking, or chewing tobacco, resting from the day's rigors. The night insects serenaded them, and there was a chill in the mountain night.

Finally Train said, "I didn't want to say nothin' while the others was around, Nathaniel, but I've seen sign."

"That so, lad?" Squire said, noncommittally.

Train had been made chief tracker just before they left their winter camp. Li'l Jim had been put in charge of the hunting. It suited their talents best. "Yep. Camp refuse, pony tracks, moccasin prints, travois markin's, more."

"*Bon.* Ye know what kind they be, lad?"

"Shoshoni?"

"Aye, lad, that they be. That be good or bad?"

"Most likely good," Train said thoughtfully, brows furrowed as he tried to remember all that Squire had taught him through the winter about the many tribes.

"Why?"

"They're mostly friendly to mountaineers." Train said thoughtfully. "They ain't so likely to try'n cause us trouble, and they got plenty of horses to trade."

"*Bon*. Ye've learned well, lad. Ye know where they be now?"

"No. I figure they're a ways over across the creek and down to the other side of the hole, but with all this fog and clouds we've been havin', I can't see smoke or other sign to be sure."

The next morning broke cold, with a chilling drizzle. But they pushed on across the valley through the murky grayness. By midday, the fog had mostly lifted, though the rain persisted.

Suddenly they spotted half a dozen armed warriors racing toward them from out of the gloom. "Whoa up, lads," Squire said. He stood in the stirrups and held out his arm, palm forward, signing peace.

The Indians slowed some, and then more when Squire stroked his beard with exaggerated movements, so they could see he was a white man. They stopped in a flurry of water and mud not far from Squire, who had resettled in his saddle.

"We wish to trade for horses with the Shoshoni," Squire said with signs.

"It is good," one of the Shoshoni men signed back. Then he said in English, "You come. We trade." He was short and squat, with a wide face and deep-set dark eyes. He had a fur wrapped around his shoulders against the chill drizzle and cap made of the head and fur of a badger. Long, looping necklaces lay on his chest, and he held a horn bow in one hand.

"It is good." Squire signed back, nodding. The Indians turned and raced away.

"Why are they so damned happy lookin'?" Train asked.

"Can't rightly say, lad. But I think they just got back from the warpath, probably with a heap of scalps, and so they be lookin' forward to tonight's scalp dance. They be full of pride, if'n that be true."

"Think we'll get to see a real scalp dance?" Li'l Jim asked. He was hardened and tough now from his months in the mountains, but he was only seventeen years old, and his youthful exuberance still bubbled up often.

"That we might." He clucked to the horse, shaking the reins lightly. *Noir Astre* moved forward, shaking the water from his great mane. The rain stopped as they neared the Shoshoni camp, but the wind blew a little harder, dropping the temperature. But the men were warmed by their welcome in the village of perhaps two dozen lodges. The camp bustled with activity as the Shoshonis prepared for their guests. Some women hurried about herding children out of the way, setting up cooking tripods with dangling iron kettles, gathering large piles of firewood. Others kept at their regular work, fleshing hides, sewing clothes, beading.

Word made its way through the village that guests had arrived and that celebrations would start soon.

Before long, Squire's men had made their own camp just to the east of the Shoshoni village. The camps were close but not intermingled. Bellows posted horse guards, noting that the Shoshonis had done the same with their horses west of the village.

Then Squire led the rest of the men toward the Indian camp.

-9-

A large fire was blazing in the center of the village. An old chief sat waiting there. The village's three dozen or so warriors were arrayed in a horseshoe behind him and his few subchiefs.

Squire took a spot opposite the old man, across the fire. His men sat behind him. The giant mountain man sat quietly as a long, thin pipe, a feather fluttering from it, was filled with kinnikinick and was lighted. The Shoshoni chief offered it to the four directions, then the earth mother and the sky father before taking a few puffs. He handed it to one of his subchiefs, who carried it to Squire. The mountain man emulated the old man. Before long, the pipe had made the rounds of all the warriors, white and red.

Then the old Indian smiled and said, "I'm Red Dog. Who're you?"

Squire chuckled. It was obvious that Red Dog had spent much time around white trappers. His English was as perfect as was the mountain man's. "I be *L'on Farouche*."

"You got whiskey?"

"A little. Ain't much left after a winter in the mountains."

"Better'n nothin'."

Squire nodded, then asked, "Ye lads been on the warpath lately?"

Red Dog grinned hugely. "Yes. Kicked the Crows in the ass. Got plenty of scalps. Counted plenty of coups. That's goddamn good, huh?"

"Aye, lad," Squire laughed, still amazed at the incongruity of this weathered old Indian talking like a white trapper. "Ye aimin' to have yourself a dance o'er it?"

"Goddamn, yes. Dancin', singin'. You bet. You stay here, damnit. We'll get drunk and watch 'em all dance." He laughed. "I'm too goddamn old for such doin's as dancin'."

"Sounds good, lad. How 'bout ye, Colonel?" Squire continued to laugh.

"Yes," Melton said noncommittally. He was a little irritated but not at all certain why. He supposed it was because he always was uncomfortable around groups of Indians. From what he had seen, all Indians were unpredictable—and that made them dangerous.

Food was brought, and they sat eating, talking of nothing important. While they did, some of the warriors went off and began digging holes near the fire. Soon poles were planted in them, and the dirt piled around so the poles would stand. More than a dozen scalps were hung on the upright poles. Drums were brought up, and several men began to pound out a rhythm.

Some of the warriors—Squire took them to be war chiefs—began dancing close to the poles, circling them, shuffling back and forth. Other warriors took up the beat, stamping their feet, beginning to sing. They formed a circle around their war leaders. Finally the women joined the chanting and dancing, whirling wildly right along with the men.

Squire and his men moved, giving the Shoshonis the room they needed. A few of the white men became entranced and stood. They uncertainly tried to emulate the steps of the Indians. Soon some of them had it down pretty well and wormed themselves into the circle of wailing, shouting, shuffling warriors. Li'l Jim was among them.

Whiskey was brought up, and Squire and Red Dog sat gulping the burning liquid. The old Indian relaxed, enjoying himself, the fire and whiskey warming him against the chill of the afternoon.

Squire stayed with him until after dark. But by then he was tired and Red Dog nearly stuporous. He pushed himself up and lurched back to his own camp, noticing that Melton was already back and sleeping by the fire. Squire entered his tipi and plopped down near the small, cheery fire.

Star Path put down the moccasins she was beading and filled a bowl with stew. She gave it to him with a promising smile. While Squire waited for the stew to cool a little, Star Path tugged and tussled off his heavy buckskin shirt. As he ate, she rubbed his massive, scarred shoulders, her stubby fingers working with certainty.

He grunted with pleasure and reached up a huge paw to pat one of her hands. "Ye sure know how to make a man be feelin' right, Star Path. Aye, ye do."

She smiled in the dimness, happy.

When Squire finally put the bowl down, Star Path pushed him gently onto his back. She peeled off his moccasins and rubbed his feet gently.

"Ye'll be puttin' me to sleep, ye keep that up, woman."

"You shouldn't drink so much whiskey," she said. She had learned to speak rather well from Hannah while they were captives and had improved it even more since. She was proud of herself for it. Her speech was still stilted and heavily accented, but in some ways it was as good as he used.

"Don't ye give me a hard time," he chastened, but the words were soft.

At last she stood and stripped off her greasy buckskin dress, tossing it carelessly to the side. She was squat and dumpy, with a thick middle, heavy thighs and well-rounded breasts topped by long, thick nipples. She looked very good to him.

Squire looked at her closely, enjoying the sight of her and her musky smell. Then he squinted and asked, "Are ye carryin' a child, woman?"

She smiled, shyly. "Yes." She was worried. She and the big mountain man had had two children before, a daughter and a son. Both children had died of smallpox almost five years before. In his grief, Squire had left Star Path. He had returned to her only last fall, while leading Melton's brigade to the mountains. Could he accept that again? Would he even want to risk it again? "You aren't pleased?"

"It be fine, woman," he said huskily. Thoughts of their children raced through his mind, too. He had left her, knowing it was not her fault that the children had died, but he still found himself unable to be with her. Not after what had happened to

Sings Pretty years ago. And then . . .

Now was another chance. This time would be better, he thought. "Aye, it be fine," he said quietly. He smiled at Star Path.

She knelt next to him and ran one of her harsh hands over his thick-bearded cheeks, and then down onto the wide, hard-muscled chest, over the scars. Both of her hands worked at the muscles, kneading them as she knelt upward a little for leverage, her breasts swinging, the nipples brushing his body.

There was a sound at the flap. Squire asked who it was, then said, "Come in, Colonel."

Melton stepped in, letting his eyes adjust to the dim interior of the lodge, saying, "I'm sorry I fell asleep while you . . ." he stopped, mouth dropping open. Then he stuttered, "I . . . I'm sorry, Nathaniel. I . . . I didn't . . ." He turned back for the flap, embarrassed beyond words at Star Path's nakedness.

"Ye got somethin' to say, Colonel?"

"I cannot, Nathaniel. Not like this."

"Ain't ye e'er seen a naked woman before, Colonel?"

"Of course. Well . . . I . . ."

"Injin women ain't so shy as your ones back home, Colonel. She ain't worried about it."

"But she's your woman, Nathaniel," Melton said, face still toward the tipi wall. "It's not right."

"Well, then say what ye got to say, lad, and be done with it. I ain't aimin' to put this off much longer."

"It's not important, Nathaniel," Melton said, cheeks burning. "I was just looking for company." Then he was outside again, breathing deeply of the cold air.

Star Path bent back to her man and whispered, "Your friend needs a woman."

"Aye, Star Path, that he does. I'll be seein' to it tomorrow. But now ye and I got us some business to be tendin' to." He reached out his powerful arms and she came into them willingly.

Squire spent most of the next day across a trading blanket with a hungover Red Dog and a few of his warriors. Melton, Hannah, Train, Li'l Jim, Bellows, and Ransom were with him.

They haggled and argued over plews, horses, trade goods, and more.

The other men lounged or cared for their equipment or slept off the effects of too much dancing or drinking from the night before. Others played the hand game with warriors, betting what meager belongings they had left after the long winter. Most had had nothing when Melton hired them, so they had little to wager with. But with a few belongings bought when a dead man's things were auctioned off, or from winning at euchre or three-card monte when they were wintered up, some of them had at least a few possibles to put on the blanket when they faced a Shoshoni bettor.

Squire showed patience in dealing with the Shoshonis, as he did in dealing with almost any of the Indian peoples, except the Blackfoot. It was something he tried to instill in his young charges, for an Indian could not be rushed.

It had dawned clear, and the sun had come on strong, warming the day nicely. In early afternoon, Li'l Jim headed off with a group of young warriors to hunt buffalo, and Squire took a break from his trading. Train and Hannah slipped off to their lodge.

Bellows and Melton sat with Squire near Squire's lodge, eating desultorily. Squire yawned and stretched, and Star Path touched his cheek in passing. He looked up at her and she smiled. He grinned and stood. Together they went into the tipi.

Outside, Melton shook his head, while Bellows cackled his bobbling laugh.

"Come on, Silver Necklace," the old cavvy handler said happily to the young, very pregnant Indian woman nearby. He stood. Taking her hand, he headed off toward his own lodge, leaving Melton sitting there alone.

Bellows had bought Silver Necklace, who was barely seventeen, from her grandfather, a Sioux chief named Sky Hawk when they had stopped in the Sioux village north of the Platte some weeks after leaving St. Louis. It was then that Squire had taken Star Path as his woman again, and a few other men had bought Indian women to take with them on the journey. Melton had turned down any offer of women in the village and had not asked one to go along with him. In fact, he had been stiffly opposed to the idea.

Finally Melton rose and wandered off. He was still uneasy being alone among the Shoshonis, though most of the other men had had little trouble adapting to the Indian way of life and moving freely among them. But Melton could not accept it, always feeling that the Indians would attack him.

He shrugged the gloom off and wandered through the village, watching the half-naked youngsters playing their games, quietly observing the women bent to their tasks, sewing or cooking or picking the few berries that were ripening already, or the men gambling or resting or caring for the horses, making or fixing weapons. There was always something to do in an Indian camp—or a mountain man camp, for that matter—he thought. But for him there was little to do.

Since the earliest part of the trip, it had become a ritual for Melton, Train, Li'l Jim, Bellows, Hannah, and Ransom to gather at Squire's lodge for the evening meal. There they would plan the next day's march, discuss that day's doings, or just relax and chat, as befitted close friends. This night Melton was almost afraid to head there, feeling so much out of place. But Li'l Jim, flush from success on the hunt, had seen him wandering around and made sure he was at his accustomed place at Squire's fire.

The Colonel sat a little stiffly, thanking Star Path perfunctorily, afraid or unwilling to look at her when she had served him up a bowl of boiled meat, nicely spiced in broth. He found he could not meet her eyes. He kept his face down throughout most of the meal, offering little to the general conversation, preferring to eat quietly. Making it all the worse, he thought the men were staring at him and the women were giggling about it.

"Ye seem a mite quiet this night, Colonel," Squire said, trying to contain his grin.

"Preoccupied, Nathaniel."

"Ye certain it ain't 'cause ye saw Star Path buck-ass naked? Maybe she be the first woman ye've e'er seen such?"

Melton felt his face flame with embarrassment as the other men chuckled. He said nothing.

The men talked quietly for a while then.

Finally Squire stood, knocking the ashes from his pipe. It was growing dark, the sun blazing in final glory over the mountains to the west. The big mountain man took the time to work some tobacco into the proper consistency in his cheek, then said, "Come on, Colonel, I be needin' your help for something."

Melton glanced up, startled, sure now that everyone was having a joke on him. "What is it?" he asked roughly.

Squire fought back a grin. "Just a wee bit of tradin' that's got to be done afore full night comes, Colonel. And ye be the only one that can help me with it."

Melton stood up. He was still embarrassed and more than a little angry. How dare they all make light of him, he thought. But going with Squire would keep him from the eyes of the others. "Then let's get it over with, Nathaniel," he said in resignation.

They stopped at a tipi and Squire called for entrance. A male voice told them to do so. They entered the warm, comfortable lodge, into the light of a brightly blazing fire, which threw orange shadows flickering around the sides. A middle-aged warrior sat on a folded buffalo robe at the fire. He motioned Squire and Melton to sit. When they did, he lighted a pipe, and the three men offered it, then smoked solemnly.

"Everything be ready, Painted Blanket?" Squire asked.

The Shoshoni nodded and signed, "It is good." He stood and left.

"Where's he going?" Melton asked. His irritation was growing.

"We don't be needin' him no more, Colonel. In fact, ye don't be needin' me no more, neither." He stood.

"What the hell are you talking about?" Melton asked, suddenly a little worried.

A young Shoshoni woman entered the lodge. She was about sixteen, fairly tall and quite striking in her beauty. Her high cheekbones and glossy black hair caught the firelight in a flickering dance. She wore a soft deerskin dress that reached just below her knees. It was heavily fringed on the bottom and on each long sleeve. It was tanned to a creamy brown and decorated with bluish-gray beads, ermine tails, small tin cones and bits of shell. On her feet were intricately beaded moccasins.

"What's this?" Melton asked, flustered.

"It be about time ye had yourself a woman, Colonel," Squire said gleefully. "It ain't right for a man to be without a woman for so long. Nay, Colonel. Such doin's'll shrink your stones up till ye can't be findin' 'em."

"I cannot. This . . . this . . . is preposterous. No. I cannot do it."

"Don't be a goddamn fool, Colonel. This be what you need."

"But I am married!" Each word was distinct.

"Where? Back East? That don't mean shit out here, Colonel. *Sacre bleu!* Ye ain't plannin' on tellin' her about this, are you?" When Melton vigorously shook his head, Squire said, "Well, I ain't aimin' to tell her neither. So, who's gonna know? 'Sides, she'll be expectin' it of ye, if'n she thinks of such doin's at all."

"But . . . but . . ." He wound down. Squire started to leave, but Melton grabbed the mountain man's arm. "Wait, Nathaniel. This isn't right. I have children as old as this girl."

"Any of 'em be girls?"

"Yes. One."

"Then she be of marryin' age, right?"

"Yes, but . . ."

"No buts, Colonel. If'n she was to have a suitor who was as old as ye—say, one of your business partners—ye'd not be puttin' him off, would ye?"

"Well, no, but . . ."

"This here girl be of marryin' age, Colonel. The only reason she ain't been plucked yet is cause her pa's been askin' a heap too much for her. I reckon he was hopin' to find some rich trapper down to rendezvous this year for her. If'n he didn't he could've given her o'er to whate'er warrior she chose and could offer him more'n a few horses."

"But this is wrong."

"How so, Colonel?"

"Because . . . Well . . ."

"*Merde.* Now ye just be listenin' to me, Colonel. This woman be waitin' just for ye. There ain't nothin' wrong in it. And she'll be makin' ye feel a heap better'n any white woman would. I guarantee that. And, hell, Colonel, it ain't like ye got to pledge your troth to her. Ye sport with her till we be headin' out of rendezvous. Then ye can sell her, or send her back to Painted Blanket."

"But that would dishonor her," Melton said. The very thought offended him.

"Shit," Squire snorted. "Ain't ye learned a thing since ye've been out here? Hell, there ain't no shame in that for her. None. Besides, ye been a gloomy ol' fart lately. This'll be cheerin' ye up." He grinned. "*Au revoir,* Colonel."

-10-

Suddenly Melton was alone with the young woman.

She seemed uncertain of her reception, but she finally took a few tentative steps forward. As she grew closer, Melton could smell the fragrant herbs she had spread on herself, and he could see the bright vermilion stripe of paint along the part in her hair.

She looked up at him and smiled, showing perfectly white teeth. Her breath was sweet from chewing mint leaves. "I am Rising-Sun-Woman," she said softly, touching his arm.

Melton almost jumped, but he managed to control himself. Rising Sun tugged at his sleeve, pulling him toward the buffalo robe bed a little way from the fire.

He stumbled toward it and then sank down onto it, almost in shock. He lay on his back, stiff. With a great effort, she pulled off his thick, leather boots and rubbed his feet and ankles. She moved up and pulled him into a sitting position. With deft, small fingers, she unbuttoned the homespun shirt he still wore. Then she slipped it off his back and tugged the bottom free from his pants.

She pushed him back down. He still said nothing, did not move.

She kissed him lightly on the forehead, eyes, nose, lips, her long, brightly greased hair tickling him as it traveled along his chest. She kissed his chest, then his ample belly, giggling a tinkly laugh a little when it jiggled under her soft lips and hands. He relaxed some as she moved her hands off his chest and shoulders and face. Then she reached for his trousers.

His hands shot forward and grabbed her. "No," he whispered, eyes pleading. "Not yet."

She smiled and rolled back on her bottom to pull off her moccasins. Then she stood and slinked out of the dress. She smiled in joy as she saw the look on Melton's face, and the beads of perspiration that had broken out on it.

Melton could not help but stare at this magnificent young woman, with creamy copper skin, perfectly shaped limbs, her full, rosy-tipped breasts leading to a mildly sloping belly.

She knelt and undid his trouser buttons. He started to protest again, but her look quieted him. She opened the front of his pants and slid them partway down his legs. Then she eased herself down on him, smiling again as he caught his breath. It was not long before he groaned his pleasure.

When the second time arrived, it was much easier for him. That time, he proudly took his pants off fully, feeling a freedom he had never in his life known. It was a night that was much too short for him.

The next morning Melton had more than a little trouble facing the other men. They had known what Squire had planned, and they ribbed him tremendously. He was in such good spirits after a night with Rising Sun that he took it good-naturedly. It all died down soon enough.

As they were heading for the center of the village to do some more trading, Melton held Squire back and said, "I'm planning to move Rising Sun into my tent," he said, almost defensively.

"*Bon*," Squire smiled.

"How do I go about paying her father for her? I have no expertise in these matters." He sounded anxious. Melton was primarily a businessman, and he wanted such things done right.

"It be took care of, Colonel. She be yours as long as ye want her. Ye e'er get tired of her, just toss her plunder out of your tent. Or ye can sell her to someone at rendezvous."

Melton looked aghast but only said, seriously, "Thank you, Nathaniel."

"*De rien*, Colonel."

They spent two more days with the Shoshonis, trading, trapping, and hunting.

When they left, they headed mostly south, trapping along the Teton River and its tributaries—Twin, Mahogany, Little Pine, and Moose Creeks, among others. Squire swung the brigade southeastward again, following the roaring Snake River, until catching the Little Greys River and onto the Grey River. They followed its winding course southeastward, still trapping as they made their slow way along it.

Eventually, Squire led the brigade east across country to North Piney Creek and followed it to the marshy, beaver-rich site where the creek joined the Green River.

"Where do we go from here, Nathaniel?" Melton asked while they were camped there.

"Depends, Colonel." Squire stretched out his long legs, easing the strain of the long days in frigid water. "Rendezvous be on the Green this year. We can just follow straight on up it mostly."

"Or?"

"Or we could trap a series of streams and such up there, be takin' the long way."

"What's your thinking on it?"

"Ye know what time of the year it be, Colonel?"

"Of course." Melton reached into a buckskin case and pulled out a small book. He opened it and quickly leafed through the pages. "Tomorrow'll be June twenty-third. Why?"

"Rendezvous'll be startin' in a couple weeks. Maybe a bit more."

"So?"

Squire grinned. "So, I reckon we be movin' straight up the Green."

Two days later, they left, working up the Green River. They took time while crossing Muddy Creek, and later Cottonwood Creek, to spend a few days trapping. Then they were moving on again.

More than once they had cut the trail of a band of Shoshonis, and twice of Utes, though they had no trouble from the latter and spent only a few days with the former. They traveled slowly, the pack-laden horses and mules laboring under their heavy loads.

Rains and the resultant floods and mud slowed them. Twice they had to wait out a norther' that blew through, pelting them with hail and rain, and dropping the temperature quickly and deeply. Still, the weather had favored them most of the way, with the days getting warm and the nights still cold.

Then one day Train rode back toward the slowly moving caravan and said, "I see smoke. It looks far off, but there's smoke for certain."

"Ye sure it ain't buffalo runnin'?"

"I'm certain. I can hear noise, too. Sounds like guns. A heap of 'em."

Squire smiled. They were close now, and he told the men that night, "If'n ye think ye had a high time whilst we visited with them Shoshonis up there in Pierre's Hole, just wait till ye be gettin' to rendezvous."

For two days they could hear the sounds of the revelry—staccato bursts of gunfire, screams of drunken joy or pain, thundering hooves of horses or buffalo, the deep throbbing of Indian drums, the higher pitched singing of the warriors.

Squire topped a rise plush with summer grass and stopped the massive black stallion. Train, Li'l Jim, Hannah and Melton crowded up behind him. "That be it, lads," Squire said. He felt a building excitement.

Out ahead of them, in the quickly gathering dusk, they could see many pinpricks of firelight.

"We gonna get there tomorrow?" Li'l Jim asked anxiously. Squire had talked of rendezvous plenty during the winter, and Li'l Jim was looking forward to the frivolity. Most of the others were, too, though they were not as vocal about it as Li'l Jim.

"Aye, lad. Early on, too, I reckon, though it'll be takin' us some time to get ready."

"Get ready?"

"Aye, lad. Ye don't think I'd be ridin' into rendezvous lookin' like this now, do ye?" He moved his hands to his sides, letting them take in the torn, filthy buckskin shirt and trousers, coated with grease, blood, and God knew what else. His beard and hair were a tangled mess and any exposed skin was filthy. "Nay, lad."

He moved the horse forward down the slope toward the

sparkling river and the groves of willows and cottonwoods down below. Behind him streamed the men, women, and animals of the brigade.

The men were used to the routine by now, and the camp was made quickly. Tipis or tents were pitched, firewood gathered and fires started, meat set to cooking, horses hobbled and rubbed down, mules unpacked, the apishamores left to dry of the mules' sweat.

Squire, amid the taunts and jeers of his fellows, headed for the river and scrubbed himself clean, grunting as the sharp soap he had carried all the way from St. Louis burned into his skin. But he endured it, and before long all the other men and women had bathed.

When Squire came out his lodge the next morning, he was a sight to behold, wearing brushed buckskin pants, heavily fringed along each outside seam, the fronts embroidered with geometric designs in beads, shells, porcupine quills, small, hollow bones and bits of metal. He wore a long war shirt of the same soft texture and creamy color. It was fringed along each arm, as well as the bottom. Scalps hung from chest, back, front and back of the shoulders. Simple bead work completed the shirt.

Under his freshly combed beard could be seen a bear-claw necklace. His hair was burnished with a thick coating of bear grease under the new cap of a wolf's head and fur. Beaded moccasins covered his huge feet, each with a small ermine tail dragging behind the heel. A wide, plain black leather belt circled his waist, holding the war shirt down.

"Well, lookee here," Li'l Jim shouted. "The great Nathaniel Squire, *L'on Farouche,* Blackfoot killer, struttin' 'round here like a goddamn peacock."

Squire grimaced. "Ye remember, lad, when ye called me fat one time. Do ye?"

Li'l Jim gulped. He had actually done that, and in doing so challenged Squire to a race. Not only had Squire beaten him handily in the race, he had also taken him and hung him from a tree to punish him. The picture was still vivid. "Yep," he said more sedately. Still, he was cocky enough to make one parting shot. "Well, shit, ya do look like some fancy-ass dandy, ya know." He grinned.

"Ye just best go on about your business, lad," Squire said roughly. But he smiled.

But by the time the brigade rode out an hour later, Li'l Jim, Train, and Hannah were decked out nearly as finely as Squire. Star Path had seen to that.

Melton had dug out the fine suit and top hat he had not worn since St. Louis. Bellows and Ransom were finely attired, too, thanks to the work of Silver Necklace.

-11-
RENDEZVOUS

"And how about ye, *mon ami?*" Squire asked Etienne Gravant across the fire. It was a hot day, though the breeze coming down out of the mountains softened it some.

"We 'ad not so much trouble as you. Killed two of the damned Blackfeets . . ." everybody grinned " . . . and brought in plenty plews. We each made more den two t'ousan' dollar for dem."

"You bank any of it?" Squire laughed.

"*Non.*" The Frenchmen all chuckled. "Why we wan' to do dat, eh?"

"What're ye gonna do once ye be too old for the mountains?"

"I die in dese mountains, *mon ami,*" Gravant said seriously. "I never leave dem. *Non. Sacre Bleu,* where would I go, eh? Montreal? Maybe Bytown. An' what would I do in one of dem cities, eh? *Non,* I stay in de mountains till de Blackfeets or de Utes get me."

They all laughed.

The laughter finally died down and Squire finally asked quietly, "Where be ol' Toussaint?"

Sadness crossed the faces of the three French-Canadians. "*Il est mort,*" Gravant said quietly. "''E is dead."

Squire nodded sadly. "I figured he was gone under when I didn't see him with ye lads. But I were hopin' he was just off to himself somewhere." He sighed. "How'd it happen?"

Gravant shrugged. "We were in de Absarokas two year ago, trapping up dere. Some of Suzette's people come by, heading to de prairie to hunt de buffalo to make meat for de winter."

He reached into the pot and pulled out a piece of meat. He popped the buffalo chunk into his mouth. He chewed loudly while he took up the tale again.

"We decided to go wit' dem since we needed to make meat, too. We found a big 'erd of dem beasts and went after dem. Dis one ol' bull, he got angry when Toussain' don' shoot him so good."

Squire could see where this was going, and he didn't like it.

"Dat bull, 'e hook Toussain's horse but good. Toussain' 'e goes flyin' off dat screamin' 'orse." He sighed, missing his old friend. "Dere wasn't much left of 'im when dem buffalo was gone off," he added softly.

"Waugh! That be a piss-poor way to go under," Squire growled. While Toussaint Robiseau's death did not affect him nearly as much as LeGrande's had, he still would miss the old French-Canadian. He was saddened, but it was to be expected out here. Every year another one of his old friends seemed to go under, but that was the way of things.

"Well," Squire finally added, "he had his time here, lads. And now he be with the Great Spirit." The sad look lifted and he said, "That ol' hoss prob'ly be fightin' Blackfoot and Rees in the other world e'ery bit as good as he did in this one."

Gravant, Ledoux, and Dumoulin smiled. What Squire said was true, they thought.

Toussaint Robiseau, *voyageur,* trader, and trapper had been a wild one right up till the end, when he was nearly seventy years old. He had not missed much in life, and while he would have preferred dying while fighting Indians, he at least went in the wilds that he had traversed for more than five decades.

The men sat quietly, letting the warmth of the summer ease the memories of winter's harshness out of them. They stretched out, relaxing, feeling their muscles unwind from the strains of the long, cold winter. Squire lay back, plucking off a blade of grass to stick between his teeth, where he worried it slowly.

He had banked a fair amount of money over the years. Always he had brought in more plews than just about anybody.

He spent a lot of the money he had made—on drink, food, foofaraw for his women, both the temporary ones and those who were more permanent—but he had had enough sense to make sure he had saved some.

As he thought about it now though, he was not sure he would ever use it. Gravant had the right idea, he figured. He thought that he, too, would end his days in the mountains, most likely from an Indian arrow or lance, or maybe a victim of rabid wolves or an enraged bear.

What other life was there for him, he thought. Living in a cramped city like St. Louis, with its stench, rushing people, hard-packed streets, and bad food? A return to his farmstead and mill in New York state, his oldest brother would own now if his parents had died?

No, he thought, this was the only place to be. There was no other place quite like it. He enjoyed the fresh breezes, abundant, succulent game, fresh, cold waters tumbling from high, snow-capped peaks. He did not think of the dangers— the Indians, wild animals, blizzards, flash floods, raging rivers and subzero temperatures. He thought only of the good things: the plush feel of prime beaver plews; the taste of seared buffalo hump; the free-spirited lovemaking of Indian women, untainted by the sanctimonious preachings of people who did not know better.

Squire grinned around the green blade of grass and pushed himself up. "Well, lads," he said. Some of the men were still talking quietly, but others had fallen asleep. A few of those, including Gravant, awoke sharply, then slowed, rubbing the sleepiness from their faces. "It be time to commence takin' part in this here *fandango*."

A few of the men whooped. Train, Hannah, and Li'l Jim leaped up and started running off, but Squire yelled, "Whoa, lads."

The three stopped and walked back. He gathered them round and said softly so that no others could hear, "Now, lads, it be your job to keep Hannah here a secret. All the lads been with us be knowin' about her. There'll be a heap of whiskey flowin'. It can be makin' for a loose tongue. Ye just make certain ye don't be flappin' your goddamn gums too much. And pass the word along to all else who's part of us that if'n they go spillin' the beans about Hannah, I'll be peelin' their hides from 'em, slow-like."

The three nodded and charged off again. Squire watched grinning but shaking his head, hoping there would be no trouble. Once more he mentally questioned his decision to bring the brigade here. Trouble was likely to ensue. But taking the easy route was not his way, never had been. He would worry about the trouble if it came. With a little luck, the brigade would get all the carousing out of their systems quickly, and they could leave. Squire grinned to himself. He liked the element of risk.

He turned. "Star Path," he called. The Sioux looked up, her soft brown eyes inquiring. "Let's go see how our own camp be, woman," he said.

Star Path nodded and stood, wiping her hands on a piece of old cloth. She walked off quietly, but Squire knew she was unafraid of him. They had been together for long enough now that her awe of him was gone. She was still an obedient Indian wife for him, but she also knew she stood high in his eyes, had better standing than most. And she was confident in knowing how Squire felt about her. It wasn't exactly love, though it bordered on it. It was more than most mountain men, or warriors, offered Indian women. In return, Star Path offered more than most Indian women offered only to a squaw man. Both were happy with the arrangement.

The camp amid the willows was placid. The horses and mules grazed nearby under the watchful eyes of several camp helpers. Other camp helpers worked around the camp. The lodges or lean-tos were scattered in the trees. Squire's skin lodge, Hannah and Train's tipi, the lodge shared by Bellows and Silver Necklace, and Melton's tent were in one small group, close enough for comfort but spaced enough for privacy.

Squire looked over the camp—and especially his lodge—with satisfaction.

Star Path had made their tipi herself of heavy buffalo hides that Squire had brought in and she had tanned. It was tight, warm in the winter, and cool in the summer, when the hides were rolled up. She kept the inside mostly free of insects with careful tending, the fire was always ready, with food available to any who visited, and everything was in its place. As with most Indian women, she took pride in her work and pride in pleasing her man. Squire was one of the rare squaw men who acknowledged it, though not in public very often.

Melton and Rising Sun, who had been walking slowly, arrived. "Are you going to the festivities, Nathaniel?" Melton asked. When Squire nodded, Melton asked, "May we join you?" He had wanted to go to the rendezvous, but was leery of going alone.

"Aye, Colonel. Ye be plannin' on takin' Risin' Sun with you?"

"Yes, I thought she'd like it."

"Aye, she more'n likely will, Colonel. But ye mind if'n I be givin' ye some advice?"

"Of course not."

"Ye'd best be keepin' your hands on her. Ye let her out of your sight, and she'll be took up in a moment by someone else. She be too pretty to be lettin' her run loose in a camp full of rendezvousin' beaver men."

"I'll do so. But would they really try to spirit her off?"

"Aye. Shit, most of these lads got no honor when it be concernin' Injin women, Colonel. 'Specially if'n they be in their cups like most of them usually is at rendezvous."

"But Risin' Sun wouldn't allow it."

"Mayhap she would. Might be that some trapper comes along and offers her a pile of foofaraw that catches her fancy, she'll shuck her dress quicker'n hell. But mayhap not. She seems right fond of ye, Colonel. Long's ye keep treatin' her good, she'll most likely be stickin' with ye. But she be young yet, and she may have her eyes set on anyone who can offer her something she wants." He shrugged.

Melton looked angry and depressed at the same time. Then he shrugged, too, and said, "I'll take the chance, Nathaniel. She'll come with me."

Squire smiled. "I thought ye'd be saying that." He paused, then said, "There be just one more thing, Colonel."

"Oh?"

"The lads here ain't gonna be havin' much of a spree till ye be givin' them their wages."

"Is that wise?"

"Aye, Colonel. They've done their jobs for ye, now it be time for settlin' up with them."

"But if I give them the money, won't they refuse to go back to St. Louis with us?"

"It was part of their deal for them to go back that far." Squire half-grimaced, half-grinned. "But I suspect there'd be some who'd cut out on us. Or try to." He glared. "I'd be makin' sure they'd head back with us. Ye remember what happened to Breen and Belknap, don't ye?"

Melton nodded, suppressing a shudder. The two men had been hired on and given a small advance on their wages. They took the money, stole two horses, and lit out. Squire had caught them, killing Belknap, and bringing Breen back to face justice.

"That would create no end of trouble, though, wouldn't it?" Melton asked.

"Aye." Squire had no desire to be forced into keeping watch over more than two dozen men every minute of the trip to St. Louis.

"That wouldn't help our enterprise any." Melton paused, looking a little ashamed. "I'm not sure I'll have enough cash for all the men."

Squire shrugged. "We can be workin' somethin' out. Most commerce at doin's such as these is conducted in beaver plews anyway. There ain't much specie to be goin' 'round." He stroked the lush beard a moment. "Ye can hold off payin' me. I got enough to last. I reckon Homer's got himself a little stash, too. Pay the rest of the lads half their wages, if ye can be doin' that much. They can be collectin' the rest back in St. Louis. It'd make certain to keep 'em from leavin' off your employ too early."

"Yes," Melton said thoughtfully. "That would work."

Squire laughed. "It'd also be teachin' 'em not to spend too damned foolishly. They'd have to be savin' a bit of money, less'n, of course, they just throw it away in St. Louis. It . . ."

Train, Hannah, Li'l Jim, and Slocum Peters arrived. They all looked glum.

"I thought ye lads'd be havin' yourselves a time," Squire said with a knowing grin.

"We ain't got no money," Train said.

"And ye know damned well there ain't nothin' here for free," Peters added.

"I knew that afore," Squire laughed. "And I were some surprised when ye skedaddled off with these here young pups," Squire said to Peters. He laughed some more.

The mountain man grinned. "Just lost my head, I reckon. I ain't used to being without specie or plews for rendezvous." Peters had thrown in whole hook, beaver pelts and all, with the Colonel's brigade.

"We'll be fixin' that soon enough, eh, Colonel?"

"Yes," he said, distractedly. Melton was surprised again at Squire. Every time he thought he had the big mountain man pegged down, Squire pulled some new trick. Like this little joke on his men. Melton wasn't sure whether to laugh at it or be appalled at its cruelty.

Other men from the brigade began drifting back into the camp. Some looked downcast, others angry, still more, confused.

When just about all the men were back, Squire bellowed, "Gather 'round, lads. It be time ye was gettin' paid some for your services."

The men whooped and hollered as they charged toward the small group.

"All right, lads, set your asses down and be still for a spell. It'll be takin' a while."

The men did as they were told, though they fidgeted. Melton entered his tent, telling Rising Sun to work while he handled business. He came out with a locked cash box.

"Men," he said loudly, fighting the roar from the rendezvous, "you've done well for me all this time. You've worked hard and fought hard. Now it's time for you to play hard. I'm afraid to say that I don't have enough cash on hand to pay you all you're due now" — he waited until the rumble of discontent died down — "but I can pay each of you about half now. The rest'll be paid after I've sold my plews in St. Louis."

"Sell 'em here," one man roared. "Pay us now."

A few others grumbled in agreement. Melton waited stolidly until once more the men were quiet. "I'd be a damned fool to sell the pelts here. Neither the Sublette-Campbell outfit nor

The Company has the cash available—and I won't trade for goods. Beyond that, even if I could trade for cash, I'd leave myself open to robbery on the trail back. It'd be hard for a few thieves to make off with all the plews we have, but the same can't be said for a chest of gold."

He did not wait for more complaints.

"Now, each of you step forward when I call your name. I'll hand out your money, then record it in my ledger, which you will sign, with an X if necessary. First, Gideon Hook."

The black youth stepped up proudly, took his money in hand and scratched an X in the book. He waited impatiently as his partner, Josiah Maxwell, gathered his coins. Together the two went whooping for the rendezvous.

It was all done quickly, and soon Squire, Melton, and Rising Sun were strolling into the rendezvous themselves.

As they walked, Squire said, "Another thing ye'd best keep to mind, Colonel, is that ye be in a hell of a lot more danger here than in the mountains." He chuckled. "Best to be keepin' alert. Anythin' can be happenin' here, and usually does." He grinned, once more filled with excitement.

Melton was astonished at the kaleidoscope of sights, colors, sounds, and activities. It was hard to take it all in. His senses were assaulted by the rendezvous. Everything seemed a blur. As he strolled with Squire and Rising Sun, though, images began to coalesce.

Voices erupted from a clump of men throwing tomahawks, attesting to their fortunes in the contest. Within moments, that had faded, replaced by the crack of weapons. The acrid smell of powder blew over him, tingling his nostrils.

They stopped for a moment to watch several men rolling dice made from lead rifle balls. A small pile of plunder lay on a blanket in front of each man. Suddenly one man took exception to another's winning toss. He flung himself at the offending mountaineer, and a rough-and-tumble fight broke out.

Worried, Melton steered Rising Sun out of the way. The two and Squire continued on their journey, leaving behind a growing knot of men wagering on the combatants.

"Do such things happen frequently here, Nathaniel?" Melton asked.

"Aye, Colonel." He laughed. He felt at home here with all the wild and raucous goings-on. To him it was akin to being in the bosom of family.

Melton shook his head, amazement increasing.

"Best step lively, Colonel," Squire said sharply, suddenly.

Melton and Rising Sun managed to get out of the way as two horses raced through the camp, their riders lashing them viciously with spurs.

When the horses roared by, the three continued their stroll, pausing to watch as half a dozen men ran by, red and white, stripped down to next to nothing. Each man had his screeching supporters or detractors.

An ever-shifting pattern of smells filled the air: wood smoke; roasting meat; rotting food; hides; blood, both human and animal; urine; manure; sweaty, unwashed, highly greased bodies; vomit.

Squire wandered to a plank bar set up in a big wall tent and tossed down a few gold coins. "Give me a jug, lad," he growled. "But I don't be wantin' none of that watered-down mule piss ye be passin' off to all these here others. I be wantin' the best ye got."

The surly man passed over a small jug. Squire lifted it, yanked out the cork with his teeth, spit the cork out and then swung the jug up. He gulped, downing nearly a quarter of the jug in one long swig. Suddenly he slapped it down on the wood.

"This shit ain't fit for an Injin to drink, lad," he snarled. "I tol' ye, I be wantin' the good stuff, some real *aguardiente*. I ain't gonna be tellin' ye again."

"That's the best we got, friend," the greasy, dark-haired bartender snapped. "You don't like it, drag your ass elsewhere."

"Now, that ain't very neighborly of ye, lad," Squire said evenly.

"I ain't here to be neighborly." The bartender spit tobacco juice on the planks, near the jug. He made no move to clean the mess up.

Melton watched, aghast. Squire wrapped his huge right fist around the neck of the jug, inverted. Suddenly he whipped it up and smashed it across the side of the barkeep's face. The man groaned once and slumped.

Robert Campbell burst out of his tent behind the bar tent, pistol in hand. "Och, what the hell ... ?" he started. He saw the bartender and looked up, bringing the pistol to bear on Squire.

"Ye aim that piece at me, Campbell," Squire said calmly, "and ye'll be one poor-sittin' niggur, after I take it from ye and stick it up yer ol' Scot's ass."

Campbell grinned thinly, but he uncocked the pistol and shoved it into his belt. "Shoot, Nathaniel, what'd ye have to go and do that for?" he asked in exasperation, his r's rolling in his thick, Scot's burr. He knelt next to his employee. "Damnit all, Squire, now I got to find another mon to tend things here."

"Hell, teach him some manners, if'n ye want him to be makin' his way through life without some aggrieved chil' rubbin' him out."

Campbell chuckled. He was relieved to find his employee still alive. The man would have a sore head for a while, but Campbell figured he was lucky. There weren't too many men who lived after tangling with Nathaniel Squire. "Well, at least he is nae dead," he said. "But he'll be hurtin' considerable for a time."

"Aye, I expect he will," Squire allowed. "And mayhap it'll be makin' him some more hospitable to folks."

"What'n hell was the problem?" Campbell asked, standing. When Squire told him, Campbell muttered, "Damn fool. The laddie should've known better." He sighed. "Hell, good help's hard as blazes to come by these days." He shook his head at the plight of the well-meaning businessman in this day and age.

"Well, wait here a moment," Campbell said. He entered his tent and returned in a few moments, two bottles swinging in one hand. He held out the bottles toward Squire. "Brandy. Straight from France. Enjoy it." He grinned. "But, Nathaniel, please try to refrain from clubbing any more of my people. I can't afford to lose any others."

Squire laughed and handed one of the bottles to Melton. From the one he kept, he drank long and deep. Melton drank a little more cautiously. Squire swiped the back of his huge hand across his full beard and bushy mustache. "It be good," he pronounced before stomping off.

The three strolled through the sprawling chaos of the rendezvous, with the two men swigging as they walked. Squire often stopped by a group sitting around a fire to chat for a spell before moving on, and the trio frequently had to sidestep brawls or games or cooking pots or meat racks or Indian women working at their various chores.

The throbbing thump of horses' hooves made them spin, and they hopped out of the way as six horses thundered past, their riders whipping the foaming mounts. Squire drained the rest of his bottle, then whooped and tossed it after the rapidly departing horses.

They found another plank bar, and Squire tossed down a coin. He took the large earthen jug of fiery alcohol and drank deeply. "Waugh!" he offered. "That goddamn shines to this ol' chil', I'd be sayin'."

Melton clung tightly to his bottle with one hand and Rising Sun with the other as they followed Squire around the camp, heading for where a large circle had formed. A fiddle, dulcimer, and small Indian drum could be heard.

As the three strolled up, they could see several men, most of them drunk, dancing either with themselves or with some Indian women, who shuffled uncomfortably to the unfamiliar sounds and rhythms.

"Hey, Nathaniel, come on and join in," Train called out.

Squire looked around and grinned when he saw Train smiling as he played a dulcimer with some talent and considerable abandon.

"Why don't you go on and join the dancin', Nathaniel?" Train said. His playing had not suffered from the conversation.

"Nay, lad. Such doin's ain't for me. Now, mayhap the Colonel and his lady here might take a shine to doin's such as them."

"No, Nathaniel," Melton protested. He was still arguing when Squire shoved him and Rising Sun into the center of the ring.

"Dance, boy," someone yelled. Others kept up their clapping, foot stomping and cheering.

Reluctantly, Melton began moving, his large body showing surprising grace. He grabbed Rising Sun and began leading her through the increasingly complicated steps. Rising Sun followed along rather well, though with her beauty, the men watching cared not a whit how well she danced.

Squire sipped and listened, the sounds bringing his mind back over the years to places barely remembered, to a people he could hardly recall. There were images of a young, bright-haired mother dancing happily with a giant, bull-necked, hard-muscled father. The giant had taken time out from his many chores to join the celebration at a neighbor's place.

With a snort of disgust, Squire turned away, his mood suddenly soured. The alcohol creeping its tortured way through his brain turned him into a brooding hulk. With jug in hand, he stomped off toward the seclusion of a small bend in the Green River. He sat heavily and leaned his back against a willow. He drank deeply again, letting the demons rummage through his mind.

-12-

He had been thirteen years old when they held the dance. It was a combination harvest festival, barn-raising, and welcome home for Squire. The youngster was uncomfortable with all the attention he was receiving, especially from his mother. Not all the attention was friendly.

Nathaniel was the youngest of the Squire children—a younger daughter had died before she was a year old—and he was his father's favorite, since he was most like him. Such did not sit well with some of his older brothers.

Even when he was young, Nathaniel was big, and he had his father's quick temper and streak of stubbornness. He was hardened by work on the family farm, and the Squire flour mill. He did not mind the hard labor of either job, but he disliked boredom intensely. Because of that, and his oldest brother's ordering him about too often, Squire would frequently sneak away to wander through the thick woods and rocky defiles of upper New York state's Adirondack Mountains.

That was how he had come to be the focus of this party. More than a year ago, he had slipped off liked he often did, strolling silently through the sun-dappled forest. The rippling of a brook caught his attention, and he drifted toward it, his mind lulled by the soothing sound.

A sudden movement to his left and a little behind him snapped him back to alertness. But it was too late.

Two men rushed him, so fast that he could not get a look at either. One came at him high and flipped a large burlap sack over his head and down to about waist level. The second grabbed him around the middle, managing to pin his arms.

Squire gave no thought to yelling for help. His father had taught him to be self-sufficient. He did try to fight, though, but he was incapable of doing much under the suddenness of the attack.

He felt himself lifted. He grunted, frightened, as his stomach landed on the hard edge of a man's shoulder. He bounced and flopped as the man ran. Squire could feel branches whipping at him. The youngster struggled and wriggled, trying to get free. Suddenly the man carrying him stopped, and Squire felt relief. Now maybe he could fight back, he thought.

His relief and optimism were but momentary, though, as he felt a blinding pain in his head. "Ease yer struggles, boy-o, or I'll put anudder knot in yer head," a voice growled at him.

Squire quit fighting then, trying not to cry from frustration, pain and worry. He felt himself thrown over the shoulder again, and then they were off and running once more.

He thought with growing fear that his tendency to skip out on his chores might be leading to serious, perhaps fatal consequences this time. No one would think twice about him being gone, at least not until supper time. Even then there'd be talk that he was still wandering out in the woods, trying to avoid the chores around home.

Finally the man stopped, but it was no relief for young Squire, who quickly found himself dumped across a saddle. The movement began again the bouncing worse now on the back of a horse.

After what seemed like hours, the horse stopped, and Squire was pulled roughly off. The sack was yanked free. He stood blinking. He was in a cave, that much was certain. But they were not very deep in the cave, since daylight streamed in behind Squire.

"Stoke the fire, boy-o, and then fix grub. It's over there." A man pointed to a jumble of bags and boxes along one wall of the cave. He was a burly fellow with a pugnacious face covered with several days' worth of stubble. He had low brows, and his leather clothing was greasy and stained.

"Don't think so," young Squire said defiantly, despite the pain in his head from being hit. His tears also had dried long ago, though he was still scared right down to his toes. But he was not about to yield easily to this filthy, rank slob.

The man smacked Squire with an open palm, then swung the arm the other way, backhanding the boy. The man was not much taller than eleven-year-old Squire, but he was brawny and powerful. Squire's head snapped this way, then that. Combined with the blow he had taken earlier, the slaps left his head ringing.

"Ye watch yer mout', boy-o, and ye do like I says," the man growled. His voice was rough from years of tobacco and whiskey.

Squire considered jumping the man. His temper was flaring, and he thought he was big enough to take him. But the thought was fleeting, since he remembered right off that there was a second man. He hadn't seen that one and had no idea where he was. The other could very well be right behind him, though he did not think so. He decided to do what he was told, biding his time.

In the week they spent in the cave, Squire was kept tied up most of the time. The second man, Simon Crump, was gone for several days, leaving Squire to the none-too-kind care of Elkanah Gill. When he wasn't bound, Squire was doing chores under Gill's watchful eyes. During those times, Gill always sat there with a pistol held loosely in hand.

"What'd ye take me away for?" Squire asked one day while he was lugging two buckets of water up from the brook.

"Got me reasons, boy-o."

Two days later, Crump returned. That night, Squire heard Crump and Gill talking softly, but he could make out nothing of what was said. The next morning, Crump untied Squire and told him to load the supplies and saddle the horses.

Soon after, they left the cave. They traveled for four long days, weaving through thick stands of birches, beeches, sycamores, and firs. The scent of pine and flowering dogwood was heavy in the air. Finally they stopped in another cave. This one was much larger than the last, a giant hole punched into the side of a granite mountain. A three-inch-wide ribbon of water rippled down the rocks inside, providing water.

Squire didn't know what to think of all this. He had figured that the men would kill him. But after two weeks, he was still alive, if rather battered. So Squire wondered just what the hell the two men were up to.

The boy began to lose some of his fear. He figured that if they had planned to kill him, they would have done so already. He was baffled by why they had taken him, though he had gotten it into his head that the two men had some half-baked idea of keeping him as some sort of slave. With that thought in mind, however right or wrong, he strived to work harder, trying to anticipate the desires of his captors. That way he hoped to avoid beatings and to lull the two men into easing up on him—then he might have a chance to escape.

The fear returned to full bloom, however, a few days later. Crump had gone off again, and when he returned, he brought a small wooden keg of rum with him. The two men tapped the keg after eating a perfunctory meal. Neither looked happy. They drank heavily while they puffed their pipes.

Shortly after eating, Squire turned in. He pretended to sleep. Crump and Gill spoke in normal tones, not worried about Squire.

"Still nuttin' from that Squire, goddamn him," Crump grumbled. "Maybe he ain't gonna pay up."

"He'll pay," Gill growled. "He'll pay." His voice faded but distinct. "It'll teach that no-good bastard to thrash Elkanah Gill and t'row me out in the street. Goddamn him."

"Why doesn't we just kill the boy now, 'stead of waitin'?" Crump interjected. He sounded like the idea held a great deal of interest for him. "Ain't no use in keepin' the little beggar alive."

"Aye, there is, Simon." Though Squire could not see it, Gill's eyes burned with an unnatural luster. "That goddamn Squire might ask to see the brat b'fore he pays up." His voice betrayed the fact that he would not allow the boy to live much beyond that, if that even occurred.

"But more'n that," Gill continued, "I want Squire to see the brat's body when I dump it off, after I get me the gold. I don't figure to cart 'round no festerin' corpse whilst we wait for Squire to gather his coins. The little bastard can serve us." He laughed harshly, thinking it sweet irony that the boy would be their servant while they waited for the ransom and then would die at their hands once they had their money.

A chill crept up Squire's back, but he kept his silence. He knew now, though, why they had taken him and what his fate was to be. He vowed he would not let their plan come to fruition.

The next morning, Gill kicked Squire after breakfast and ordered him to pack up the supplies.

"We movin' again?" Squire asked innocently.

"Jus' do what I tol' ye," Gill responded, punctuating the statement with another boot to Squire's rear end.

Squire almost exploded in rage. For more than two weeks, he had been subservient. He was not even that way with his family. It was eating at his young soul, and he wanted to lash out. Only a fragment of common sense—the legacy of his mother, he figured—kept him still. He nodded and went to work.

But as he packed the supplies, he slid out a knife that he found in one of the packs. He dropped it on the ground and kept working. When Gill and Crump went outside for a few minutes, Squire hastily fashioned a slipknot at each end of a long rawhide thong. He scooped up the knife and slid each slipknot over the wooden hilt. Then he hung the thong around his neck, so the knife was inside his shirt, dangling against his belly. He smiled grimly to himself. Simon Crump and Elkanah Gill were in for a rude and fatal surprise one day soon.

They traveled another three long days, heading mostly westward, but a little southward, too. They stopped in another cave and set up their camp. That night, Gill and Crump started drinking rum, tapped from the keg into tin mugs. Squire turned in, pulling his one thin blanket around him. He was shaking with excitement. Tonight, he thought. Tonight will be the time.

He waited until he figured the two men were pretty well drunk. With anger, expectation, and fear coursing though his young veins, he finally slipped the cord over his neck and carefully pulled the knots loose and then off the hilt. He cast off his blanket and rose, smiling disarmingly as the two men blearily looked in his direction. The knife was held casually behind his back.

"Where're you goin'?" Gill asked, gravelly voice slurred.

"Got to piss," Squire said. He wiped his eyes, trying to pretend he was sleepy. He was such an incredibly poor actor that he wouldn't have fooled anyone but a couple of men so besotted by alcohol they were barely aware someone was there at all.

"Go on with ye, then," Crump snapped. He laughed, knowing the boy did not have long left to live.

Squire shuffled forward, still trying without much success to feign tiredness. As he passed by Crump's back, he found the streak of savagery his father had warned him might be hidden deep in his soul. He suddenly stopped, whirled, knocked off Crump's ancient tricorn, grabbed the man's hair and pulled his head back. The knife moved in a blur and suddenly a long gash appeared in Crump's throat.

Squire shoved the man's head to the side. Gurgling and gasping, Crump fell. He tried to get up, spraying blood all over.

Squire was not paying any attention. As soon as he had flung Crump away, he stepped forward. Not worrying about the pain, he stuck a boot into the fire and kicked some of the burning wood and coals at Gill.

Gill had gone for the pistol in his belt as soon as he saw Squire acting. He had the flintlock halfway out when the burning shower hit him in the chest. With his left hand, he slapped at the embers that singed his hair and set his homespun cloth shirt on fire in several spots. But that did not stop him from continuing to pull the pistol.

Squire walked through the fire and kicked out. His boot caught Gill's arm, and the pistol sailed away. Gill surged up, small flickers of flame still on his shirt. He punched Squire in the chest, his anger and strength lessened only by his drunkenness.

The boy staggered back under the power of the blow. He stumbled through the fire, nearly falling over Crump, who lay in a heap, blood still seeping out of his neck, pooling on the rock and snaking toward the fire, where it hissed.

Squire almost dropped the knife, too, but managed to keep it. Gill charged at him, but he was not too steady on his feet. It allowed Squire to get himself set and brace himself. When

Gill plowed into him, Squire was ready. He took the jolt, only giving way a few steps. But at the same time, he jerked the knife upward.

Gill grunted when the blade punctured his belly flesh. His bloodshot eyes widened and glared angrily at the boy. His hands sought out Squire's throat. Latching onto it, Gill squeezed.

Squire jerked the knife free and plunged it into Gill's belly and chest three times. By then, he could feel Gill's hands loosening and slipping away from his throat. Gill began to fall, and Squire gave him a push.

The boy stood there, breathing heavily. He was shocked that he had accomplished what he had. He was more stunned that he had been so savage in dispatching the two men. Shaking, he dropped the knife and went outside. He vomited several times. When he was finished spitting the foul residue out of his mouth, he urinated. With some trepidation, he went back into the cave. He curled up in his blanket, hoping the remains of the fire and the human smell would keep any scavengers away from the bodies.

He looked without fear on the bodies in the morning. Indeed, he found he had an appetite. He ate well, then packed the supplies. He took Gill's pistol and rifle, as well as powder horn and shooting bag. He saddled one of the horses and hooked the others, including the pack horse, to it with rope. Then he rode off.

He had no idea of where he was. He only knew that in all the traveling Crump and Gill had done, they had ridden mostly west. So he turned east, trying to find a path or a trail.

Two days later, he pulled to a stop when he heard a strange noise off the trail. He sat listening for a minute before he realized it was a bear. Not wanting to get mixed up with a bear, he started the horses moving again. Then he heard a voice.

He slid off the horse and quickly tied it to a bush. With rifle in hand he ran for the sound. He slammed to a stop, heart pounding in fear, when he saw a black bear mauling an Indian boy just a few years older than himself. The boy was fighting wildly, trying to stab the bear wherever he could reach. He was mostly silent, shouting only once in a while.

Squire was an excellent shot already, but Gill's rifle was unfamiliar to him. Still, he could not just stand here and let the bear make a meal out of this Indian. He threw the rifle up to his shoulder, tried to steady himself, and fired.

He knew he had hit the bear full on, but the bruin seemed to be unaffected. It whirled and charged at him.

"Providence save me," Squire whispered as he dropped the rifle and pulled the pistol. He fired. That ball hit the bear, too, but the animal did not stop. The next thing Squire knew, the bear was sinking its fangs into his shoulder. Squire bellowed in surprise, ripped out his knife and began stabbing at the bear.

He didn't know if the Indian had weakened the bear or if it was his bullets, but the bruin's gnawing and slashing at him slowed. Suddenly the animal gasped and fell dead right atop Squire.

The boy scrambled to get out from under the animal's weight. When he managed, he looked at his wounds. There were several spots bleeding, but he didn't think any of them were too bad. He hurried to the Indian boy.

Squire had never been close to an Indian. The Indians where he lived had long ago gone away. The boy was not as frightful looking as Squire might have thought. He was pretty hurt, though, and looked at Squire with a combination of pain and fear in his eyes.

"Where's your people?" Squire asked.

"Southwest," the boy said, surprising Squire in that he spoke English. "Near the Genesee River."

"I don't know where that is," Squire said apologetically. "You well enough to show me?"

"Don't know. Go southwest. In three or four days you'll come to the river."

"Hope I can make it that long myself," Squire muttered. "What be your people?"

"Seneca."

Squire bound up the youngster's wounds as best he could and then went to get the horses. He helped the youth onto a horse. "What's your name?" he asked.

The Indian rattled off a string of words in his own tongue, then, "Among your people I am called Tin Kettle."

Squire nodded. "I be Nathaniel."

• • •

Squire remembered little of the trip after that first day. All he knew was that he grew progressively weaker from loss of blood, especially when he had to help Tin Kettle so much. He sort of remembered riding along slumped on his horse.

He awoke in a Seneca lodge, not knowing where he was or how long he had been there. He was afraid. Then Tin Kettle and two men came in and sat near his pallet of furs and blankets. They patiently explained to him in halting English that he was in a Seneca town on the west bank of the Genesee River. That he had come in, barely alive, with Tin Kettle. The Senecas had nursed both youngsters back to health. Tin Kettle had recovered more quickly and told his people how he had come to be in his condition and how Squire had helped him home.

One of the two older warriors told Squire that he had been adopted into his family. "You will be my son, as equal as my other sons," he said seriously.

"I got a pa," Squire said weakly. "And I'll miss him somethin' awful."

"Then you will stay until you are well enough to travel," Tall Birch said. "We will send an escort to return you to your father."

But by the time Squire had regained his full health, winter sat over the harsh land like an angry spirit. Squire spent the winter months getting to know the Senecas some. In the spring, he decided he could wait a little longer before leaving, since he was enjoying his time here.

Then a visitor came, a tall, regal-looking Shawnee named Tecumseh. Squire was privileged to sit in the Seneca councils to listen to the visitor, but he did not understand enough of the Indian languages to really follow what went on.

Late in the summer, Squire decided it was time to leave. The Senecas seemed agitated after the visit by Tecumseh, and he no longer felt comfortable in the town. Besides, he missed his father and mother. Tin Kettle and three other young warriors accompanied him until he was near the farms a few miles from the town where the Squire family had their farm and flour mill.

There was great rejoicing when Squire appeared at his family's home, just in time for supper. He suffered his mother's well-meaning ministrations and his oldest brother's annoyance as he filled his belly and recounted his adventure.

Two weeks later, they had the celebration.

The boy was different, though. He had been out in the world, had killed two men with only a knife, had saved someone from a bear, and had lived with Indians for a year. All of which served to make his oldest brother, Joshua, even more antagonistic to him than before. Joshua ran the family farmstead and the mill with an iron hand when their father, Ezekiel, was not around. That was happening more and more as Ezekiel took more of an interest in local politics and turned his attentions there.

Squire could see right off that Joshua was trying to drive his brothers away to ensure that he would have it all to himself. As the eldest Squire, it was his right anyway. He made Nathaniel's life as miserable as he could, though with Nathaniel's great size and wild temperament, he could not be pushed far.

Things were bound to come to a head between Nathaniel and Joshua, but that was more or less avoided two years later. Nathaniel was caught with his pants down and his ardor up in his neighbor's loft with the neighbor's daughter. He left home to save his family any disgrace.

He headed southwest, looking for the Seneca village. He found where it had been, but it was long deserted. He trekked west, but he never did find his adoptive people.

Early the next spring, he signed on with Manuel Lisa's men heading up the Missouri River.

-13-

Squire awoke on the riverbank with a throbbing head and a sour stomach.

"Waugh," he muttered, pushing himself up so that he was sitting. "Goddamn ol' fool. Think ye'd know better after all this time, wouldn't ye, goddamn ol' coon like ye."

There was, he knew, little that could be done about the effects of last night's drinking spree. But at least the demons that had visited him in the night were gone.

He did not often sink into depression, though when it came upon him, it usually was intense. And, during those times, folks who knew him gave him a wide berth. He felt a sense of relief in knowing that none of his brigade had come across him. He did not want any of his men to find him in such a state.

He pushed himself up gingerly. "*Merde*," he muttered as he felt the earth spinning wildly in front of him. He blinked hard and sucked in air. Finally the world stayed put, more or less. He took two steps toward the Green River, then sank heavily back down, resting on his hands and knees.

"*Merde*," he muttered again. Then he vomited.

He remained on his hands and knees for a while. Then, with a mighty groan, he shoved himself back up until he was on his feet. He stumbled the remaining few feet to the creek and plunged into it, head first.

"Waugh!" he bellowed, surging up from the cool water,

shaking his great mane. He dunked his head a few more times and gulped down some of the fresh, cold water, trying to ease the burning sourness in his belly.

At last, he waded out and headed for his camp, gaining strength as he walked. There were still plenty of buffalo to be had in the vicinity, and he hoped someone had managed to bring in some fresh meat. There was nothing like some fresh roasted rump or tongue or ribs to settle a man's alcohol-churned stomach, he thought.

When Squire strolled into his camp, Train had some meat hanging over a fire. Squire settled himself down, saying, "Mornin', lad." He sighed heavily, hoping his discomfort was not evident. "Ye lads be lookin' right fresh."

Train and Hannah grinned. "Can't say the same for you, Nathaniel," Train said with a big, friendly smile. "You look like you've been wrasslin' a polecat."

"Smells like it, too," Hannah offered. She wrinkled her nose in mock offense.

"Weren't no polecat I was wrasslin', lad," Squire said rue-fully. He felt no regret for having gotten drunk, only for the aftereffects. "It were Lightnin'. The devil's own brew, goddamnit. This chil's gotten a mite ol' for such doin's. Was a time when I could wrassle with *aguardiente* all the night and still be comin' out the winner. Waugh!"

He shook his head carefully, not wanting to start up the reverberation that would roil his stomach again. "But all this here talkin' makes my head hurt." He reached out and sliced off some meat with his knife. Leaning back against a log, he chewed and swallowed slowly. He was hungry and enjoyed the taste of the half-raw meat, but he wanted to give his stomach a chance to adjust to it.

"What'd ye two lads do last night?" Squire asked between bites. Then he laughed and said, "Reckon there be no need to be askin' ye two such a thing, eh?"

Hannah blushed and looked away, but she was smiling; Train grinned in cocky manfulness.

"But I meant aside from such doin's," Squire added, still chuckling.

"Played some music mostly," Train said, returning the smile. "And did a bit of dancin'."

"Where in hell'd ye learn to play that thing, lad?" Squire asked, surprised.

"Back to home. I come from hardscrabble mountains in Kentucky, and I been playin' one since I could remember. Ain't seen one in a while, though."

Squire nodded. "Where'd ye find it?"

"Borrowed it from some ol' feller. It's been a heap of time since I played one."

"Ye done well from what I heard of ye."

Train nodded. "It's somethin' that don't seem to leave a body." He shrugged and grinned. "Hell, I were even thinkin' of tryin' to buy it from the ol' coot."

"Ain't such a bad idea, I 'spect." Squire nodded. "You might find him in a game one time and out-euchre him for it."

Train's eyes blazed in interest. He had precious little money. Even with what the Colonel had given him, and what he still had coming. He had Hannah now, and he had to think of the future. But if he could win the instrument . . . The possibility pleased him.

"Where be the Colonel?" Squire asked. "And Homer, Li'l Jim, and the others?"

"Ain't seed hide nor hair of Li'l Jim," Train chuckled. "I think he's got himself a squaw. Homer left a bit ago. Didn't say where he was goin'. And the Colonel," Train added with a snigger that was echoed by Hannah, "is still in his tent."

"That ol' fart just can't get enough of that little Injin gal, can he?" Squire said with another chuckle. Then he moaned as the hangover forcefully re-asserted itself, twisting into his innards.

"I don't think that's exactly right, Nathaniel," Train said after a momentary bout of laughter. When the big mountain man looked at him quizzically, Train said, "You'll have to see for yourself."

Squire nodded. "Well, I reckon I'd best be seein' if Star Path can be fixin' me somethin' that'll ease off this goddamn painin' in my head and such."

He stood gingerly, then looked around. "*Merde,*" he suddenly snapped.

"What's wrong?" Hannah asked, not too concerned. She figured it was just that the hangover was plaguing Squire.

"Star Path be some powerful angry, lads," Squire muttered. "Aye, that she be."

"How do you know?" Hannah asked, surprised. She and Star Path had become good friends when they had suffered through their ordeal with the Blackfeet together, and whenever she was not with Train, she tried to stay by the Sioux woman. But when she had seen Star Path this morning, she could not tell that anything was wrong with the woman.

"She's throwed all my plunder outten the lodge," Squire said. He pointed. "Means she be wantin' me outten her life."

"No!" Hannah gasped, startled. "She wouldn't ever do that." She cared deeply for both Squire and Star Path and would hate to see them split apart. Her allegiance was stretched.

"Aye, Hannah, she would," Squire said. The others could not tell whether he was bothered by it. "But I aim to see about patchin' things up with her right off."

Squire wandered off, walking slowly. Star Path came out of the lodge and squatted to her work. By the time Squire loomed over her, the Sioux woman was busy, her stubby fingers beading a pair of moccasins. When she did not look up, Squire gingerly knelt and lifted her chin with his finger. She snapped her head away and looked to her work again.

"Come on now, woman," Squire said softly, "don't ye be actin' this way."

She spit an epithet at him in Sioux.

"I ain't e'er lodgepoled ye afore, Star Path," Squire said with a slight edge to his voice. "But I be of a mind to mayhap start now. Just tell me what your problem be. We was apart for too long afore. Now ye be carryin' my chil', and I ain't fixin' to let ye go out of my life less'n ye be havin' a damned good reason for it."

The words suddenly boiled out of her mouth: "Where you go last night? You with another woman? Eh? I'm not good enough for you no more? You leave me here with baby in belly while you lay with some dirty Shoshoni. Or maybe a Nez Perce bitch. Goddamn. I know these things. You no care . . . you no good, goddamnit. You not come home . . . must be laying with other woman. Then I not want you no more. You take your things and go. Goddamn. Not come back. I find another man . . . One . . ."

"What'n hell are ye talkin' about, woman?" Squire exploded. He slapped a huge hand over her mouth to cut off the stream of her words. When she quit her struggling to continue her outburst, Squire said quietly, "I ain't been with no other woman. I got ye, Star Path. That be enough for me. I don't need no other woman. Where'd ye get such a goddamn foolish notion anyway?"

He released his hand, and once more the words tumbled out of Star Path on top of each other: "You didn't come home. I made special food for you, but you stay away . . . All night. You don't come to the lodge . . . And my bed. I wait . . . But you don't come . . ." Her voice was rising.

Once more the big hand dammed up the river of words. "*Merde,* woman, ye got to be slowin' down. And keep your voice down, damnit. Ye be gettin' too loud."

She mumbled against his hand, and he removed it.

"You afraid others hear?" Star Path asked, almost haughtily. "I don't care. Let 'em hear. Then they'll know what kind of man you are." She stopped on her own this time, and her voice had been quieter.

"Ye know better'n that, Star Path. I don't much give a shit who hears. But, goddamnit, I got me a head feels like a buff'lo bull did himself a war dance on it. I was comin' to ye to be seekin' some relief from this with your herbs and such. I can't set here and take this nonsensical jabberin' ye been makin'. Now, will ye shut your trap and let me try'n talk to ye?"

When she nodded, Squire breathed a sigh of relief. He felt worse than he had ever felt after such a night, and he had the momentary worry that he might be getting old. He brushed the thought aside. "Now, ye just take a good look at me, woman," he said. "Does it look like I been layin' with someone else?"

"Well . . ." Star Path mumbled.

"Goddamnit," Squire snapped. Then he groaned and held his head in both hands for a moment. He raised his head and looked blearily at Star Path with bloodshot eyes. In a much quieter voice, he said, "I weren't with no one else, Star Path. I got me piss-eyed roarin' drunk and went off down by the creek to be myself. I've done that afore, ye know that. That fire water filled my head and my heart with a heap of bad spirits last night, woman. That be all."

"You get sick?" It was more of a statement than a question.

"Aye." He grinned ruefully. "Puked half my guts out in the doin', too, like as not. And I got it all over this here fine shirt ye made for me. For that, I be sorry, Star Path."

"I'll clean it." She stared suspiciously at him for a few moments, but then decided to believe him. He was not the type of man to lie. Had he been with another woman, he would have said so, and then tried to talk her into taking him back. He would not sit here and whine and plead for forgiveness in any case. He would own up to whatever it was.

She put her work down and took his hands. "Come," she said, rising. "I'll give you something to make you better. It'll drive those bad spirits out."

"What about all my plunder?" he asked, pointing to all his goods.

"We'll see to it later," Star Path said huskily.

Inside the lodge, Star Path made Squire lie down. She went to a *parfleche* and took out a small leather pouch. From it she got an odd-looking root. She put it in an old pot with some water. While Star Path made the decoction of prairie ground root, Squire sat with his eyes closed. Finally it was ready, and he gulped down the hot, musky liquid. He followed it with two quick but healthy drinks of whiskey from a jug Star Path had handed him.

After he had taken his medicine, Squire rested his head. Star Path knelt next to him, gently massaging his forehead and temples. Thinking he had dozed off, Star Path started to rise, but Squire grabbed her and pulled her playfully down on the robes. He kissed her several times and then shoved her dress up as far as it would go.

"No," Star Path said, not very sternly. "Take time. Make good."

Anger flickered in Squire's eyes for just a moment. Then he relaxed and smiled. "Aye, woman, make good."

He lay back down, hands behind his head. Star Path stood and shrugged out of her dress. There were little signs of her pregnancy, but her earlier childbearing had left her breasts heavy, the nipples thick and dark against her dusky skin.

Her flesh was ample, but Squire had always liked her that

way. He enjoyed the feel of her thick, silky thighs, the weight of her full breasts and wide buttocks. He could never understand how a man could be satisfied with some emaciated scarecrow of a woman.

She leaned over him, her pendulous breasts swaying over his face. He darted his head upward and nipped at her left nipple. Star Path gasped in delight and arched her back as Squire's teeth and tongue worked on first one and then the other. His hand shoved between her nude pubic area and his pants-covered groin, fingers searching. She gasped.

After screeching in delight twice and feeling herself warming up again, Star Path finally scooted back and off Squire. She frantically scrabbled to yank down his buckskin trousers. He was ready for her. She thought for a moment of pleasuring him a little before climbing onto him. But she decided she could not wait. She rose, squatted over him, and then sank down onto him with a drawn-out moan.

Squire grunted with emotion. He grabbed her and rolled, until he was atop her. It was not long before both were yelling in their ecstasy.

Soon, Squire fell asleep. Star Path smiled, teeth bright in the dim lodge. She cradled him against her bosom. He snored softly as she stroked his hair.

But his weight soon became too great for her, and Star Path wriggled out from beneath him. He awoke, and she calmed him, slid out, and made sure he was asleep again. Humming a soft, happy tune, she slipped on her dress and stepped out of the tipi into the bright sunlight.

-14-

When Squire awoke two hours later, his things were back in the lodge, neatly placed where they belonged. He could hear Star Path singing softly outside. He felt much better as he adjusted his clothing. Outside, he stroked Star Path's cheek with a big, calloused finger before heading off. With a little bit of a smirk, he headed toward where some of the others were sitting around a fire.

"How be ye lads . . . ?" he started jovially. Then he stopped, eyebrows raised, and asked in surprise, "*Merde,* what'n the hell happened to ye, Colonel?"

Melton sat at the fire, a grimace covering his mottled face. "Nothing," he mumbled.

Squire half grinned. "Now, ye know goddamn well I ain't gonna be believin' such a thing, Colonel," he said joyfully. By the evidence, he had taken a considerable beating. That could mean trouble. But Squire would not worry until he knew all the particulars.

"Ye have a run-in with a griz?" he asked after a moment's pause. "Or mayhap your sweet little Risin' Sun set on to ye after ye tried some doin's that didn't set well with her?" He snickered. The thought of Melton doing something so offensive to Rising Sun to make her attack him was quite ludicrous.

"Neither," Melton snapped indignantly. His usually jovial face was bruised and discolored. He worried his tongue over a loose tooth as he sat, head down.

98

"Why don't ya tell him, Colonel?" Train urged with a laugh. "Else I will."

"Don't you dare," Melton threatened, lifting his head to glare balefully at Train.

"What're ya gonna do to stop me, Colonel?" Train said, continuing to laugh.

"I still hold a goodly portion of your wages, young man," Melton said. It was surly.

"Hell, I ain't ever had no money anyway," Train said with another laugh.

He paused, making sure he had all attention, then he said cheerily, "Well, seems like while the ol' Colonel here was kickin' up his heels, some other coon took a shine to Risin' Sun. At first that chil' just wanted to *fandango,* but then he got more'n more drunk, till he was startin' to grab her and all . . ."

Colonel Melton was a man slow to anger, and it gave the hectoring, offensive mountain man courage—that and the bottle he drank from constantly.

"Come, Rising Sun," Melton had finally said. "We'll go."

"Like hell ya will, boy," the mountain man said nastily. He grabbed Rising Sun's arm and pulled her toward him. "Ye just come wit' me, lassie," he said sharply.

"Unhand her, you son of a bitch," Melton snarled, surprising even himself with his vigor and anger.

"And what if I don't . . . ?" the man started. He had turned, a sneer on his face.

Melton punched the man, sending him sprawling. A growing crowd cheered and hooted. "Come, Rising Sun," Melton said sternly. He took the woman's arm.

But the circle of mountain men and warriors would not let them pass. "Y'all started somethin' here, ol' son," one mountain man said. "It'd be best was y'all to finish it."

"Now you listen to . . ." Melton started. Then the mountain man who had been pestering Rising Sun slammed into his back, knocking his wind out. The man pounced on the Colonel, smashing Melton's face into the rough dirt, pounding on the back of his head.

Melton was aware of the roaring crowd, even as disembodied as the cacophony was. Still, he could make out individual voices or statements from time to time:

"Hit him agin, George."

Or "Carve him, Parker."

Even an occasional "Get up and go at him, Colonel."

Melton regained his breath and shoved himself up, knocking Parker loose as he did. He spun to face the mountain man, who was scrambling to his feet.

For the first time, Melton really looked at his adversary. George Parker was of medium height, with long, scrawny arms ending in extremely large, knob-knuckled hands. His chest was broad and his neck bull-like. He had very large ears, where Melton could see them under the hat, and long, lank, greasy hair. His beak-like nose had long ago been pushed well off center.

Melton took a few moments to regain his breath. He was a big man, too, but was something out of shape for such endeavors as these. In addition, he was used to civilized fighting. He had been an officer and would always retain that haughty feeling. He was not used to scrabbling around in the dirt like a common thug.

Parker moved forward, closing the gap between him and Melton. Suddenly he kicked out, boot aiming for Melton's groin. The Colonel managed to turn enough to catch the kick on one broad thigh. But when he thought of how close it had come to doing him permanent damage, he blanched. It hurt but nothing like it would have otherwise. He lashed out with a fist but missed.

Parker leaped into the gap and pounded Melton three times in the face.

Melton stumbled to the side from the blows. He whaled out wildly with his fist, but hit only air. Parker laughed and hit him twice more.

Melton suddenly spun and grabbed Parker in a bear hug, squeezing for all he was worth.

Parker wheezed, as the pressure threatened to crack his ribs. Suddenly he reared his head back and then jerked it forward. His forehead smashed into Melton's. The Colonel gasped with the pain and loosened his grip.

Parker landed, grabbed a lungful of air, and then waded back in, pounding lefts and rights on Melton as the Colonel tried without great success to cover up. Finally he fell.

The mountain man tried to kick Melton in the side, but the Colonel grabbed Parker's foot and twisted with all his might. Parker howled and fell. He kicked Melton in the face with his other foot to get free. He stood, favoring the wrenched ankle. As he lurched forward, he pulled his knife.

Suddenly a large knife was quivering in the dirt less than an inch from his left foot. Train moved up, stopping right in front of Parker.

"Sheath your knife, boy," Train growled. "There's no call for you to be tryin' to carve my friend. You've whupped him pretty good without it so far."

"Get outten my way, sonny, or I'll gut ye all the way to the Green River."

Train calmly bent and pulled his knife from the dirt. Then he slowly wiped it clean on his shirt, all the while staring hard into Parker's eyes.

"This isn't your fight, Abner," Melton said from behind him.

"I know that, Colonel," Train answered. He still had not taken his eyes from Parker's bloodshot ones. "I ain't aimin' to fight your battles for ya. I just aim to see it's fair is all."

"Let'em fight," someone yelled. Others growled agreement.

"Soon's this niggur sheaths his blade," Train said calmly. "Less'n someone's of a mind to come out here and change my mind for me." It was a challenge.

Several men started out from the crowd. But suddenly Hannah, Li'l Jim, Josiah Maxwell, Gideon Hook, and two other men from the brigade were at Train's side. The others stopped.

"What's it gonna be, boy?" Train asked, still glaring at Parker.

Parker spit at Train's feet, then shoved his knife back into the sheath. "Now, get outten my way, boy. I got me some business to finish up here."

Train sheathed his own blade. He and his friends stepped back into the ring of mountain men and Indians. But the delay had given Melton time to recover a little. He moved a little slowly, but so did Parker, now that his ankle was damaged.

As Train had passed Melton, he had said quietly, "Ya got to fight like he does, Colonel, or you've had it."

Melton nodded imperceptibly. He had known it, of course. Still, it went against his grain, and he did not want to admit it. But it was clear now—either fight like Parker did, or get killed.

Suddenly he charged, barreling down on the smaller man. Parker, caught unaware and unable to move quickly, was not ready. Melton plowed into him, slamming him down on the hard-packed earth.

The Colonel began beating Parker's face and chest, sometimes missing the man and pounding on the dirt instead. But he hit more often than not, and it began taking its toll.

Parker squirmed and lashed out. Twice he tried to bite Melton's nose, but the Colonel avoided it both times. He did finally manage to drive a greasy thumb into Melton's eye, sending the Colonel stumbling and reeling away.

Parker got up and charged at Melton, who stood his ground, one eye clamped shut. He rained blows on Parker, who finally stood toe to toe with him and tried to match the furious flurry of punches.

But the two were weakening fast. Parker went down first, sinking to his knees and then slumping to the side. Melton staggered and swayed before crumpling in a heap.

A hoot and holler went up from the crowd, and money and other goods passed from hand to hand as wagers were paid. It had been a good fight, even though dark was nearabout full on them now and some of the finer points had been missed.

Train and Li'l Jim came forward, grabbed Melton by the arms and hauled him up. The Colonel tried to look around, but the one eye was all bloodshot, and both were puffy. He had trouble breathing through his nose, and all his joints ached. The world swam before him, but he managed to slow it enough to see other men helping Parker up.

"You keep away from my woman, goddamnit," Melton managed to gargle. "You hear me, boy?" He had tried to snarl but did not have the strength.

Parker nodded weakly.

"Come on, Colonel," Train said with a low chuckle. "Time for you to hit the robes."

Train and Li'l Jim supported most of Melton's weight as they walked off toward camp. Rising Sun looked frightened as she followed closely behind them, while Hannah, still in her male guise, escorted her.

-15-

"Well, I'll be damned," Squire said with a hearty laugh. "So ye set yourself to fightin' just for your squaw's honor. Goddamn. And ye, who didn't want nary to do with Injin women not so long ago." He shook his head in mock amazement.

The others laughed hard as Melton just groaned with the pain of his injuries. His mind was eased, though. He felt more a part of the men than he ever had.

"Ye'd best be havin' someone see to them injuries, Colonel," Squire said more seriously. "Star Path has some learnin' of herbs and such, but I be thinkin' ye be needin' more'n that. I can check with some of the tribes, see who might be willin' to have their medicine man look ye o'er."

"That won't be necessary, Nathaniel," Melton said defensively. He was in agony but did not want to admit it. He had seen some of the other men in the brigade, and years ago, too, in the Army, who had been wounded far worse, and yet who had kept their composure. He did not want to be belittled in front of his men. "It's mostly cuts and bruises. They'll go away with time."

"Mayhap they will. But ye can get someone who knows ways to ease the pain so's ye can commence to healin'."

"If you think it better, then, Nathaniel." Melton sounded dejected again.

"Ye needn't be ashamed of any of this, Colonel," Squire said consolingly.

"I acted the fool, Nathaniel," Melton snapped. "I am supposed to be the leader of this expedition, to set an example for the others. Yet I find myself fighting in the dirt like a common savage." He sighed. "Hell and tarnation."

"Shit, don't take it to heart so, Colonel," Squire said with a chuckle. "It be the way of things out here. Look at them others—Bridger, Fitzpatrick, the Sublettes. They all be partisans, owners of a fur company, yet those lads'll be fightin' at the drop of a hat, like as not. Ye was protectin' your woman. Ain't no harm nor shame in that."

"But she isn't my wife."

"It be the closest ye'll be findin' to one out here, Colonel. And ye'll nary be findin' women who're better for a man than an Injin woman. Ain't no white woman gonna compare to 'em." He grinned hugely. " 'Cept maybe Hannah here."

"I suppose you're right, Nathaniel," Melton said with a touch of regret.

"Aye, lad, that I be. And ye should get used to seein' fightin' here. It be part of rendezvous. All these young bucks runnin' around, full of *aguardiente* and boilin' blood. Worse'n goddamn buff'lo come ruttin' time. Always ready to fight."

Squire stood. "Well, lads, I'd best be seein' if I can find someone to tend to the Colonel."

He was back in less than an hour. "Ye be in luck, Colonel," he said.

Melton glanced up at him, worried when he thought he detected a hidden grin lurking on the big mountain man's broad, weather-beaten face. "Oh?" he asked warily.

"Aye. Risin' Sun's people rode in this mornin'. Their medicine man, Blue Rattle, says he'll be helpin' ye. For a fee, of course."

"And how much will that be?" Melton asked. He was wary.

Squire shrugged. "A pouch of tobacco maybe. Or a knife or somethin'. Ye'll have no trouble findin' somethin' small he'll be wantin', Colonel."

"Well, I'd better get on over there," Melton said. He stood, sighing with aches and weariness. His face contorted with the pain, but he looked proud when he had accomplished the maneuver. He stood for a moment to get his bearings. "Where's their camp?" he asked.

Squire pointed north, up the river.

"Rising Sun," he called. "Come on. Your people are here, and we're going to go see them. Come now. Hurry." He was ever the commissioned officer.

Rising Sun, eyes expectant, hurried up, and the two left, walking slowly.

When they were gone, Train said, "I didn't want to say nothin' while the Colonel was here, Nathaniel, but I think we might have a bit of trouble arisin'."

"How so, lad?" He pulled a piece of meat from the fire and popped it into his mouth.

"I saw Farley Walker and Tom O'Neely near the packs of furs last night. And again this mornin'."

"So? They got plews in there, too, though they don't rightly belong to them two."

"Well, when I went to look after those two was gone, the packs seemed messed up some, like somebody had pulled a plew or two out of the middle of several packs."

"Don't mean too much, I reckon," Squire allowed. He betrayed no emotion, though he was annoyed. "I expect they've run out of their cash already and figured they could make off with a couple of plews to cash in. It won't hurt us much, but we'll want to see it don't happen again. We can afford to lose a couple of plews now and again, but we can't stand to have it be happenin' regular."

Squire stretched and yawned. "This ol' coon's gettin' lazy just settin' 'round here like this." He rose to full height. "I aim to go find me some action."

"Can we come?" Li'l Jim asked.

"Aye, lads."

Cradling their rifles, they walked over to Etienne Gravant's small camp.

"Eh, *mes amis,*" Gravant said, "you are ready for de celebrating now, eh?"

"*Oui, mon ami,*" Squire said. "I aim to be winnin' me some shootin' contests, goddamnit, and mayhap try my medicine at the hand game somewhere."

"Don' play de 'and game wit' de Flat'eads dis year. *Non.* They winning everyt'ing."

"They ain't met up with this ol' niggur, Etienne. *Allons.*"

They walked through the throngs of people toward Campbell's tent to buy some whiskey.

Campbell was inside the big tent, toting up goods and such. He greeted Squire and his companions jovially, his burr thick and pronounced.

"Och, laddies," he said, "come for some refreshments, have ye?" He jerked his head, and the bartender—a different one from the last time—placed several bottles on the plank bar, where he awaited the appearance of some cash.

Squire handed Campbell a few coins and reached for one of the bottles. He drank deeply. "Waugh! That be prime, Robert. Plumb prime, I'd be sayin'." He passed the bottle to Gravant.

"Och, it ought to be, laddie. It come over from me own dear Scotland."

"It's come a fair piece then."

"Aye."

"Not as far as that milk that time, though."

"Milk?" Train asked, unable to refrain.

Campbell's usually dour face brightened at the remembrance.

"Aye, lad," Squire said. "It was three year ago, I be thinkin'. Mister Campbell's partner, Bill Sublette, brung himself a heap of wagons to rendezvous."

"So?" Hannah said, unimpressed. There were wagons all over rendezvous. Anyone could see that.

"It was the first time, laddie," Campbell said. "No one had ever brought wagons out this far before."

Hannah nodded. Then she looked up, eyes full of question. "But what about the milk?"

"He brought a goddamn milk cow that time, too," Squire said with a laugh. "We stood 'round passin' about a bucket of milk from that damn critter."

"Shit," Li'l Jim snorted, "I got me a heap of better things to do than stand around here listenin' to you boys jaw about milk for chrissake. Damn." He grabbed a bottle and hurried off.

Squire laughed and took another drink. "Where be Bill this year? He ain't ailin' is he? I heard he took a ball in that little ruckus ye had with the Blackfeet after last rendezvous."

"Och, was but a wee scratch, Nathaniel." He looked around to be sure he would not be overheard. "William's up on the Upper Missouri. Building forts."

"Forts?" Gravant asked, surprised. "What's 'e wan' to go and do dat for?"

Campbell's lips curled in what was supposed to be a smile. "William has it in his head to take on The Company."

Squire's eyes glistened. "And ye be agreein' with him, lad?" he asked, masking his interest.

"Aye." Another furtive glance. "Those laddies need to have their tails pulled a wee bit."

Squire poured a portion of Scotch whiskey down his gullet. "Here be to yer success, lad," he said. He had an intense dislike for the American Fur Company. He wasn't sure why, exactly, but it had a lot to do with The Company's business practices, which he knew were deplorable, both with Indians and with white traders and trappers. Dealing with The Company was never pleasant or safe for anyone.

Squire and his friends headed toward where the shooting contests were taking place. As they drew nearer, they could see a large crowd. With each shot, there was a chorus of cheers and a corresponding one of groans from men who had lost their wager.

"Somebody be doin' right well, I'd be sayin'," Squire commented. After pushing through the crowd to the front, he could see a slight figure standing next to three horses, two squaws and a small mountain of supplies.

"It's Li'l Jim," Hannah said excitedly.

"Aye. I always knew the lad could shoot some." They stopped near to Li'l Jim and watched as the cocky young man fired several more shots. They started taking bets from anyone still foolish enough to bet against their friend.

After Li'l Jim's next shot, Squire leaned over to him and said, "Best be givin' your rifle a rest, lad."

Startled, Li'l Jim looked around. With a smirk, he said, "Why? I'm doin' just fine."

"I can see that, lad. But if'n ye don't let your rifle cool some and wipe it down, it'll not be throwin' plumb center for ye much longer."

"Aw, let me be, Nathaniel."

"Ye can be doin' what ye want, lad. But your rifle's gonna get too hot to throw plumb center. 'Sides, a few more shots, and you'll be havin' no one bettin' against ye, once word gets around." He grinned. "Take your plunder and be givin' yourself a rest.'

Li'l Jim grinned back. "Reckon you're right." He was cocky, and often defiant. But he could also see common sense when it was thrust under his nose. "You aim to take my place here?"

"I had thought on it," Squire said dryly.

Li'l Jim nodded. "Good luck to ya, Nathaniel."

Squire laughed arrogantly. "I don't be needin' any, lad. But thankee for your concern."

Li'l Jim motioned to the two Indian women, telling them to start loading the horses. As they did, he stepped back from the crowd a little and ran a greased patch through the barrel with his wiping stick. He would clean it better back at camp.

He was proud almost to the point of awe in owning the rifle, and so took excellent care of it. When he had left St. Louis in September, the Colonel had supplied all the men with muskets good enough to do the job but nothing extraordinary. Li'l Jim had showed his aptitude with the musket early on and had quickly become one of the brigade's main hunters. As he improved, Squire knew Li'l Jim needed a better weapon.

Squire had wondered where they could find a new, proper rifle for Li'l Jim. But after the battle at the Blackfoot village, the answer came to him. Still, he hesitated a while, mulling it over. He and the others had made their way back to the cabin old LeGrande had been sharing with Slocum Peters. There, quietly and by himself, he built a scaffold, Indian-style, and laid his friend to rest with a few things to carry him on his journey. He stood there a long time, tears of loss in his proud blue eyes. He was unaware of the bitter cold and the biting wind.

Finally his pain was assuaged some, and he turned back to the cabin. Star Path took his buffalo robe and his hat. She got him seated in front of the fire, worried about his blue hands and the ice on his beard. She gave him a mug of coffee. He looked up and smiled softly at her. When she placed a hand on his shoulder, he patted it.

The others said nothing. Train, Hannah, and Li'l Jim were too afraid and worried to speak. Peters simply had the sense to keep his mouth shut.

Squire finished his coffee, set the cup down and stood. He strode across the small, one-room, crude cabin. He bent and rummaged in LeGrande's blankets a moment before standing and walking back toward the fire.

"Li'l Jim," he growled, "bring your lazy ass o'er here." When a frightened Li'l Jim presented himself in front of Squire, the big mountain man handed the youth LeGrande's rifle. "I reckon it be about time ye had yourself a proper rifle, lad," Squire said gruffly.

Li'l Jim took the rifle with something approaching reverence. It took some moments before he was able to speak. When he finally could, he said in a voice cracking with emotion, "I can't take this, Nathaniel. This's Mister LeGrande's rifle."

"Aye, lad." Squire's voice was stronger. He was more certain now that what he was doing was right.

"I . . . I . . . Damnit, Nathaniel, I ain't worthy." Li'l Jim might be arrogant, but he had sense and decency.

"I think ye be, lad," Squire said. "How about ye others? What be yer thinkin'?"

There were some moments of silence. Then Hannah went to Li'l Jim. She placed a hand on his shoulder. "You remember back in that village, when Abner was havin' doubts about me?" she asked.

Over Hannah's shoulder, Li'l Jim could see Train wince at the remembrance. Train had, indeed, been having doubts about accepting Hannah back. Li'l Jim had stepped up and offered to be Hannah's man. "Yeah, I remember," he mumbled.

"You're worthy, Li'l Jim," Hannah said. "Don't ya never doubt it." She kissed his cheek.

Li'l Jim looked up at Squire, who stood smiling softly at him. Li'l Jim was torn between a feeling of unworthiness and abject pride. He was close to tears. He ran a hand up the fine, polished maple of the rifle's half-stock. "I'll . . ." he started. He stopped to work up some spit. "I'll try to live up to what Mister LeGrande was," he finally said.

Star Path had made him a case for the .54-caliber Hawken of softly tanned elk skin with two-foot-long fringe on the lower half. A few beads, some bits of metal, and a feather completed the decoration. Li'l Jim slid the rifle into the case now. Seeing that his new horses were loaded, he set off for his camp, whistling.

He had shown them, he had. Made 'em come pure as goddamn snow. He grinned.

-16-

The bunched leaden skies had opened, and the rain cascaded down in blinding curtains. The rendezvous camp was a dismal, quiet place, with most of the men opting for the smoky warmth and comfort of their lodges, where they huddled around their fires to drink and yarn.

By midmorning, Train, Hannah, Melton, Peters, Bellows, and Ransom had gathered around the fire in Squire's lodge. Rising Sun joined Star Path to the side, where they worked quietly, one ear attuned to the men, ready to wait on them should the need arise.

"You hear about them fellers was wolf-bit the other night?" Peters asked in general. "Couple days afore we pulled in here?"

"I heard a Snake Injin was bit by a mad wolf over to his camp. Yep. Sure did," Bellows offered.

"Some ol' hoss tol' me it was a Rocky Mountain Company chil' that got it," Squire said.

Peters nodded. "I were talkin' with Campbell just a bit ago. The ol' Scottie said was both got bit. Maybe a couple other boys, too. Shit, maybe a couple of Company boys got it."

The rendezvous was made up of three camps, spread along ten miles of the Green River. The most southerly camp, near where Squire's brigade was, belonged basically to the Rocky Mountain Fur Company and its associates. About five miles up the river, was the American Fur Company camp, and five miles north of that was Fort Bonneville, with Captain Ben Bonneville's men.

Squire and the others enjoyed a laugh before settling.

"Waugh!" Squire said. "I'd as soon have some Blackfoot shovin' his war lance up my ass as to be gettin' bit by a mad wolf."

The others were unanimous in their agreement.

"What happened to them poor bastards?" Bellows asked.

"Campbell tol' me the Snake was out with some of his *amigos* a couple days afterward, when he all to a sudden flung himself off his pony and started foamin' at the mouth and such. They hauled ass back to camp to get that hoss some help, but when they got back, he was long gone. Just yesterday, a couple boys said they spotted an Injun some miles from here. They gave chase, but he disappeared. I expect he's gone beaver by now."

"How about the other 'un?" Li'l Jim asked nervously. The thought of being bitten by a rabid wolf was not a settling one.

"Campbell said he went out of his head and ran off into the brush last night. His *amigos* let him be."

They were all silent, chewing on meat, thinking of the horrible demise of a man afflicted with rabies. None of them liked the idea. Finally Squire asked, "How ye be feelin', Colonel?"

"A little better, Nathaniel, thank you. The day of rest did me well, as did the ministrations of Blue Rattle."

"Aye, I thought so. But ye be lookin' perplexed. They hurt ye?"

"Oh, it's nothing." His eyes drifted to the slim, buckskin-covered back of Rising Sun. "It just seems that Rising Sun's family . . ." He trailed off.

"They be gettin' pesty?" Bellows asked with a chuckle.

"Yes, Homer. They . . ."

"That's the way Shoshonis track, Colonel," Bellows cackled.

"Aye, Colonel," Squire added, "that be the lay of it. Once ye set onto one of their women, ye've got the whole goddamn family latchin' onto ye. Ye'll be giving 'em foofaraw for all the time ye be with 'em."

Melton almost groaned, Squire and the others laughed.

"Don't be takin' it too much to heart, Colonel," Squire said. "We'll be settin' out afore long, then ye'll be shed of 'em. Ye either can give Risin' Sun back to her folks, or ye can sell her to somebody and let him be worryin' about her people. If'n she ain't too troublesome a woman, ye can be gettin' a couple of good horses for her, or maybe a good Hawken gun."

"I couldn't sell her," Melton said, aghast.

"Then just give her up. Or take her with you. Her folks ain't gonner to be trailin' along after us."

Melton looked thoughtful, and Bellows said, "Don't you go frettin', Colonel. They'll not follow. Nope. And no one'll look at you crosswise in St. Louis for bringin' her, neither."

"But what will I do with her there?"

"Same as ye'd be doin' here," Squire said. "Sell her, or just put her up somewhere till ye head back into the mountains, if'n ye be plannin' to." The last was a question.

"I'm not sure I will, though I've thought of it. But what'll I do with her when I return home to see my backers and visit my wife?"

Squire laughed again. What a strange man the Colonel was, he thought. A man of the wilderness, a soldier, adventurer, Indian fighter, now squaw man, worrying about a wife who was two thousand miles away in Boston, doing everything not to think of what her man would be doing in the wilds. He could not understand it.

But all he said was, "Ye ain't likely to be havin' no time for visitin' home, Colonel. Not if'n ye plan to make beaver shine again next season."

"Why?"

"Ye been trackin' the days for us all along, Colonel. What's the date?"

"July. About midmonth."

"Aye. As I thought. We'll be havin' just enough time to be gettin' back to St. Louis, sell our plews, have us a wee spree, load up supplies for the new season, hire on men and get back on the trail within a month or so. If'n ye be wantin' to avoid some of the poor doin's we faced this year."

"What about this crew?"

"No tellin' if'n they'll be stayin' on with ye, Colonel." He did not say it, but he had no intention of spending another year with such a big brigade. Maybe he would take a few of the young men he trusted and head off, or maybe just go back to his solitary ways. But the telling of it would come later. "I know there be a few that don't seem likely to sign on again. And if'n ye don't be payin' 'em all before we get back, ain't too many of 'em gonna be in your debt. They just might be signin' on with somebody else.

"I reckon we ought not to be stayin' much longer here, anyway. The specie ye paid these lads ain't gonna last but a bit what with the prices here bumped up so high. Ye're either gonna have to pay 'em the rest or risk 'em stealin' our plews, horses, and anythin' else they can be sellin' for money."

"How long?"

"A week, maybe. Less'd be better."

"You seem troubled, Nathaniel," Melton said shrewdly.

Squire stroked his beard, thoughtful, before saying carefully, "It be makin' me uneasy havin' Hannah here amongst all these men. I be afraid one of our lads'll be gettin' a snoot full of Lightnin' and open his goddamn yap about her to all." Squire had put it out of his mind sometime back, but the worrisome thought had re-asserted itself.

The other had tried not to think of the possibility, but now that it was in the open, worry began to flood over them.

"Is that a serious danger, Nathaniel?" Melton asked. Were it not for the seriousness of his countenance, he would have looked almost comical. His face was bright with mottled purplish bruises, interspersed with yellow and blue. They had faded a little, though, in the past couple of days.

"Ain't certain, Colonel. Most of the lads be pretty loyal, but ye never can be tellin' what a man'll do when he be in his cups. And there'll always be one or two in any bunch that'll be lookin' to gain some advantage for themselves whate'er way they can."

Train spoke up, "Then let's leave, Nathaniel. I can't see riskin' Hannah for a longer spree for the men. They've seen rendezvous. They can have a spree in St. Louis."

"What be your thinkin' on it, Hannah?" Squire asked.

"I ain't goin' nowhere, Nathaniel. And I'm not lettin' me spoil everyone else's fun. I'll take my chances."

"After what happened to ye afore?"

She shuddered at the thought of Elk Horn, the big, hard-handed warrior who had forced himself on her repeatedly while she was a captive in the Blackfoot village, and at the thought of the treatment she had received from the Blackfoot women. But she shook her head roughly. "I ain't lettin' that stop me. There's nothing can be done to me that could be any worse than what I've been through already."

Squire's lips cracked in the barest of smiles. "I thought that'd be where your stick'd float. Colonel?"

Melton looked around at the determined faces, his own small woes forgotten. "What would be the consequences if these others found out about Hannah?" he finally asked.

Squire shook his head slowly. "Can't be sayin'. Most of them ain't seen a white woman—or at least one close enough to get next to—in years. And to find a white woman who be livin' like a squaw, 'specially if'n they find out she's been bedded by a buck . . . Shit, I figure it be likely she'd be havin' a hard time of it."

"Surely they'd consider her sex and her color as defenses," Melton exploded. "They'd not treat a white woman that poorly, would they?" His voice let it be known he could not believe such a thing.

"Normal times, I'd be sayin' that's true," Squire said reflectively. "But I ain't so sure. If'n most of these lads met her in the settlements, they'd be as polite as can be and not bother her none." He paused.

"But we be miles from any city," he continued. "I figure that these lads'd figure that even if'n she be white, she's been layin' with a mountaineer and shared her bed with a Blackfoot, even if it weren't willin', they ain't gonna have no respect for her. I reckon they'll take to her just like she was a squaw, only they'd be fightin' o'er her, since she be white."

He glanced over at Hannah. She was ashen-faced, and her knuckles were white where they were clenched. But there was determination on her face, too.

"Perhaps we should leave now," Melton said. He sounded worried.

"It be up to Hannah, Colonel." Squire turned to face her. "What do ye say, girl?"

"We'll stay," she said tightly. "Any man thinks he can have me just for the askin', may end up not bein' much of a man at all." She fingered the deer-antler hilt of one of her knives, her face sharp in the gloom.

The men nodded, and Squire stared at Hannah. His face was hard, but there was a strange light in his eyes. He wore a look of pride, mixed with deep respect. She would be all right, he knew. "*Bon*," was all he said though.

The silence grew heavy, as if the others were afraid to speak, but finally Slocum Peters said, "Well, this here quiet's no good for a body. Ain't nobody got some winnin's from yesterday they're bustin' to crow over? Or, hell, even some good losin' somebody wants to howl about?"

Everybody looked expectantly at him, so he said with mock humility, "Well, boys, it seems that this ol' chil' had luck ridin' with him yestidday, for sure. I tore into some Flatheads at the hand game, nice as ye please. I . . ."

-17-

Squire blotted out the voice, listening instead to the sizzling of the fire and the rhythmical drumming of the rain on the tipi. He was no longer sure he should have brought the men here; it would have been better to have gone straight on to St. Louis, especially this late in the summer. But he had wanted the men to have a good time—and he did, too.

But the problems were compounding. First there was Hannah. He was not really sure what the men would do if they found out about her. Most of the mountain men, even as wild as they were, treated white women with respect—or at least standoffishness. But out here, miles from civilization? How would a camp of more than two hundred white men, plus half-breeds, *mestizos, métis,* and Indians, nearly all of them either drunk or hungover, aching for release after a harsh winter, react?

And Squire was certain they would find out about the girl. His whole brigade, trapper and camp helper alike, knew about her, and few of them could be expected to hold their liquor. It was only a matter of time before one of them spilled it. What then?

He was especially concerned with Farley Walker. Though Walker had kept it hidden from the others, Squire knew that the young man was still obsessed with Hannah. More than once Squire had seen him surreptitiously lurking about where the girl would be coming to get water or firewood, or when the months warmed up, where she would bathe. Squire did not know how far Walker would go to slake his passion.

Worse, though, he knew that many of these men were not the best sort to begin with. Many was the man who had made his way out to the mountains to escape the law back in the settlements. They were the kind of men who would rape and plunder back there under any circumstances. Out here, without the constraint of any law, they could be uncontrollable.

Still, he had brought the men anyway, self-assured or arrogant enough to think that he could handle anything. Something in him had always pushed him into taking risks; he had been that way all his life.

Squire looked from face to face. In each, except Melton's, he saw recognition and understanding. They all felt the same way as he did; even Hannah. Or maybe her most of all. She had been as cruelly abused as any woman ever had, yet she had not let it defeat her. Melton was far more bothered with her past than she was.

"How 'bout you, Nathaniel?" Peters asked. "You got somethin' to tell?"

His voice broke Squire from his thoughts. He drew in a breath and then let it out slowly. There was no use in worrying, he thought. He could do nothing now that they were here. If Hannah was found out, they all would deal with it. Worrying about it would not prevent it nor change it.

Squire smiled with a little regret. "I reckon the lads be plumb tired of my yarnin'." They weren't, but he was of no mood for spinning a tale. "How about ye, Colonel?" he added. "Mayhap ye'd break out your book."

Everyone looked at Melton with expectation. "Well, if you boys really want me to continue . . . ?" Melton asked.

They all did, and so the Colonel dug into the pouch at his side and pulled out a small book. He had carried the small volume all the way from St. Louis. He had not had an opportunity to read it until the brigade was in its winter camp. One night just before spring had arrived, he had brought it out and was reading it to himself.

Squire had seen him and said, "Why don't ye start readin' to the lads of a time?"

"I didn't expect them to have any interest," Melton said, surprised.

"Hell, any mountaineer will be sittin' and listenin' to readin'—leastways if'n it be an excitin' story."

"This most certainly is that," Melton said enthusiastically, holding up the book.

"Then ye can begin readin' to 'em tomorrow night."

The next night, Melton nervously sat on a stump before the eager group of trappers and camp helpers who had crammed into his small cabin. He opened the book, licked his lips, and began: "*Frankenstein, or the Modern Prometheus*. By Mary Wollstonecraft Shelley." He paused a moment, then continued, "A letter to Mrs. Seville, England. You will rejoice to hear . . ."

As he read, he had been pleasantly surprised to find that Squire had been right. It was all he could do to stop reading after an hour or so each night. He had read to the men a little just about every night until they had gotten to rendezvous. The story was spooky and heart-stopping enough to keep the men enraptured.

He opened the book now to the page he had marked, and he started: "The voyage came to an end . . ."

Once again the men were enthralled. The rain pattered on the smoky tipi, sometimes heavily, at other times with just a soft thrumming. The wind rose and fell in bursts, occasionally whistling through the flaps of the smoke hole. All of it added to the scariness of the story.

As he listened to Melton's infectious voice, Squire was mostly at peace.

In late August, when he had been approached by the Colonel to lead this expedition, he had turned Melton down. But then he had suddenly changed his mind and took on the job of hauling these untested young men to the mountains. There had been plenty of times during that fall and the long, harsh winter when he had regretted ever getting involved. Now, though, he was . . . well, not glad, really, but not unhappy, either, that he had taken the job on.

Some of the men had turned out to be worthy companions, others acceptable; only a few had gone bad. He was happy in the company of such old friends as Peters and such new ones as Colonel Leander Melton, Homer Bellows, Abner Train, Li'l

Jim, Cletus Ransom, and of course, Hannah Carpenter.

It was late in the afternoon and the men were excitedly discussing the chapter that had just been read when someone called at the flap of the lodge.

"*Entrez-vous,*" Squire said.

Gravant, Ledoux, and Dumoulin entered quietly, shaking off the rain. They pulled off their knit caps and long, colorful capotes. They tossed the garments aside and sat. Star Path and Rising Sun hurried to make sure they had food and then retreated back into the shadows and their work.

"Damn rain," Gravant said as he dropped the bowl Star Path had given him. He leaned back and lighted his pipe, letting the puffs of smoke cloud his face. From behind the cloud came his voice: "'Ave you been tellin' dese boys your lies, *L'on Farouche,* eh?"

Squire laughed. "And what if I have?" Even if he had denied it, Gravant would not have believed him.

"I t'ink you did not tell dem some of de stories I know about you, eh?"

"Like what?"

"Like the time dem 'Rapahos chase you for miles across de prairie, eh?"

"What for?" Train asked. He was interested.

"Dem 'Rapahos thought *L'on Farouche* was bad medicine," Gravant said with a chuckle. "Just after he come to de village, de storms come. Rain, hail, big winds. *Sacre bleu,* all dese storms ruin de hunt de 'Rapahos were planning. So dey blame it on *L'on Farouche.* Hah, you should 'ave seen 'im run."

Squire rocked with laughter, unable to help himself. He picked up a honing stone from the possible sack at his waist and began sharpening his tomahawk.

"And ye couldn't be keepin' up with me, either, could ye, ye ol' fart?" Tears glittered in Squire's eyes from the laughter. "More'n once I had to come back for ye and drag ye along or ye'd have been butt-humped by them 'Rapahos for certain."

The two laughed for a while, joined by the others.

But finally Train asked in some exasperation, "Well, what happened, damnit?"

"We dug us some holes in a riverbank," Squire said, still full of humor. "We hid out till them 'Rapaho peckerwoods give up and went home. After dark we snuck back to their village and stole back all our horses, traps, and other possibles."

He started laughing again. "And we kilt two of the chief's horses and left 'em for ol' Blue Arm to find in the mornin'."

"'E's not been back dere to dat village since, either," Gravant said with a chuckle.

"Well, neither have ye, best as I know."

When the laughter finally died down, Squire said with a wide yawn, "Well, lads, it be robe time for this ol' chil'." He slipped away the tomahawk and whetstone. Then he stood. "Ye lads be welcome to stay here the night if'n ye don't feel brave enough to be out there facin' the storm."

There were hoots and hollers of derision as the men and two women stood and filed out into the downpour.

When the last of them had left, Star Path said with a sigh of relief, "I am glad they're gone."

"Me, too," Squire smiled. "Now come on over here, woman, where ye belong."

-18-

Squire strolled across the sodden rendezvous grounds. He had been bored as all hell with sitting in the lodge and took the first break in the weather to get out. Things were quiet compared with what they had been, but there was plenty of activity.

Suddenly he heard a savage scream. As he whirled, ready for action, a heavy body slammed into him. Squire did not go down, though his attacker had. The man righted himself and charged at Squire again.

Squire recognized the Crow. It was Kills Many, the war chief who had presided over the battle between Train and Fox Spirit after the Crows had stolen the brigade's horses.

Squire sidestepped the bellowing warrior and clubbed him down.

Kills Many was slow getting up. Squire took the opportunity to ask roughly, "What'n hell're ye tryin' to do, lad, turn yourself into gone beaver?"

"I kill you," Kills Many hissed in rage as he stood. "You bring shame on my people. On me." The scar on his face was vivid. He pushed off the hood of his capote, shaking his hair.

Squire shrugged. "That be tough shit, lad," he said harshly. "Ye shouldn't have sent them peckerless bastards to steal my horses, they'd still be breathin', and ye'd be sittin' in your lodge now humpin' some unfortunate woman."

"Killing Fox Spirit not all bad," Kills Many admitted. "He fought well." The Crow shrugged. "White-eyes warrior fought better." His eyes grew hard, looking like glittering dark stones. "But you not have to kill Stands-Twice-Against-the-Enemy."

"He was a buff'lo's ass," Squire sneered. Kills Many hit him. Squire was surprised, and the punch rocked him a little. Then Kills Many was all over him, swinging and kicking.

Squire fended off most of the blows and blocked the kicks. Finally, he managed to shove Kills Many, sending him staggering back through the mud. Then he lashed out and smashed Kills Many in the face. Blood spurted from a badly cut lip, but Kills Many would not give up.

Kills Many was not a tall man, but with his powerful chest and bull neck, he was as strong as a mountain lion. And as wily as a fox. He leaped closer and hit Squire three times in the face. Squire only grunted a little, then grabbed the shorter man. He squeezed hard, pushing Kills Many's air out.

He pulled his head back and whipped it forward, slamming his forehead into Kills Many's nose. He released his bear hug, and Kills Many fell to the mud, groggy. Squire held out his hand.

Kills Many tried to push himself up, ignoring the hand. "Ye got a chance to be makin' your peace with me, lad," Squire said quietly. He could see no purpose to be served by killing the Crow.

Kills Many shook his head a few times, trying to clear away the fog. He finally managed to get to his feet. He stood, weaving.

Squire knew the Crow wouldn't quit, and he knew he should just kill the Indian straight off. But this was supposed to be rendezvous, a place for celebrating and having a good time, so he wanted to give Kills Many as much chance as possible.

Kills Many untied the belt of his capote and let the garment fall to the muddy ground. The action had given him a little time to recover his senses. He pulled a war club and began chanting his death song, the sound eerie though somehow fitting in the gray, gloomy day.

"These doin's be plumb foolish, lad," Squire said flatly. "I got no feud with ye or your people."

Kills Many suddenly charged, as if he had not even heard Squire.

The giant mountain man shrugged. He had gone out of his way to spare Kills Many's life; it was more than he usually did. But his peace overtures had been rebuffed. Now Kills Many would have to pay the price.

As Kills Many charged, war club raised high, Squire dipped his right shoulder. Suddenly he jerked the shoulder forward, slamming it into Kills Many's side a little under the armpit. Several ribs cracked, and Kills Many's club sailed over Squire's back to land with a splash in the mud.

At the same time, Squire pulled back and launched his right fist. It smashed into Kills Many's stomach, rupturing the diaphragm. Kills Many sank to his knees, unable to breath.

Squire whirled and shoved on Kills Many's back with the flat of his foot. Kills Many's face fell into a muddy puddle. Squire stepped up and placed a foot across Kills Many's neck, keeping his face in the two-inch-deep puddle.

Less than a minute later, Kills Many was dead. Without emotion, Squire lifted the soggy body and carried it to the Crow camp. He explained briefly to several war chiefs in council what had happened.

Some of the Crows wanted to kill him. Angrily Squire's eyes narrowed. "Ye peckerwoods want to be comin' against me, best get it done. But I'll be tellin' ye now, ye do that, and there'll be one hell of a heap of dead Crows after we finish it."

That shut the warriors up momentarily. They had sense enough to know that if they killed Squire now, they would have to face a couple hundred angry mountain men soon after. And they would jeopardize many of their trading opportunities. They began talking quietly among themselves again.

"Now ye best be listenin' to me, lads," Squire interjected into the Crow discussion. "I could've took Kills Many's hair and left him layin' out there for the buzzards. But I didn't do that. I brung him here for ye so's ye could give him a decent buryin'."

The Crows finally acknowledged that Squire had acted properly, and they pledged to remain peaceful toward him.

"*Merde*," Squire muttered as he walked back to his camp. He hoped this would blow over, and not add to his problems. It was bad enough he had every Blackfoot in the world half froze to take his hair, he didn't need the Crows feeling the same way.

He smiled when he saw that Star Path was waiting for him. She fed him fresh buffalo and hot, black, heavily sweetened coffee. As Squire ate, she cleaned his buffalo robe, then pulled off his moccasins and cleaned them. She rubbed his feet when he had finished eating, and they spent the rest of the morning in amorous pursuits.

About midday, Train and Hannah arrived with fresh buffalo meat—a tongue, liver, hump meat, and ribs.

"I see ye lads've done all right."

"Weren't easy," Train said. "I hate huntin' in this damned rain."

"Well, at least we got fresh meat now, lad. That shines with this chil'. Now set yourselves down and be havin' some of that hot coffee."

When they did, Squire threw the buffalo tongue on the coals, then he split the liver with his two companions and Star Path. They ate it raw, smacking their lips in pleasure. The rest of the meat was hung over the fire to slowly roast.

Not soon after, Melton, Rising Sun, Bellows, and Silver Necklace entered, shaking the rain from their coats and caps.

"Ye lads be just in time. There be fresh buff'lo tongue just right for eatin'," Squire said. This morning's encounter with Kills Many was all but forgotten.

He speared the delicacy with his knife and tore off a big chunk with his teeth without bothering to wipe off the ash. He passed it to Melton, who did the same and passed it on until each had two large bites.

"That goddamn shines, it does," Squire said happily. The others agreed.

They talked idly while the women worked and chatted. About an hour later, Li'l Jim called for entrance. When he stepped in, he looked tired. Squire laughed and said, "Ye been findin' out that two women can be drainin' ye fast, lad?"

The others joined in with remarks, hoots, and catcalls, while Li'l Jim smiled ruefully and sat. "Them two damned women don't never get enough of me, I'm tellin' ya." He ignored the suppressed giggling from Star Path, Rising Sun, and Silver Necklace.

"Mayhap ye ain't the man ye thought ye was, lad," Squire said. "Ain't ye got the balls to shine with them women?"

"Bit off more'n you could chew, eh?" Bellows laughed, his Adam's apple bobbling merrily.

"And I thought you stronger than that," Melton threw in. "You've always acted the banty rooster. Is it that you can't live up to that?" He chuckled. He was slightly embarrassed at the bantering, but after his fight over Rising Sun, he felt more like one of the men and wanted to fit in with them.

"Leave off ridin' me now, boys," Li'l Jim warned. His face grew more red than could have been blamed on the firelight. "I've done what I could." He sounded angry, and disappointed.

"Oh, go shit in your cap, boy," Train joshed, starting to laugh again. "Just admit ya ain't so much of a man as you thought."

Li'l Jim turned angrily on Hannah, saying, "Well, I reckon you got somethin' to say, too, girl," he snapped.

Hannah snickered. "Nah, it ain't my place to tell ya I'm plumb shocked at ya. Nor is it my place to say you've gone an' disappointed us all with your inability to live up to the standards set . . ." she blushed at the words, but she also giggled.

"I've heard enough from you, girl," Li'l Jim snapped. "I've got a good mind to take you over my knee and . . ."

"Shoot, you ain't got enough strength left in ya," Hannah laughed.

"We'll just see about that, girl." He started to rise, but stopped in midcrouch when he realized that he was not going to hurt Hannah. Even if Squire or Train would let him try. He plopped back down and angrily tore off a piece of meat and stuffed it into his mouth. He chewed harshly, ire stamped on his face.

The others drifted onto other subjects, ignoring Li'l Jim for the most part, though each kept a wary eye on him, waiting for him to explode.

But as time passed, they saw the rage dwindling in him. Finally, during a lull in the talk, he said sheepishly, "I done went and made a goddamned ass of myself again, didn't I?"

When the others nodded in joyful agreement, he said, "Well, ya don't have to rub it in, damnit. Besides," he said with an impish grin, "I ain't never seen any of you boys with two wives." He crowed, proud as could be, while the others joined him in laughter. "I held my own with 'em for a spell."

The afternoon dragged on. The men were sick of the rain, but in no mood to spend much time out in it. So they sat, talking quietly, working as they did—cleaning rifles or pistols, sharpening knives or tomahawks, repairing weapons or traps. They gambled a little, playing hand or three-card monte. Squire was not adverse to wiping out his friends and did pretty well until the others began dropping out.

Except Li'l Jim, who had lost a lot, but still wanted to keep on playing. Finally Squire said to him, "Ye be losin' a heap, lad. Why don't ye leave off?"

"Nope. I won me plenty the other day at the shootin', and I can do it again, but I ain't givin' up."

Squire suspected there was more to it. "Why, lad?" he asked shrewdly.

" 'Cause I aim to be losin' at least one of them damned squaws I picked up," he said, sparking a burst of laughter from the others.

"Ye'd be doin' better to keep 'em for a while and then sell 'em to somebody once things get goin' again." Out of the corner of his eyes he could see Star Path looking evilly at him. "For I ain't aimin' to win neither one of 'em from ye, lad. I'll be takin' your horse, your possibles, e'en your money, if'n ye be havin' any. I'll take your weapons if'n ye was so foolish as to bet 'em against me. But I be wantin' no truck with either of them goddamn squaws of yours."

"Damn, Nathaniel," Li'l Jim said in mock anger this time. "I thought you was my friend. Friends is supposed to help friends."

"I ain't that good a friend, lad," he laughed, though both knew it was not true.

As the gray day faded into the dull black of the night, Gravant called from outside.

"*Entrez,*" Squire called. When his friend stepped into the lodge, Squire said jovially, "*Comment allez-vous, mon ami . . .*" His voice petered out when he saw the look on his friend's face. "What be wrong, Etienne? Ye be all right?"

"*Oui.*"

"The others?"

"Dem, too."

"Then what is it, *mon ami?* Tell me."

Star Path handed Gravant coffee, and the French-Canadian sat. "I 'ave bad news for you, *mon ami.*" He paused, taking a sip of coffee. "I saw Abel Carney ride in a little while ago."

Squire stiffened. "The others?" he asked tightly.

"I did not see dem, my frien'. But if Carney is 'ere, de odders must be, too."

Squire stood, calling, "Star Path, my buff'lo robe." He reached for his rifle.

"Where're you goin'?" Gravant asked.

Squire said nothing, the answer was clear on his hard face.

"Don' play de fool, Nathaniel. It is dark an' you don' know where 'e is."

"I'll be findin' him."

"Wait. If 'e is 'ere, 'e will stay. Then you can face him. If 'e does not stay? Eh, so what?" he lifted his arms and shrugged his shoulders.

"Ye be knowin' goddamn well, what," Squire growled.

"*Oui.* But now you are ready for 'im, *non?*"

"*Oui.* I be ready." He sat back down, fire burning in his pale blue eyes.

"Who is this man, Nathaniel?" Melton asked.

"Nobody who needs concern you, Colonel."

"Everything you do here concerns me, Nathaniel," Melton said tightly. "I'm still in charge." He was not sure of that, though, and hadn't been for a long time.

" 'E will not say anyt'in' about it," Gravant said. "But I will. De first time Nathaniel sees this Abel Carney was ten, twelve year ago. *L'on Farouche* an' me an' Marcel and ol' Toussain' were trappin' on de Gallatin River . . ."

-19-
DAYS GONE BY

Nathaniel Squire had left St. Louis with his woman, a Nez Perce named Woman-Who-Sings-Pretty. He had found her three years earlier in a village on Lolo Creek in the Clearwater Mountains. He was taken with her right away—with her industriousness, the singing voice from which she had gotten her name, and her looks. She was fairly tall and slender, with attractive features. She had cost him three good horses, a winter buffalo hide, two tins of powder, a bar of lead, a bolt of blue cloth, and three trade knives. But he had been happy with her. She worked hard and was caring of him. The clothes she made for them were serviceable or beautiful, depending on their use. The pelts she cured were lush, her cooking varied, her ways of making love were thoughtful and considerate.

Their son had been born almost a year later, a strapping infant with Sings Pretty's hair, dark-copper skin coloring and features, and Squire's size and washed-out blue eyes. They called him Blue Mountain Squire.

The three had left St. Louis in late summer. Some miles west of the city, along the Missouri River, Squire met his mentor and old friend, Emil François LeGrande. Not even Squire knew much of his background. About all Squire knew about his mentor's past was that LeGrande was from Montreal and that he had joined the Northwest Company when he was nineteen. After that, things were murky, and LeGrande never talked about his past.

The slight fifty-two-year-old French-Canadian was accompanied by Yellow Kettle, his young Flathead woman. LeGrande had God knew how many children by an equally unknown number of women, but he could not stand traveling or wintering with children once they were past four or five years old, so he usually left them with their mother's people.

Squire and LeGrande trapped their way up toward the hot springs, geysers, and bubbling mud pits of Colter's Hell. They decided to winter on the lower Yellowstone River, near where Mountain Creek entered it. They found a good-size cave and decided it would do.

Within a week, Squire and LeGrande had gathered what they hoped would be sufficient forage for the horses during the winter, had put up meat in addition to what they had made along the way, strung hides across the front of the cave mouth to keep out the snow and wind, and hauled logs into the cave to be cut into firewood as winter progressed.

Then Etienne Gravant, Marcel Ledoux, and Toussaint Robiseau arrived with their horses, plews, women, and children.

"*Bien venue, mes amis,*" LeGrande said joyously. It had been at least four seasons since he had seen his friends. He and Gravant went back some years, to the Northwest Company.

"*Bien venue.* You are winterin' 'ere, *mes amis?*" Gravant asked.

"*Oui,*" LeGrande said. "Come, join us. Stay wit' us 'ere, eh?"

"It would be too much trouble, *mon ami.* We 'ave many horses. Many mouths to feed."

"We'll be findin' enough, Etienne," Squire interjected. "We got a heap of forage set up and a heap of meat made. It be lookin' like ye have a passel, too. It ain't snowed more'n a dozen times so far. Ye'll be comfortable."

LeGrande nodded his agreement with these facts.

Gravant grinned. "Den we will do it." He turned to his companions and said, "*S'occupez des chevals*—see to the horses." He slid out of his saddle and handed the reins to his woman, a Cree named Light Walker with whom he had been for at least ten years.

Soon the men were all seated around a fire inside the cave, being served fresh elk that Gravant and his men had brought in. They chatted idly while they ate, ignoring the yelling children and the happy gossip of the women who managed to talk amongst themselves quite easily despite the barrier of several different languages.

But it was time for the men to get back to work, and work they did, that day and for the next week and a half. More forage had to be gathered, sending them farther afield; additional firewood had to be brought up and covered to keep it from the wet snow that was already coming more regularly; extra meat had to be made into jerky and pemmican; trap lines still had to be run; the season's catch tanned and cached.

They were comfortable, however, when the big snows came and the streams and rivers froze over, stopping their trapping for the winter. The winter passed like it always did, slowly and tediously. But it ended, as it always did, and this year a little earlier than usual. The men were out on their trap lines as soon as the ice broke, pulling in scores of lush winter pelts. Buffalo returned to the valley, and they ate well.

But soon enough it was time to move on, and they headed northwestward along the Yellowstone, past the weird, dripping formations of odd-colored stones and the sputtering, erupting mud volcanos. They spent three days trapping near a particularly violent one before turning west through Hayden Valley. The buffalo and elk were plentiful in the broad, grass-covered valley.

They spent several more days trapping at Gibbon Creek near the Virginia Cascades. The day after they left, they hit Obsidian Creek and took it north, past the imposing Obsidian Cliffs. They set their trap lines in that area, pulling plews from Obsidian Creek, near Appollinaris Spring.

They slipped through snow-clogged Fawn Pass the day after, and caught the headwaters of the Gallatin. They trapped there, moving on in late afternoon a few miles each day for the next day's trapping. The beaver were plentiful and had fine winter pelts that would bring in the best price. It took them two weeks to make the thirty or so miles to a place of tall, red cliffs. It was here that they decided to spend a few more days, to trap and to give all the plews they had already taken a chance to be cured properly. The women had their hands full with all the work.

They set up a small, comfortable camp in a grove of aspens and junipers, with the Gallatin at their backs. The women set up their lodges facing the east. Meat racks were hastily built for some of the fresh buffalo they brought in—it was always best to have a supply of jerky and pemmican handy. Willow hoops were hung from trees by the dozens, stretching the beaver pelts.

Just after the group arrived, two other old friends showed up—Pierre Druseau and American, Samuel Syrett. These two had done well, too, and soon enough their plews were hanging in the trees to cure.

The men decided that a small *fandango* was in order. Before long, a raucous emanation of LeGrande's fiddle and Druseau's squeezebox was wafting up into the bright blue sky.

They were in Crow country, but none of them had ever had any trouble with the Absaroka's. In fact, they had all traded with some of the many bands of Crow throughout Absaroka. They were wary, however, since the Crows would steal a horse any time they were given a chance. But the camp was so comfortable, the days so warm, the times so peaceful, that they let down their guards a little.

Squire was crotch-deep in a freezing, snow-fed stream when he first heard the shots. He looked up at LeGrande from the trap he was setting. LeGrande stood on the bank, watchful, on guard, skinning the beaver Squire would throw his way. "Huntin' buffalo?" Squire asked.

LeGrande shrugged, seemingly unconcerned, but his head swiveled as his senses picked the air for any sign. As usual, he and Squire had paired off for trapping. So had Ledoux and Gravant, and Pierre Druseau and Robiseau. Syrett, the odd man out this day, stuck close to the camp to watch over the women and children.

Squire bent back to his trap, setting the spring carefully before dousing it well with castoreum. But a second volley made him look up in alarm. "Shit, that ain't . . ."

The sound of pounding hooves stopped his speech. But he started moving. He dropped the trap, mumbling, "*Merde.*" He splashed heavily through the water, the rushing stream pulling at his heavy blanket pants.

LeGrande, already mounted, held the reins of Squire's horse. Squire swung himself into the saddle of a big bay. His own horse was a huge roan gelding. Like *Noir Astre* to come, the reddish horse was very large, well-suited to Squire's massive frame. But he had left it in camp to rest. They were off in a rush, racing as fast as they could through the thick stands of aspen, junipers, cottonwoods, and pines.

It was quiet when they pounded into camp ten minutes later. Ledoux and Gravant soon raced in from the west. Moments later, Robiseau walked in.

They found Druseau dead. LeGrande's woman, Yellow Kettle, also was dead. Syrett was seriously wounded, as was his woman, Deer Woman. Squire slid cautiously out of the saddle to check on an infant, whose brains had been dashed against an oak. It was Little Paw, Robiseau's third son by the Sioux woman, Blue Robe.

Gravant's woman, Light Walker, stepped timidly from behind a tree, accompanied by her two children, Blue Robe, and four other children—two of Druseau's, one of Ledoux's, and one of Syrett's.

"*Qu'est-ce q'eu lieu ici?*" Gravant asked urgently, harshly. "What happened here?"

Light Walker answered in an amalgam of Cree, French, and English, but the men understood enough: a number of men had fired at the camp, downing Druseau and Syrett, then they attacked, stealing the horses, what bales of plews they could quickly load and whatever women and children they could grab. Sings Pretty and two others, White Feather and Red Leaf, had been taken.

"Dey went nort'," Robiseau added. "Pierre and me, we were coming back 'ere, finished wit' our trappings for today. I stop a little to tighten my saddle. But Pierre, 'e don' wan' to wait. You know him, 'ow impatient 'e is." Robiseau smiled wanly. "I 'eard de shots, and started 'ere. Den I 'eard many coming my way, and I cached behind a tree. Men passed, carrying women and chil'ren. When dey pass by, I come." He shrugged. "An' 'ere I fin' Pierre."

Toussaint Robiseau might have been handsome were it not for the lower part of his face. The grotesque appearance was compliments of an Arikara war club. He was about fifty years old, though he still possessed a youthful look about him. He and Druseau had been partners for some years. He would miss his garrulous old friend.

"Crows?" LeGrande asked, surprised. He could not believe the Crows would do such a bloody thing. Even though LeGrande and the others also had close ties with the Sioux—the Crows' traditional enemies—they had remained friendly with the whites. They might steal horses, or anything else lying around, but a brutal, planned attack like this was unlike them.

"*Mais non,*" Robiseau said, anger bending his already mis-shapen face. "It was white men. Damn Britishers," he spit. "Wit' a few *Pied-du-noir.*"

"*Merde,*" Squire shouted as he took to the saddle.

"No, *mon ami,*" Gravant shouted. "We need you 'ere."

Squire ignored him and kicked his horse into a run. Sign was not hard to find, and he quickly cut the trail. In a minute, LeGrande was with him, the hatchet-faced French-Canadian's face tightened in anger.

In fifteen minutes they caught up to the thieves. Squire jammed his horse to a stop and slid out of the saddle fast. Slinging the big .58-caliber rifle over the saddle, he took careful aim and fired. The thundering crack of the shot bounced off the mountains and came back at them before fading. But one of the men ahead, one of two in the rear herding the stolen horses, went flying from his saddle and lay still on the ground.

Squire did not bother to reload; he swung himself back into the saddle and took off again. Two more of the men who had attacked the camp turned back to help fight off the attack. They fired their rifles hastily, not hitting anyone. But Squire and LeGrande were closing in, and the enemies drew their pistols.

Squire pulled the big horse pistol he carried and fired. But the charge was bad and the weapon misfired. An enemy fired at him, and he felt the ball nip his hair.

Another fired, and Squire saw LeGrande slammed backward off his rushing horse. Squire screamed a war cry and yanked out his war club—a pointed stone fastened with rawhide to a thick oak staff covered with otter fur. He had taken it from a Blackfoot he had killed several years ago.

He ducked as the third man fired a pistol, then he was on one of them—a man with a permanently etched sour look on his face, bad teeth, and yellowed eyes. The war club caught the man squarely between the eyes, pulverizing his face. He did not even have time to scream as he fell backward, rolling off the horse's hindquarters.

The stolen horses were more than a mile away now as an enraged Squire turned on another of the white men he faced. He fended off a tomahawk blow with his war club, then used the semiflat top part to rabbit-chop the man in the face. The foe tumbled down, and Squire yanked the horse around, trying to face the last of the enemies. But the horse was not his usual roan and was unused to either his size or his commands. He was slow in responding.

He never did know exactly what it was that hit him, but something heavy thudded into the back of his head. He reeled in the saddle before toppling, darkness closing in on him. He also never knew that Abel Carney stood over him for a few moments, empty pistol in hand, tempted to reload and put the finishing bullet into Squire's brain. But the stolen horses and his comrades were more than two miles away and still moving fast. A bullet flew by him, tugging his shirt lightly a moment before he heard the report. He whirled and saw a skinny, grizzled man, the one who had been shot earlier, dropping his rifle and pulling out a pistol.

Carney did not hesitate. He leaped into the saddle and raced off, taking Squire's and LeGrande's horses, as well as the ones from his slain companions. He left the bodies to the wolves and the vultures.

-20-

Squire awoke slowly, the world still spinning around him. He sat up cautiously, trying not to move his head too much. He was surprised when he heard, "Well, it's about time, *mon ami*, eh?"

He turned carefully, smiling when he saw LeGrande sitting up, a jolly smile brightening his lean face. "How long I been out?" he asked.

"Maybe 'alf a day."

"How are you?"

LeGrande shrugged. "I took a ball in de shoulder. Is not so bad, eh. But I can do little with it."

"Ye seen any sign of the others?"

"*Non.* But I 'ave spent de time trying to keep de wolves and de vultures and de coyotes away."

"*Merci,*" Squire said flatly, grimacing as pain blinded him momentarily. He stood, wobbling a bit, and then lurched to LeGrande. "Let me be havin' a look at that shoulder, *mon ami.*"

He sliced through the greasy cloth shirt, baring the oozing wound. He looked around the back of the shoulder. "Went through clean. Ye be lucky, lad. But I reckon there be bits of your shirt in there. There ain't shit I can be doin' for ye here, though. Can ye walk?"

"*Oui.*" LeGrande hawked out some snot, then wiped his eagle-like nose clean with two fingers.

"*Bon.* But first I'd best be bindin' up that shoulder so's it don't go floppin' about on ye. Ye've lost some blood, but I reckon ye'll be makin' out."

He sliced LeGrande's shirt into strips, then bound his friend's shoulder tightly to his side. He retrieved his war club and rifle. He had been lucky he had kept it in one hand or else it would have been run off with the horse. His father had given Squire the .58-caliber flintlock with the full stock of curly maple when Squire had left home nine years ago. He loved the rifle and took excellent care of it, since it was his only link to his home and family.

"Ye be ready, *mon ami?*" he asked finally.

"*Oui.*"

"*Allons.*" They marched off, Squire carrying both rifles. It was still only a little past noon, and the sun beat down harshly on them. Within half an hour LeGrande began to falter. Squire caught him before he hit the ground and lifted him easily. The lean, hard LeGrande was a small burden for the mighty strength of Squire.

They were less than ten miles from their camp, but it took the better part of that day to make it. They arrived just before nightfall. LeGrande was weak but lucid. Squire ached and his head throbbed.

"*Sacre bleu!*" Gravant exclaimed when he saw them. "I t'ought you was dead, de bot' of you."

"Well, we ain't," Squire snapped. "How be Sam?"

"Bad, but alive still. Deer Woman has died."

Squire nodded. He had always liked Deer Woman, who had been with Syrett for four or five years now. She was quiet, shapely, and a hard worker. "Ye know who it was who done it?"

"*Mais non.* I t'ought you might fin' out when you chased dem."

"Nay, *mon ami.* I ain't never seen the three we killed; nor the one what got away."

"I see some of dem before," LeGrande said weakly from his place on the robes near a fire. "One of de dead ones was called Sam Oxley. 'E runs wit' a man is call Abel Carney. He is partner wit' Duncan Maclish."

"I've 'eard of dem," Ledoux said harshly. "Dey is wit' de 'Udson Bay Company." His voice betrayed his hatred. "We Nor'westers 'ad run-ins wit' dem before."

"Well, I don't give a buff'lo's ass who they be workin' for," Squire snapped. "I aim to be findin' them shit-eatin' sons a bitches."

"Now?" Gravant asked. "We 'ave no horses, and dey are miles away by now."

"An' dey deal wit' de Blackfoot." Ledoux offered. "Ain't many white men can do zat."

"Waugh! I don't give a shit if they be dealin' with the goddamn devil and all his buff'lo-humpin' minions. I ain't afeared of no goddamn piss-yellow Blackfeet, nor even of ol' goddamn Lucifer himself."

"Why you wan' to do dis, *mon ami?*"

"They took my woman, my chil', my horses, and all my goddamn plunder, includin' a heap of plews."

"Dere are odder women. You are a big man," Gravant said. He laughed crudely while grabbing his crotch. "You can 'ave many more chil'ren, eh? And dere are more 'orses, and dere are plenty of beaver in dese mountains."

"Them bastards also put under Ol' Druseau and Deer Woman. And it looks like Ol' Sam'll be gone beaver afore long, too. Ye aim to let them *fils des garces* be gettin' away with such doin's? Are ye?" His voice had risen, but he brought it under control. "Shit, ye and Druseau go back nigh onto twenty year."

"It is de way of t'ings out 'ere, *mon ami,*" Gravant said seriously. "You know dat."

"Aye, lad, that I do. But I didn't let the goddamn Blackfeet get away with puttin' Ol' Marchand under a few years ago, did I?" His face was livid with rage. "Goddamn, ye be turnin' into an ol' woman, Etienne. Got no more balls."

The French-Canadian's face suddenly was mottled with rage. "'Ow dare you say such a t'ing to me." He pulled a knife and stood in one fluid motion.

Suddenly Ledoux stood in front of him. "Don't be a goddamn fool, Etienne," Ledoux said quietly, but with force.

Gravant spit. "I will show him I am *le grand homme.*"

"We've seen enough blood shed 'ere today," Ledoux said calmly. "Dere is no reason to spill more among ourselves. If you wan' to show *L'on Farouche* 'ow much of a man you are, den go wit' 'im to find de *immonde fils des garces* who killed Pierre."

"And you, *mon ami?*"

"I am going wit' *L'on Farouche*. Dey 'ave taken my Marie— White Feather—and my chil'ren, both of dem."

"Den I will go, too. Though I 'ave lost only plews, I will go wit' *L'on Farouche* and show 'im what a man I can be."

"*Bon.*"

"How many plews did we lose?" Squire asked harshly.

"About all what we all took," Ledoux answered. He turned to face Squire. "Dey knew what dey were doing, and dey were fast."

"We'll be cachin' the rest here. I'll set to it after I've ate. We'll be leavin' afore daybreak."

"What about Sam?" Ledoux asked roughly as Gravant sat there, still angry.

"If'n he ain't gone under, we'll be takin' him with us. We got three horses left. We can be makin' a travois for him. If he's gone under . . ." Squire shrugged. "LeGrande can be makin' it, I expect, if'n he gets some rest. Eh, *mon ami?*"

"*Oui,*" LeGrande said heatedly.

Squire fed himself in angry silence, bolting down chunks of beaver tail.

When he was done, he grabbed one of their small shovels and headed off into the thickets. He worked through most of the night, but by morning, he had cached all their plews. And he had done it so well that not even an Indian could find the cache.

Syrett died during the night, so Squire dug graves for him, Deer Woman, Druseau, and Yellow Kettle. When the bodies were wrapped and buried, Squire plunged head first into the cold stream, letting the freezing water splash away the grime of dirty work, the sweat of long, distasteful toil, and the fatigue of long, hard hours.

He bolted down another meal of fresh beaver meat, washed down with the only whiskey they had left—they had used a considerable amount in cleaning their various wounds—and then he marched off without a word.

Gravant, Robiseau, and Ledoux followed him silently. LeGrande, on a travois with what little supplies they had, rode, as did the smaller children. The older children walked alongside Light Walker and Blue Robe.

-21-

They followed the valley of the Gallatin River as it moved northward. It took a week to reach a place a few miles east of the Three Forks area, and they were exhausted. They made camp, and the men hunted fresh meat, getting enough to last several days.

"You know we will never catch dem now, don' you, *mon ami?*" Gravant said their first night there.

"I'll be catchin' em, lad. One day or another, I'll be catchin' up to them." Determination was written on Squire's face.

"We cannot go on like dis," Robiseau said.

"Why not?" Squire growled.

"Emil's wound is causing 'im some trouble. But even more dan dat, de chil'ren can't keep up."

Squire sat thoughtfully, stroking his lush beard. He was so immensely strong, especially when obsessed, that he had a hard time seeing that others were not possessed of his great strengths.

Finally he nodded and said slowly, "Mayhap ye be right, *mon ami.*" He paused. "I reckon I'll be goin' on alone from here. Ye lads stay put till LeGrande gets better. Then ye can build yourselves some bull boats and take the Missouri down to Fort Atkinson or back to the settlements. Ye'll be findin' someone there to stake ye. Then ye can head on back here and get the plews.

"I'll be takin' only a few supplies. A bit of the jerky we

142

made, my powder, lead, and such. I'll e'en be leavin' my traps and such with ye so's ye can make yourself some comfortable."

"I am going wit' you," LeGrande said, stoking the fires of his hatred. "Dey mus' not be allowed to get away wit' dis. *Non!*"

"Ye be too weak, *mon ami*," Squire said. "I'll be doin' it on my own."

"*Non!* I will come!"

"You will not," Gravant said, the shame of Squire's words of a week ago still stinging him. "*L'on Farouche* is right. You are too weak. You will stay 'ere wit' Marcel, Toussain', and Light Walker, Blue Robe, and de chil'ren. When you can travel well, do as *L'on Farouche* says. I will go wit' *L'on Farouche.*"

"*Bon,*" Squire said with finality, brooking no more argument from LeGrande.

Two days later, they set out on foot, heading north along the Missouri River. Several days after they left, they began seeing plenty of sign. They followed the Indian sign up the Missouri River for several weeks. They worked around the great falls on the river and followed its source as it curled northeast. A few days beyond, the trail they were following turned almost due north along the Marias River. They finally spotted a Blackfoot village in a tight bend of the River. They worked their way into some timber and watched the village a quarter of a mile or so up the river. When night fell, they crept forward until they were just outside the horse herd. Two sleepy guards kept a desultory watch.

The guards rode their way lazily around the herd, one clockwise, the other counterclockwise. Squire and Gravant split. Soon two Blackfeet were unconscious on the ground, and two white men had three Indian ponies and were moving silently away. When they were about a mile from the village, they jumped into the saddleless ponies and quirted them into action. Squire held the rope of the third horse.

They rode northwest, still following the Marias. It was easier traveling after they had passed the great falls and the land had flattened some. And the horses were a godsend.

"What're we going to do now?" Gravant asked after they

had been out two days. "We do not know where dey went. Dere is no sign to follow."

"Mayhap we'll just be talkin' to some Blackfeet."

"Hah. Dem Blackfeet ain't going to talk to nobody like us," Gravant snorted. "We will be lucky dey don' steal our 'orses and take our 'air."

"Then we'll just be findin' us one to talk to. Them lads've been dealin' with the Blackfeet. Or so Emil said. One of these red niggurs'll be knowin' where those shit eaters be."

"An' 'ow will you do dis, eh?" Gravant asked skeptically. "Ain't no Blackfoots going to 'ave a *tête-à-tête* wit' us. Dat's for goddamn sure."

"Don't ye be frettin' about that, *mon ami*," Squire said with deadly, low tones.

Gravant looked at him surreptitiously. He had known Squire for some years now. He also knew how Squire had gotten his nickname of *L'on Farouche*. The Blood faction of the Blackfoot nation held a great fear of *L'on Farouche* because of that. If he and Squire could capture a Blackfoot, the Indian most likely could be convinced to talk. Gravant shuddered, though, knowing it might not be a pleasant thing to see.

At the confluence of the Willow Creek and the Marias River, Squire instinctively turned up Willow Creek, following its slightly northwest course. They saw plenty of Indian sign, but nothing that would lead them to the men who had raided their camp.

Two weeks later, they camped in a grove of willows and cottonwoods along Willow Creek. Squire was uncommunicative, had been for days. His face looked like a thundercloud.

"I t'ink it is time to go back, *mon ami*," Gravant said that night. He and Squire were sitting at a small, wind-whipped fire, sipping on coffee and puffing on pipes filled with kinnikinick. "We 'ave learned not'ing in all dis time."

"Mayhap, lad," Squire growled. "But I be havin' the feelin' that we be gettin' closer to them niggurs all the time." He wasn't sure he believed that, but he was not going to give up now.

"You are being a fool, Nathaniel. Why you do dis, eh?"

"I don't let no chil' count coup on me, steal all my goddamn plunder, and make off with my woman and chil'. That don't shine with this hoss the least goddamn bit. I'll be raisin' hair on those critters for certain, *mon ami*. Ye can set your sights on that."

"Others 'ave counted coup on you before."

"Aye," Squire snarled. "And e'eryone of them bastards paid the full goddamn price for it, too. I've made the goddamn Blackfeet come more'n once, goddamnit. This chil' give out with the best of 'em, and I thought Bug's Boys had learned their lessons well, goddamn 'em. Any others who've set agin me know better, if they still got their topknots, which most of 'em ain't. Mayhap these red niggurs need another dose of *L'on Farouche*'s medicine."

Gravant laughed roughly. "*Oui, L'on Farouche, mon ami.* You 'ave earned dat name. I will stay wit' you a little longer then, eh. We will find dem an' pay dem back for all de troubles dey 'ave cause."

They rode on the next morning. They began seeing more sign of Blackfoot activity and so grew more wary over the next two days. They spent a few nights with their sleep broken by watchfulness, but they were not molested. Two days later, Squire asked, "Ye reckon ye know what time of year it be?"

"*Mais oui.*" Gravant had always made himself a calendar, using a piece of elk hide, and scratching off each day with a rub of charcoal. It wasn't perfect, but it was mostly accurate. "It is late in July. Maybe early August. Why?"

"We been seein' one hell of a heap of goddamn sign, and I been tryin' to figure out why. Now I know what time of year it be, I be certain I know the lay of it."

"De Sun Dance, eh?" Gravant said with a nod.

"Aye. We got Blackfeet comin' from all over creation to meet at some village, which I don't expect is but a couple mile away, for it. And we be sittin' plumb in the middle of 'em."

"What do you t'ink we should do, *mon ami?*" Gravant asked with an edge of sarcasm.

"Can't rightly say. If'n them lads we be followin' ain't here, one of these red niggurs ought to know where they be."

"You plan to jus' ride in dere and find out?" Gravant's sarcasm was thick.

Squire grinned viciously. "Wouldn't be the first time. But I be thinkin' not this time. I reckon we ought to be holin' up till dark. Then we can be takin' us a little looksee."

"*Bon.* Now let's go."

They found a tight stand of willows, wormed their way into the brush, and hunkered down, chewing on jerky. Each napped fitfully, dozing in short stretches. Only once did danger near, when five laughing Blackfoot warriors drifted by. Squire and Gravant jumped up, slapping hands over horse muzzles to keep them quiet. Both men stood like rooted trees, unmoving as the warriors passed. Squire's face was twisted with a desire to lash out at the Blackfeet, but he knew that would be foolish. So he restrained himself.

When the warriors had gone, the two mountain men flopped back onto the ground to while away the lingering daylight hours. When night began its slow descent, they moved slowly out. All they had to do was follow the sounds of the throbbing drums and ululating voices.

"We'll not be molested this night," Squire said. "They all be too busy having themselves a *shivaree.*"

"*Oui.* But de young bucks might be out, looking for some *jeunes filles* to 'ump."

"Then they'll be a heap too goddamn busy to be payin' us any mind," Squire chuckled humorlessly.

They worked their way up a slight wooded rise and peered out through the trees at the large camp laid out ahead of them, about half a mile away. "*Mon Dieu!*" Gravant breathed. "Look at all dem 'orses."

It was full dark now, but there was a full moon, bright and bulbous in the sky. Combined with the flickering light of scores of fires in the separate but bunched together camps, they could see quite well. And what they could see, beyond the dozens and dozens of tipis were thousands and thousands of horses, ranging far and wide.

"Give me your glass, Etienne."

Gravant pulled out the collapsible telescope from his possible sack and handed it to Squire. Squire squinted through the glass. He never did like these things, but they did have their uses sometimes. Methodically he swept the camp with the glass.

"You see anyt'ing?" Gravant stood with his arm draped over

his horse's neck. He picked at his teeth with a sliver of wood in the other hand.

"Nay. Other than they ain't watching their camp very well. They be too interested in their *shivaree* for that. That means them horses ain't gonna be well looked after."

Squire snapped the glass closed and sat. "Best be restin' your bones, *mon ami*," Squire said, looking up at his friend. "We might be havin' us a full night ahead."

"Are you planning to just go down there and look around?"

"Mayhap, lad."

"*Vous êtes fou.* You're crazy."

"That be why they call me *L'on Farouche*." It was a fact, and stated as such.

Gravant laughed a little and sat, amazed still again at this giant. He was as ferocious as a wounded grizzly and as tenacious as a badger.

The noise from the village finally began to die down. Squire stood and put the glass to his eye again, scanning the spread out village carefully. Then he looked beyond, checking the lay of the land, the position of the horse guards, the shifting of the horses themselves.

"*Sacre bleu,*" he muttered.

Gravant jumped up, "*Qu'est-ce que?* What is it?"

"My horse."

"Where?"

Squire handed him the telescope. "Over there, by that small clump of cottonwoods, down where the crick be curving back around this away."

"*Oui.* I see him." He slid the glass away. "But what are you going to do about it."

"I aim to go get him."

"Against all them goddamn Blackfeet?"

"*Oui.* Them Blackfeet don't scare me none. Most of 'em'll be asleep soon, including the horse guards. Ye be stayin' here. I aim to be takin' me a looksee in that camp afore I fetch up my horse."

"Don't be de fool, Nathaniel."

"I'll be back before long." Squire said, paying no mind to Gravant's words.

"If you don't get killed."

-22-

Squire grinned. He stripped off his war shirt, exposing the scarred, broad back and chest. He spread a little bear grease on his torso and arms to help hide his smell. He put his shirt back on.

Then he vaulted onto the horse's back and rode out. He wasn't worried about the Blackfeet waking up, it was the dogs that gave him concern. Every Indian camp had hordes of yipping, barking, snarling, snapping, vicious, cowardly beasts that were suffered until they were ready for the cook pot.

He wondered whether the many mongrels would set up a ruckus at his scent, but he was liberally coated with grease on his body and buckskins, and he smelled of blood and dirt. He was riding a Blackfoot pony, too, which would help.

He rode into camp as if he belonged there, and the dogs mostly left him alone. A few inched toward him, sniffing warily before slinking back into the shadows.

Squire let the horse gingerly pick a course past sleeping, snoring bodies. Once in the large camp, he slid off the horse and moved silently about on foot. He passed through the village like a wraith, pausing a moment at each lodge to listen briefly and then move on.

Suddenly he stopped, ears perked. Then, he heard it again— a voice speaking in English, a version of English as rough as his own fractured variety, but somehow different. But it was not from the lodge he was next to. He moved on some more, listening intently. There, again. He had it pegged. He glided to the tipi from which the sound came and stopped, waiting.

He heard a woman's soft giggle, then a man's deeper-pitched, quiet laugh. Squire smiled savagely and grasped the edge of the door flap. He wondered if the man and woman were alone. He would find out soon enough, though he realized he really didn't care.

He yanked aside the heavy skin flap and slid in, close to the ground. The glowing coals of the fire gave him enough light to see all the lodge in one quick glance: the white man, his pale skin glowing eerily in the firelight, about to enter the young, broad-faced woman; the rifle, pistol, knife, and tomahawk, far enough away from the love bed that the man wouldn't be able to reach them, the empty bed places; stacked bales of plews, traps, and clothing scattered carelessly around. It was obvious in that first glance that this was a white man's lodge. The jumble was one giveaway, but there also were no altar or weapons rack or scalps hanging proudly from a standing lance or from the lodgepoles.

Squire took it all in in less than a second, then he was moving again. The man had heard something. He was on hands and knees between a woman's legs, and he started to turn his head up and around to see what it was. Squire's massive fist broke the upper side of his face. As he slumped to the side, the woman tried to scream, but Squire swiftly clamped a paw over her mouth.

The woman was young and scared. Still half covered by her lover, she could not move easily. Squire grinned wickedly. "Ye understand English, girl?" he asked. When she nodded, he said, "Will ye set to screamin' if'n I let my hand off'n your mouth?" She shook her head. "Just remember what I done to this here lad," Squire warned.

Her eyes widened even more, but she said nothing when he removed his hand. He quickly found her dress and sliced off strips of it. Then he bound her hand and foot and gagged her, still nude. He tossed her a little to the side.

Squire found a gourd full of water and poured it over the man's head. The man sputtered and awoke groggily. He tried to say something, but groaned at the pain it brought.

"What be your name, lad?" Squire asked, yanking the man up into a sitting position.

"Ezra Smith." The words were edged with pain.

"Who ye run with?"

"Bunch of free traders under contract to the Hudson Bay Company."

"Who be your leader?"

Smith thought to argue, but the pain in the side of his face made him think better of it. "Abel Carney."

"How many of ye be there?"

"Was a dozen. Three—no, four—were killed a few weeks back."

"Who be the others?"

"Duncan Maclish, an educated half-Orcadian, half-Blackfoot named William Isbister, a half-breed Cree called Blue Turtle, a métis we know as Dufrain, another Orcadian, John Tomison; and Abel's two younger brothers, Seth and Noah."

"An educated Blackfoot?" Squire asked, surprised despite himself.

Smith nodded. "His old man was an Orkneyman—the company hires many a lad from the Orkney Islands, over in the north of Scotland. Don't know why exactly, though they're hard workers." He sighed. "Will's old man married some Blackfoot slut and kept her *à la façon du pays,* as a country wife, even though the company frowns on such things."

His eyes closed for a moment as he battled the pain. "Blue Turtle's father, a crazy chap from Northumberland, left Blue Turtle with his mother's people more often than not. But Will's father made sure he was educated and learned civilized ways."

He laughed just a little, sending a gale of pain floating through him. "You ever want to get him riled up, call him by his Blackfoot name, Weasel. Pretentious bastard hates that."

Squire nodded, though he had not been all that interested. Still, he had not wanted to shut Smith up. With this much pain, and talking more or less comfortably, there had been a chance Smith might let slip some important information. That he hadn't did not matter now.

"Where be the others?" Squire asked, when it became apparent Smith was not going to say any more.

"Off somewhere." The pain rocketed through his head, growing until it almost engulfed him.

"Where?"

"Don't know." He shook his head slowly, as if hoping the pain—or his head—would fall off.

"Best be answerin' me, lad." The voice was quiet, but there was steel behind it.

"Different places." The words were more mumbled now, as the cracked bones in his face shifted. "Some to Canada, others to St. Louis, the rest . . . someplace . . ." The voice trailed off. Smith fought back the agony and whispered, "Why?"

"Ye got a shitload of gall, lad, to be asking such a thing of me. After ye'n your friends come agin our camp, killin' women and kids. Ye like seein' women die? Mayhap ye'd like to see this here little Blackfoot *chien*—dog—die."

"Let her be." The effort seemed to strengthen him a bit. "She's done nothing."

"That be too bad, for I ain't lettin' her free to go'n tell her people. Less'n, of course," he said with a gleam in his eye, "I be gettin' some help from ye."

Smith waited silently, not wanting to talk more than he had to.

"Where be my woman and child?"

"I don't know what . . ."

Squire pulled his knife.

" . . . We all used her some, but we didn't touch the kid none. Abel finally took the woman over for his own. Then he sold her to some Blackfoot war chief in a camp on the Milk River. In or near Canada. Can't tell for sure. The border ain't well defined thereabouts." He sank back, drained.

"The child?"

Smith could only nod and whisper, "Him, too."

"Ye be knowin' the name of this here chief?"

"Two Bows, I think."

"He be here for the Sun Dance?"

Smith shook his head carefully. "Stayed in his village for it, I think. He's an important bastard, so I expect it's true. I heard others chatting of going there for the celebration. Ain't sure."

"*Bon.*"

"You'll let Song Dancer go, mate?"

"Aye, lad."

Smith, who had pushed himself up a little, sank back again in resignation. He knew he was going to die, but it didn't matter too much. Song Dancer would be freed.

Without expression or feeling, Squire grabbed Smith's throat and quickly squeezed the life out of him. With the same flat look on his face, he turned and plunged his knife into Song Dancer's heart. He did not like doing it, but he was not about to let her get free and spread the alarm. Not when there were maybe two hundred Blackfoot warriors against only him and Gravant.

Gently he lifted the slight young woman and placed her neatly and carefully next to Smith. He covered them with a robe. He cleaned off his knife, slipped it away and eased himself out after checking carefully. He headed toward the horse herd. There was no more he could do here, he knew, not if all the others were far away.

He walked through the camp almost unmolested. One dog trotted up and sniffed, then growled at the strange smell. Squire brained it with his war club and kept walking.

Past the outermost lodges, he dropped to the ground and slinked forward. There were few horse guards for this many animals, and most of them were asleep or not paying much heed. Who would be so foolish as to attack them here, with so many warriors? So why should they be stuck here watching the horses, when all the others were comfortable in their beds, maybe asleep, maybe not . . . ?

One warrior apparently was daydreaming of such things when Squire shattered his head like an eggshell. Another was dozing on horseback when iron-like fingers suddenly wrapped around his throat. Still another was thinking of becoming a father for the first time, it would be anytime soon, or so his woman said. A knife in the heart ended his thoughts.

Squire waded into the milling mass of horseflesh, looking for the huge stallion. The animal was not hard to find. The horse snickered when he caught his master's scent.

"Easy, boy," Squire said, letting the horse nuzzle his neck. He grabbed a fist full of mane and vaulted onto the horse's back. Then he roared and thumped the big horse's sides with his heels. "Come on, lad, run for it," he shouted.

The big reddish steed exploded into action, Squire directing him by knee toward the sleeping village. There were often troubles with riding a stallion, Squire knew, but there were other times, like now, when it was an asset. As big as the roan was, he could easily become the master stallion in a pack. Even in a large herd. So most of the mares would follow him, and then the others. It made stampeding easier. And once started, the surging mass of horseflesh would be almost impossible to stop, he could get away in the confusion.

Thousands of horses wheeled and snorted, breaking into a run that made the ground tremble with their hoofbeats. Squire and the big roan led the way.

The wall moved forward, tentatively at first, but gaining momentum as it raced over the grassy sward. The few remaining horse guards were yelling, trying to turn the tide back, but it was of no use, the horses were upon the village. With no place else to go, the animals smashed into tipis, knocking them over, entangling themselves in the buffalo skins, tipping over racks of drying meat, scattering ashes from scores of fires.

Horses snorted and whinnied as they rammed into each other in their mindless bolting for freedom, driven by nothing other than the press of animals behind them.

Blackfoot men, women and children, most of them naked, raced out of their lodges. The women and their babies ran, followed by the older children, and then most of the men. They scattered wildly, trying to escape the flood of hooved flesh that bore down on them. More than a few were trampled under foot as the teeming mass of horses kept coming.

Embers from the fires were kicked up, starting a fire on a downed tipi here, another there. Soon numerous lodges were burning, sending ugly coils of black smoke looping into the night sky.

Squire looked back at the confusion and grinned wickedly. He was almost alone now, with only a few mares still tagging close by. The other thousands of horses were jammed in knots in the midst of the village, or were racing across the open while Blackfeet tried to trap and catch them.

Squire slowed the roan. "Ye done good, ol' hoss," he said. "Now come on, let's be findin' Etienne."

Within minutes he was back with his friend, letting the roan breathe. Two mares cropped grass a few feet away. "Well, *mon ami,* what do you think?"

"You made dem come, now, you did, eh." He laughed. "Dem bastards was running like chickens when dere heads is lop off."

"We'll be havin' no trouble from them lads this night, I'd be sayin'."

"*Oui.* And for the next few days, too."

-23-

Just before dawn, Squire and Gravant rode down from their small, cottonwood-covered hillock through what was left of the huge Blackfoot camp. Most of the men were still off chasing horses while the women were searching the scattered remains of their lodges for whatever belongings they could salvage.

"Where away we heading?" Gravant asked.

"Toward the Milk River, I reckon."

"You t'ink you're still going to get your woman back, eh? An' de odders, too?"

"I aim to be tryin'."

"You are *fou, trés fou*." Gravant shook his head.

"Ye've said that afore, *mon ami*. But I ain't givin' up now."

Gravant shrugged. He had known Squire for a long time, and he knew how hard-headed the mountain man could be. There was no give-up in the American once he set his mind on something. Gravant could not understand it. Sure, Sings Pretty was a good woman, but Indian women were as easy to come by as beaver. Easier, since they were a hell of a lot more willing. Squire could have his pick—Sioux, Nez Perce, Flathead, Shoshone, Ute, Crow.

And what of the child? Gravant shrugged in his mind. The boy probably would have been raised as a Nez Perce anyway. Once the boy had gotten old enough to go to war, Squire most likely wouldn't even have seen him again.

He shook his head in resignation. Squire had helped him out of some serious scrapes more than once, he would not turn his back on his friend now.

They sat a little, letting the horses drink and wondering which way to go. Here, the Milk ran east and west. Squire finally shrugged. Instinct had worked for him so far, he could see no reason to go against it now. He turned west, following the river's winding, brushy course.

A day later, they camped at the juncture of the Milk and its northern branch. The next day they followed the Milk as it turned southward and a little west. Several days beyond, they spotted the Blackfoot village nestled in the foothills of the Rocky Mountains.

They took to riding the brushy river bank as much as possible once they began seeing a lot of sign. But it was not an easy trip, cutting through the muck and mud, tangled brush, and fallen tree limbs. Finally they were forced away from the river, out onto a flat.

There was nothing they could do but press ahead boldly. Suddenly some Blackfeet appeared ahead of them. There was no place for them to hide, so Squire and Gravant kept going. The Blackfeet saw them and charged. Calmly, Squire pulled himself up as high as he could on the back of the horse and held out his left hand, palm outward. He thought they might think him one of Carney's men. It didn't work.

An arrow nicked one of his fingers. Angrily he leveled the long flintlock rifle and fired. A Blackfoot flew back over his horse's rump as the ball plowed into his breast.

Another arrow thunked into Squire's possibles bag as he kicked the big roan into motion, heading toward the enemy. He took one hasty, sidelong glance at Gravant and saw that the French-Canadian had dropped his rifle after firing. Then Squire had to turn his attention back to the Blackfeet.

Squire jerked out his war club and let out a whoop. Three arrows suddenly thudded into the roan's big, broad chest. As Squire went sailing over the horse's head, he heard the crack of a rifle and thought he could hear a ball hitting bone. Then he hit the ground, bouncing and flopping, the wind knocked out of him.

Before he could rise, half a dozen Blackfoot warriors were

on him, brandishing their knives. They screeched in victory. Amid them was a white, hairy face, shouting almost cheerfully, "Don't kill him, now, lads. Don't kill him."

Squire found himself trussed up like a Christmas turkey, the rawhide thongs wrapped tightly around him. Then he and a battered Gravant were hauled off to the Blackfoot camp.

It was a bigger village even than the one they had seen the last time, with more than a hundred lodges scattered through the wooden valley. Horses by the thousands grazed on the lush grass. Hunters left in small groups, lances upright and gleaming in the sun, or returned with fresh buffalo and elk and deer.

Many of the women jeered and spat on Squire and Gravant as the two mountain men were brought into the village. A few threw stones at them. But the novelty wore off quickly, and they went back to work, scraping hides, cutting meat, sewing clothes, carting firewood, hauling up water. There would be time for sporting with the two captives later.

The two men were tied to poles in an open space. Their hands were bound behind the poles. Several wrappings of rawhide were also made around their chests and the poles. Their legs were spread and pegged down with rawhide thongs and wooden stakes.

Nearby, some of the young men were preparing themselves for the Sun Vow, chanting or entering sweat lodges tended by old men. A few had already had their flesh pierced, the skewers pushed through and heavy buffalo skulls attached to the pegs by rawhide thongs. They chanted and danced, blowing on eagle-bone whistles and shaking rattles as they wandered throughout the camp.

Squire grimaced in annoyance as he heard two criers riding through the circles of smaller camps that made up the larger village, announcing their arrival and that a council would be held to decide what to do with the two white men.

"These doin's don't shine with this chil' a-tall," Squire said, squinting up at the merciless sun.

Gravant let out a string of curses in French that even Squire could not follow.

They waited, thirst creeping up to clutch at them after several hours. They watched in interest as the warriors held their council not far away. Each warrior got his full say and usually took his time about saying it. But the white man that Squire had seen earlier finally began taking a hand, riding roughshod over the talk.

Squire wondered how a white man could get away with such doings. He remembered that LeGrande had said this Carney worked for the Hudson Bay Company. Since the Hudson Bay Company was reported to have some strong influence with the Bloods and other northern bands of Blackfeet in Canada, Squire supposed that was how this white man held the upper hand here. Still, it was unusual.

Then Squire also recalled that Smith had said that one of Carney's men was a half-breed Blackfoot. The two factors combined probably would account for it, he decided.

Before dark, the council broke up, and the white leader and two others came over to where Squire and Gravant were tied.

"I'm Abel Carney," the one said, "and these are my brothers, Seth and Noah."

"I be Squire."

Abel Carney laughed, showing a great expanse of shining white teeth behind the tawny beard and mustache. He was a handsome sort of fellow, a year or so older than Squire. He was of medium height and build, but he looked like he could carry his own.

He also was well dressed for a man who spent so much of his time in Indian camps. It was obvious that he was a trader, if he actually did any trading, and not a trapper. Judging by the fine wool trousers, crisp white shirt, and swallow-tailed coat, Carney also had aspirations of becoming a factor of one of the Hudson Bay Company posts.

"I know who the hell you are, old boy. You're that goddamn bloody big ox some of these chickenshit Injuns call *L'on Farouche*. Seems like the Blackfeet are scared of you, old chap, but for the life of me, I bloody well can't see why."

"I be figurin' to show ye afore too much longer, lad," Squire said in tightly controlled anger.

Carney laughed again. "I like that. I surely do. But I have my doubts you'll be doin' anything like that, old boy. I just came to inform you that the Blackfeet have got some bloody special doin's planned for you two chaps." He laughed again, a warm, deep laugh that might have been pleasant under other circumstances.

Squire spit at Carney. The sticky phlegm landed on his left cheek. The laughter stopped as if the man's throat had been cut.

Without a word, Carney kicked Squire in the crotch. It wasn't as hard as it could be, but it was brutal enough.

Squire sagged against the rawhide holding him up. Air whistled through his teeth.

"That's just a taste of what you're going to get, you bloody bastard," Carney snarled. He spun, and with his two brothers in tow, stomped off.

"Foolish son of a bitch," Gravant grumbled. "*Comment allez-vous,* Nat'aniel, eh?" he asked.

With an effort, Squire pushed himself up. The pain was subsiding some, but he had never felt such agony before. Even when he had been arrow shot it hadn't been that bad. His scrotum ached with a steady pulse, and he could feel it swelling. He vowed, though, that he would not let the others see his pain. By morning, it was an aching but fading memory, and all but forgotten as a horde of Blackfeet, and a few white men, came toward him and Gravant. Most of them sat or kneeled or stood in a great semicircle around the two trussed-up men.

Abel Carney stepped up close to them. In a voice that all could hear, he said, "Now comes the time to show what you chaps are made of. Especially you, *L'on Farouche.* It's a real bloody coup for these lads to have taken you. The Blackfeet'll gain a heap of honors after they've done with you and have removed your hair."

"I ain't dead yet, lad, so don't ye be countin' your coups afore ye took any. I made four of these chickenshits gone beaver already, and I'll be doin' the same to ye one day. Of that ye can be certain, lad."

"That's good, Squire," Carney laughed. "Yes, bloody god-damn good." His teeth gleamed. Carney actually seemed to be having a good time. "I hope you'll keep that bloody frame of mind once the Blackfeet get to workin' on you."

"Don't ye be worryin' your head o'er me none, lad," Squire said nonchalantly.

Carney was pleased. Squire knew how to play the game. Unlike so many others. He would be an interesting experiment. Carney turned and nodded at several Blackfoot standing nearby. "He's all yours, old chaps," he said.

Several warriors stepped up and began slicing the clothes off Squire and Gravant. They did their work none too gently, and more than once a blade sliced through human skin as well as buckskin.

Squire breathed deeply, building up his resources of strength and will. Already the sun was blazing down on them, and thirst scratched at his throat.

The warriors paced off about twenty-five yards and began shooting arrows at the two captives, trying to come as close to their flesh without doing too much actual damage. The two major targets on each were the head and privates.

Sweat broke out on Squire's forehead as arrow after arrow thunked into the post, only to be removed by the rough hands of women and children. The removers hoped to make the captives flinch. He glanced at Gravant out of the corner of his eye occasionally.

The French-Canadian had a look of pain etched permanently on his face. But he shouted at the Indians, as did Squire, with each shot. The Blackfeet would cheer, and the two captives would taunt them on their woeful marksmanship until the two could barely speak through parched throats.

Then an errant arrow thudded into Gravant's left leg, just above the knee. He hissed with the pain but kept himself standing. The hiss was not heard over the roar at the shooter's poor aim.

"Is that the best ye assholes can be doin'?" Squire croaked, trying to work up some spit.

But the game was soured now, and the arrows soon stopped.

"Ye dumb bastards had enough?" Squire yelled as loudly as his thirst-weakened voice would allow. More quietly he asked, "*Comment allez-vous, mon ami?*"

"*Pas mal*—all right." Gravant sounded weak.

"Ye certain?"

"I've been better, eh?" Gravant almost managed a grin. "But I've been worse, too."

Squire glanced up, wondering why they were being left

alone. The Blackfeet were paying almost no attention to them now. It made Squire wonder what they were planning. He flexed his shoulders and biceps, testing the strength of his bonds. There was no give in the rawhide.

A commotion made him look up again. The three Carneys were heading toward him and Gravant. The other white men followed closely behind, and the Blackfeet set up a cacophony of hooting and jeering in anticipation.

"I expect you were wonderin' where she was, weren't you, old chap?" Abel Carney asked with a sneer. He stepped back to reveal Sings Pretty. The woman was battered, her eyes hollow-looking from the treatment she had received.

"I give her to old Two Bows," Carney said with a rough laugh. "But I just bought her back from the bloody old savage." He nodded, and his brothers sliced off what was left of the woman's ragged buckskin dress, leaving her naked. Her moccasins and leggings had long since been lost. Like her face, her breasts, belly, and legs were a latticework of purple and blue bruises.

Squire bit back the rage that boiled up in him like a geyser. Only the narrowing of his eyelids showed the anger that seethed inside him.

"She's a bloody good-lookin' piece, I'll give you that, old boy," Carney said with a leer. "But, goddamn, you treated her bloody poorly for someone's supposed to be a big goddamn man." He nodded again, and his brothers and two other men threw Sings Pretty down and held her spread-eagled. "I suppose you should see how a bloody real man should treat a squaw."

Abel Carney strutted toward the woman. As he knelt in the V of Sings Pretty's legs and unbuttoned his drop-front wool pants to expose his rigidness, the other men whooped and hollered. With a cruel smile on his lips, he jammed himself into Sings Pretty. It was over before long, and Sings Pretty did not utter a sound.

Carney still looked pleased with himself as he stood. He crowed before stuffing his dripping member back into his pants and buttoning them. Then he grinned. "Your turn, lads," he said joyfully, watching Squire's face.

He was disappointed when Squire showed nothing. The

huge mountain man simply turned his head and began chatting casually with Gravant.

"You're good, Squire, I'll say that for you," Carney admitted, half in anger, half in admiration. "But you'll have to watch these bloody, goddamn activities sooner or later." He kicked the young woman, making her yelp once at the surprise of it. Carney smiled wickedly when Squire's head turned that way. Carney nodded again.

Seth Carney stood as another man took his place holding Sings Pretty. He, too, took the Nez Perce woman with far more viciousness than was needed. Then came Noah Carney and the eight other white men. Then the Blackfeet started on her, and they made the whites look pleasurable by comparison. Most battered Sings Pretty around as they ground their bodies against her, hoping for a reaction.

Squire watched on and off, blanking his mind when he could no longer look away. There was a deep-seated core of rage in his breast, but there was nothing he could do about the situation. He simply turned his mind off what was happening to Sings Pretty, while still recording and noting everything. There would come a time to pay back these men for all this, he vowed. And his retribution would be a fearsome thing to behold, indeed.

He occasionally let his mind drift to his son. He had not dared mention the boy or ask about him. He simply hoped that the boy was still alive and had been adopted by one of the Blackfoot families.

He tried to keep his mind off what was happening to Sings Pretty, and he tried to keep his thoughts off the scratchy dryness of his throat and mouth and the blood dribbling down Gravant's leg and the pain that lingered in his tender genitals. He thought only of escape and revenge.

Others began to tire of the woman's debasement, and they turned their attentions back to the two mountain men. Knives traced light, bloody patterns on their skins or peeled away slim strips of flesh as the Blackfeet watched intently for any sign of weakness or pain.

Squire and Gravant would let none of their pain or discomfort show. Indeed, both insulted and demeaned their hosts as regularly as their parched mouths would allow.

-24-

The Blackfeet broke off their festivities at nightfall. Squire wondered about it, but was grateful for the respite. He would take whatever chance to rest that he could, since he knew they would be back in the morning, if not before. He supposed they simply were trying to prolong the torture, letting the two men have time to think of what devilish things the Indians would come up with next.

It also helped that the Blackfeet had gotten drunk on whiskey supplied by Abel Carney and his men. Before long, most of the warriors were snoring loudly all over the camp.

Sings Pretty had been dragged off late in the afternoon, and now Squire and Gravant were all by themselves.

"Ye be all right, *mon ami?*" Squire asked.

"I will live," Gravant said. He laughed harshly and spat. "At least for a little longer, eh?"

The camp was full asleep, except for the bored horse guards and a few wandering drunks, when Squire saw Sings Pretty crawling toward him. He waited, aching to help her, but unable to. Finally she reached him, and cut through the bonds holding his feet.

Pulling on his flesh, she managed to stand. She was wobbly and had to clutch one of his iron arms as she sawed feebly at his bonds. She moaned a few times, and she dropped the knife once. She could barely manage to get upright again after retrieving it, but she did.

She finally had cut through the thongs, and Squire was free. He stood, rubbing his arms to restore his circulation. He rolled his great shoulders and flexed his chest and arms and legs. He was sore and a little weak, but he would be able to manage.

He took Sings Pretty in his arms and held her. She whimpered. Quickly he held her out at arms' length and looked at her in the full brightness of the starry night. Her face and body were a mass of bruises and welts. He turned her around and saw that her naked back and buttocks and been scraped raw. Blood oozed out and mingled with the scraps of dirt and grass.

"*Merde,* woman, what've they done to ye?" Squire asked. He almost moaned as the pain of what she had been through swept over him. That hurt more than anything the Indians had done or could do to him.

"Is all right," she whispered. "You go now."

Squire took the knife from Sings Pretty's hands, noticing that the hilt was covered with blood. "From me?" he asked showing it to her. "Or from you?"

She shook her head. "Neither. Two Bows took me back to his lodge," she gasped. She made a slicing motion with her hand. "Now he no longer a man." She tried to smile but could not.

"*Bon,*" Squire was pleased with that thought. It was small enough retribution for their travails, but retribution nonetheless. He began sawing at the rawhide binding Gravant. "Can ye be gettin' us horses, woman?" he asked.

Sings Pretty shook her head. "No guns either. You run. Now. You must go."

Gravant was free, and Squire grabbed him when he began to fall. "*Merde,*" he muttered again. He looked at Sings Pretty. "I ain't leavin' here without ye, lass."

Sings Pretty shook her head again.

"Don't be arguin' with me, goddamnit, woman. You'll do . . ."

"She won't make it, Nathaniel," Gravant interjected. "She knows dat, even if you don'."

Squire stood rooted. He knew in his head she could not make it fifty yards, let alone the trek they would have to undertake.

He thought he would carry her, but he realized Gravant would need help. He did not think he could carry them both, not in his condition. But in his heart he knew he could not leave Sings Pretty here. She would die as soon as Two Bows was found. Her death would not be an easy one, either.

"Time passes, *mon ami*."

"I know."

"Go," Sings Pretty said. Her voice was a mere whisper. She sank down, wincing as her raw buttocks hit the ground. "Go. Hurry."

"*Allons, mon ami*." There was urgency in Gravant's voice.

"Kin ye be walkin'?" Squire asked. The urgency of the situation caught up to him.

"I will try."

"*Bon*." Squire scooped up Sings Pretty. Tears flooded her pain-racked eyes.

He took off at a run.

Gravant got half a dozen steps before he fell on his face. "*Merde*," Squire hissed. He raced back to his fallen friend and scooped him up.

"Leave me," Sings Pretty whispered. "Take Etienne."

"No." Squire snarled low in his throat. "This ain't gonner be easy," he muttered. Aloud, he added, "This might pain ye some, Sings Pretty, but it's got to be done."

She started to argue, but Squire wasn't listening. He had made up his mind, and so was obsessed. He set her on her feet, never fully letting her go. "Can ye stand, Etienne?" he asked.

"*Oui*." Gravant's voice was weak but determined. He did it, asking, "Where?"

"Next to Sings Pretty. *Vite*."

Gravant shuffled next to the woman and stopped with his right shoulder almost touching Sings Pretty's left one.

Squire bent and reached out his arms. One appendage went around each of the others. "Bend forward," he ordered. They did, and when he straightened, Sings Pretty dangled over his left shoulder and Gravant over his right. He turned and trotted off. He ran easily for a man burdened as he was and suffering from thirst, pain, and hunger. He slowed, however, when he reached the horse herd. He set Gravant and Sings Pretty down and took the knife Gravant had been holding.

"Stay here," Squire whispered, sliding forward silently. He crept up on a Blackfoot horse guard who was sitting, back against a cottonwood, thinking he was unseen. Suddenly Squire clasped a hand over the man's mouth and with the other hand slid the knife across the Blackfoot's throat. The Indian struggled but a few moments before he was still. Squire yanked off the man's breechcloth and shook it vigorously to get rid of some of the lice before he put it on. He took the Blackfoot's knife and war club, as well as the pouch with flint and steel in it.

He moved through and around horses, until he found another guard. Squire cracked the warrior's head with the club. He took that Blackfoot's loincloth for Gravant. Squire prowled a little while longer but saw no other horse guards nearby. Finally Squire took three Blackfoot ponies, careful not to disturb the other horses. He led them back to Gravant and Sings Pretty.

Sings Pretty looked bad when Squire returned. He knelt at the woman's side.

"She is near *morte, mon ami*," Gravant said quietly.

"I know," Squire responded in kind. "But I ain't leavin' her here."

"You will only bring her more pain, *mon ami*."

"Aye," Squire said roughly. "But I can't be leavin' her to the tender mercies of them red niggurs and those bastards who took her and all our plunder."

"Dere is only one t'ing to do." Gravant reached out and tapped the knife with a finger.

Squire knew it was the only reasonable thing to do. Sings Pretty would never recover, even if they could get her to a place of safety alive. Still, he was loathe to do it.

"Dey will be 'ere soon, *mon ami*," Gravant said.

Squire looked at Sings Pretty, his heart near to bursting with the pain of his decision.

Her eyes opened and looked straight at him. She had been nearly unconscious, but she had heard it all. "Yes," she whispered, trying to smile in reassurance.

"*Je t'aime*," Squire whispered. He plunged the knife into her heart.

Sings Pretty's eyes never left Squire's, until the light faded from them. She tried to smile once more, but it was feeble. Then she died.

Squire stood, feeling like he had a lead weight on his chest. Absentmindedly he wiped the knife on his breechcloth.

"We must go, *mon ami,*" Gravant said, urgently struggling up.

"Aye." Squire dropped the knife and war club and helped Gravant onto one of the horses. He gave the knife to Gravant. Then he picked up the club. With it in one hand, he bent and scooped Sings Pretty up.

"I ain't leavin' her here to be butchered by those sons a bitches." He leaped onto a Blackfoot pony. He let the third horse go. It drifted back toward the herd. Cradling Sings Pretty's body, he said, "*Allons.*"

They moved off slowly.

After they rounded a hillock and passed through several groves of cottonwoods and oaks, they smacked the horses hard. Through the night they pushed the horses, heading southwest, until the animals dropped of exhaustion. Squire's, carrying the extra weight, went first. When he felt the horse begin to stumble, Squire pulled to a halt. He slid off the pony, set Sing's Pretty's body down and dropped the war club. Gravant tossed him the knife. Squire slit the horse's throat and then hacked off some meat.

Squire handed the bloody bundle of meat up to Gravant. He stuffed the knife and war club into his breechcloth. "Ride, *mon ami,*" he said.

"What about you?"

"I'll follow."

Gravant matched the pony's gait to Squire's long, sure strides. He did not want to leave his friend behind. He also thought that maybe the slower pace might help the pony.

Soon after, Squire suddenly stopped. He set the body down and walked toward the edge of a cliff, where piles of boulders lay in immense profusion. He looked over, seeing the cliff wall slope outward toward the bottom. At the bottom of the twenty-foot-deep cliff, on the opposite side, was a cave.

"*Bon,*" Squire muttered. He went back and got Sings Pretty.

"What now?" Gravant asked in exasperation.

Squire ignored him. He went down the sharp, rock-strewn cliff as carefully as he could. He slid and slipped most of the way. He gently placed Sings Pretty's corpse in the cave. He wished he had something to see her on her journey, but she was going to the afterlife as naked and poor as she had entered this life.

The climb up was harder than the one down, though Squire was unburdened. He did it as quickly as possible, not wanting to allow himself time to think about Sings Pretty. Not now.

At the top, he paused only long enough to catch his breath. Gravant sat on his pony, watching him. The French-Canadian knew for certain now that Squire was crazy. Squire ignored him. He put his shoulder to a huge boulder. Tensing, he strained, sputtering with the effort.

Slowly, ever so slowly, the boulder moved an inch. The movement increased fractionally, then even more. Suddenly it started to roll, and Squire almost went down after it.

The boulder rumbled down the cliff crashing into other rocks and stones, sending them tumbling downward with a roar and a cloud of dust.

When the smoke of the dust blew away or settled, Squire looked down. He nodded with satisfaction. The cave could not be seen. Sings Pretty would be safe now.

"Come, *mon ami,*" Gravant said quietly.

Squire nodded and strode off, looking like he had not a care in the world. But a core of hatred and loss burned in his heart.

A few hours later, Gravant's pony went down. They left it to the wolves and vultures.

-25-

They pressed on, Squire carrying Gravant more often than not, marching on bare feet over the rough grass or prickly pear cactus, over rocks, across streams. It was a nightmare with the sun beating mercilessly on them for the first three days. Then came a torrential, freezing downpour that lasted several days. More than once they had to scramble out of a coulee as a flash flood roared down on them, twice they almost drowned crossing a river swollen by the deluge.

The sun returned as they headed southward and a little eastward. Wildlife abounded—buffalo, elk, rabbit, deer—but they ate lean. It was not easy to bring down a fleet elk or a buffalo with a war club and knife. But they managed to survive on carcasses they could scare the wolves from and on berries and nuts, roots and tubers.

Twice more Squire snuck into Blackfoot camps and stole horses. He and Gravant, though, rode the ponies to death before long, putting them afoot again.

Finally, though, they entered Crow land. They had traded with the Crows plenty in the past, but they had nothing with them now, so they were not about to approach some Crows and hope they could talk those Indians into just giving them some ponies. The Crows most likely would just laugh at them and chase them out of the camp.

169

So, Squire stole a couple of ponies from one band. But they were far enough from the Blackfoot to go easy on the horses now.

Four weeks and a day after they left the Blackfoot village, they found their old camp on the Gallatin.

LeGrande, Robiseau, and Ledoux were waiting for them with a rather comfortable camp. They had traded with the Indians for a few horses, and they had had considerable luck in hunting buffalo and elk, so meat was plentiful.

"And what will you do now, eh?" Ledoux asked.

"I be goin' after them again," Squire said flatly.

"I told you 'e was *fou*, eh," Gravant said. "Forget dem, *mon ami*. You'll be better off, I tell you."

"'E is right, my friend," LeGrande said flatly. "Your woman and son are gone. You won't get dem back. She is dead, *mon ami,* and de boy will be raise by de Blackfeet as one of dem."

"I ain't lettin' that happen."

"But . . ."

"Oh, let him alone," Gravant said. "'E will not listen to you. He is *sourd*—deaf. We chase the Blackfeet all over an' all we get is pain and hurts. I got an arrow in de leg, and him, he got feet full of cactus thorns. They counted coup on us but good, *mon ami*."

"*Oui*. And I aim to be returnin' the favor, in spades."

"Maybe some day you will," Gravant said in exasperation. Never in his life had he met anyone so hard-headed and stubborn. "We will see dem again if dey are in de mountains, eh. One day, we ride along, nice as you please, eh, and dere dey will be, just like we were—unready. Den we will pounce on dem like de cat on de mouse, *non?*" He snapped his fingers at the simplicity of it all.

"We all 'ave somet'ing to settle with dem, Nathaniel," Robiseau said. "Dey killed ol' Pierre and Sam and Deer Woman and one of de chil'ren. You say you could not fin' White Feather and Red Leaf. Dey, too, are gone, whether dead or living wit' de Blackfeets." He paused. "Dose Blackfeets will pay. But it is no good for you to be like dis, *mon ami. Non!*"

"And just what do ye lads aim to be doin'?"

"Take what plews we 'ave," Robiseau said. "Dere are still plenty in de cache. Enough for a *shivaree* in St. Louis, eh." He laughed a little. "Den we get more supplies and come back 'ere. Next season we do plenty good, *non?*"

"*Oui!*" Ledoux and Gravant said in unison.

"Can't you see it, *mon ami?*" LeGrande said, painting a picture with his hands. "The good food dere in St. Louis, eh. And de whiskey." His voice oozed with honey. "And de women!" He and his companions laughed heartily. "Ah, *oui*, de women. Clean ones dere, smelling of *parfum*, and not of bear grease, eh."

Squire was starting to grin, too. He was still angry beyond words, but it had been a long time since he had had a woman, and a longer time since having a good spree. "*Oui*," he growled in ascent.

Squire counted *leve* on them early the next day, and before long they were on their way. Two days later they made a camp on the lower Yellowstone. There they killed several buffalo and used the hides to make bull boats. It took a week, but they got it done. They loaded all their furs and traded off the horses to a band of Crows, who promised to care for the horses until they returned in the fall—if they did.

The trip down the Yellowstone, and then the Missouri, was an uneventful one, as far as such journeys went. They saw nothing out of the ordinary in having to shoot the many stretches of white water, in the portaging, in the drenching rainstorms they endured, in the race past Assiniboines and Arikaras, and later Pawnees. The careful hunting to preserve the rapidly dwindling supplies of DuPont powder and Galena lead, the vast swards of mosquitoes that came over them in choking clouds until they were bleeding all over, the poisonous snakes and savage grizzlies, to them such things were a natural part of life, and not even worthy of discussion over the small fires they made at night. Instead, they talked of important things, of battles with Blackfeet or Rees or Pawnees; of women they had had; of memorable hunts.

But the talk came a little harder around the fires these days. There was no tobacco for chewing or to fill their small clay pipes. They tried to make do smoking cottonwood bark, but it was not the same. Four days down the river their coffee ran out. Their flour and sugar had done so long before.

They stopped for two days in a Sioux village. LeGrande and Gravant had traded with the band before, so the visitors were welcomed. But the Sioux were not willing to part with much food or anything else. Not with winter so near, and after finding out that the whites had nothing to trade. The group left quickly, heading down the river again.

But finally they pulled into St. Louis, women and children still in tow. They had beaten winter, but not by much.

They traded in their plews and sold the bull boats. Gravant and Robiseau, with their women, set up their lodges on the outskirts of town, near enough to be handy but far enough so the women and children would not be bothered. Ledoux picked up an Osage woman someplace and set up his lodge near the others.

Squire and LeGrande, whose Yellow Kettle had died, found cheap, wretched lodgings near the waterfront.

The men had their spree, wenching and drinking and fighting and roaring for two splendid weeks. But then their money dwindled, and winter quickly settled over the land. It was November already, and they hunkered down to wait for spring.

With little money and a bellyful of hate, getting through the winter was an ordeal, for Squire especially. He roamed the waterfront, frequently lashing out in drunken rages. He worked at whatever miserable job he could find to keep himself supplied with food and liquor. He hoped the latter would ease his pain somewhat. It didn't.

Squire endured, though, and spring eventually arrived. He had not gotten over the loss of his woman, child, and possibles, so he told the others, "I'll be headin' out on my own this time, lads."

"But why, *mon ami*?" LeGrande asked. He seemed hurt by the notion. "We 'ave been together a long time."

"Aye, that we have. But it's somethin' I got to be doin'. Your stick floats in a different place than mine, and whilst ye'll be a headin' up for the Sioux villages on the Missouri and then beyond, I aim to set out across the flats this time."

They looked at him quizzically. "You will not take de river?" Gravant asked, in disbelief. Always they had come back to the great river of rivers. "You will get lost out dere."

"Buff'lo shit. I'll be followin' the Missouri up a ways till I be hittin' the Platte. Then it be on to the Sweetwater and the Shinin' Mountains. Less'n I can be finding me a different way to go."

"Why?"

"I aim to be lookin' for them murderous bastards. And I can't be doin' that from no dugout or bull boat bein' towed up river or bouncin' back down it."

"But we will get 'orses from de Crows or de Sioux," Gravant said. "Jus' like we always do."

"Aye," Squire acknowledged. "But it be too risky for me to be lettin' chance decide whether I can be findin' me a horse that suits me in some Crow village."

Squire was such a big man that he needed a truly large horse, one that could carry his weight under the harsh demands of the plains and mountains. The three French-Canadians usually traded with Indians for horses, and there were not that many big ones in Indian camps.

They argued with him, trying to convince Squire of his foolishness in heading for the mountains alone. But he had done it before, the first time for several years after his first mentor, old Marchand, had gone under. Then, once again when LeGrande had gone back to Montreal on family business. Afterward the two usually trapped and wintered up together. Occasionally, Squire would ride out alone. LeGrande and some others had found him injured after a fight with Blackfoot up on the Marias once when he had done that. He had an arrow embedded in his chest and had lost a lot of blood, but six Blackfoot warriors were scattered about, a testament to Squire's strength and ferocity. After they had nursed him back to health, Squire decided that being alone was not as safe as being in a group, and so he had joined them again.

Now, though, he had determined it was time for him to move on alone again, and there was nothing any of them could say that would change his mind.

LeGrande finally threw up his hands in despair, muttering French curses under his breath. "Den we will go with you," he said, uncertainty ringing in his voice. "You will be rub out if you go alone." He sounded like a parent trying to shame an errant child into behaving properly.

"I don't want your help, *mon ami*. This here be somethin' I got to be doin' on my own. Ye've got your own shit to see to."

LeGrande thought for a moment, then he nodded. "*Non*. It is settle. We go wit' you," he said with finality.

But the next day, Squire was up well before the dawn. He was packed, saddled, and miles away by the time dawn cracked and LeGrande counted *leve* on his friends. They had the sense not to follow.

-26-

Squire looked forward to rendezvous. It was late June, maybe early July, 1826, and he was headed toward Willow Valley. This would be only the second rendezvous ever held—and the first full-blown one. Squire and his friends had not heard of the small train of supplies that had kicked it all off a year earlier on Henry's Fork of the Green River, not until that small rendezvous was long over. They had heard about this one, though, and had determined to make it here.

Squire was far out ahead of the others, scouting out the trail and looking for fresh meat. He was moving slowly, since he was still at least three days' ride from Willow Valley, and he was in no hurry. LeGrande, Gravant, Ledoux, and Robiseau, along with the women and children, were a mile or so back, leading the long string of pack animals loaded with plews. In the past year, since the rendezvous had started, the French-Canadians had come around to Squire's way of thinking—that horseback was a better way to travel out here.

A curl of smoke half a mile ahead brought Squire to a halt. He studied it a moment, then shrugged and rode on, heading toward it. Eventually, he spotted several tipis. At the distance, he took them for Blackfoot lodges, but there were only a few of them.

With his usual fearlessness and arrogance, Squire rode into the camp.

Then he saw Abel Carney and the others.

It had been five years since Carney's men had attacked Squire's camp on the Gallatin River. In those five years, Squire had hunted constantly for Carney and his men, though he never relented in his trapping. Mostly he trapped, traveled, and wintered alone, though at times he threw in with LeGrande, or even with Gravant's small crew.

His trapping sometimes took him west into the land of the Flatheads and Nez Perce. But those times were difficult for him, bringing back the painful memories of Sings Pretty and of their son, Blue Mountain. Those painful thoughts kept pushing him to find Carney.

Because of his obsessive hunt for the men who had taken so much from him, Squire had spent most of his time prowling through Blackfoot country. He kept mostly to himself, unless the Blackfoot bothered him. Or unless the wind brought him a whisper about a Blackfoot boy with light hair and blue eyes. Then he would go on a rampage, tearing through Blackfoot villages and war parties like a hot Bowie knife through buffalo fat.

With LeGrande's harping whenever they were together, and with the passage of time, Squire's passion for revenge had ebbed some. It never went away, but after a while, it did not cling to him with the tenacity it had at the beginning.

He had even begun to feel the pang of loneliness again. Three years ago, on his way out west from St. Louis, he had stopped by Sky Hawk's Sioux village. He had half hoped he could find a woman there, at the same time, he almost hoped he wouldn't.

LeGrande was in the village, full of life and humor like always. "I know dere's a woman 'ere for you, *mon ami*," he said with a ribald laugh. "We will fin' you one, dat's sure."

Squire had several choices. A few of the women were lithe and comely, two of them never married. But all were giggly and lacked restraint. He did not need nor want such a woman now. His only other choice was a dumpy, pleasant-faced widow. Thirteen months later, Star Path gave birth to Falling Night Squire. The child was near two in the summer of 1826. Having a wife and young daughter helped calm Squire's desire for revenge even more.

They saw him at the same time and swung as a group to

stand near a lodge, jugs and food in hand. Several had their arms around the shoulders of Indian women.

Squire stopped his horse about twenty yards in front of the six men. He pulled his right leg up over the horse's neck and slid off the massive black animal, his two-year-old .66-caliber percussion Hawken in his right hand. He let the reins drop to the ground. He had had *Noir Astre* almost three years now and trusted him. The horse would not go anywhere without him.

"Well, look here, lads," Carney said, a vicious, humorless grin showing his still perfect teeth. "If it ain't bloody, goddamn big-shit Nathaniel Squire himself come callin'. Welcome, old chap."

"Hey, Squire," the larger, meaner looking of the two half-breeds shouted, "I see ya got yourself another woman. Why don'tcha just send her over here? I'm bloody tired of this dirty Blackfoot bitch and could make do with someone else."

Squire spit some tobacco juice as the others laughed harshly at Isbister's jibes.

"*Oui,*" DuFrain threw in around the guffaws, "Since you don' 'ave ze balls, give 'er ovair to some who do." He laughed, showing many missing teeth. He started raising the jug for a drink. He never made it. A ball from Squire's rifle punched a big hole just under DuFrain's left eye, exploding out of the back of the métis's head.

DuFrain spun with the impact, the jug of liquor flying out of his hand to smash on the hard-packed earth. The Blackfoot woman he had been clinging to screamed as he crumpled.

Squire stood there calmly pouring a measure of powder into his rifle. Then he stretched some patch material over the muzzle, as Abel Carney said, "That wasn't very bloody nice, Squire. DuFrain was a good man."

Squire slipped a ball onto the patch material and tapped it with a starter, pushing the ball just below the lip of the muzzle hole. As he sliced off the excess patch material, he said, "DuFrain was a worthless piece of shit who should've been put under years ago." He pushed the ball the rest of the way home, seating it. Then he pulled the hammer back to half cock and slid a cap on the nipple. "Where be the other two of your men?" he suddenly asked. "Maclish and Blue Turtle?"

"Around somewhere." Carney shrugged. "They'll be here

by and by." He grinned devilishly.

Squire's eyes narrowed, but did not show his worry. Nor his excitement at finally having found his long-time enemies. He cradled the rifle in the crook of his left arm, right hand wrapped near the trigger, thumb resting on the hammer. "I been lookin' for ye lads for some time," he said with a faraway sound in his voice.

"Whatever for?" Carney asked in mock surprise.

Squire took a deep breath and let it out slowly to settle his racing pulse. "Where be my son?"

"He's a Blood Blackfoot now, old chap," Carney said slowly, seriously. "Adopted by one of the families."

"Who?"

"I'm goddamn bloody well not going to tell you that, Squire. Just think of him as gone under. Like that bitch of yours. What was her name, anyway?" A smirk lingered on his face.

"Sings Pretty," Squire growled deep in his throat.

"Ah, yes, now I remember." He laughed. "She sure made bloody Two Bows come, old boy. Whacked his whole bloody works off sure as shit. Too bad you made off with her, old chap. I was considering the notion of seekin' more pleasure with her." He shrugged.

Squire's chest tightened with the power of his rage, but only his eyes revealed the fury that burned like hellfire inside him. "I asked ye where my son be, lad," Squire said through compressed lips. "I still be waitin' for an answer."

"He was taken in by a Blood war chief, a chap named Black Bull." Carney finally said.

"Be they here?"

Carney shook his head. Then he laughed and said, "What're you planning to do, huh? Go and get him from a goddamn camp full of bloody Blackfeet? How about that, lads," he said, still laughing bitterly. "Crazy goddamn *L'on Farouche* was going to take on a whole goddamn Blackfoot encampment just to get back some bloody little half-breed."

The others joined in the laughter while fury spread up and over Squire's face.

Then Carney said, "That's enough goddamn questions from you, Squire." He spit. "Now, you've caused me too much trouble already."

"I caused ye troubles?" Squire questioned dryly. He was almost incredulous at the thought.

"Yes, goddamnit," Carney snapped. "You should've just taken your death honorably, old chap, instead of running off like you did. Damnit all." His anger was rising fast. "You have those bloody Blackfeet scared of you, sir," he added. "Once I saw it was you we'd caught up there by Two Bows' village on the Milk, I figured I could show those goddamn stupid savages that you were, after all, just a man."

He paused, running a hand over the stubble on his face. Then he said, "I had them all about bloody well convinced, too, old chap, until you went and disappeared. That was bad enough, but you went and rescued your friend, that Nor'wester son of a bitch, and you took the goddamn woman. Jesus, Squire, you made me look bloody awful in front of all those Blackfeet."

Squire shrugged. "Ye'll be breakin' my heart, lad, ye keep up with this tale of woe," he said with an absolute lack of sincerity.

"Hell, me and the other chaps had to hie on up to the North Saskatchewan for a few years to let the poor Blackfeet get over their disappointment. Stayed up there near Edmonton House until Meisner and Will Isbister smoothed things over with the damned bloody redskins." He smiled. "Now all's light and sweet once again."

Carney could not understand Squire's obsession with revenge for his mistreatment in the Blackfoot village. The way Carney saw it, he had been put upon as much as Squire had. He was willing to forget it all and go on with his life. He started to turn away, saying, "Come on, boys."

"Ye be movin' another step, damn ye, and I'll crack your spine with a lead pill," Squire hissed.

Abel Carney turned back. As he did, his brother Seth brought his hand around for the .45-caliber flintlock pistol stuck into his wide, black leather belt. Squire shook his head once, almost imperceptibly, but Seth Carney saw it. His hand hesitated, then grasped the pistol.

Squire grinned tightly and leveled the massive Hawken. The rifle thundered and a ball crashed into Seth's chest, sending him staggering back until he rammed into William Isbister, whom the ball just missed after tearing a huge hole in Seth's back on its way out. Seth's jaws worked, but no words came. He slid down Isbister's front, leaving a trail of blood and bits of flesh on Isbister's tan buckskins.

Almost as one, Abel Carney, Noah Carney, Isbister, and John Tomison reached for their pistols. Squire leaped, not giving them a chance to draw. He ran and then jumped, bringing down all four of them in a tangled heap of arms and legs.

Squire was first to his feet, but he had John Tomison clinging to his back. Tomison, a wiry combination of fury and fierceness, clamped his teeth on Squire's left ear. Squire howled and reached back his left hand, grabbing Tomison behind the head. Then he jerked his right fist up and around and snapped his left shoulder forward, smashing his fist into Tomison's forehead. Tomison let go of Squire's ear, hollered, and slumped to the ground.

Squire yanked out his stone-headed war club and his new metal tomahawk. He saw a movement finally and spun to see Noah Carney scrabbling in the dirt for his pistol, which, like the others had fallen when Squire slammed into the horde. Squire took two giant steps and brought the stone war club down on Noah's upturned face, smashing it into a blood-spattered profusion of splintered bones.

Squire was hit from behind by Isbister, whose own bulk slammed Squire down. They struggled, Squire trying to use the war club or tomahawk, Isbister a large butcher knife. Abel Carney jumped in, landing on Squire's tomahawk arm. He pounded Squire in the face two or three times. Squire mostly ignored him and concentrated on the war club. Suddenly Isbister's hand slipped, and Squire's arm, holding the club, was free. He brought the club up as hard as he could from his awkward position, smashing it into the side of Isbister's bronze head.

The big half-breed groaned and fell off to the side, rolling onto Carney. Squire yanked his arm free, but lost the tomahawk. While Carney struggled to get out from under Isbister's weight, Squire turned his attention to Tomison. The small man was up and frantically trying to put a new cap on the pistol he had dropped and recovered.

Squire ripped out his big-bladed knife and threw it. The knife tore into Tomison's shoulder, making him yelp and drop the pistol. In a few strides, Squire was on him and crushed his head with the war club.

The huge mountain man grunted when a pistol ball creased his left leg. With an angry roar, he pivoted and saw Abel Carney trying frenziedly to reload. Squire ran at him and engulfed Carney in his huge arms. He squeezed, straightening with the effort.

Carney wheezed and struggled, kicking out, trying to break the bear-like embrace, but he could not. Squire squeezed harder. Suddenly he let go; Carney fell to the ground. "That be too easy for ye, lad," he muttered. Then he proceeded to beat Carney, his massive fists thundering down on Carney's face, chest, and back as the smaller man weakly tried to wriggle out of the way.

Finally Squire stood over the inert body of Carney. He slowly pulled his scalping knife. Then he grinned savagely. "First the scalp," he said low in his throat. "Then the other. For Sings Pretty. She'd be likin' that."

Suddenly he felt the fire of a pistol ball cut through his beard to one side. Then Blue Turtle, the Cree who was nearly as big as he was, slammed into him, knocking him flat.

Blue Turtle stood over him, a French pipe-tomahawk clutched in his right hand. "I kill you now," Blue Turtle snarled in a gravelly, fractured voice.

A second later he was dead, the front of his face gone from where a ball from a .56-caliber Leman had exited after boring a hole in from the back.

Squire looked up to see Toussaint Robiseau sitting a horse, smoking rifle in hand, a wide grin on his face. "*Bonjour,*" he said.

Squire stood and looked at LeGrande, Gravant, Robiseau, and Ledoux. "Took ye lads long enough to get here." Suddenly he looked a little nervous. "Where be Maclish?"

"Gone," Gravant shrugged. "When he see us come, he took off like de rabbit."

Squire nodded and turned. Isbister was gone, too. "Well," he said picking up his scalping knife, "There be unfinished doin's here."

"What you going to do?" Gravant asked.

"Take his hair."

"I don' think he is dead." He did not sound concerned.

Squire shrugged. "He'll be so afore long."

"You better be quick about it," LeGrande said nonchalantly.

Squire was having trouble bringing himself under control. He always did when the blood lust rode high in him like it was ow. "Why?" he asked in a low growl.

LeGrande pointed. "Because we're about to be ass deep in Blackfeets *bientôt.*"

Squire whirled and looked. At least a dozen Blackfoot warriors were racing across a meadow toward them. He looked at his friends, an evil grin parting the heavy facial hair. "More hair to be raisin'," he said, almost dreamily.

"Dere are more," Gravant said, pointing in another direction. "And dere, too."

"*Merde,*" Squire mumbled. If he was alone, he would have stood and fought, but he did not want to risk the lives of Star Path and Falling Night. He turned and neatly sliced off the whole scalp from Carney. Spinning, he held the grisly trophy aloft as a challenge to the charging Blackfeet.

Squire glanced down at the bloody, battered thing that had been Abel Carney. His old nemesis was dead, of that he was sure. Still, he wanted to mutilate the body some more.

Then Gravant said urgently, "*Vite, mon ami.* Hurry."

A glance at Star Path's impassive face convinced him. He scooped up his rifle, then jumped on *Noir Astre*'s back, and the group lumbered off, pack animals slowing them.

As they trotted off, Squire looked back. Most of the warriors had stopped at Carney's camp, but a dozen or so were still coming fast. Unhampered by furs, they were closing the gap rapidly. Squire turned back and stopped. As he checked his rifle, he noted Robiseau pulling up alongside him.

"We will make dese bastards come now, eh?" Robiseau said. He grinned. He was already old and did not fear death. He was full of life, energy, and wildness.

"Aye, goddamnit," Squire sat there, rifle in his hands and mean gleam in his eyes. Less than ten minutes later, half a dozen Blackfeet were being carried, dead, back to the village where their families wailed and hacked at themselves in grief.

That night, when they made their camp, Squire was still

angry. He had avenged the death of Sings Pretty, but now Blue
Mountain was almost assuredly lost to him forever—unless he
could find a Blackfoot warrior named Black Bull, or maybe
the man named Meisner whom Carney had mentioned.

His rage flourished as he sat by the fire, tearing at chunks
of meat.

Finally Gravant said quietly, "Forget dem, Nat'aniel. Bot'
of dem. Dey are gone to you now."

"I can't," Squire snapped.

"You 'ave a new woman. An' a chil'. Dat should be enough.
De odder is dead, an' de boy is Blackfeets now. You can'
change dat."

Squire knew all that was true, but he could not accept it.
And having Gravant rub his face in it did nothing more than
to pique Squire's already hot temper.

"Ye be lucky ol' Robiseau just saved my hair, or I'd tear
ye limb from asshole, all of ye," Squire spat.

The three French-Canadians looked bitter, angry, or hurt, as
was their own way.

That was the beginning of Squire's feud with Gravant. It was
he who angered Squire the most. LeGrande was his old friend
and mentor, Ledoux had offered to stick with him five years
ago, and Robiseau had stood by him now. Only Gravant had
tried to make Squire accept Carney's heinousness.

Two years later, Star Path gave him a son, whom they called
White Bear. But the child and his older sister died four months
later. In his grief, Squire left Star Path, wandering aimlessly,
halfheartedly searching for Blue Mountain, his long lost son,
even though he knew the boy was lost to him forever now, after
seven years.

He became more of a loner, avoiding even his old French-
Canadian companions—except LeGrande. Then he met a man
full of determination, a big man named Leander Melton, and
saw something in that man to make him want to join up with
an outfit again.

-27-

RENDEZVOUS

The fire crackled and snapped, sounding loud in the dank lodge now that Gravant had finished his tale. Li'l Jim shifted self-consciously.

"Where is he?" Squire asked in a flat voice. "Ain't no Hudson Bay critters gonner be showin' up here."

Gravant shrugged. "One of de *hommes* said 'e is working for de Company now." He spit. He disliked the American Fur Company about as much as he did the Hudson Bay Company.

Squire and the others felt about the same.

The real problem, though, with that news was that taking Carney would be more difficult if the man and his companions were working for The Company. They would have a heap of protection in The Company's camp almost five miles upriver from here. There would be plenty of Company men there, and trying to take Carney might precipitate an all-out war, one in which Squire's men would be seriously outnumbered and outarmed.

Squire decided that the numbers would not deter him. He would go alone, so as not to endanger any of the others. "Well, lads," he finally said quietly, "it be robe time for this ol' niggur."

The men and their women filed out into the decreasing drizzle. The young men and Hannah were amazed once again at the wild man they followed, the older mountain men knew what the look on Squire's face meant. But all of them were worried.

"What will you do?" Star Path asked as she eased herself into the robes next to Squire.

"Ye be knowin' the answer to that, woman."

"There has been much pain. You don't need to fight them no more."

"Waugh. What d'ye know, woman? I want to find my son." He sighed. "All the years I've thought he was gone fore'er. Now I be havin' another chance."

Star Path patted her stomach. "You will have a new son. Soon. Yes. A son."

"How can ye be certain, woman?" he said, feeling the strain in his chest ease a bit.

"A woman knows these things."

Squire smiled and stroked her cheek. But the black thoughts crowded in on him again. "Hell," he muttered bitterly, "it'll only be took from me anyway."

"Don't say that," Star Path said in alarm. "No! He'll grow strong and proud. Big. And a mighty warrior. Like his father."

"I wish it were so, woman," Squire said softly, his voice filled with pain. "I've planted seed for three other young 'uns, and all be lost to me now."

"It'll be all right." She stroked his temples and then slowly slid her blunt, work-hardened fingers down onto his bushy cheeks. They moved onto his chest, and then lower. The tightness of anger in Squire's chest was replaced by another kind of tightness, and he reached out to roughly pull Star Path over on top of him.

The morning broke clear as a bell, the sun rising high over the grass-hugging mist that soon burned away. The air had a sparkle to it, a fresh smell that invigorated a man.

Despite the fine day, Squire was still in a black mood. After a breakfast of buffalo and coffee, he grabbed his Hawken and headed toward Gravant's nearby camp.

Train and Hannah stepped in front of him. "We need meat, Nathaniel," Train said, standing squarely in front of him.

"So grab some of the lads and go get some. Ye know how to hunt by now, don't ye?"

"We'd like you to come with us, Nathaniel," Hannah said. If anyone could get to him, it would be she.

"I be havin' business to tend to."

"We've been cooped up in these damned lodges for two whole days," Hannah snapped, her green eyes flashing bright. "You—and we—need to do somethin' other than sittin' on our behinds all day."

Squire started to argue but Hannah overrode him: "Besides, *Noir Astre* needs some work. He's stood fallow for more'n two, three days now. You don't get him out soon, he'll be no good for nothin'."

A slight grin cracked Squire's stern visage. "Ye be right, girl," he said quietly. "But it don't mean shit to me right now." He shoved roughly between the bulky boy-man and the small, slim girl-woman.

"You just can't go traipsin' off looking for old ghosts, Nathaniel," Train said.

"I be lookin' for my son, lad," Squire said harshly, stopping.

"Let it go, Nathaniel," Hannah said. She and Train moved in front of Squire again. "He ain't your son no more. You should know that. He was a babe when he was taken, if what Etienne said was right. He'll be what, thirteen, fourteen now? Almost a warrior. He's been raised by the Blackfeet, leave him to that life."

"Best be movin', girl."

"I'll move when I'm damned good and ready," Hannah snapped. "You're bein' a fool, Nathaniel."

Squire raised a massive arm, calloused palm open.

"Go on and hit me," Hannah said defiantly. She was quite certain he wouldn't, but there was a seed of uncertainty.

"Get out of my way," Squire mumbled gruffly, shoving past her again and stalking away, ignoring the girl's shouted, "Nathaniel Squire, you get back here! Get back here, I tell you, you pig-headed old . . ."

Finally, he was out of earshot. In an increasingly surly mood, he stomped into Gravant's small camp. Gravant and Ledoux looked up at his towering height. "*Bon jour*," they said in unison. Then Gravant said, "Sit down. Eat somet'ing."

"Nay."

"Then why're you here, eh?"

"I be goin' for Carney. I thought mayhap ye lads'd like to be joinin' me in the fun."

"I 'ave no quarrel with Carney no more. Dat was a long time ago. Best to forget," Gravant said.

Rage percolated through Squire. He knew deep inside that to go on was pure foolishness, but something drove him. And he did not like that, which made him all the more angry. He would not back down. "He still be in The Company's camp?"

"I don' know. I saw him 'eading dere las' night, but I don't know where he is now." He looked defensive. "I ain't his keeper."

"Ye'll not be helpin' me look for him?" The old anger at Gravant was reborn in all its former glory.

"*Non.*" It was said with finality, as if the saying of it would end Squire's crusade.

"*Bon.*" The anger was controlled now. Squire spun on his heel. He stalked back to his own camp and saddled *Noir Astre*. The others watched him with a mixture of fear and awe. Then he pulled himself onto the giant black horse and left.

He rode boldly into The American Fur Company camp. He knew many of the men, could even call a few of them acquaintances, if not friends. He acknowledged them as he searched around tipis, through groups of men throwing knives and tomahawks, shooting rifles and pistols, playing euchre, or monte, or hand; he sidestepped foot races and horse races and wrestling mountain men, both those doing it for fun and those trying to kill each other.

Squire found no sign of Carney, though, nor any of the men who rode with him. With growing disgust, he headed north. He rode unmolested through the huge Shoshoni camp strung out for more than a mile, and he passed through the camps of Flatheads, Nez Perce, Bannacks, and Crows. But he found nothing.

He kept going, heading for the pitiful place facetiously labeled Fort Bonneville by its creator, Colonel Benjamin Bonneville. Along the way, he waded through more Indian camps. Still he had no luck.

In the early afternoon, he finally turned back for his own camp, taking his time to search some more as he moseyed through The Company's camp. Empty-handed, he moved on. He unsaddled *Noir Astre,* then headed for the Rocky Mountain Fur camp—and the festivities, which were centered more or less on the wagons brought by Campbell. He stopped to talk with one of Campbell's men, when he heard a commotion that rose above the normal cacophonous uproar of rendezvous.

"Reckon I'll see what that be," Squire said to the man.

"Wish I could go," the man said. "But if'n I leave these supplies, Campbell'll have my hair."

"Aye, that he will, lad." He strolled off, watching as the ring of shouting men grew and grew. It was a fight, he reasoned. He edged up, then pushed through the knot of men. He loomed over most of the others, so he could see what was going on.

"*Merde,*" he mumbled when he saw Hannah in a rough-and-tumble fight with a medium-sized mountain man.

The two tussled and rolled in the dirt, oblivious to the shouts of encouragement or derision from the circle of sweating men.

The man, whom Squire recognized as one of Jim Bridger's men named Josiah Acker, landed a good punch to Hannah's head, knocking the back of her head onto the dirt. But she kept her wits and dodged the next punch and squirmed enough to slip from Acker's grip and stand, where she kicked Acker in the side. She went to do it again, but he grabbed her ankle and yanked her down. She fell heavily, yelping.

Acker squiggled forward on his knees. With his left hand, he shoved her chest, pushing her back down. With his other hand he grabbed for her crotch. The fight had been going on for ten, maybe fifteen minutes, and he was getting tired. He wanted to end it soon, and what better way than to grab a man where it hurt most and yank hard, he figured.

Hannah yelped again, Acker's eyes widened in surprise. He staggered up and stumbled back a few steps. The circle of men shouted, and few of the jeers wormed their way into his consciousness:

"Hit him!"

"Ye ain't scared, are ye?"

"Take his hair!"

"This hoss wants to see some blood!"

"It's a woman, damnit. A woman!" Acker screamed.

The din lessened as men looked at Acker, who stood ashen-faced. Finally the noise sputtered to a halt as comprehension arose.

"What's that ya say?" someone in the crowd shouted.

"It's a woman, goddamnit. A goddamn white woman."

Hannah stood slowly, her green eyes flashing insolence. Slowly she pulled her knife and looked at the sea of eyes—some of them touched with hate, some with curiosity, some with newborn lust.

Before Hannah could say anything, Train was standing at her side, tomahawk in hand. "Any of you boys here like to make somethin' of it?" he challenged.

Squire bulled his way through the crowd to take a place next to them, saying nothing. He heard a rifle being cocked and he searched for the source, while automatically bringing his own Hawken up and thumbing back the hammer. Then he saw Li'l Jim, rifle barrel stuck in some mountain man's ear. The man eased the hammer down on his rifle, looking a little sheepish.

"Let's be goin', lads," Squire said as they moved as one toward the circle of men, which split to let them pass. Once past the ring, Squire said hastily, "Abner, go'n find the others. And move your ass about it. We'll be havin' a council soon's e'erybody gets back to camp."

"What about Hannah?"

"I'll be seein' to her, lad. Now get." He turned. "Li'l Jim, best help Abner. Move it, lad."

-28-

Less than half an hour later everyone was gathered around a fire outside Squire's lodge. As always, food was cooking, ready for whoever wanted to eat.

"Well, lads," Squire said, "this here be some damp goddamn powder, and there ain't no use in sayin' nay to it. Hannah's secret be out, lads. Aye, the whole goddamned rendezvous be knowin' of her now."

"What're we gonna do?" Gideon Hook asked. The others grumbled agreement with the question.

"That be up to ye lads. We can be stayin' here another few days, hopin' it'll pass over without trouble. Or we can be ridin' out."

"I say we stay," young Cletus Ransom said. "We can protect Hannah from these fractious sons of bitches if it comes to that. Ain't that right, boys?"

Most growled assent, but Billy Von Eck asked, "Why do we have to get involved? It's her problem."

"She be one of us, lad," Squire said quietly. "Hannah's been with us since the beginnin'. She's pulled her weight, same as e'eryone. A man can't be askin' no more'n that."

"Can ya tell us what it means, Nathaniel?" Hook asked.

"Can't be sayin', lad. Some of them lads could be thinkin' of causin' us trouble. Many of 'em ain't seen a white woman in quite a spell. Knowin' one's amongst 'em could set some of 'em to havin' black thoughts. Mayhap nothing'll be happenin'.

Bridger, Fitzpatrick, Campbell, and the others'll do what they can to keep their lads in line more'n likely. A few free trappers might think to be tryin' something, though. And ye ne'er can tell about those bastards from The Company, if they was to get wind of it, which I suppose be done already."

He shrugged. He really wasn't expecting trouble, but it paid to be cautious. "Well, ye lads set here and jaw it over for a spell amongst yourselves."

Squire leaned a little back, munching on roasted hump meat. Star Path set a small earthen jug wrapped in beaver fur next to him. He nodded thanks. When he finished a mouthful of buffalo, he lifted the jug and tilted it back, drinking deeply of the honey-flavored alcohol. He ignored Colonel Melton's reproving look.

Squire was torn, sitting there thinking. He had never run from a confrontation in his life, and he wasn't keen on the idea of doing so now. But that was the least of his worries—few would be the men who would call Nathaniel Squire a coward. He could deal with that.

What was most difficult for him was the prospect of putting the others in more danger. Hannah especially, since she was the focus of all this. But Train, Li'l Jim, Ransom, and a few of the others would gladly battle every man at rendezvous—white, red, or black—to protect Hannah. Nor would they complain at going under in such a noble venture.

Squire would even be willing to join them. He considered Hannah, Train, and Li'l Jim almost as his children. As such, he did not want to see them dead or even hurt, not for a foolish reason, and staying here any longer, putting them in unnecessary danger, was foolish.

On the other hand, now that he knew Abel Carney was alive his obsession to find his son was reborn. Leaving the rendezvous now would force him to forget Carney and possibly any chance of ever seeing Blue Mountain again.

Squire sighed heavily as he gulped down a little more whiskey. It was not an easy choice, but he realized the others were right. Sings Pretty was long dead, and Blue Mountain would be all Blackfoot by now. He had killed several of Carney's men and dozens of Blackfoot warriors, and he had carved the topknot off Carney himself. It should be enough retribution. He wasn't sure that it was, but it didn't matter right now. His loyalties and interests lay with this new group of young men and women now. They had earned his respect and his allegiance. He could no longer be so devoted to his ghosts.

One day, though, he vowed silently, I'll be extractin' a full measure of vengeance for ye, Sings Pretty. And ye, Blue Mountain. He closed his eyes a moment, trying to blot out the past.

When he opened them again, he saw Gravant and Ledoux heading toward him. He scowled, the old anger returning. The two French-Canadians arrived and sat facing him, nodding their thanks when Star Path handed them food.

"Ye lads be wantin' somethin' here?" Squire asked when they had eaten a little. His voice held little hint of warmth.

"Carney's gone, Nathaniel," Gravant said with hesitation.

"Where?"

"To de *nord,* I t'ink. One of de *hommes* from Suzette's band said 'e was 'unting dis morning, up to de nort', across de river. 'E said 'e saw a camp of *Pied-du-noir.* A *trés grand* camp. Many Blackfeets dere, 'e said. Maybe two hundred, t'ree hundred warriors."

"And ye be thinkin' that's where Carney's got off to?"

Gravant shrugged. "Where else would 'e go where dere is a camp of so many Blackfeets near?"

It seemed likely, but Squire was still not convinced. "What'n hell're so many Blackfoot doin' here anyway?" he wondered aloud.

"Maybe dey come for you, eh, *mon ami?*" Gravant said. He almost smiled.

Squire burst out laughing.

"Don' laugh, *mon ami,*" Gravant said seriously. "He 'ates you after what you did to him." He brushed a hand across his skimpy white locks. "But who knows? Dem Blackfeets 'ave bad 'earts dis year. Dey are still half froze for a fight wit' anybody after dey got dere asses kick but good up in Pierre's 'Ole after de rendezvous last year. It wouldn't take much for Carney to get dem stirred up."

He paused to hawk out some snot. Then he grinned roughly. "Especially not when de prize is de 'air of *L'on Farouche.*"

"Ye be talkin' out of your ass, ye ol' fart," Squire growled. He wasn't sure whether to put any stock in Gravant's idea, but he was convinced of what he had to do.

"The Blackfeet here for serious?" Peters asked.

"What you t'ink, eh?" Gravant said. "Two Fingers said 'e saw *Schim-aco-che*—High Lance—and Old Dog, Bull Tongue, Black Knife, Wolf Skin, Falls Down, and . . ." he paused a moment for effect " . . . Elk Horn."

"*Merde,*" Squire muttered as the others snapped to fuller attention.

"Them others as bad as Elk Horn?" Train asked, voice caught with anger.

"Aye, lad. They be the cream of the Blackfoot war leaders."

"How can you be sure they'll attack?" Melton asked.

Squire shrugged. "Them critters didn't come all this way to be breakin' bread with the likes of us, Colonel."

"Won't the other trappers stand with us?" Melton asked.

"Sure. Most of 'em. 'Cept for those chickenshits with The Company. They wouldn't spit to help the Rocky Mountain boys or most of the free trappers. Especially now that they be makin' a play for the Blackfeet trade." Squire sighed. "But, I reckon them Blackfeet'll be sittin' on their asses out there somewhere, waitin' till rendezvous breaks up. Then they'll try'n catch us on the trail alone."

"What do you suggest, Nathaniel?" Melton asked.

"That we be leavin' now."

"But you just said . . ."

"I aim to be outfoxin'—or outrunnin'—'em, Colonel. They still be up north, and they'll not be expectin' us to be leavin' here early. We'll be headin' south afore cuttin' east. Mayhap we can be throwin' 'em off our trail. Ye know how far off them lads be, Etienne?"

"*Non, mon ami.* All I could tell from Two Fingers is dey might be a day's ride. Maybe a little more, maybe a little less. Who can say?"

"All right, lads," Squire snapped, "listen up. We'll be setting out come mornin'. I don't aim to let them Blackfeet be gettin' my hair. We'll be movin' hard. Best be seein' to your possibles and be gettin' some robe time early. And," he bellowed as they began standing, "nobody be leavin' camp."

"Homer . . ."

"No need to be tellin' me nothing, Nathaniel. Nope. I know what's got to be done. Yep. I do. Me'n Cletus'll be seeing that everything's set and ready, though I don't know why I put up with that boy, I purely don't. He's the worstest of them all, he is. Yep . . ."

"Oh, quit your jabberin', ya old coot," Cletus said with a tight, nervous grin.

The two of them were still going at it as they walked away. Squire allowed himself a slight grin. The two—one an old hand, the other still only sixteen—were invaluable. And their vituperative camaraderie was already becoming legendary.

"Hannah," Squire said, "Ye'd best be stayin' in your lodge as much as possible till we pull out. Abner, ye be stayin' close to her, but ye'll be needed to be doin' work." He turned. "Slocum, are ye with us?"

"Sure, Nathaniel. I ain't ary turned my back on a friend. I'll be dipped in buffler shit afore I'd begin now."

"*Bon.* I wasn't certain. This here ain't really your fight."

Peters shrugged. "Killin' Blackfeet's always my business," he said. His tone indicated that anyone who thought differently was not worthy of being called a mountaineer.

"It sounds as if you expect a battle, Nathaniel," Melton interjected.

"Aye, Colonel."

"But, you said we would outfox or outrun them."

Squire grinned viciously. "There be times things don't work out like we plan, Colonel." He turned. "Etienne? Marcel? How 'bout ye lads?"

"*Non,*" Gravant said immediately. "I wan' no part of dis. I still 'ate de Blackfeets, but I've been trapping in their lands, an' I don' want dem 'aving bad 'earts for me. *Je regrette.*"

"Marcel?"

He took a few moments to speak, and when he did, he sounded regretful. "I will stick wit' Etienne."

Squire nodded curtly. "Then ye'll not be mindin' if'n I be tendin' to business, eh?" There was bitterness in his voice.

Gravant and Ledoux stood and began walking away, aware of the many eyes on them. They stopped and turned back when

Squire called. "You won't be tellin' nobody of this, will ye, lads?" he asked. His voice was hard with warning, and it was not really a question.

"*Non*," Gravant answered for both.

"*Bon*." Squire turned his attention back to his companions.

-29-

Squire stepped out into the coolness and breathed deeply of the fresh air. It was at least three hours before daylight, maybe a little more. He nodded with satisfaction, seeing that Bellows and Ransom were up and directing the camp hands, who were busy packing panniers and loading bales of beaver plews on mules. Others were tending the fires, cooking meat. Pots of harsh coffee were ready.

"*Bon*," Squire muttered as he headed for Melton's tipi, calling softly, "*Leve, leche lego*—Wake up, turn out." He repeated it at Train's and Hannah's lodge, then Li'l Jim's, Peters's, and so on until the whole camp had been roused.

"Best be eatin' hardy, lads," Squire said, moving from one fire to another. "This'll be a long day for ye, and it may be a time afore we be stoppin' for a real meal again."

He sat at his own fire with Melton, Train, Hannah, Li'l Jim, and Peters. Bellows and Ransom were still busy. Squire wolfed down large bolts of hot, greasy, half-seared meat. He washed it down with several cups of thickly sweetened coffee. Wiping the greasy hands on his calico shirt—with which he had replaced his buckskin war shirt—he belched and gave the order to strike camp.

Canvas tents and buffalo-hide tipis came down easily and quickly. Within an hour of the time that Squire had stepped from his lodge, he and his men were riding out of the rendezvous, skirting by a wide margin the huge Rocky Mountain

Fur camp and a few vast Shoshoni and Nez Perce horse herds. They wound their way southward along the Green River.

The going was slow with this many animals, some of them balky after almost a week of doing nothing. The men were a little out of practice for such a hard push, so Squire called a halt fairly early that day. They had made just over ten miles.

There was no reason for Squire to tell the men to hit their sleeping robes early. All of them were exhausted and voluntarily turned in, except for the assigned horse guards, soon after eating.

They made no better speed the next day, but they did make better mileage, since Squire kept the men in the saddle for close to twenty hours. They camped in the brushy, cottonwood-speckled V close to where Cottonwood Creek emptied into the Green River.

The brigade struggled across Cottonwood Creek after an all-too-short night of rest. The creek was only two or three feet deep here, but it had a shifting bed, and the current was strong as the creek bubbled into the Green River not far away. Several mules and horses protested the chilly crossing and had to be practically dragged over to the far bank.

Squire gave the men a brief break before forcing them up and moving again. He pushed the men on without a rest, driving them by sheer force. He had Train, Li'l Jim, Hannah, and Hook out hunting, since the brigade had next to no meat left in their packs.

Finally, Squire pulled up on *Noir Astre,* along the river bank.

"Something wrong, Nathaniel?" Melton asked, stopping alongside the big mountain man. He looked worried.

"Nay, Colonel," Squire said. "Just gettin' the lay of things."

"And, what've you decided?"

Squire pointed. "Ye see that sandy bank o'er yonder?" When Melton had nodded, Squire said, "I reckon we'd best be crossin' the Green right there."

"Now?" Melton asked, surprised and more worried.

"Nay, Colonel." Squire sighed. "I reckon the lads can be usin' some rest. 'Sides, we'd ne'er get all these animals and plews and all across afore dark." He turned *Noir Astre* and began passing the word that camp would be made here.

Since the nights were clear and warm, no lodges were set up. The men and women opted instead to sleep under the stars. They were too tired to be bothered with putting up lodges and then striking them four or five hours later.

The men groaned when they looked across the wide, swift-flowing Green River. They knew they faced a daunting task.

"Are you sure this's wise, Nathaniel?" Melton asked nervously. Melton was not a timid man, but sometimes Squire made him wonder, what with some of the things he pulled.

Squire shrugged. "We could be followin' the Green all the way down to Mexico and visit some bean eaters, was ye of a mind to."

Melton ignored the jab. "What then—after we get across?"

"We be facin' some hard doin's, Colonel." Squire pulled off his wolf fur hat and stuffed it under thongs behind his saddle. It was too damned hot to wear it anyway. He ran a hand through his long, greasy, sweaty hair. "There be a stretch of maybe fifty, sixty miles that's drier'n old women's breasts. We make that, we'll hit the Big Sandy, where there ought to be water."

"Can we make it?"

"Ain't much choice," Squire said with a shrug. "The Blackfoot be waitin' for us to the north, we can't afford to go west into the mountains—not as ill-supplied as we be—an' there be nothin' south of here but mean-ass Injins and then Greasers."

"Then let's proceed," Melton said firmly. "What's first? Do we just plunge in there?" He sincerely hoped not.

"I've thunk on it, Colonel, since we be pressed. But I reckon it'd be dumber'n shit to lose them Blackfoot only to have half the men get rubbed out crossin' a goddamn river."

"Rafts, then?"

"Aye."

Minutes later, most of the men were chopping down cottonwoods. As soon as some were made into logs, other men began lashing them together. Squire figured half a dozen would be enough—he didn't want to waste any more time at it, especially since it took the better portion of the day to get the six crude rafts finished.

At the same time, the women began making several bull boats.

"Enjoy your leisure, lads," he said late in the afternoon. "And ye best eat hardy." The brigade's four hunters had been quite successful, and there was plenty of fresh buffalo and elk.

"Time to show what ye got, boy," Squire said softly. He patted *Noir Astre*'s great neck and eased the horse into the rushing water of the Green River. Looped around his saddlehorn were coils of rope. The men had taken all the spare rope in camp— rawhide, grass, or hemp—and tied the lengths together into one long rope.

One end of the rope was tied to a sturdy cottonwood. The coils on Squire's saddle played out as *Noir Astre* moved.

The horse got caught up in the swift current. For a few moments, those on the shore thought the big man and the midnight stallion would be swept away. Then the great beast caught himself and began swimming with surety.

Squire had not been concerned, he had a lot of faith in *Noir Astre*. The people back on the west bank of the river had been worried. Especially Melton. Hannah sat quietly, but her heart was in her mouth. Star Path was confident in her man. She did not bother to watch, instead, she kept busy making sure their supplies were well-packed.

Noir Astre finally climbed up the far bank. Squire slipped out of the saddle, rope in one hand. He patted the stallion's shaggy mane. "Ye done good, ol' hoss," he muttered. "Get ye some rest now." He swiftly tied the rope to a cottonwood, then waved his hat as a signal to the brigade across the way.

As Bellows, Ransom, and Peters began directing the men into the rafts and bull boats, Squire loosened *Noir Astre*'s saddle. Then he pulled his rifle out and set about drying and reloading it. He sat and watched the progress across the river.

Three men with three animals went aboard each raft. One of the men held the animals steady; the other two hauled on the rope, towing the raft across the river. At least one of the two made sure he did not let go of the rope, lest the raft be swept swiftly down the river.

Ransom was on the first crude raft across and brought the horses up onto land. He stayed to care for the horses and mules on Squire's side.

The other two men turned and started towing their way back across. As soon as they touched land, three of the other five rafts began making their way eastward. As they did that, the others were loaded. It took a long time, but they could not keep a steady flow of rafts going because the current would smash them against one another as they passed.

When about half the animals were across, some of the men stayed on the east side to watch the beasts. In addition, Homer started sending over bull boats loaded with plews and other supplies. The deep, round-bottomed boats of cottonwood branches covered by buffalo hide, carried a substantial load of plews. However, the more weight in each, the more difficult it was for the haulers to control it. Because of that, Bellows kept the loads small.

Star Path was on the first bull boat across. She wanted to be near Squire and had indicated that to Bellows in no uncertain terms.

As more supplies, animals, and precious plews made it to the east side, more men also stayed to protect their investment. The Colonel was among them, as were Train and Hannah. Li'l Jim had stayed on the other side, though his two Indian wives were on this side.

Melton inquired about that when they sat to a late meal around the fire. Train laughed. "He's some grateful for the respite," Train said. "Seems them two been sappin' him good. Now," he boasted, "was it me, the story'd be a heap different."

Hannah swatted him on the arm with her hat. "Hoo, listen to this," she said in feigned offense. "You can't even take care of one little lady, let alone two lusty Injuns."

Train blushed in embarrassment, but he laughed.

"I thought he'd planned to give up at least one of the two," Melton said. He chuckled a little, but he was embarrassed, since he was sitting there watching Rising Sun at her work.

"He was fixin' to," Train said, stifling a chuckle. "He told me he was dickerin' with some ol' hoss over one of them. I reckon he didn't have time to get the deal set afore we left out from rendezvous."

Squire was amused by the banter, but he was concerned, too. He didn't like having his forces split like this. He didn't really expect to see the Blackfoot at all, least of all here and now, but one could never be certain. There was nothing could be done about it. He did, however, make sure there were extra guards out that night, and he impressed on them the need for added vigilance.

It took until almost noon to get the remainder of the men, animals, and supplies to the east bank. Though the men had never done this before, they had been working together for a long time now. Combined with the iron direction by Nathaniel Squire on one bank and the oath-accentuated orders of Homer Bellows on the other, the work proceeded apace.

Bellows, Peters, Gideon Hook, Josiah Maxwell, and Li'l Jim were the last over, all in one bull boat. They had left two bull boats and three rafts on the far side. Those were the ones brought back before Bellows could stop them. But the men on those rafts had not known there were no more to bring over and had crossed.

"You want I should cut the towin' rope, Nathaniel?" Train asked as the final group stepped on shore.

"Nay, lad," Squire said. "If'n the Blackfoot're followin' us, they'll take fore'er to get across usin' them things. If they ain't, well, mayhap the rope and all'll do some mountaineers some good one day."

The brigade needed meat, so Train, Hannah, Hook, and Li'l Jim prepared to head out on the hunt. As they did, Melton approached Squire. "Would you mind, Nathaniel, if I was to join the hunt today?"

"Well, nay, Colonel," Squire replied, somewhat surprised.

"I know it's strange, Nathaniel," Melton explained. "But I feel the need of getting away from all the men, the horses, this infernal damned confusion and bustle."

"Aye, Colonel," Squire chuckled, "that do be a pleasure of a time. But ye'll need a partner."

"I'll go with him, Nathaniel," Peters said.

"*Bon.* Cut yourselves a couple extra horses for carryin' meat. Then report to Li'l Jim. We'll be noonin' for certain today, lads, so best be back come high sun."

"We'll be here," Peters promised. "Come on, Colonel."

Squire could hear Bellows's and Ransom's curses growing some and knew the mules were packed and ready. "Let's be goin', lads," he called out, swinging into the saddle.

-30-

It was just past noon when Hannah and Train came riding in. Hannah had given up all pretense of being a man now, though she still wore the buckskin pants and shirt Star Path had made for her. She was unfettered under her shirt and felt all the better for it.

"There ain't nothin' out there for cover," Train said. "No sign of nothin', neither, 'cept some buffalo. Not many of 'em, but enough to feed us a spell, I guess."

"They movin', lad?"

"Yep. But slow."

"How far away?"

"A mile or so," Hannah said. "It looked like they was headin' southwest, toward the Green."

Squire nodded and looked around. They had been following a stream that became Cottonwood Creek, across the Green. There were a few stunted trees on the bank here, but they did not provide enough shade for the men or animals. The sun blazed down hot and red. Dust and shimmering heat waves rose from the flat land.

"Well, lads, I reckon this'll have to be doin'. I can't see backtrackin' a couple miles to that grove we passed. I just hope them buffalo don't take to spendin' too much time at the river."

Li'l Jim and Gideon Hook rode in as the men were loosening

the saddles from their horses, letting the animals cool in the slight but steady breeze.

"Ye see anything, lads?"

"Not shit," Li'l Jim snapped, sliding off his horse. He pulled off his felt cap and wiped his sweltering brow on one buckskin shirt sleeve. He would learn in time, as would the others, to bring an extra cotton or linsey-woolsey shirt with him next time, as Squire and most of the other old-timers did. Buckskin was too hot and uncomfortable for wearing in such weather. "Some Injun sign."

"What kind, lad?" Squire asked, perking up.

"Ain't sure, Nathaniel. It was old, and there's been a heap of buffalo run over it. There ain't enough left to tell what Injuns they was, only that there was some passed by."

"How old?"

Li'l Jim shrugged and scratched at his still patchy beard. "Couple days at least, I'd say. The Colonel back yet?"

"Nay, lad." He was worried some, but he didn't show it. "You two lads go on and water your horses and yourselves."

Li'l Jim and Hook wandered off, pulling their horses slowly by the reins.

"Where do you reckon the Colonel and Slocum are, Nathaniel?" Train asked.

"Can't be sayin', lad. Reckon they just found part the herd ye saw and took after it."

"I ain't heard no gunfire."

Squire shrugged. "I reckon they'll be all right. Slocum's a tough ol' niggur and knows his way around."

The men drank heartily from the creek, though they ate lightly of jerky. Many splashed into the shallow creek, enjoying the welcome coolness. Most stretched out, heads resting on saddles, for a *siesta*.

About a half-hour later, they heard shots far to the northeast. "There, lads, ye be hearin' that. I reckon them two old coons was just waitin' for the right shots."

Another hour passed, and then another, yet Melton and Peters did not return. The men roused from their naps and were anxious to be moving again. The sun was unmerciful.

Hannah strolled off by herself to drink from the creek. Farley

Walker approached her, saying softly, "If I might have a few words with you, Miss Hannah."

"What do you want, Farley?" Since their fight during the winter, Hannah had been very cautious around Farley. She was not afraid of him, only wary. She did not want to give him any excuse to think she was encouraging his attentions.

"Sit," he said politely, waving a hand magnanimously at the sparse grass. "Please."

Hannah looked nervously back toward where the others were, then shrugged and sat.

Walker did likewise. "You know," he said with a tremor in his voice, "that I've wanted you for a long time now . . ."

Hannah started to rise but he grabbed her arm, pleading, "Please, hear me out." She settled back down and he continued: "I know you've wanted nothin' to do with me, but what I'm gonna tell you might change your mind. Our lives'll be changin' right soon, Hannah. Most everybody here's for the worse. But yours can be for the better."

"What do ya mean?" she asked suspiciously, worrying her lower lip with her teeth.

"There's a heap of Blackfeet just waitin' for us a few miles from here."

"Where?"

"A few miles. Never you mind exactly. But they're there, don't you doubt that, young miss."

"So?" she asked, drawing the word out. She had to get him to tell her more, so she could kill him and then inform the others.

"So—I've throwed in with Abel Carney and his men. I'm tired of Squire and that fat old Colonel and everybody else tellin' me what to do all the time. 'Specially Li'l Jim and that big, dumb son of a bitch you're so attached to. But with Abel and Duncan Maclish and Will Isbister, I'll be a big man. Even the Blackfeet'll listen to me." He achieved a cocky, self-satisfied look.

"Hmmm. I can see that. But how do you know where they are? We ain't seen anyone. Not even sign."

"I slipped out of camp the night before we left and told 'em which way we'd be comin'. So they headed out across the Green a little north of the rendezvous. Then come down this way. One of 'em left me a sign last night."

"So they're up river from here still?"

"Yeah. They're . . . no, I'd best not say nothin' more. But I'm askin' ya to go with me."

"You got to be crazy," she burst out. "After what those heathen bastards did to me, you expect me to just ride into a camp brimmin' with those savages?"

"Quiet down, Miss Hannah," Walker said urgently, looking around furtively. "You'll be with me this time. I won't let nothin' happen to ya, I swear I won't."

"So," she said with a sneer, "you think you can talk down a whole passel of Blackfeet, is that it?"

"I'm partners with Abel now. They'll listen to me."

"You're a goddamned fool, Farley Walker." She stood, fighting her temper. "Now you best leave me be *and* forget all this nonsense, or I'll go tell Mr. Squire."

Walker leaped up and backhanded Hannah on one cheek, knocking her down. Then he ran. He vaulted into the saddle of a horse he had had ready and roared off in a cloud of dust. The other men, startled, looked up at his passing.

Hannah jumped up, rubbing her face and ran for her horse. It was not saddled, but she did not care. She leaped, slapping her hands on the horse's spotted rump and landing on the animal's back. She yelled wildly and smacked the horse's hindquarters. The animal bolted, and they raced after Walker.

"Hannah!" Train bellowed as she thundered past, head low over the horse's neck, holding tight onto its mane. "Damnit, what's she doin'?" he said to no one in particular.

He had been saddling his own horse in preparation for going back on the scout when Hannah roared by. He hastily yanked the rigging, tightening the saddle. He grabbed his rifle from where it lay on the ground and, with one leap, was in the saddle.

"Don't do it, lad," Squire yelled, hastily yanking tight the cinch on *Noir Astre*. But Train was gone. "*Merde*," Squire said, finishing his task. Then he, too, was in the saddle and pounding across the grassy prairie, Hawken in hand.

Gradually he caught up to Train, *Noir Astre*'s great legs

eating the distance. Ahead, Walker disappeared into a ravine and then appeared again. Hannah did the same.

Far off, now mostly to the north, Squire could see a great cloud of dust. The buffalo herd, he surmised. Somebody must have stampeded it, hurrying it along. But who? he wondered, though he had a growing suspicion.

Suddenly Squire saw a dozen Blackfeet appear from another ravine, about a mile away.

Walker rode through them and kept on going.

-31-

Hannah yanked at her horse's mane with all of her strength, and screamed, "Whoa, damn ya. Whoa!" The horse rammed to a stop, almost squatting.

Hannah jerked the animal's head around and thumped its ribs with both heels. "Come on, horse," she yelled, urgency in her voice. The horse got moving, but it was too late. Blackfeet warriors surrounded her. One grabbed her and tried to pull her, belly down, onto his war pony.

She would have none of it. She slapped his hand away and then spit in his face. He tried to smack her, but she ducked and kicked out, knocking the warrior from his horse. The others laughed as the infuriated warrior stood, pulling out a trade tomahawk, brass with a pipe bowl.

"No," another growled. The warrior looked up at the war chief with hate smoldering in his dark eyes. He pointed back at Train and Squire racing after them. The warrior slid the tomahawk away and with one fluid motion was on the horse's back.

The war chief clubbed Hannah on the side of the head with a fist and then roughly hauled her onto his horse, holding her face down across the horse's neck. The other warrior dropped a grass rope around the neck of Hannah's horse. He looked across the dusty land and yipped at the mountain men, now only about three hundred yards away.

Squire had caught up with Train, coming up on the young man's right side. He reached across and grabbed the reins of the racing horse and then shoved Train on the shoulder. Train went sailing. He landed hard and bounced a little.

Squire pulled up and trotted back to where Train lay. He looked out at the Indians yelping their victory at him. "*Merde,*" he muttered. He dropped the reins of Train's horse and brought the big Hawken up.

"No!" Train screamed, jumping up.

But the big rifle boomed, the sound fleeing across the wide expanse, the Blackfoot holding Hannah's horse tumbled backward off his horse, a bright red stain blossoming on his breastplate-covered chest.

Noir Astre reared, shaking his great head, as Squire yelled his own war cry. The Blackfeet scattered.

"Now they'll kill Hannah, damn you," Train moaned.

"Buff'lo shit. Now get back on your horse and move out."

"I'm goin' after her."

"Don't ye be arguin' with me, lad, goddamnit. We got mayhap three hundred goddamn Blackfoot warriors aimin' to raise our hair. We have to think of that first. Now mount up, before I tie ye to your horse."

An angry Train swung into the saddle, and the two men hurried back to the brigade.

The others crowded around, asking questions all at once. "Pipe down," Squire yelled. "There be no time for such foolishment. Less'n ye lads want half the goddamn Blackfoot nation to be comin' down on us, ye'd best be gettin' your asses movin'."

"I told 'em we'd have to do that. Yep. I did," Bellows shouted.

"E'erything ready?"

"Yep. Sure is."

"Then let's be movin', lads. We'll be headin' back for that grove about two miles back up, near the Green. That be pretty good cover."

The men rode hard, spurred by the thought of so many Blackfoot warriors after them, though they did not see any of the Indians for the first mile. Then the Blackfeet hove into view behind them, racing after them.

"Ride, lads, ride!" Squire bellowed. "Li'l Jim, Abner, come on." The three pulled up and rode back trail a little, before stopping. Squire slid off and threw the Hawken over *Noir Astre*'s saddle. Li'l Jim and Train followed suit. Squire fired first, and a Blackfoot toppled. As he rapidly reloaded, Li'l Jim fired. Another warrior went down. Train's shot was a little off, killing a Blackfoot war pony, sending its rider flying.

Squire fired again, thankful that not all the Blackfeet were coming at them. There were maybe fifty, he could see, minus the four he and Li'l Jim had just killed. Train's rifle boomed, and another Blackfoot fell dead from his horse.

A few arrows thunked harmlessly into the ground around them as each man fired successfully one more time. But by now the Blackfeet were within a hundred yards of them. Squire threw a hasty glance behind and saw that his men had just about reached the thicket.

"Ride!" he roared, swinging into the saddle. He jabbed his heels into *Noir Astre*'s sides. The big horse leaped forward in a burst of speed. Li'l Jim and Train raced alongside. Squire looked back over his shoulder; they were gaining a little on the Indians, who screamed war cries at them.

They were about a hundred and fifty yards from the copse when Train's horse went down, several arrows buried in its hide. Train hit and rolled, coming up on foot, running hard.

Squire and Li'l Jim spun their horses and raced back at him. Train stopped and turned, firing off his rifle. The Blackfeet were almost on him; running would do him no good. He tore his pistol from his belt and blasted a Blackfoot off his horse.

As Squire and Li'l Jim pulled up on either side of him, the Blackfeet swept around them like a tidal wave. Li'l Jim fired his pistol, killing another; Squire shot one down and clubbed another off his horse.

The Indians swept around them in a dizzying blur of color and sound. They might have killed three mountain men easily with their superior numbers, but their numbers also made it almost impossible to fire bow or gun without hitting each other. One warrior, a burly man whose hair was long enough to sweep down onto his horse's rump and whose painted face was etched with battle scars, whacked Li'l Jim with his curved, otter-fur-covered coup stick. The blow knocked the young man off his horse.

The Blackfoot yipped, shaking his coup stick in the air in victory.

"You son of a bitch," Li'l Jim yelled. He swept up onto his horse from the right side. He shoved his rifle into a buckskin scabbard and pulled out his cheap trade tomahawk. But the warrior was lost in the chaotic knot of Indians, dust, and noise. "Damnit," he muttered as he fended off a blow from another coup stick.

Train was scared; more so even than when he and the others had attacked the Blackfoot village last winter. He was afoot amid too many snorting, prancing war-blooded horses eager for action. He ducked a swung coup stick, then another, bumped and bounced between several horses. Suddenly he lashed out and grabbed a young warrior by the breastplate and yanked hard, pulling the Blackfoot down on the ground.

Before the Indian could really struggle up after falling, Train's knife flashed in the sun and plunged twice into the Blackfoot's heart. Within seconds he had swung on to the Blackfoot pony's back and had drawn his trade brass tomahawk.

Squire split the skull of one warrior and grabbed the coup stick of another, pulling the man down, where *Noir Astre* stepped on him several times with nervous hooves.

But the three were terribly outnumbered, and the Blackfeet were losing patience with their inability to kill the white men. They pressed the attack harder, maneuvering their fleet, nimble ponies in, though the three mountain men had brought their horses together to form a small, tight triangle.

Squire lashed out with tomahawk and big knife, hacking at anyone foolish or unlucky enough to get within reach of his long, powerful arms. Train used his trade rifle as a club, swinging so widely he almost hit Li'l Jim more than once.

Li'l Jim kept up his end with a stone-headed war club he wrested away from a warrior, struggling face to face, their noses almost touching, their horses bumping and jostling.

The three fought desperately under the harsh, broiling sun. The dust from hundreds of hooves welled up and settled in their nostrils and mouths making it hard for the men to breathe.

Squire slowly butchered a path through the Blackfeet, forcing *Noir Astre* through the bloody aisle, with Li'l Jim and Train in his wake. Then his head snapped up, as did the others', at the sound of rifle fire.

Train bellowed in surprise and pain as a war club bounced off his right shoulder. The semipointed stone club moved fast, winging for his head, but he managed to bring his rifle up in both hands and catch the hickory handle of the club on it and shove the weapon away. He whipped the rifle around and smashed the Blackfoot in the head with the barrel, knocking him off the horse and under the hooves of horses that bunched in an attempt to flee.

Squire received a cut on his arm when his concentration was momentarily broken. He lashed out angrily with his tomahawk which bit into the Indian's shoulder, near where it met the arm. The Blackfoot howled and yanked his horse back. Then he fled, with all the other Blackfeet, who scooped up their dead and wounded as they rode hellbent across the dusty plains. They left behind only two of their friends, whom they could not get to.

A few fired arrows as they raced across the prairie and into a gully. One arrow lodged itself in Li'l Jim's right calf. He gasped, and his face turned white. Then he saw that the arrow was buried only three-quarters of the head into the leg. He laughed in relief and pulled it free.

"What're ya gonna do with that arrow, Li'l Jim?" Gideon Hook asked as he, Josiah Maxwell, Billy Van Eck, and Tom Douglas rode up.

"Save it for a souvenir. How came you boys to be here?"

"I just couldn't set and let them Injins put you boys under, now could I?" he said with a grin splitting his handsome black face. "Took me a spell, though, to get a few boys weren't afeared of comin' 'long."

"Well, I do 'preciate it, Gideon, I purely do. It was gettin' some close there for a spell. We could've handled it, though . . . We would've licked 'em good. Well, I was just ready to start . . ."

"Look," Hook shouted, interrupting him, pointing to the east and northeast.

A line of Blackfoot warriors, each mounted on his favorite war pony, stretched in an arc from northwest toward the river around to the east. They were painted and dressed in their finest war clothes. They had made their medicine and felt invincible.

"We'd best be gettin' back to them trees, lads," Squire said, edging his horse forward.

It was a good place for cover, with thick cottonwoods and willows bunched closely together. Bellows and Ransom had worked the pack animals as far into the middle of the wooded section as possible, keeping them well out of the way of almost any arrow or rifle shot. The horses were next. The men hastily threw up bulwarks of logs, branches, and scooped up dirt. Then they waited.

With the Green River to the west and the creek to the south, they had only to watch two sides, helping to keep the men from being spread too thinly, for there were less than two dozen mountain men and perhaps seven camp hands who might be of some help against more than a couple hundred Blackfoot warriors.

At about two hundred yards the warriors charged, coming in from two sides, racing their horses, roaring war cries, and firing arrows and a few trade rifles.

"Hold steady, lads," Squire said.

When the Blackfeet were less than a hundred feet yards away, Squire roared, "Now!" His big Hawken and five other rifles barked, and six Blackfeet went down. Two got back up, though their horses did not, and ran back the way they had come.

While Squire, Li'l Jim, Hook, Van Eck, Hannah and Train reloaded quickly, six other guns roared. Three more Blackfeet went down as the horde swirled around the outskirts of the copse, the Indians howling, riding off the sides of their horses, presenting almost nonexistent targets.

"Choose your shots well, lads," Squire shouted over the din.

But the Blackfeet broke off the attack soon, scampering back about three hundred yards. There they shouted insults and made obscene gestures to the white men.

"They're makin' fun of us, Nathaniel," Li'l Jim said angrily, his dander up. "I ought to take one of 'em down from here. That'd show them."

"Do it." Squire said softly.

Li'l Jim looked at him in surprise. Li'l Jim was a cocky little man, full of braggadocio. But he was a dead shot, especially since he had been given LeGrande's old rifle. His cockiness fled a little now. "Ya really think I could do that?"

"Aye." There was no doubt in Squire's voice.

Li'l Jim hefted his Hawken, then laid it carefully on the log he was laying behind. He pulled back the hammer and carefully took aim. To the others, he seemed to take forever. Then the gun boomed, rocking Li'l Jim's shoulder.

Nothing happened.

"Damnit," Li'l Jim muttered.

"You tried," Hook shouted over to him.

"Didn't do no damned good," he said, his confidence shaken some.

"Ye be needin' a bigger charge of powder, lad," Squire said. "Mayhap double what ye be usin' regular."

Li'l Jim nodded. He poured an extra measure of powder down the barrel before seating a patched ball. Again he laid the rifle barrel over the log and calmed his breathing. The gun slammed hard against his shoulder, and he winced. But he kept his eyes on the Indians to the north. He jumped up, whooping and doing a little dance when one of the Blackfeet fell from his horse, as the mountain men cheered.

The celebration ended soon after, with another charge by the Indians. Again it was repulsed, with at least half a dozen Indians dead or wounded. One of the camp helpers died with an arrow in the throat, and a trapper was nicked in the shoulder by an arrow.

"That be showin' 'em, lads. Aye. We'll be breakin' their medicine for good before long." He was not as confident as he sounded. There were still a heap of Indians left.

-32-

WAR PARTY

Panic ripped through Hannah's mind when the small band of Blackfeet suddenly loomed before her. But she fought it back. She had been a Blackfoot captive before and lived through it; she would live through it again if need be.

She remembered slapping the one and, soon after, feeling the sharp pain in her head. She did not really lose consciousness, but her recollection was foggy. She bounced on a horse's neck, face down, for not very long before being dumped on the ground. She shook her head, trying to clear away the fuzziness.

"Welcome, girlee," a man said.

She looked up. Standing before her were five white men, or rather, four white men and a half-breed. They were semicircled by painted Blackfoot warriors.

"I'm Abel Carney," the man standing in front said.

He was about Squire's age, Hannah had heard, though he looked much older. Some of the youthful handsomeness remained in the weathered, lined face, but the eyes and thin lips were cruel.

The man pulled off his black felt, wide-brimmed hat with the feather in the band and wiped at the ridges of scars that covered the top of his head. Hannah gasped involuntarily. She had known Squire had scalped this man. She had seen many men being scalped, but never one who had lived through it and the horror it looked like.

"This bother ya, missy?" Carney asked.

"No," she muttered, standing shakily, looking at the other men. Farley Walker and Tom O'Neely she knew too well, the other two she had never seen before. She took them to be Duncan Maclish and the half-breed, William Isbister. Maclish was a little better than medium height and thin as a rail. He had a prominent nose and sunken, gray eyes. His long hair was curly, as was the tangled mess of a beard and mustache, which were graying heavily though he did not look very old. Isbister was not what she would have expected. He was a little shorter that Maclish, but blockily muscled. His long, black hair was slick with bear grease. He wore fringed buckskin pants. His chest was bare, his dark bronze skin almost gleaming in the sun.

Maclish wore buckskin pants and shirt, while Carney had on wool drop-front trousers and a linsey-woolsey shirt.

"She's not half-bad for a scrawny girl," Isbister said, bulling his way forward. "Let's see how she'll hold up after I get done with her."

"You're not . . ." Walker gasped. "You can't. She's my woman." He was scared, but he stepped in front of the bulky half-breed man.

"I plan to have my fill of this bloody bitch, old chap, and I'd suggest you keep your ass out of my way lest I take my steel to your vitals."

To Hannah, the voice and diction were so odd, coming as they were out of the mouth of a dark-faced, half-Blackfoot.

"Abel, you got to stop him," Walker pleaded, fear spreading over him.

"No time for such things, Will," Carney said.

"Won't take long," Isbister answered, grinning.

"I said not now!" Carney barked. "There'll be plenty of bloody goddamn time for that later. Now, strip her down so she'll not take to runnin' and throw her in that lodge."

Isbister moved forward, pulling his knife, grinning savagely. As he grasped the top front of Hannah's buckskin shirt, Carney said roughly, "And Will, don't touch her."

Hannah breathed a small sigh of relief as the knife slid harshly through the shirt, exposing her breasts to all. She gulped nervously as Isbister started on the pants. But she stood defiantly, proud of her body and its effect on men.

"Take a good look, Farley," she said bravely, thrusting her breasts toward him a bit, "for it's all you're ever going to get from me."

Walker stood with dry mouth, unable to speak. Isbister licked his thick lips and whispered, "You're going to be a tasty piece, missy. Oh yeah." Then he pushed her shoulder until she had turned and taken a few steps.

"Just remember what I told you, Will," Carney said.

"I heard you," Isbister said icily.

"That's good, for if you don't, old chap, you'll be no good to any woman ever again."

Isbister seethed but said nothing. He just shoved Hannah forward. She walked with head up until she spotted Elk Horn, who moved in front of her, looking down at her in wonder.

Hannah shuddered at the remembrance of this greasy, high-smelling savage's attacks on her body. She shrank, her hands coming up in an attempt to cover her nakedness. But she knew it would do little good, and she dropped her hands. She stared back up at the Blackfoot, whose long, greasy black hair dangled to his knees. He looked a little older and much more weary. And she realized Squire's attack on Elk Horn's camp and the Piegan leader's defeat had cut him deeply. But this war party, she could also see, was doing much to help him regain his self-confidence.

"I will come for you," he said to her in Blackfoot, "when the mighty *Siksika* have killed the dogs." He pointed to the way she had come from. "I will keep you from these others."

"Go to hell, you heathen son of a bitch."

Elk Horn smiled. "I will come," he said in English. "For you."

He stepped out of the way, and Isbister shoved Hannah's back, moving her along. Hannah was not surprised to see no women around the camp. She knew the Blackfeet did not bring their women along on war parties, and this was a bigger war party than anything she had ever heard of. She pushed it from her mind, though, when she saw the lonely figure tied to a pole.

"Colonel Melton," she breathed in shock.

He raised his head slowly, painfully. He had been terribly abused, Hannah saw, his body covered with blood, some of

it dried, some still seeping from the knife wounds. Flayed
skin hung from his shoulders where he had been frightfully
whipped with riding quirts. He was naked, and it shocked
Hannah more than her own exposed flesh. The sun had burned
much of his skin. Melton's eyes were blurred from pain, the
heat, and thirst.

Hannah started to go to him, but Isbister grabbed her by the
back of the hair and held her. Then he shoved her forward
again. "Get your pert, little ass in there, missy," he said when
they stopped in front of a greasy, unpainted tipi. It was the
only one in the camp.

"Ain't you coming with me?" she asked, turning.

Isbister licked his lips again. Carney would not have to
know. He knew the three Blackfoot warriors who accompanied
him, and should be able to talk them into keeping quiet. After
all, they were practically family. But no, there would be time
later, he thought, when it would be safer. "Just get on in there,
missy."

"Come for me tonight," she whispered in what she hoped
was a sexy voice. They had left her calf-high moccasins on; a
knife was hidden there in each. She could make sure he would
never molest another woman.

Isbister smiled, but it froze on his face. There was something
in this young woman's eyes, something . . . "Get on in there,"
he snarled, shoving her roughly through the flap.

She poked her head out of the lodge occasionally. She was
not guarded. There was no need for it; with this many warriors,
she could go nowhere. Warriors came and went through the
camp all day, and she could hear sporadic gunfire and knew
the brigade was under fire. Drums pounded almost constantly,
and there was a ready supply of dancers at all times.

Darkness finally came, but she had no way to make a fire.
She had nothing to eat, either, and no one brought her anything.
There were a few lice-infected, greasy blankets tossed to the
side, and she finally crawled onto them and drifted into sleep,
plagued by dreams of Elk Horn or Isbister coming to visit
her.

But it was Carney who came, and it was morning when he
did. "Did you spend a nice night, missy?" he asked, oozing
with civility.

"Not very."

"Maybe you'd like company. I expect that me'n a few of the chaps here," he waved to the three Blackfeet who were with him, "could stop by."

"Don't bother."

"That's not very bloody nice of you, missy."

"It's the nicest you'll get from me."

"I don't think it's fittin' of you to speak to me in such a bloody awful way, missy."

"I didn't know you could think."

He smacked her, knocking her backward. Then he leaped on her, pinning her arms down with his own, getting his weight atop her. She could feel his excitement through his drop-front trousers, and a sick feeling crawled through her belly.

"Got the fight in you, do you, lassie? We'll just see about that, then. Maybe you'll keep my fires burnin'."

Hannah struggled, trying to kick, bite, scratch, anything. Carney chuckled and then clamped his lips on hers, forcing his tongue past her teeth. The Blackfeet laughed and shouted encouragement.

Carney freed his right hand, letting her swing with her left; it had little effect since she could not build up any momentum. He loosened the front of his pants and pulled back a little in preparation of plunging into her. Hannah gasped, more in disgust and anger than in shock or fear.

Then suddenly there was a deep voice, and Carney's weight was gone from her. Faced by a livid Elk Horn, Carney stood, hastily fastening his pants, which was difficult in his state.

The big Blackfoot war chief was dressed and painted for battle. He wore only buckskin pants, moccasins, and a hairpipe breastplate. His face was a frightening mask of red, yellow, and white. The part in his long hair was painted vermilion, and his scalplock was greased and inviting to any warrior who had the courage to come and take it. He carried a hardened bullhide shield on his left arm, and in his right hand he carried a lance with an iron point. Across his back was an unstrung bow and a puma-skin quiver filled with arrows. At his waist hung a big knife and a stone war club.

"This woman mine," he said in halting English. "You not touch her."

"Horse shit, Elk Horn," Carney said, agitation growing in his voice.

"No touch." Elk Horn wiggled the lance just a little.

Carney breathed deeply and tried to relax. He realized how much danger he was in. This war chief was angry, had made medicine, and was feeling invincible. And Carney had left his weapons on the ground, except for his knife and tomahawk. He was not about to challenge Elk Horn under these conditions.

"All right, Elk Horn," he said placatingly. "I'll leave the bloody strumpet be for now. But when we take care of those chaps out there, I'll buy her from you."

Elk Horn's eyes were glittering black stones. He said nothing. The two men faced each other silently for a few moments before Carney picked up his rifle and pistol and stalked out.

"He leave you alone now," Elk Horn said to Hannah. "You mine. After battle, I come for you."

Hannah shuddered and had to force back the bile that rose in her throat. The Blackfoot left, but he had thrown her some jerky. She picked it up and began gnawing hungrily at it, watching out the front of the lodge as the warriors rode off. The jerky was terrible tasting and covered with dirt, but it was sustenance, so she choked it down.

She could see Melton, too. He was still tied to the post, and he looked worse. Hannah had heard the Blackfeet screeching with delight the night before, and though she had heard no sound from the Colonel, she knew they were torturing him again. She wanted to rush out and free him, to soothe his wounds as best she could. But that would be folly now. She would wait. She was determined to get out of here. After Elk Horn's visit—and promise—she figured it had better be soon.

She heard more gunfire, and she fretted. She was worried most about Train, but she also was concerned about Squire, Li'l Jim, and all the others. She was anxious about herself, too, and about how she would get away. She was troubled about Melton, who was wounded and suffering out there under the broiling sun, and she grieved for Slocum Peters. Since he was not here, she figured he had been killed when Melton was captured.

Several hours passed, and the warriors returned. Another group prepared to leave.

Hannah made up her mind. She slid out one of the knives, a handy little Green River with a five-inch blade, and slit a small line in the back of the tipi. She peered through. There was nothing but a few stunted trees and plenty of sagebrush. She lengthened the slit and slipped through it, ducking behind the scant cover of a large tuft of buffalo grass.

Suddenly she stopped. She had to try getting Melton away from here; she just had to, though she knew in her heart that it was hopeless. Hannah squatted behind a bush, surveying the camp. It was virtually deserted right now, with only two or three warriors crouched at a fire to her left.

Hannah moved fast, slinking and slithering toward Melton. The Colonel seemed unaware of her presence until she popped up almost directly in front of him. His body shielded her from the warriors at the fire.

Melton stirred, thinking the Blackfeet had returned to torment him some more. Squire's words burned through his brain, telling him that he must give back as good as he got. He worked up a little spittle, but just before he expelled it, Hannah's countenance filtered through to him. His eyes were dimmed with pain, fatigue, and sweat.

"I'm gonna get you out of here, Colonel," Hannah said.

"No," he finally moaned.

Hannah looked at him in surprise.

"Go," Melton said, a little more firmly.

"But, Colonel . . ."

"No buts, Hannah," Melton insisted. "I can't walk, and you couldn't support my weight all the way back to the others. Save yourself."

"No. I'm . . ."

"Don't argue, Hannah," Melton said almost fiercely. "Do it. Bring help, if you can."

Hannah nodded. She knew it was their only chance. She turned and slid away.

She worked her way from bush to bush, ignoring the scratches she received. Suddenly she heard voices heading toward her. She forced her way partly under a clump of sage and then froze. She could feel sweat trickling down to drip off her chin, and running down her sides. Five warriors, laughing and talking, passed within five feet in front of Hannah. When the warriors had passed, Hannah finally breathed and then moved on.

Hannah slithered from sagebrush to clumps of gramma grass. The short, scrubby grass and the rough, stony dirt scraped at her soft flesh. Her hands and knees bled, and she winced each time she landed on a stone or thorn.

The heat was fierce and raised an all-powerful thirst. She had had nothing to drink since the day before, and soon it felt like her tongue was swollen almost to filling her dry mouth. Her throat was constricted from thirst and the dust.

She cautiously raised up on one knee in the sparse, brown grass. Then she stood. Checking her bearings, she moved on at a good-paced jog, plodding across the rugged, undulating land. Cactus and rocks tore at her feet, and she was glad she still had her moccasins on. More than once she sidestepped a hissing, rattling swarm of snakes, and once she startled a solitary old buffalo bull. He glared at her, snuffled, and pawed the ground, then he swung his great head and lumbered off to the northwest.

The sound of gunfire grew louder as she trotted, and she knew she was getting nearer. She ran down a small gully and popped up on the other side, less than fifty yards from where some of the Blackfoot warriors were sitting on their ponies. The warriors were taking a short break, watching their brethren at the fight.

She dropped flat on the short, rough grass. Letting her heartbeat slow as much as possible, she inched forward, praying that none of the Blackfeet would pay any attention to the barren grassland behind them. When she was barely five yards behind a young warrior, she calculated her chances. They were not very good, but neither were the chances of having this all just go away if only she sat and hoped hard enough.

-33-

Hannah pulled out the Green River again. She took a few deep breaths, then stuck the knife between her teeth. She sprang up and ran flat out, realizing for one fleeting, almost giggly, moment that she liked the feel of the wind on her naked, sweaty flesh.

Her hands slapped the horse's rump and she flew onto the pony's back before it or any of the warriors knew she was there. Her left hand shot out, grabbing the young Blackfoot's hair. She yanked his head back, exposing his throat. She grabbed the knife from her mouth at the same time and swiftly slid the blade along the exposed, throbbing arteries in the man's neck.

Hannah shoved the bleeding Indian off the side of the horse and jabbed her heels into the pony's flanks. "Come on, horse, run your damn hide off," she yelled.

The animal bolted, and Hannah flattened out along its neck. Arrows flew at her, but none hit her or the animal. She glanced behind and saw a dozen Blackfeet racing after her.

"Run, damn you," she shouted into the wind at the horse. "Run!" She kicked the pony even harder.

She glanced back again and saw that three of the Blackfeet were almost on her. She heard three rifles crack, and all three Indians fell off their horses, dead or dying. She whooped and brought her face back around. A hundred yards to go . . . fifty . . . twenty-five . . . and then she was roaring into the thicket and pulling the horse up hard. She slid off the animal and, unmindful of her nudity, into Abner's arms.

"There be time enough for such doin's later," Squire said dryly.

Train would not release Hannah. He realized that his woman was stark naked in front of all the other men. To let her go would be to expose her completely to the men. At least while he was still holding her, all they could see was her bare buttocks. That wasn't as bad as the other, even as bad as it was. "Well, one of ya give me a blanket, damnit," he roared.

The other men, suddenly embarrassed, turned away as Star Path hurried up with a blanket. Hannah nodded thanks as she took it and wound it about her. "I'll need somethin' better soon, though, Star Path," she said. "I can't fight in this thing."

The Sioux woman nodded and hurried off.

"It sure is good to see ya, Abner," Hannah said, fighting back tears of joy.

"They be comin' again, lads," Squire shouted calmly.

The men turned back, and some fired a volley. The others fired while the first batch reloaded. The Indians came again and again. Then quiet finally descended in the grove.

"Has it been like this since yesterday?" Hannah asked.

"Aye, girl," Squire answered. "That bunch has been here a spell now. I reckon they'll be headin' back to their camp soon and sendin' out the others again."

"Why don't they just all attack at once and keep on comin'?"

"Ye've lived with Injuns, girl. Ye know about their medicine and such. 'Sides, I think they be figurin' we'll be runnin' out of powder and ball afore long."

"Will we?" Hannah asked bluntly.

"I misdoubt it'll be too soon. I saw to it we was well-supplied with both afore we left rendezvous."

"Can we make a run for . . ." Her eyes suddenly widened. "Slocum!" she gasped in surprise as Peters walked up.

"Welcome back, Miss Hannah," Peters said with a lopsided grin parting his wild red beard and mustache.

"How'd you get here? I thought you was gone under."

"So'd the Blackfeet. But I'm afraid to tell you that it was most likely the Colonel was rubbed out."

"No he ain't," Hannah burbled. "He's in the Blackfoot camp."

"What?" Squire exploded.

"He's alive, I tell ya. He's been abused somethin' awful. They been torturin' him since at least yesterday. But he was alive when I skedaddled out of there."

"I'll be damned," Peters breathed. "Me'n him was out, as ya know, and had just shot us a fat cow. We was settin' to butcherin' that critter when all to a sudden maybe a dozen of those savages all hove into view over a ridge. I yelled for the Colonel to light out, but they was on him afore he could get mounted. I were in the saddle and ridin' hellbent for here. Three of them niggurs lit out after me, but I got that herd of buffler 'tween them and me.

"They turned back, then, figurin' they had one caught, and that was enough. Weren't no tellin' how many more of them red devils was hangin' about those parts. Then my horse hit a chuck hole. Snapped his leg clean as hell. Sent me flyin' ass over topknot. Knocked me cold. Next thing I knowed, it was dark. I wasn't banged up too bad, so I got my saddle and possibles bag from my horse and walked on in. I figured the Colonel'd been put under certain and had his hair took by them savages. It's good hearin' he's still alive."

"He might be that, but I don't know how much longer he'll stay that way," Hannah said. She looked from one to the other of the men with pleading in her eyes, finally fixing her gaze on Squire. "Ya got to do somethin' for him, Nathaniel," she said urgently. "He was tied to a pole in the center of that damned camp when I got there. He was still there when I took off. Ever' time one of those critters gets a mind to, he goes over there and slices off a piece of skin or does somethin' else awful. He's got no shade." She was fighting back tears. "He's been treated powerful poorly, damnit."

"There's nothin' can be done for him, Hannah," Squire said softly, looking hard at her. "Leastways not by us, not now." The other men looked away.

"He'd try to help you, if he could."

"Aye, girl, he would. The Colonel shines, he does. I'd be tryin' to help him, too, was I able. But there's nothin' we can do right now."

"Can't we get help?"

"Where?"

"Rendezvous, maybe. The boys there'd be willin' to help us, I'd wager."

"Aye, Hannah, mayhap they would. But it be two, maybe three days at best to get there, and the same back. Figure a week. We might all be gone under in a week. 'Sides, most of them boys'll likely be gone by now."

"Well, yeah, . . . but . . . " Hannah sputtered and fumed, but she knew he was right.

An hour later the Blackfeet made another run at them, and then another and another. But darkness was coming on, and the warriors seemed to be losing enthusiasm for it.

Squire gathered the men around him just after dusk. "Now be the time to fetch back the Colonel," he said quietly but fiercely.

"How?" Hannah asked, surprised.

"Me and a few of the boys'll be makin' a little *paseo* o'er to that village and pluck him out of there," Squire said with practiced nonchalance.

"Who're ya takin'?" Li'l Jim asked with a low growl.

Squire half-grinned. "I expect ye'd like to be comin'?" he asked rhetorically. "I reckon that'd suit this chil'." He paused, looking thoughtful. There was no need for it, really. He had thought about this all afternoon and had mentally chosen his small assault force. "Ye'n Abner, mayhap Gideon and Josiah."

"And me," Hannah snapped.

"Nay, girl," Squire said softly.

"You ain't leavin' me behind, damnit," Hannah said fiercely.

"Why're ye so all fired up to go?"

"Hell, Nathaniel," Hannah snorted. "You shouldn't need to ask that." She paused. "I've been took by them savages twice. I aim to make sure Elk Horn and maybe Farley Walker—he's gone over to them, ya know, him and Tom O'Neely—don't molest no more folks." Her slim fingers swept along the wood hilt of her Green River knife.

Squire nodded. His shaggy mustache and long beard wiggled, as if he was smiling. "All right. Josiah, ye be stayin' here." He spit some tobacco juice. "Slocum and Homer be in charge here."

Hannah quickly explained the lay of the Blackfoot camp, and within fifteen minutes the small group was moving swiftly across the scrubby ground.

Hannah wore an old pair of Li'l Jim's buckskin pants and a shirt of Hook's. They all left their rifles back in camp, not figuring the weapons would do them much good on this jaunt.

There was no actual village to infiltrate, it was more a matter of slinking past fires at which small groups of Blackfeet sat eating and talking. With some, it was easier than others, but they made it to the pole to which Melton was still tied.

While Li'l Jim, Train, Hook, and Hannah crouched in the darkness, ready to spring into action, Squire rose up behind the Colonel. "Ye'll be all right, Colonel," Squire whispered.

Melton was too dulled with pain to respond with more than a small, surprised moan.

With one massive arm, Squire held Melton, with the other he sliced the rawhide binding his friend and then slid the knife away.

Melton would have fallen had Squire not been holding him. He sagged, grateful for Squire's strength.

Squire bent and scooped Melton across his shoulders, startling the agony-filled Colonel.

"No," Melton groaned, barely able to speak. "You can't carry me all the way . . ."

"Shut your trap, Colonel," Squire growled.

"But . . ." Melton protested. He weighed a good 250 pounds, a portion of it fat, and he worried that not even the immensely strong Nathaniel Squire would be able to bear his weight for long.

Squire was moving already, though, stalking slowly forward through the camp.

Melton thought he saw darker shadows flitting nearby and was about to warn Squire when he realized the figures were his friends.

Train, Li'l Jim, Hook, and Hannah moved along and then suddenly disappeared into the night. Melton was only dimly aware that they were gone.

As they had arranged before leaving their own camp, the four headed toward one of the fires. Four Blackfeet squatted around it. With studied ease and ruthlessness, the three whites and one black crept up on the four Indians. There was a fast, silent rush and suddenly four Blackfeet were lying dead with their throats cut. Moments later the Indian corpses had their scalps gone. Then the four shadows hurried on, albeit one of them reluctantly.

Hannah wanted to kill more Blackfeet. The more she thought of her captivity at the hands of those savages, the more she burned with blood lust. There was one in particular she wanted to take her knife to, but Elk Horn was not in sight. The desire to kill, however, kept her from being afraid as they slipped out of camp.

The crouching walk-run across the scrubby desert was more nerve-wracking, since the blood lust lessened with each step.

In a break in the cloud cover, the four young people caught a glimpse of Squire's huge form, and they hurried to catch up. Squire was moving effortlessly with great strides. The others had all they could do to keep pace.

Then they were in their camp. Back among the trees, Squire set Melton down on a buffalo robe that had been placed there in readiness. He rose, looking none the worse for his exertions. Star Path and Rising Sun Woman hurried to Melton's prostrate figure.

"Blanket," the Colonel mumbled in some agitation. Despite his wounds and the pain he was in, he was conscious of his nudity, and that bothered him.

"Eh?" Star Path asked.

"Blanket," Melton croaked. "Cover me."

Star Path nodded. With a few quick signs, she made her wishes known. Cloudy Moon, one of Li'l Jim's women, rushed off. She returned moments later with a blanket and set it gently over Melton. Star Path began to work on a calmed Melton.

"The rest of ye lads best get some robe time," Squire said. "We'll be needin' it come mornin', I'd be sayin'." He grinned savagely. "I reckon them red niggurs're gonna be more'n half-froze to raise our hair after tonight's doin's."

The men began to drift off.

"What about Colonel Melton?" Hannah asked.

"What about him?" Squire responded.

"He gonna be all right?"

Squire shrugged. "He be a strong lad, and he be gettin' the best care we can be givin' him. Can't no more be done here. We'll just have to see if he be strong enough to pull through."

Squire and Train stayed while the two women looked after the Colonel.

-34-

When dawn broke, nearly two hundred angry, painted Blackfoot warriors moved forward slowly on horseback toward them.

"*Merde*," Squire said.

"What's wrong?" Train asked.

"Them critters mean business this day, lads. Best to be spreadin' out more'n usual."

"What're they gonna do?" Hannah asked. She still wore her hand-me-down buckskins. They would do till something better came along, if she lived that long.

"Most of them be chantin' their death songs, Hannah. I reckon it means they be plannin' on overrunnin' us. There'll be no stoppin' them from a distance this day, lads. They'll be amongst the trees with us afore long. Set your sights to takin' down as many of them as ye can whilst they still be ridin'." He paused, then roared, "Homer!"

"I'm right here, goddamnit." Bellows snapped from a few feet behind Squire.

"Fetch up blankets, lad," Squire said, nonplussed. "Enough so e'erybody's got one. *Vite!*"

The light of recognition blinked on in Bellows's eyes. He nodded and hunched off, roaring orders. Most everyone else either watched him in wonder, or looked out at the massing of warriors, frightened.

Moments later, Bellows and Ransom were handing out blankets. The men stood holding them, dumbfounded.

Squire dropped his belt and pulled off his long war shirt. He grabbed the four pointer Ransom tossed at him. He hurriedly folded it so it was long and narrow. Then he wound it around his torso, covering his chest, stomach and back. He punched holes through the blanket with his knife, then jammed two small pegs through to keep it pinned in place. He bent to retrieve his shirt.

The men shrugged and followed suit. Many wondered what it was all about; however, most of them figured they'd find out but now was not the time for questioning it.

Squire had finished adjusting his belt. "This'll be protectin' ye some from them Blackfoot arrows. At least from a distance." He turned to face the enemy.

"You don't expect us to live, do ya, Nathaniel?" Hannah asked, voicing the words that were in all of them.

Squire turned back. "Can't be sayin', girl. We be ass-deep in a suckin' swamp for certain. But," he added with a crooked grin, "goin' under this way purely beats dyin' slow and lonesome back in the settlements, now don't it? And if'n I be goin' under," the grin widened, "I'll be takin' a passel of Blackfeet with me when I cross over to the Spirit Land. I be promisin' ye that."

He spun, yelling, "Come at me, then, ye shit-eatin' bastards. I be *L'on Farouche,* and I be fearin' no man, red or white. Have at me if'n ye got the balls for such doin's!"

The Blackfeet heard him and sent up an ululating wail of war cries. They broke into a run as Squire's men spread out amongst the trees. There were no goodbyes, though Squire, Train, Li'l Jim, and Hannah had made their wills verbally with friends during the night.

The mountain men got off two volleys, killing or wounding at least a dozen Blackfeet, before the Indians washed into the copse like a tidal wave. Some of the Blackfeet headed for the horses and mules; others went straight to battling.

Squire yanked his pistol from his waistband and blasted one Indian into the Spirit World. He tossed the weapon down and pulled out his tomahawk and biggest knife. With both in hand, he ranged through the grove like a vengeful demon, slashing and hacking his way through the cream of the Blackfoot nation.

Over the roaring din, Squire could hear Bellows's bobbling shouts. "Get away from my animals, ya goddamn savages. Get, I tell ya. Go on, ya heathen, shit-eatin' devils, ya. Get away now."

And through the haze of dust he could see the horse handler swinging his musket for all he was worth, fending off the charges of Blackfeet who came on horseback and foot to steal his horses and mules.

And nearby was his protégé, Cletus Ransom, the young wiry little buck who was full of fire, deftly wielding a burning log, a savage among savages.

But one quick glance was all Squire could afford as a Blackfoot swept down on him on horseback. He ducked as the Blackfoot swiped at his head with a stone war club, then he lashed out in a backhanded blow of the tomahawk, biting deep into the Indian's back. Squire did not see the Indian fall and try to crawl away, he was too busy.

Most of the Blackfeet were afoot now, seeing the futility of fighting atop horses in the dense copse.

Squire spotted Peters battling hand-to-hand with three Blackfeet, and he sprang in that direction. Two quick blows of the razor-sharp, iron-headed tomahawk, and a brace of warriors crumpled dead to the ground.

Peters kicked the third in the groin. As the Indian doubled over, Peters brained him with his own war club. "*Merci,*" he mumbled, grabbing up his tomahawk, as Squire spun and ran, looking for more Blackfeet to fight.

They were not hard to find. Squire waded into a group of about a dozen that had surrounded Train, Hannah, and Li'l Jim, who fought desperately with knife and tomahawk and war club.

"Get away from those lads, ye bastards," Squire bellowed, flinging Blackfeet this way and that, hacking and slashing. "Do ye hear me now? Do ye? Come on ye red niggurs, get away."

He lived up to his nickname in his fury. No sooner had he cleared out the Indians surrounding his three friends than he sprang into action against a small knot of Blackfeet crowding Hook and Josiah Maxwell, and then on to help others.

Squire was indefatigable, invincible. He was everywhere at once, or so it seemed to both his own men and the Blackfeet. One large warrior finally smashed into him from behind, knocking him onto his hands and knees. He lost his knife, but kept the grip on the tomahawk.

Two other Blackfeet rushed up. Then three more. *L'on Farouche* was the key, they knew. Kill this mountain of a man, and the others would be of no consequence. Two of them leaped onto Squire's back. He bellowed and surged up, massive legs giving him the strength. Both warriors fell off, but the other three jumped at him, knives flashing in the tree-dappled sunlight.

Squire blocked one knife thrust with his left arm, feeling the steel slice through shirt and flesh. Another missed, and the third was blocked by the tomahawk. A quick flick of the wrist, and the tomahawk was buried in one Blackfoot's brain. He yanked the weapon out in time to block another thrust of a knife. With his left hand, he punched an Indian in the face, breaking the man's nose, spraying his face with blood. He kicked another in the knee as the first two came at him again.

But now he had a little room and could swing the tomahawk with reckless abandon, which he did. One warrior got too close, and the weapon bit a chunk off the side of his head. He howled and stumbled away, clutching his bloody wound.

Another came in behind Squire, but the mountain man sensed it and swung around, lashing out wildly with the tomahawk. The Indian almost lost one arm completely to the weapon, and he fell away, shock dulling his eyes.

The remaining two grabbed up their dead companion and, with help, the two seriously wounded ones. They fled, calling sharply for their companions to follow them.

The call was not necessary. The Blackfeet were streaming out of the copse, on foot and on horseback, running for their camp. There was little glory for them this day, though they had made off with twenty horses, several mules, and even a few packs of beaver pelts.

Squire stood, chest heaving with exertion and emotion, his hands on his knees, slightly bent. A small fire burned on his arm where the knife had cut him. The other men began gathering around him. He straightened, the old gleam coming into his eyes.

"Ye done well, lads," he said harshly. "Aye, ye made 'em come now certain. Anybody be hurt?"

Hook and Li'l Jim had taken arrows, both in the blankets. They wandered up, arrows sticking out of their middles. They laughed about it. Nearly everyone else had been at least nicked by knife or tomahawk. Two had broken bones—one man some ribs, the other an arm—from being hit with war clubs.

Billy Halsop and Maxwell were dead, as were two camp helpers. Another pork eater was wounded seriously enough that he would not live out an hour.

"What now, Nathaniel?" Train asked.

"We be waitin' some more."

"I don't think that's a very goddamn good idea," Bellows said. "Nope. If they come back again, we can't hold 'em off. Nope, goddamnit. We only got enough powder and lead to last a little while, but there's little food left. And everybody is hurt. Yep. Goddamn savages anyway."

"Ye be havin' any suggestions, lad?"

"Maybe we should attack them bastards."

"You're crazy," Li'l Jim sputtered.

"Nope. They won't expect that from us." He chuckled, the sound a harsh cackle. "Nope. They won't be ready for it, damn 'em. We'll surprise the livin' hell out of 'em."

"Aye, that we would," Squire said unpleasantly. "But then they'd put us all under for certain. Then there'd be nobody to watch o'er the Colonel and the women. We'd have no cover out there, *mon ami*. At least we be havin' that here. If'n they want to be raisin' our hair, they'll have to workin' for it if'n we stay here."

"But . . ."

"Don't be givin' me no buts, Homer. We'll be doin' it my way for now. Mayhap the time'll come when your idea'll be used. But for now, let's see to gettin' e'erybody's wounds bound up. A few of ye be seein' to the buryin' of Billy and Josiah. Li'l Jim, I want ye to set out to see if'n ye can make meat. Go on up toward the Green, but not too far. Take Abner with ye."

"Abner, ye'll be his lookout for the Blackfeet. Don't ye worry yourself none over tryin' to make meat. Ye be lettin' Li'l Jim do the worryin' o'er that. Ye just keep your eyes peeled for them red niggurs. Ye see any, both of ye head your tails right back here. *Vite*. Understand?"

They both nodded and headed off to saddle a couple of horses.

The day wore on, the heat and mugginess oppressive. Squire wished for rain. He thought it might break the back of this heat. But there was not a cloud in the sky.

"Riders comin'," Peters called from his spot behind a tree. A few minutes later, he said, "It's Abner and Li'l Jim."

The two young men rode in with three antelope slung over the back of a pack mule. The men in camp murmured worriedly in appreciation. The women soon had the meat cooking over fires, but the men were so hungry, most of them gobbled down chunks of it before the fire had barely warmed the flesh. To them all, it was delicious and filling.

By the shank of the afternoon, it seemed obvious that the Blackfeet would not attack again that day. Squire and a few of the others went to check on Melton.

The Colonel was badly sunburned from head to toe and covered with dried blood and sweat. He winced frequently as the salty perspiration worked its way into the numerous cuts.

His tongue was swollen from thirst, and his lips bloated and cracked. His hand shook as he reached out to touch Train's arm. "It's good to see you, boy," he croaked.

"Don't talk now, Colonel."

Soon men were back with canteens of water. Squire forced the liquid into the semiconscious Melton until he vomited most of it back up. "Be takin' some more, Colonel," Squire said soothingly. "It'll be doin' ye a heap of good."

Melton drank and vomited again and then drank some more. This time he kept most of it in him.

-35-

Squire sat on a blanket facing the east. He could just see the beginnings of dawn rising far off, that first tinge of pink on the horizon. Hannah and Train walked up quietly and sat beside him, one to a side. Behind them, the rest of the camp was beginning to come awake, the sounds of it wafting over the three.

Squire had been up early, well before the dawn, as he usually was. With the warm, clear nights, he and Star Path were sleeping without a tipi. She woke with him.

Star Path had made him some coffee, sweetening it with the last few sprinkles of sugar in the packs. Then she had set meat to roasting. He had finished eating not long ago and walked just out beyond the edge of the trees and spread his blanket. He sat, watching and waiting. He was still doing so when his two young friends joined him.

Soon, Li'l Jim, Peters, and Bellows arrived and took places on the ground. They all watched the rising dawn.

"How's the Colonel, Homer?" Hannah asked.

"He'll live," Bellows said wryly. He didn't really expect any of them to last more than a few hours longer, at most.

"What's gonna happen?" Train asked. He sounded concerned, but not worried.

Squire almost smiled. "Them red bastards'll be comin' for us today, sure as shit," he said. He sounded almost wistful, as if he couldn't wait for it to happen. "Aye, lad. And they won't be none too goddamn friendly about it neither."

"Shit, we'll turn them red sons a bitches back again, just like we did yesterday," Li'l Jim said with his usual cockiness.

"That'd be mighty unlikely, I be thinkin'," Squire said quietly.

"Huh?" Li'l Jim asked, looking sharply over at him.

Squire almost smiled. "Them sons a bitches'll be throwin' all they got at us this day, lad. Waugh! They're madder'n a griz with his balls in a knot after what we did to 'em yesterday. They'll not be thinkin' kind thoughts about us."

"The hell with 'em, goddamnit," Li'l Jim growled. "The first one of them red niggurs comes at us, I'll sprinkle him with a little death dust." He grinned ferociously. "And a goddamn lead pill waits for them that comes after."

Squire laughed. He had no fear of dying. Indeed, he found it hard to conceive of such a thing, even when the odds were so high against him and his tough little band.

The others could not really believe they would die either: Bellows and Peters because they had cheated death often enough to think they could get away with it forever; Train and Hannah and Li'l Jim because they were too young to really believe it.

"Jis' be sure you don't miss with them lead pills, boy," Peters said with a harsh chuckle.

"Shit, I'll outshoot you and any goddamn body else, and you goddamn well know . . ."

Squire rose. "It be time, lads."

The Blackfeet had ridden into sight, still a ways off. They made a frighteningly compelling sight in their war bonnets and paint, with their painted horses.

"Come on, ye red devils," Squire muttered. His hands twitched, anticipating the action. He looked at each of his friends. One by one, he clapped them on the shoulder and nodded. They were good people, all of them, and he was proud to call them friends. It wouldn't do, though, to tell them so. The gesture would suffice, especially when the smile was returned by each.

Then they faded back into the trees and brush, heading for the places they had held yesterday.

Star Path was waiting for Squire with his heavy Hawken rifle in her hands. As he took it, his hand brushed hers, and he smiled. He was pleased with the Sioux woman named Star Path, always had been. She was nowhere near as slim, trim, and youthfully attractive as Sings Pretty had been, but Squire still found her more appealing. He didn't understand it; he just accepted it.

Squire reached out his huge right paw. His hand could have covered her whole face, but he instead softly cupped Star Path's chin and left cheek. It might have seemed a strangely gentle gesture for a man so large and ferocious. But to those who knew *L'on Farouche,* it was entirely in character.

The couple said nothing to each other. They knew their duties and places. Carrying her trade rifle, Star Path headed toward where Bellows and Ransom, with the help of the other Indian women, would be keeping the horses and mules. Star Path would watch over Colonel Melton, protecting the agony-filled Melton to her last breath, if need be.

Rising Sun was already at Melton's side. She looked worried about her man. Star Path smiled reassuringly at her, and then at the Colonel. He returned it; Rising Sun tried but could not.

Squire settled in behind a stunted cedar. It would offer him some protection, but it was not so big a tree as to get in his way. He checked his rifle, then his shooting supplies, then he settled in to wait.

Not far away, Train and Hannah unabashedly hugged brief-ly before seeing to their weapons. Train felt funny inside. It was something he was becoming familiar with. He worried about Hannah and wanted to protect her. Such a thing seemed instinctive to him. At the same time, he knew that she was as capable as he in taking care of herself. She was nearly his equal with rifle or pistol, and far better with a knife when the fighting got close. She was not as strong as he was, seeing as how she was so much smaller, but she made up for much of that with speed and plain feroc-ity.

They stared out across the barren expanse of broken land, trying to blot out the fear and anticipation.

The Blackfeet presented an awesome and frightening specta-cle as they spread out. Were it not for the small, swift-running creek with the marshy banks, the small island of mountain men would have been surrounded by the Indians.

The Blackfeet moved slowly forward in their arc. Their lances and guns gleamed in the glow of the new morning sun.

"Li'l Jim," Squire called out.

"Yeah, Nathaniel?" There was no fear in the young man's voice. In only a year he had faced more danger than most men faced in their lifetimes.

"Ye see that red niggur there on the big skewbald horse?"

"The one with the buffler horn headdress settin' out there near the middle?"

"Aye, lad. Put a lead pill in his meatbag."

Li'l Jim smiled a little. He had a streak of cruelty in him that burst forth only occasionally, but it was there. He lifted the old Hawken rifle and sighted down the long barrel.

Everyone knew the act would mean nothing in the overall scheme of things. But they also knew that it would make a statement that they were not about to sit here and be overrun by the warriors.

Li'l Jim fired, and the warrior spilled off his pony. The animal bolted and raced off, heading toward the white camp. The mountain men ignored the horse, especially since the Blackfeet seemed to use the death as a signal.

There were a few moments of silence as the sound of the gunshot faded into the morning's warmth. Then the warriors suddenly charged. They came quietly at first, and slowly. But they picked up speed.

"Now, lads!" Squire bellowed when the warriors were about halfway to the copse.

A volley of gunfire roared out, and several Indians fell from their saddles. While those men reloaded, the other half prepared to fire.

The small group got off three more volleys before the Blackfeet crashed into the camp. More gunfire erupted as men shot with pistols before taking to fighting with knife, tomahawk, club, or anything else that came to hand.

Once again, the mountain men battled with a fury borne of despair and desperation.

Squire was, as usual in such situations, the fiercest of the fierce. He seemed to be everywhere at once. Whenever one of the men ran into trouble, looked like he was about to go under, suddenly Squire was there, flinging Blackfeet about like sacks

of wheat. No individual Blackfoot, nor even any group of warriors, could dent the savageness of the huge mountain man.

One warrior who felt the giant's full rage was one who
managed to get through and count coup on Colonel Melton.
Star Path had fired her rifle, killing one Blackfoot, but as she
hurried to reload, another warrior was looming over her and
the helpless Melton.

Star Path was no match for the burly warrior, who whacked
Melton with his rifle, then grabbed the woman.

"Waugh!" Squire roared over the din of the battle. He had
glimpsed the warrior grabbing Star Path. The mountain man
raced that way.

While Star Path was no match for the warrior's strength,
she was not about to cooperate with him either. He struggled
to drag her away, figuring she would be a good prize for later.
Still, she was creating too much of a fuss, and the warrior was
tiring of it. He dropped his rifle and pulled out a war club,
ready to bash her head in.

Then he felt his arm being bent in an unnatural way. The
pain was intense. He glanced down, almost stupidly, to see the
massive hand clamped around his forearm. He released his grip
on the woman, figuring to spin and relieve himself of this new
burden.

His arm snapped, and he grunted with the suddenness of it.
He glanced up into the savage, grim eyes of *L'on Farouche*.
Wolf's Foot was afraid now, though he tried not to show
it. He had heard the stories about this giant, wild man. He
had only half believed them, thinking them the product of
some warrior's alcohol-besotted brain. His band had never
encountered the mountain man and had no real reason to fear
him, other than the stories.

Wolf's Foot realized with dread that all the stories about
L'on Farouche probably were true. The man had just broken
his arm as if it were a small twig. And now . . . now . . .

Squire dropped the warrior's arm and clamped a hand on the
man's throat. He squeezed. In moments, he dropped the body.
Wolf's Foot's larynx was crushed, and if he had any life in
him when he hit the ground, it would not last long.

Star Path did not stop to say thanks. She simply hurried back
to her post and finished reloading her rifle. Squire would not

expect her thanks. Besides, he was already gone, off to slash and hack at other warriors.

The mountain men fought so savagely that the Blackfeet were pushed back into the open. The Indians remounted their ponies and raced off out of rifle range to lick their wounds.

"Tighten up the lines, lads," Squire roared. "Be seein' to your partners. Make sure they be all right. Fill in where need be."

The men retook their original positions, as much as could be. Several were wounded, but none so badly that they could not make another stand. Partners tended to one another, wrapping cloth around wounds.

It was unbearably hot, even in the shade, and the men wiped the sweat from their faces. Two of the camp helpers went around with skin buckets of water. The men sipped the liquid gratefully.

The wait this time was not that long. After an all-too-brief breather, the Blackfeet swept over the white men's camp again. They were enraged at having been repulsed twice, at not having eradicated these ferocious mountain men.

Squire figured the end was near for all of them, but he was determined to sell his life as dearly as possible. But there was no time for thinking of anything now.

Squire fought solely on instinct. He saw everything and yet nothing. He could pick out all the sounds very distinctly, despite the cacophony around him. Still, he was not conscious of any of those sounds. He felt no pain, though he knew he had been hit at least twice by arrows.

He had no idea of how much time had passed. He simply slashed and hacked, bit and punched, kicked and butted. He moved from place to place like the Grim Reaper, felling Blackfeet wherever he went.

Something, though, changed, and he wasn't sure for some time what it was. Slowly the blood lust drained from him, clearing his vision. He realized that the Blackfeet were fleeing, racing away on their ponies. But they were heading mostly north and east, rather than straight eastward toward their camp.

Squire sensed another someone charging up behind him, and he whirled, tomahawk in one hand, war club in the other.

"*Bon jour, mon ami,*" Etienne Gravant said with a wide, gap-toothed grin.

Squire did not return the smile. "What're ye doin' here, ye Flathead-humpin' bag a shit?" Squire asked, hiding his surprise and his sudden distaste.

"Me an' dem odders t'ought you might need some 'elp wit' de Blackfeets," Gravant said testily. He surveyed the small camp. "Looks like I t'ought right about dat, eh?" He chuckled, but it was a brittle sound.

"*Merde,*" Squire said. He turned to watch the two hundred or so Shoshoni and Flathead warriors still racing after the fleeing Blackfeet.

-36-

Li'l Jim edged up toward Squire and Gravant as the Frenchman dismounted.

The young man whooped. "Goddamn," he crowed. "You boys see them damn Bug's Boys runnin'?"

Train, Hannah, Peter, and Hook strolled up. The rest of the men moved in their direction, but stayed a respectable few feet back. They wanted to be close enough to hear what might be said, but not so close as to be in the way if Squire went on the rampage again or something. They could never be sure he wouldn't.

"What're you doin' here, Mister Gravant?" Hannah asked. She was still rather stunned by the sudden appearance of a couple hundred friendly warriors who had quickly saved their bacon.

"Come to 'elp you and de odders out, *mademoiselle*," Gravant said graciously, though he was still stung by the cool reception Squire had given him.

"But how'd you get all them chickenshit Shoshonis and Flatheads out here with ya?" Li'l Jim asked with a combination of wonder and condescension.

"Hell," Gravant said with another brittle laugh, "It was mostly your doings, boy."

"Mine?"

"*Oui.*" He grinned at Li'l Jim's blank look. "Dem two women of yours. *Mon Dieu!* Dere families was angry, said

243

you didn't give dem enough foofaraw. Damn Nez Perceys.
Dey wanted to come looking for you." He spit. "De Colonel's
woman, too. Old Painted Blanket took a likin' to de Colonel.
Dat old son of a bitch wanted to see if de Colonel an' his
daughter, too, was all right."

"And what made you change your mind, you cowardly
shit?" Squire said.

Gravant's back stiffened, and his face colored darkly with
anger. "You 'ave no right to say such a t'ing to me, *ton débile
mental*—you half-wit. I will not . . ."

"Dat is enough, Etienne," Ledoux snapped, riding up. He also
dismounted. "*L'on Farouche* is right. We should be ashamed for
not standing wit' him and dese *hommes* before. We 'ad every
reason to hate Abel Carney and de Blackfeets. We should 'ave
come at de first."

"Den we would be dead now, and everyone," Gravant hissed.
He was enraged at the insinuations and insults Squire had
heaped on him. It made him forget momentarily just how
large—and dangerous—Nathaniel Squire could be.

"Maybe," Ledoux growled. "But we would have our 'onor."
He spit angrily. He had been more than half-convinced right
from the start that he should ride with Squire and the others.
But Gravant had been far worse mistreated by Carney and the
Blackfeet than he had, and if Gravant was not going, Ledoux
figured he should not either. Now he regretted it.

Some of the friendly warriors, led by Painted Blanket and
Pierre Dumoulin, rode into the camp. The Indians were whooping and yipping, displaying bloody trophies. They moved back
to where their families were setting up a camp back up along
the creek, toward the Green River.

"It's all right, Mister Gravant," Hannah said with quiet
intensity. If anyone could salve over this growing rupture
between Squire and his old friends, it was she.

"Hell, this young hoss is plumb glad to see you boys," Li'l
Jim added with his usual joyous bravado. " 'Course, you and
them warriors hadn't of come along when you did, I would've
had me a time killin' more of them goddamn Blackfeet. Hell,
I was just warmin' to such doin's."

"Hah," Gravant said, his ruffled feathers soothed only a little. "You would 'ave lost your 'air and *les bijoux de famille*."

He grabbed his crotch and laughed rudely.

Li'l Jim felt sick at the mere thought that such a thing could happen, but he kept the audacious smile plastered across his face. " 'Least I got me some balls to be took, you dried up ol' fart."

More Shoshoni and Flathead warriors filtered into the camp. The noise was almost as bad as it had been during the heat of the battle. Horses snuffled and pawed the ground; warriors screeched and hollered in victory; women shouted to each other as they set up the camp.

As Hannah, Train, Li'l Jim, and Peters bandied words with Gravant, Ledoux, and Dumoulin, Squire turned and silently strode away. His blood still roared with the want of battle, his hands itched to kill more Blackfeet.

He stopped and knelt at Melton's side. Star Path stood behind him, a blunt hand stroking his long hair. He had lost his hat somewhere in the fight and had had no time nor inclination to search for it.

"How ye be feelin' Colonel?" Squire asked.

Melton was awake, and from the look in his eyes, in considerable pain. But there was no give-up in him either, that was plain for all to see.

"Better than some others, I suppose," Melton said softly. He coughed, wincing as shards of new pain cut into his chest and sides. "Will the Blackfeet be back?"

"I'd be thinkin' not, Colonel. Not with this many Shoshonis and Flatheads around." Squire rose. "Ye just rest easy now, Colonel," he said quietly.

Melton did not like the sound of that. He looked up sharply. "What're you planning, Nathaniel?" he asked.

"Got some folks to go see."

Star Path set down her rifle and moved off, almost unseen by the small group.

Melton looked at him, wondering what the huge mountain man meant. Then it slowly dawned on him. With Rising Sun's help, Melton struggled to his feet. "That's a foolish notion, Nathaniel," he said through gritted teeth. "Stay here." He knew, even as he said it, that he was wasting his breath.

It was as if Squire had not heard him. "Star Path and Risin' Sun'll be takin' good care of ye, Colonel. With Homer,

Slocum, and the others about, ye'll be safe enough. Soon's ye be able to travel, ye get on the trail. E'erybody knows their duties now."

"And you?" Melton asked. He was in agony, and wanted nothing more than to lie back down for a few hours or days or weeks. But he would not give in, not while there was a chance to convince Squire of the folly of what he was contemplating.

"I'll be by when I'm done. I'll meet up with ye down the trail somewhere."

"And if you don't . . . ?" Melton did not want to think of the alternative.

Squire shrugged. "*C'est la guerre*," he said quietly. He didn't foresee it, though.

Melton was weaving, and Squire set down his own rifle and grabbed the Colonel. He eased the big man down onto the blankets again. "Don't ye worry none, Colonel," he said in his usual grumble of a voice. It was calm and assured, like always. "I'll be just fine."

Squire rose as Star Path walked up, leading *Noir Astre* by the mane. Squire nodded. He and Star Path headed toward where they had set their camp. As Squire grabbed his saddle and blanket and walked back to the horse, Star Path began going through their supplies.

Train and Hannah walked up and stopped on the other side of the animal from Squire. "Where in hell're you goin'?" Train asked as Squire was saddling the great black horse.

"Got business to be seein' to, lad," Squire said without stopping his chore.

"Doin' what?" Hannah asked.

"Damn fool's goin' after Carney and the others," Melton grumbled from his blanket pallet.

"Hell, Nathaniel, you ain't got to do that," Train offered.

Squire said nothing.

"Why?" Hannah asked calmly.

"It's business that should've been finished a long time ago, lass," Squire said softly.

Hannah came around the stallion and placed a hand on Squire's arm. She looked up at him, eyes pleading. "Let it go, Nathaniel," she said earnestly. "Let it go."

"I can't, lass."

"Damnit, Nathaniel, yes you can!" Hannah snapped. She was about the only one in the world who could get away with talking to Squire in such a way.

Squire jerked the cinch tight and pulled the stirrup down from where he had hooked it over the saddlehorn. He turned to face Hannah. "No, I can't," he said. "I got this one more time to try'n find my boy."

Hannah had forgotten about Squire's son, the boy stolen from him so many years ago. She gasped when she remembered, but then she grew solemn again. "There'll be other times, Nathaniel. It's been so long now, a while longer won't hurt none."

"I don't find him now, lass, I'll ne'er do so."

"Why?" Train asked, coming around the horse to join Hannah.

Squire stroked the long, lush beard. "Abel Carney's the best—and only, I reckon—chance I got of findin' my boy. He'll know where the boy's kept, if anyone knows."

"So?" Train asked, surprised. "You'll be able to cut that old bastard's trail anytime, I'd expect."

Squire came close to smiling. "Shit, lad, how long ye think them goddamn Blackfeet're gonner be lettin' Carney and his lads live? Hell, after the ass-kickin' they got from us over the past couple of days—brought on by Carney's doin's—Bug's Boys're gonna be more'n half froze for them lads' hair." He did smile then. "'Course, Carney ain't got not hair to be took, but you catch my meanin'."

"You aim to catch 'em before the Blackfeet kill 'em," Hannah said. It was not a question.

"Aye, lass."

"We'll be ready directly," Train said firmly. Nathaniel Squire was his best friend in the world and had done more for him than even his parents had. He was not about to be like Gravant and Ledoux and not back up Squire when the mountain man was about to go off on such a quest. "Soon's we get our horses saddled."

Squire nodded. "Make sure ye got enough powder and ball. Best bring some buff'lo jerky and a bit of coffee, too. Homer'll see to it ye get what ye be needin'."

Train nodded solemnly. He and Hannah hurried off.

Star Path had walked up during the exchange. Now she handed Squire the buckskin bag she was holding. "Food," she announced. "And powder, lead. All you need."

Squire smiled softly at Star Path as he took the bag and hung it over the saddlehorn. He touched her cheek with a big, sausage-size finger. "Ye be a goddamn good woman, Star Path," he said quietly.

Star Path said nothing, but Squire knew she was bursting with pride inside.

"I expect ye to have me a good camp when I get back, ye hear me, woman?" Squire said with mock severity.

Star Path nodded solemnly. She knew he was not as gruff as he was pretending to be. Not with her. She also had no doubts that he would return.

Melton, watching the exchange, was amazed, as he always was when he saw the two together. Though he had been with Squire almost a year, he still could not reconcile the maniacal warrior with this soft-spoken, gently caring giant.

Squire looked around and saw Train and Hannah talking with Li'l Jim, Peters, and Hook. He swung into the saddle. "Homer and Slocum'll make sure things be fine here, Colonel," he said. "Ye've been with 'em long enough now to know ye can be puttin' your trust in 'em."

"I'm not worried about them, Nathaniel."

Squire nodded. He tugged on the reins, and the great black horse moved.

"You're not going to wait for them, Nathaniel?" Melton asked. He was not really surprised. Such a gesture would be unlike Squire.

"This here be business I'll have to be seein' to myself," Squire said flaty. "'Sides, ye'll be needin' 'em here."

Melton nodded. He was in too much pain to worry too much about such a thing. He also found it hard to think that anyone even such a large group of Blackfeet—could kill Nathaniel Squire.

Melton also was comfortable with the service he would get from Abner Train, Hannah Carpenter, Li'l Jim, and all the others. Still, he always felt better when the huge mountain man was with them.

"*Bon chance,*" Melton said. "God go with you, Nathaniel."

Squire shrugged. He turned *Noir Astre* and rode through the trees and brush, not wanting to announce his intentions to the young people who were determined to follow him.

Hatless and with rifle cradled in the crook of his left arm, Squire moved slowly past knots of women working to put up tipis, build fires and in other way set up a camp. Warriors sat in small groups, crowing about their abilities and bravery.

Squire swung northeastward, across the sage-studded flats, heading toward the Wind River Range that could be seen dimly. Once out on the dry, barren flat, he picked up the pace.

-37-
SQUIRE'S RAGE

Li'l Jim, Hannah, and Train were enraged that Squire had gone off without them, particularly Li'l Jim. He felt left out of so much, though he knew that was not true. He had had as many adventures as any of the others. Still, he could not help the hurt feeling, since he was pretty well convinced that Squire favored Train and Hannah.

Favoring Hannah he could understand. She was all that most men could want in a young woman, and more. More than once Li'l Jim had regretted that it had not been he who first found out Hannah's secret. Then she might've been his. It made him hate Train on occasions. But whenever such thoughts came over him, he would smile and shake his head, annoyed that he could think so poorly of Train, who was his closest friend. Besides, he was more than half certain that Hannah would've had nothing to do with him. Mainly because he would have done something stupid, he figured, and turned her against him right from the start.

Li'l Jim could not help but wonder, though, why Squire seemed to favor Train. He wanted to show Squire that he was every bit as good as Train.

"Well, goddamnit," he announced after several minutes of fuming, "I'm goin' after that overgrown son of a bitch."

"No," Melton said. He was still lying down, looking up at them. He had at first thought to stand when he told the three— as well as Bellows and Peters—what Squire had done. Then

250

he had decided against it. He had been on his feet several times today already. He did not need to do it any more for a while.

"The hell you say," Li'l Jim snapped.

"Watch your tongue, boy," Peters growled. "This here's the Colonel you're sassin'."

"I don't give a damn."

"Li'l Jim," Train said with a strong note of warning in his voice.

The young man was still furious, though. That, combined with his normal lack of tact and sense, made him unmindful of the trouble he was brewing. "Leave off me, goddamnit, the both of ya," he snapped. "I ain't lettin' that goddamn big ox leave me out of these doin's."

Peters clobbered him one, sending Li'l Jim sprawling. "Best mind what you say and who you say it to, boy," Peters said calmly.

Li'l Jim scrambled up, drawing out his well-used Green River knife. "I'll gut you, goddamnit," he snarled. He took a step toward Peters.

Suddenly Hannah was between the two potential combatants. "Now, you just hold on there, Li'l Jim," she said calmly.

Li'l Jim froze. He would have killed anyone who got in his way, except this woman. He could not do that. But the fury still pulsed through his veins, goading him into action.

Hannah moved slowly forward, until she was close enough to lay her hands on his arms. They were about the same height and could look easily into one another's eyes. "Put your knife away, Li'l Jim," she said softly. When he resisted, she said, "Do it."

Li'l Jim could not defy those searching green eyes or the insistent, firm voice. He slid the knife away. Still, nothing had quelled his rage. "I'm goin'," he said defiantly.

"No," Melton said. He moved in front of Li'l Jim. Train had him under one arm; his other rested on Rising Sun's shoulder. He took a moment to catch his breath, waiting, hoping, for the pain to subside some. "I need you here, son," he finally said softly. "All of you."

"You can get by without me," Li'l Jim insisted.

"Maybe," Melton allowed. Then his voice hardened. "But you're under contract to me, son. I expect you to live up to that."

"Shit," Li'l Jim snapped, "Squire's under contract to you, too, and you let him go traipsin' off any time he goddamn well feels like it."

"Reckon I do," Melton said with a small smile. "But I figure I have a much better chance of stopping you than I do him."

Bellows guffawed from behind the Colonel. That didn't make Li'l Jim feel any better, though he did realize the wisdom of it.

"Don't you give a damn about Nathaniel?" Li'l Jim asked, suddenly switching tacts. He might not have all the sense God gave a person, but he had some, and it occasionally asserted itself.

"Of course I do," Melton said, startled. "Why would you think I didn't?"

"You say you like Nathaniel, yet you let him go off to fight half the goddamn Blackfoot Nation all by himself?" He sounded a note of incredulity. "Shit, I expect you don't really give a damn about him at all."

"I'll knock you on your ass, boy, you keep talkin' such to the Colonel," Peters snapped, shoving past Train.

"Quiet, Slocum," Melton said thoughtfully. "Li'l Jim's right." He was shrewd enough to know that Li'l Jim was trying to manipulate him, but that did not lessen the fact that the young man had a point. He stood, grateful for Train's and Rising Sun's support, thinking. Then he nodded, as if the decision was suddenly clear.

"I suppose you others'd like to go after him, too?" he asked.

Peters, Train, Hannah, Hook, and even Bellows nodded.

"Well, I can't let you all go," he said slowly. "Some of you'll have to stay." He drew in a deep breath, both to ease the pain and to give himself time to think a little more.

"Well, I'm goin' for goddamn sure," Li'l Jim snapped. "I don't much give a shit who comes along." He thrust his chin out defiantly.

"The Colonel's right, Li'l Jim," Train said. "Some of us got to stay and help out here. It's our duty."

"Then stay here, goddamnit," Li'l Jim snarled. "I don't need ya. I'll go my own goddamn self."

"Like hell," Hannah interjected. "Ye ain't goin' without me. I got a few things to settle with any Blackfeet I can find."

"I didn't say I *wasn't* goin'," Train growled.

"That's where my stick floats, too," Peters offered.

"Looks like you get to keep Homer here to watch over ya, Colonel," Li'l Jim said with something of a smirk.

"I can't allow that, Li'l Jim," Melton said.

"Too goddamn bad. You . . ." He spied Gravant, Ledoux and Dumoulin, who had been keeping their distance. "Keep them here with ya," he said, pointing at the three French-Canadians.

While Melton pondered that thought, the three stepped up closer. "We will be going, too, *Monsieur Colonel*," Gravant said gravely.

Melton nodded. "I suppose I can't stop you and your boys, Etienne," Melton said. "But I can ask you to reconsider."

"*Non.*" It was said flatly.

"We mus' go, Colonel," Ledoux added. "We 'ave much to make up for with *L'on Farouche*."

"You've done enough for Nathaniel," Li'l Jim said blandly. He stared back at three sets of dark eyes.

Gravant and Ledoux did not know whether Li'l Jim meant what he had said or if he was ridiculing them for not having helped Squire in the old days.

"That's true, you have," Melton said. "Bringing the Sho-shonis and Flatheads like you did. We would've been in more severe difficulties without your timely arrival."

Gravant shrugged. "We did nothing." He shifted his rifle in hand. "*Allons, mes amis.*" He turned.

"Wait," Li'l Jim called after him.

When the three Frenchmen looked back at him question-ingly, Li'l Jim said, "I was there when you come up," he said darkly. "Seems like Nathaniel wasn't all that happy to see ya."

"Dat is none of your concern," Gravant said stiffly.

"Buffler shit. I reckon he don't think too goddamn highly of you for not backin' him before." Li'l Jim pulled himself straighter and sneered at Gravant. "I ain't got much likin' for chickenshits, neither."

Gravant looked as if he had been slapped. He ripped off a stream of French that only his two companions understood.

When Gravant ground to a halt, Li'l Jim said mercilessly, "I got no idea what you just said there, boy, but I don't reckon you was complimentin' me on my handsome good looks." He paused a second. "And if'n ya start up in that tone again, I'll blow a hole in your belly big enough to run a buffler bull through." His eyes never left Gravant's.

Gravant looked liked he was ready to go berserk, but Ledoux spoke first. "No man likes to 'ave 'is man'ood question. Certainly not when 'e 'as proven it since long before de accuser was off 'is mother's tit."

"Should've thought of that before ya run out on Nathaniel." There was no sympathy for the three in Li'l Jim's voice.

"*Oui*," Ledoux said sadly. "Dat is why we fix to go 'elp *L'on Farouche* now. We wan' to make it up to 'im, if we can."

"A job here is yours, *Monsieur* Ledoux," Melton said into the sudden breach of silence. "And your friends."

"*Non*," Gravant spit. "We will go after *L'on Farouche*."

Melton nodded, not liking any of this. "I can't keep you three here," he said. He was facing a tough decision; one he did not want to make. "But I can do so about the others."

"Like hell," Li'l Jim snapped. "I'm goin', and that's that."

"I can't let all of you go, Li'l Jim," Melton said reasonably. "And you damn well know that."

"Maybe. But I'm goin'. All these others can stay, if they're of a mind to."

The men fell silent for the most part as they struggled with their wills and their consciences.

The three Frenchmen talked quietly among themselves, their French grating on the Americans' ears. They finally stopped, and Ledoux said softly, "I t'ink we 'ave a way to do dis, Colonel." He paused, looking from one to the other. "Pierre will stay 'ere wit' you. Me and Etienne will go." He almost grinned at the anger that swept across Li'l Jim's face again.

"And Li'l Jim and *Monsieur* Train. De rest can stay wit' you, Colonel. What do you say about dat, eh?"

"No," Hannah piped up. It was not said sharply, but no one could dispute the determination on her face.

"Hannah . . ." Train started, a note of warning in his voice. He shut up fast when she glared at him. He knew better than to even think of questioning her bravery or abilities.

"I'm goin', Colonel," Hannah insisted.

Melton drew in a deep breath and then blew it out through pursed lips. He was tired, and his body still ached like nothing he had ever felt before. He was in no mood for such arguing. "You mind stayin' behind, Slocum?" he asked.

"I'd rather be killin' Bug's Boys," Peters admitted. "But I reckon I've put enough of those bastards under for one day. I'll stick here."

"Homer?"

"Someone's got to mind the animals, Colonel. Yep," Bellows said firmly. "Can't leave it to them other no-good pieces of mule shit. Nope. Sure can't."

"Gideon?"

Hook had said nothing all the while. He almost jumped out of his skin when Melton addressed him directly. "Reckon I wouldn't be put out none to stay and he'p out here," he finally managed to say.

Melton nodded, relieved. "Then it shall be. Make sure you boys have enough supplies for a couple days. Homer, cut 'em all out an extra horse."

"We 'ave our own, 'Omer," Ledoux said.

Bellows nodded and moved off. The others, having saddled their horses before, began to pull themselves on. Train and Rising Sun eased Melton down onto the blankets.

As the others waited for Train, Gravant pulled up alongside Li'l Jim. "When dis is over," he said, voice scratchy with anger, "I will kill you."

"Any goddamn time you want to try, you just come on at me, old man," Li'l Jim said evenly. He was afraid of no one, except maybe Squire.

Gravant grinned viciously. "It will be fun to carve you up, eh," he said roughly. "I will make it slow and painful for you and do it in front of dese odders 'ere." He swung his right arm in an arc to encompass the long, winding camp.

"Like hell you will," Hannah said calmly. "Even if you could best Li'l Jim, you'd have me and some of the others to fend off." She paused for a heartbeat. "You see, Mister

Gravant, we don't leave our friends off in times of need."

Gravant was torn between rage and self-disgust. The rage won out, though he knew he could do nothing with it now. He vowed to himself, though, to kill Li'l Jim, and maybe this uppity young female, too, as soon as all this was over.

"Let's go," Train said harshly. He had overheard the exchange while he was mounting his horse.

"You do not give me orders," Gravant rasped. "You are not de *bourgeois*."

"Yes, I am," Train said simply as he pulled his horse's head around and rode off.

-38-

A blind man could have followed the Blackfoot trail, and Squire never even bothered to look down at it for the first several miles. He passed a few Blackfoot bodies, ones that the warriors had been unable to retrieve before fleeing. All were scalped and mutilated.

He also saw numerous patches of blood on the short, yellowed grass, quickly soaking into the dust.

In addition, clusters of Shoshonis or Flatheads moved by him, heading back toward the camp on the creek. He knew many of them and nodded in greeting. The others he ignored. A few of the warriors helped wounded comrades, and Squire saw two bodies slung across pony backs. All in all, he thought, the friendly warriors had fared well, if they lost only a few in such a fight.

Squire kept up a good pace, but not a punishing one. He figured the Blackfeet had only about a half-hour head start. Of course, the Indians were riding as hard as they could, and he was not. But he was relentless and would not give up. He knew the Blackfeet, who had been fighting as long as he had, would have to slow down sooner or later.

After half a dozen miles, Squire began keeping a keener eye on the trail. As soon as the Blackfeet shed the attacking Shoshonis and Flatheads, they most likely would split up and travel in smaller groups, Squire figured. At least until they reached a point where they thought they might be safe for a little while. They would want to regroup to move through Crow territory to prevent or withstand an attack—unless they took a different path, where they would not have to be concerned about the Crows.

Squire's biggest concern, however, was that Carney and his men would end up out of his reach. There was the possibility that they would flee as soon as they got a chance. A far more likely possibility was that the Blackfeet would kill them at the first opportunity. Carney and the others would have no chance without being with the Blackfeet for the time being, so they would still be with the war band. But for how long would the Blackfeet continue to protect them, Squire wondered.

Shortly after noon, Squire stopped to let the horse breathe. He had passed no other friendly warriors in more than an hour, and he figured the Blackfeet would be splitting up soon. In addition, the trail had curled to the northwest. He scanned the ground, pacing in an arc while *Noir Astre* wandered nearby, cropping at the sere grass.

Not only was Squire looking to see if the Indians had divided, he also wanted to try to pick out some sign of Carney's passage. Finding nothing, he climbed back into the saddle and rode on, moving slowly, scanning the ground.

It was easy to pick out where some small groups of warriors had branched off. It was not so easy to find any trace of Carney or his men. They might be riding Blackfoot ponies, like the warriors were, which would give Squire little to go on. Even if they had shod horses, it would be hard to trace them, since the Blackfeet had some stolen horses, plus the sheer number of horses they had would obliterate any clear sign.

Still, he persevered, pressing ever onward. In midafternoon, he stopped again. This time he loosened the saddle on his black stallion, letting the animal breathe. He sipped from the gourd canteen of water. Then, while looking around, he gnawed on a piece of elk jerky.

He was angry, but he kept the fury on a tight rein. Flying off in a rage would do nothing to further his cause. Still, he was getting frustrated. He had been following the Blackfeet for several hours and was no closer to catching them than he had been at the start. Or so it seemed.

He tightened the saddle and mounted, riding on. He still followed the wide swath of the trail. It continued to head northwest, back toward the Green River. If it continued, it would cut the Green some miles north of where the rendezvous had been held. To Squire, it made sense for the Blackfoot to go that way. Heading east, they would run into the Wind River Range, which it would be damn near impossible to cross. But by heading northwest and catching the Green, the Indians could follow that river for a while, then cut across land and on to take Togwotee Pass or Union Pass or one of the other passes that offered a relatively easy way through the Wind River Range.

As he rode, he once again began swinging in a wide arc. It was time-consuming action, but it was the surest way to find other groups that had cut off. It was only that way that he thought he could find Carney or his remains.

He was almost back in the mountains by the time darkness overtook him. He pressed on, not tempted to stop except for a brief time to let the horse rest. Urgency rode on his shoulder like the fringe of his war shirt. He was thankful for the full moon and the generous coating of stars. They provided enough light to see fairly well. It slowed him a little, but would not stop him.

An hour or so before dawn, when the usual dark was deepened by the towering peaks around him, Squire pulled to a stop. He unsaddled *Noir Astre* and let the animal graze. Squire built a small fire and put coffee on. Then he set some pemmican to heat in an old fry pan. He ate, had two cups of coffee, and then smoked a pipe with a third cup of thick coffee. He broke down and cleaned his rifle and pistols one at a time, then reloaded them all. With a shrug, he refilled and lighted his pipe.

Finally, though, he knocked the ashes from his small clay pipe and rose. He kicked dirt casually over the fire. Then he slowly saddled the horse. "We'll be catchin' them bastards today, ol' hoss," he muttered, half to himself, half to *Noir Astre*. Then he was on the move again. Dawn had broken, giving him some light.

He passed several dead ponies, all of which had been scavenged heavily during the night. Then he spotted a trail winding off into the trees to his right. The beginning of it was barely visible, but his eyes picked it up. He stopped for a moment, then nodded. It seemed the kind of place Carney would cut off from the Blackfoot, probably during the dark of night. He and his men could slip away without being seen and be long gone by the time any of the Blackfoot leaders realized it.

Squire pushed *Noir Astre* through the foliage and onto the trail. A quarter of a mile down the trail, Squire stopped and dismounted. He checked the trees, bushes, ground, everything. His lips tightened when he saw a horseshoe print he thought he recognized. It was of a horse that Tom O'Neely had used regularly when he was with Melton's brigade—before he had fled with his friend Farley Walker.

"Your time be runnin' out, lads," he muttered as he swung into the saddle.

He pushed harder now, still not overworking the horse in the oppressive heat, but making good time. He was certain he was on the trail of the men he wanted, and he wasted no time in seeking sign.

Squire felt the excitement grow. He fully expected to end years of searching and frustration soon. He could almost feel his big, hard hands around Carney's neck, squeezing ever tighter as Carney's eyes bulged. It was a pleasurable thought.

An hour or so later, he entered a glade that was a little more than a quarter of a mile long and a half mile wide. Squire started across it, but he moved slowly, cautiously. He sensed something, but he couldn't figure out for certain what it was.

He moved on, all his senses alert.

He tensed as he neared the far side of the glade. Within moments he would be back into the thick cover of aspens, blue spruce, and Douglas firs. He would be glad for that for several reasons. First of all, despite the altitude, it was hotter than the gates of hell out here in the open. But more importantly, he would be safer in the trees. Out here, it would be so easy for someone like Carney to just sit behind a tree trunk and blast him out of the saddle. In the trees, it was still possible to get ambushed, maybe even easier, but it would have to be close up, where he would be able to defend himself.

There were some small trees and tall brush before the real stands of aspen and spruce. As he moseyed past one particularly large sagebrush, Duncan Maclish suddenly launched himself at Squire from behind the bush.

Squire swatted the attacker with the barrel of his Hawken swung with a stiff right arm. At the same time, he pulled the horse up sharply and slid off the left side. He smacked *Noir Astre* on the rump, and the horse trotted off a few feet.

With a quick look around, he took the two steps to Maclish. The man was on his hands and knees, trying to get up. He was having a difficult time of it, and blood dripped from his broken face onto the dust.

Squire took another fast look around then grabbed Maclish's hair and yanked the man up to his feet and held him. "Where be the others?" he asked harshly.

"I don't know," Maclish mumbled.

"I'll be askin' ye one more time, lad, then I'll be tearin' your head off for ye. Now, where be the others?"

"Right here, Squire," Carney said, stepping out from behind the cover of trees. He had a rifle in his hand, pointing loosely in Squire's direction. Carney was flanked by William Isbister, Farley Walker, and Tom O'Neely. They, too, had rifles pointed in Squire's general direction.

Squire shoved Maclish forward. He stumbled a few steps and then fell. He rose slowly, then took his place alongside the others, facing Squire. His face was covered with blood, which had splattered down onto his dirty cloth shirt.

Carney was wearing a bandanna wrapped around his head, pirate-fashion. He reached up, pulled it slowly off, and dropped it on the ground at his feet. His scarred skull gleamed unnaturally in the sunlight. He ran a hand over the ridged skin.

"It's past time we ended this, old chap," Carney said. "You've been doggin' my trail for too bloody goddamn long."

"Ye been hard to find."

Carney grinned. There was no real humor in it. "With a bloody crazy bastard like you after us, we took our arses up to Canada, to Edmonton House, for a bit. Traded with the bloody natives up along the North Saskatchewan. A couple of years ago, the HBC turned against us, so we came down this way and threw in with The Company, as you Americans are so fond of calling it."

"Don't be lumpin' me in with those shit-eaters," Squire growled.

"All Americans are alike, don't you know, old chap."

Squire shook his head. "Ye've made yourself a lifetime of mistakes, ain't ye, lad?" Squire said nonchalantly.

"Shit," Carney said with a rattling chuckle. "Had my times, I suppose." He grinned. "But I reckon I've outlasted you."

"How so?"

"You big, dumb shit, you came ridin' right into our little trap here," Farley Walker said scornfully.

"That's so," Squire said rhetorically. He set the butt of his Hawken on in the dirt and leaned his forearms casually on the muzzle.

"Yep, goddamnit." Farley was feeling full of himself. He figured that after they dispatched Squire, he would try to talk Carney and the others into heading back south so he could retake Hannah.

"Should I piss my 'skins now, lad?" Squire said humorlessly.

Carney and Isbister guffawed, and Walker flushed. "Goddamn, Squire," Walker snapped, "you're lucky Abel said to leave you for him or I'd kill ya myself."

"Shut up, Walker," Carney snarled.

"But, Abel . . ."

"I said shut up, goddamn you," Carney roared. He swung his head around to glare at Walker. "Half the goddamn bloody Blackfoot Nation couldn't kill him, you think some pissant little chap like you will be able to do it?" He turned back to face Squire and shook his head at the audacity of some people. "He's right, though, about one thing—I have reserved the pleasure of killin' you for myself, old boy. And rest assured that it'll be slow and painful, too."

"I expect ye'll be havin' your hands full in the doin'," Squire said dryly. He spit some tobacco into the dirt. "I might recommend ye send a few of your lads against me first to sort of soften me up some."

"I've considered just such a thing," Carney said evenly, nodding in agreement. "And I've concluded it'd be the proper thing." He paused, smiling unctuously. "I'd be full of goddamn bloody appreciation, though, if you were to place that Hawken rifle on the ground, old chap."

"So one of your lads can be shootin' me down easy?" Squire asked in mock surprise.

Carney waved one hand, and the others dropped their rifles, some more reluctantly than others. They all pulled their pistols and dropped them, too.

Squire straightened and let the Hawken fall to the grass. He eased out his own big pistols and dropped them. He never even considered using them. This was a job that needed doing by hand.

"Let's be startin' this *fandango*, lads," Squire said quietly. He stroked his beard as he waited.

-39-

Isbister, Walker, and O'Neely charged. Maclish, who was still hurting from being smashed by Squire's rifle, moved up more slowly. He hoped to circle the giant mountain man like a vulture, sweeping in when it appeared there was little danger left.

Squire took a blink of time to set himself. His main concern was Isbister, who was the biggest, strongest, fiercest, and most experienced of the attackers. Squire basically discounted the two young men who had been members of his own brigade. He knew they would be little problem.

Still, they could be annoyances, given an opportunity. Squire decided to take care of them first so he could concentrate on Isbister.

All this took place in the span of perhaps a second. Squire glided smoothly a few steps to his left, away from Isbister and toward Walker and O'Neely. He interlaced his fingers and swung the locked fists up behind his left shoulder. Then he whipped the huge ball of flesh and bone forward.

The hard, knotted fist smashed O'Neely in the right side of the face, shattering his cheek and jaw bones. O'Neely was knocked sideways, where he crashed into Isbister, pushing the half-breed a few steps out of the way.

O'Neely fell, moaning and whimpering. He was not dead, but he wished he was.

Squire paid no attention to O'Neely once he hit him. He

simply spun and lowered his right shoulder. Walker's stomach and chest plowed into it, and he came to a sudden, sharp halt. He gasped as his breath exploded out from the impact. He was having trouble getting any air back in.

Squire gripped Walker roughly by the crotch with one hand and squeezed. He grabbed Walker's shirt with the other meaty fist, hoisted the screeching young man over his head, half turned, and then flung him several feet to the left. Walker hit with a yelp and rolled. He, too, then lay there moaning, still trying to breathe right, and clutching his aching crotch.

Squire spun just in time to have Isbister slam into him. The half-breed was not nearly as tall as Squire, but he was not a small man, either. He was solidly built and held a lot of power in his stocky frame. His bare torso also was slick with sweat and grease.

The two men sprawled, with Isbister half atop Squire. Isbister's blunt, hard hands went for Squire's throat. They made it, but lingered only for a fraction of a second, as Squire slammed a forearm backward across the side of Isbister's head. The half-breed fell off.

Isbister grinned insolently. He slid out his big butcher knife. "Time to bloody see what you're really made of, old boy," he said with an almost pleasant growl.

"Be comin' at me, then, ol' hoss," Squire said easily. He grinned back scornfully. "Best be makin' sure that blade of yours be sharp, since it'll be a heap less painful for ye when I be stickin' it up your ass for ye."

Isbister half laughed. He had no fear, despite Squire's reputation. He was afraid of no man, white or red. He charged, knife upraised.

Squire stood his ground. As the knife descended, he swung both hands up. He grabbed Isbister's wrist with one hand. As he twisted Isbister's arm some, his other hand went for the knife. Then he felt a short, sharp pain just under the ribs on his right side.

Squire looked down and saw blood. At the same instant, he saw Isbister swinging back his left hand for another jab with a small patch knife. Squire wrenched the arm he still held.

Isbister yelped as ligaments and tendons tore. His dark, nerveless fingers could not hold the big knife, and he dropped it, but he kept his wits and lashed out with the patch knife. Twice more it sunk into flesh. He was not sure, though, that he had hit anything vital in the big man's innards.

Squire twisted Isbister's arm sharply down and around and stepped a little to that side at the same time. The latter maneuver accomplished two things: it kept his stomach out of the way of the small blade, and it broke Isbister's arm.

"Shit," Isbister gasped. It was the only sign that he had felt any pain when the bones snapped.

Squire let go of the arm and spun back in front of Isbister, where he launched a strong right fist at Isbister. The gnarled ball crashed into Isbister's solar plexus, lifting the man a foot off the ground.

The half-breed's face screwed up in pain, and with his body's sudden realization that it could not inhale or exhale. The paralysis seemed to radiate out from his stomach, clutching at his heart and groin. He sank to his knees, trying to breathe.

Squire let him be. He moved, instead, toward Walker, who was showing some signs of reviving. Squire kept an eye on Carney standing ahead of him some yards away, rifle still in hand. Carney was doing nothing except watching.

Walker had risen and was standing there. He was dazed, but seemed to be regaining his senses. Wary of Carney, Squire headed toward Walker.

The young man pulled his cheap tomahawk. He tried to glare at Squire, but fear simply made him look foolish.

Squire shook his head at Walker's stupidity. "You be a goddamn fool for throwin' in with this scum, lad," he said quietly.

Walker shrugged, too afraid to talk.

"Now ye'll be payin' for your foolishness." He stalked toward Walker.

The young man swung his tomahawk up and then out, seeking Squire's head. Squire threw up his brawny left arm and blocked the blow. Walker's wrist hit Squire's steel-like limb, and the tomahawk went flying harmlessly out of his hand. Squire clamped his hands on Walker's throat and within moments had squeezed the life out of him. Squire dropped the corpse dispassionately.

Suddenly Isbister was on Squire's back, his legs wrapped around Squire's middle and his powerful left forearm clamped across Squire's throat. Isbister's other hand dangled uselessly at the end of the broken arm.

Squire balled his right fist, twisted it back, and started throwing punches back over his shoulder. He couldn't get the leverage he wanted, but he still gave Isbister a good battering, mashing the man's splayed nose, bouncing punches off cheeks and jaw. At the same time, he swung his mighty left hand up and grabbed Isbister's forearm. Sucking in as deep a breath as he could manage, he exerted all this strength. Slowly, the pressure on his Adam's apple eased.

Then he jerked the arm loose. One more mighty punch from the right hand, and an already weakened Isbister slid off Squire's back like grease out of a hot skillet. Squire whirled and smashed Isbister in the face. His rage boiled; Squire hated Isbister almost as much as he did Carney. He pounded Isbister again and again, driving the half-breed back.

Isbister grunted with each punishing below. His mind was blank to the pain, his animal cunning furiously trying to find a way out of the certain death that faced him.

Finally Isbister went down, flat on his back. His dark face was almost unrecognizable. Most of his teeth were gone, and nearly all the facial bones broken. He lay, making no sound other than a raspy, bubbling breathing.

Squire knelt at Isbister's side. "Killin' be too good for ye, ye son of a bitch," he hissed as the blood rage came over him again.

Isbister mumbled something, but it was unintelligible.

Squire slid out his knife. "Ye got to be payin' for what ye done to Sings Pretty, lad," Squire said. He was almost in a dream state, barely conscious of anything around him. "Not only in this world, but in a later one, goddamn ye."

He jabbed the knife into the inside of Isbister's thigh. He pulled it free, then slid the tip into the bloody hole in the pants. He sliced the pants open, exposing his genitals. Isbister wriggled feebly; it was all he could do.

"Ye ain't gonna be fit for shit in the spirit world, lad." There was a harsh, nasty edge to his voice.

Suddenly Squire heard a gasp. Then something hit his shoulder and fell. A moment later came the crack of a rifle.

Squire glanced over his shoulder and saw Maclish's body

lying there, a large hole in the head. Another glance across the meadow, and he could make out a few horses and a few men standing, all facing in his direction.

He shrugged and looked back at Isbister. "*Adieu, le merde,*" Squire snarled.

Isbister screamed once maniacally, then clamped his lips shut, as Squire remorselessly emasculated him with the big knife. Squire grabbed the bloody pile in one hand and forced Isbister's mangled mouth open. Then he half shoved the obscene mass into the cavity.

"Ain't nothin' can ever be squarin' accounts for what ye did to Sings Pretty," Squire growled, thoughts of the treatment his young first wife had received almost blinding him with rage. "But I expect this be makin' some small difference in the afterworld."

Squire stood and started turning toward Carney. Another rifle barked, and he felt a searing pain in his left leg. He whirled, favoring the leg only a little.

Carney was standing, clutching a bloody hand. His rifle, a thin curl of smoke rising from the muzzle, was in the grass near his feet.

Squire glanced down at his leg. The ball from Carney's rifle had only grazed him. He looked back at the other figures. All were mounted and racing this way.

Squire stalked toward Carney. Along the way, he passed O'Neely. The young man was still alive, though in intense pain. Squire could see no reason for O'Neely living, with pain or not. He set his big right foot on O'Neely's throat and pressed.

O'Neely whimpered feebly once, and then his larynx cracked and splintered. A moment later he was dead.

Squire proceeded toward Carney again. Before he reached his old enemy, Li'l Jim, Train, Hannah, Gravant, and Ledoux rode up and pulled to a stop. It was a grim-looking group. Squire looked at them, grimacing sourly a little when he saw Gravant. As his friends dismounted, Squire strode up to Carney.

Carney had pulled a knife in his left hand and a tomahawk in the right. The hand was bloody, and Squire noticed that Carney no longer had a pinky on that hand.

"Where be my son?" Squire asked in a rough, flat voice. He stopped a few feet from Carney.

"With the bloody Blackfoot," Carney said coolly. He knew he was going to die, but he had been waiting for that for a long time. His only wish was that he take Nathaniel Squire with him.

"What band?"

Carney shrugged. He was determined that Squire would get nothing out of him.

Squire smiled cruelly. After all the years he had hunted this man, and with all the pain the man had brought him, he was glad Carney was being recalcitrant. It would make the slow, agonizing extraction of information all the more gratifying.

Squire moved up, not pulling a weapon. His bare hands would do. He crouched, arms outstretched, fingers slightly curled.

Carney came in fast. At the same time, he jabbed straight outward toward Squire's brisket with the knife and swung the tomahawk high at Squire's head.

Squire glided to his left, and the knife whistled through the air, not touching him. As the tomahawk descended, Squire zipped out his right hand and clamped it on Carney's arm. He swung around toward Carney's back, jerking Carney's arm up behind him, tearing ligaments and muscles. Carney gasped and involuntarily let go of the tomahawk.

At the same time, Squire snapped his left forearm around Carney's throat and applied a bit of pressure. "Drop your knife, lad," Squire said calmly.

Carney held onto the weapon defiantly. Squire applied more pressure to his neck and at the same time twisted and jerked Carney's arm up high behind him. Carney groaned and let the knife fall.

Squire let go of Carney's throat. With a none-too-gentle push, Squire shoved Carney around and away. With Carney facing him, stunned from the pain in his arm, Squire stepped up and kicked Carney with all his might, smashing the bottom of his foot against Carney's left leg, just above the knee. The leg bone fractured loudly, and Carney crumpled.

As Squire knelt alongside Carney, his friends gathered grimly, silently. They squatted in a circle around Carney. The fallen

man's teeth were clenched against the pain. He had seen how
Squire and even the old man Gravant had taken the torture in
the Blackfoot village so long ago. He was determined to take
anything Squire could mete out with the same nonchalance as
Squire had shown back then.

"Where be my son, lad?" Squire asked calmly. While the
blood lust and rage still boiled in his veins, it, like any pain
he might have felt, was not seen on his face or in his manner.
At least not yet.

"Told you, old chap," Carney hissed. His arm burned like
fire, and his leg pulsed as if someone were beating it steadily
with a hammer.

"Ye have a heap to be payin' for," Squire said, still calmly.
"Aye, lad, that ye do. And I aim to be seein' ye pay it in full
measure."

"Go to hell, you bloody, goddamn, piss-drinking son of a
bitch," Carney snarled low in his throat.

"Such talk ain't mannerly," Squire said quietly. He sighed.
"Mayhap ye don't be takin' me serious here, lad." His voice was
chillingly polite. "Your ol' pal, Isbister, seemed be thinkin' the
same a while back." He shook his head. "Now he be lyin' o'er
yonder there with his pecker and balls stuffed in his yap."

Gravant and Ledoux grinned harshly. To them it was appropriate retribution. But Li'l Jim and Train looked a little sick at
the thought. Hannah showed no emotion, though secretly she,
too, was glad for it. William Isbister was a vile man, and after
the threats he had made against her, she was not bothered by
what had befallen him.

Carney showed nothing either. He had seen such things far
too often. He was concentrating on controlling the pain and
trying to devise a way to kill Squire before he was put under
by Squire's friends.

"Where be my son?" Squire asked again. His voice had
taken on a note of harshness.

Carney spit at Squire.

-40-

Squire's face was a mask of rage and long-seated hate. He balled his right fist and smashed it down on Carney's broken leg. It brought an involuntary moan from Carney. But Squire did not stop there. He continued pounding Carney's body, cracking ribs and further shattering the fractured leg. He stayed away from blows to the face and head. He wanted Carney conscious and mostly coherent, not with his brain pounded to mush. When he thought Carney had had enough for a spell, he rocked back onto his heels, watching.

Carney took the beating mostly silently. Occasionally a grunt escaped. He concentrated on keeping his wits. Slowly, knowing Squire's attention was occupied, he worked his one good arm upward, so the hand was sliding behind his back. He tried to make the action look like an involuntary response to the pounding.

Finally his fingers found what they sought, and it was with some relief that he felt the solid wood and metal. He jerked himself up into a sitting position, while yanking out the small, .36-caliber pistol with the two-inch barrel.

But Squire's punches had taken their toll, and he was not very steady. He fired. The ball clipped the upper part of Squire's right shoulder, near where the shoulder and neck meet.

"Them was foolish doin's," Squire said coldly. He took the pistol from Carney's unprotesting fingers and tossed it far

271

away. Then he punched Carney as hard as he could in the side, crushing several ribs and knocking the wind out of him, putting Carney flat on his back again. Carney's breath came raggedly, and he groaned.

"Such foolish doin's that I be of a mind to prolong your sufferin'." He grinned, but it would chill the heart of even the devil himself. "I've learned a few things from the Injins, too, lad."

"You'll . . ." Carney said slowly, painfully, "get . . . no . . . screams . . . from . . . me . . . old chap." He sucked in a breath and tried to get a sentence out all at once. "No matter what you bloody do to me." He tried to spit at the big mountain man again, but was unsuccessful.

Squire pulled his Green River and sliced off Carney's shirt. With a grimly amused look, he began peeling the skin off the man's chest, a small strip at a time, the way the Blackfoot had once done to him.

Carney grimaced but no sounds uttered from his lips, other than an occasional agonized hissing.

"That's enough, Nathaniel," someone said.

Squire looked up with animal-like eyes. They seemed to gain a bit of their normal light, instead of the crazed look. "This be none of your affair, Hannah."

"Like hell, Nathaniel. I got reason to hate this bastard, too. So does nearly everyone of us here. But we ain't savages, nor Blackfeet."

Blood lust burned deep within Squire. It was almost uncontrollable. But he battled it back. He wiped the knife off and put it away. "Reckon ye be right, lass," he said quietly. With another chilling smile, he reached out one huge hand and grabbed a handful of Carney's crotch. He applied some pressure.

Carney gasped and lay rigid as a board. Any fight from him would bring only intense pain.

Squire squeezed harder. "Where be my son, lad?" he asked in a deadly monotone.

Carney sucked in a breath as his eyes widened immensely. He was unable to say anything, since he was trying to block out the pain of his testicles being crushed in Squire's viselike grip.

Train and Li'l Jim squirmed uncomfortably. Train looked almost sick at the thought of what Carney was enduring. Li'l

Jim felt the same, but he kept his face blandly impassive.

"Ease up," Carney finally managed to croak.

Squire relented, but only a little. "Tell me," he ordered.

"You'll kill me fast, old boy?" Carney asked. There was no pleading in his voice despite the pain reflected in his eyes.

"Aye."

Carney wasn't sure he could believe the giant, but if there was a possibility of going under without so much pain, he would like to take it. "He's still with Black Bull, a Blood war chief."

"Where's Black Bull be settin' his village?"

"Beyond the Milk River." He paused, licking his lips. He was still afraid to move, since Squire still had a grip on his crotch. "But you don't need to go all the way up there." He wished for the peace of death, and the sooner the better.

"Why?" Squire asked, masking his surprise.

"He was with the war party."

"Black Bull?"

"Yeah. Your son, too. He became a bloody warrior this summer."

Excitement pulsed through Squire's veins at the very thought that his son might be relatively close by. "Which way'd Black Bull and his boys go?" he asked, trying to hide the excitement.

"I've said enough," Carney commented. He grinned malignantly.

Squire's eyes colored with red as rage caught him again. He gave Carney's testicles a powerful squeeze.

Carney eyes widened so much they looked like they would split at the sides. Then the eyeballs rolled upward, and he passed out from the agony.

Squire leaned back. "Ye lads bring food?" he asked in normal tones.

"*Oui,*" Ledoux said with a nod.

"We'd best be eatin'. I be havin' some travelin' to do. Reckon a full meatbag'll be makin' it some easier."

Hannah and Train headed for the supplies on the horses. Li'l Jim went for firewood. Ledoux and Gravant moved to start unsaddling their and their traveling companions' horses.

Squire watched them a few moments before standing and stomping to *Noir Astre*. He unsaddled the great horse and then took some time rubbing the animal down.

By the time he was finished with that, the other animals also were unsaddled and grazing on the dying grass. A fire was going several yards from where the unconscious Carney lay. A coffeepot was sitting on a flat rock in it, and meat was hanging over the flames.

The six people ate silently. Afterward, while sipping at coffee, Squire lighted his pipe. Then he bluntly asked, "What're ye two ass lickers doin' here?" He looked from Ledoux to Gravant.

"Come to 'elp you—and get back at dose bastards," Ledoux said.

"Shit, had you goddamn chickenshits threw in with me years ago, we'd have took care of all this then." He spit into the fire.

"That ain't fair, Nathaniel," Hannah said.

"Hell, what do ye know about it, girl?" Squire growled. Hannah had become over the past several months about the only person who had ever been able to befuddle Nathaniel Squire. He had no clear idea of how to handle her. She was as fierce as any man when the need came, and she could take hard times with equanimity. She frequently was quiet, but when she had something to say, she said it, and more often than not, she hit the point right on the head.

"I know enough," Hannah said, only a little heatedly. "If it wasn't for Mister Gravant, you'd be dead now."

"Oh?" Squire didn't like where this was heading. He sighed. "Maybe ye best be tellin' it from the start."

By the time they had left Melton's camp, they were more than an hour behind Squire. Unlike Squire, though, they kept getting stopped by returning Shoshonis and Flatheads who wanted to tell of their exploits. Since Li'l Jim, Gravant, and Ledoux were married into one or the other of the bands, they could not be impolite to warriors who might also be family. Such things slowed them.

So did trying to follow the myraid trails that branched off. Now they were not just following Blackfoot sign, they were also trying to follow the sign of one person. That made it more difficult.

But after riding for an eternity, they finally came out onto a small glade, and they stopped, spotting some figures across the way. Ledoux had an old spyglass, which he brought out quickly. "It is him," he announced. "And 'e is facing several of de enemy."

"Carney and his men?" Train asked.

"*Oui.*"

"*Allons,*" Gravant said.

They started across the glade, Ledoux stopping every few feet to stare through the spyglass. Suddenly he gasped, and said, "*Merde.*"

"What is it?" Hannah asked, worried.

Before Ledoux could say anything, Li'l Jim shoved his horse forward. "Get the hell out of my way." He slid off his horse and brought up the old, finely made Hawken rifle. Swiftly he snapped back the hammer as he knelt.

Gravant wanted to tell him that the shot at this distance was impossible, but he did not want to spook the young man. It was with some sadness that he awaited the death of *L'on Farouche.*

Everyone else waited, too. They could see what was going on, but at the impossible distance of almost four hundred yards, it was hard to tell much.

Except for Li'l Jim. The young man was the best shot any of them had seen, except maybe for Squire, and part of the reason was his exceptional eyesight. He sighted down the long barrel of the rifle and held his breath, waiting for just the right moment. He could see the man advancing on the bent-over Squire as if the man was ten feet away instead of more than three hundred yards.

The man out there in the distance suddenly stopped right behind Squire. As he starting lifted the tomahawk to brain Squire, Li'l Jim fired.

There was a heart-stopping instant before the man sprawled, all akilter. Li'l Jim dropped his eyes, and let out the full lungs' worth of breath. He was by nature a cocky man, but he had had no certainty that he could make a shot like he just had. He had amazed even himself.

"*Allons. Vite,*" Gravant growled.

Li'l Jim looked up, half wanting to crow, half in a daze at his accomplishment. Then he nodded once. He was suddenly moving swiftly, swinging into his saddle without reloading. The five raced toward Squire and the others.

Then Li'l Jim yelled, "Look!" He pointed, cursing himself silently for not having reloaded his rifle.

Gravant jerked his horse to a stop and dropped over the side. He cocked his rifle, threw it over the saddle, sucked in a breath and fired.

The others, who had caught a glimpse of Gravant stopping, swung to either side so as not to be in his line of fire. They stopped as quickly as they could and watched, worried. They saw the figure with the rifle jerk and then drop the rifle. It was evident the man had been hit; it was also obvious he was not fatally hit.

Gravant let off a string of French, the only word of which the three Anglos understood was *merde.* He climbed into his saddle, and they raced onward. They finally reached Squire as he was stalking toward Carney with mayhem in his eyes.

"So you see, Nathaniel," Hannah said with an edge to her voice, "if it wasn't for Mister Gravant, you'd likely be dead now."

Squire almost smiled. "Shit, that old fart be luckier'n hell he hit anything, bad as he's been known to shoot." With food and coffee inside him, and a soothing pipe, Squire was feeling slightly more benevolent toward his old friend. Not much, but enough to abide him for a while.

Gravant grinned. He knew Squire retained a considerable amount of dislike for him, but would see that his old friend's mind eventually changed about him.

Squire looked at Li'l Jim. "That was some shot, if Hannah be tellin' true."

"Ah, hell, Nathaniel, it wasn't nothin' special." Li'l Jim was suddenly embarrassed as the attention turned on him. That was strange, since with his natural arrogance, he generally liked being the center of attention. He couldn't understand his sudden reticence.

"Buff'lo shit," Squire growled. He always found it hard to thank people. "I be obliged, lad." He relaxed. Saying thanks to a good friend wasn't all that hard. "It would've been some piss poor doin's was I to go under here."

Li'l Jim looked like he would burst with pride, but he said nothing.

Ledoux was the first to speak. "Well, wha' do we do now, *mon ami?*"

"Ye lads go back and help the Colonel."

"*Et vous?*" Ledoux asked, certain he knew.

Squire said nothing.

"We're goin' with ya," Hannah said flatly. Before Squire could say anything, she looked at him, her glittering green eyes boring into his. "And don't go makin' no speeches about how we ain't. We've been through such doin's too many times. We're all your friends here, and friends do for friends. We're goin' with ya, and there ain't nothin' you can say or do—short of puttin' us under—that'll prevent that." She downed the last of the coffee in her cup.

Squire almost grinned. Hannah Carpenter had spunk, that was sure. He nodded, knowing it would do no one any good to argue. Indeed, deep inside, he was glad they would be coming. He was, by nature, a solitary man, but he enjoyed company of a time. And having help, especially dependable people, when going up against an army of Blackfoot warriors certainly was a good idea.

"Where do we look?" Train asked.

"I'll be findin' out, lad," Squire said. His voice had taken on that hard edge again. "Hannah, ye and Abner start cleanin' up our things."

She started to question him but then decided against it when she saw the look on his face. They rose and started.

Squire stood and walked to Carney. The scalped man was still unconscious. Squire started urinating on Carney's face. Gravant and Ledoux joined him. After a moment's hesitation, Li'l Jim did the same.

The splattering warm liquid woke Carney, though he was still groggy. After readjusting his pants, Squire knelt alongside Carney. "If'n ye be thinkin' ye felt pain before, lad, ye just try to be avoidin' my question again. Now, where can I be findin' my son?"

"With Black Bull." He was having trouble focusing.

"Which way's he headin'?" Squire asked.

"Not sure."

"He planning to be meetin' up with the other bands somewhere?"

"Yes."

"Where?"

Carney hesitated, partly because his concentration was shaky, partly because he knew that once he talked he would be dead. He did not have the strength to yelp when Squire jammed a thumb in an eye. "Northwest. Up where Cottonwood Creek and Fish Creek flow into the Gros Ventre."

"*Bon*," Squire said with a nod. He rose. "*Allons.*" He spun and headed toward *Noir Astre*. He quickly saddled the horse and mounted. The others were right behind him in finishing.

"What about him?" Ledoux asked, pointing to Carney.

Squire shrugged. "My business with that chil' be done," he said with finality.

"But he ain't dead," Hannah said with some horror.

"He will be soon enough," Squire said flatly. He turned the stallion's head and rode off.

-41-

They crept up on more than half a dozen Blackfoot bands before they finally found the one they wanted. Ledoux knew of Black Bull and was able to recognize him.

It was late in the afternoon when they heard the sounds of a camp. They crept up a forested hill, moving warily on the precarious footing, until they were overlooking the camp being built on some unnamed stream.

Gravant stayed behind around the peak, on a grassy flat, watching over the horses, while the other five went and sat on the hill, checking out the camp. Finally Ledoux pointed, "Dere 'e is."

"That fat ol' son of a bitch be Black Bull?" Squire asked.

"*Oui.*"

Squire nodded. He kept watching the camp. Suddenly he stiffened. Coming out from behind a screen of brush, with a deer carcass across his shoulders was a young Blackfoot warrior. The warrior had light hair and was taller than most of the men. Squire guessed he had blue eyes.

Hannah had spotted him, too. "That your son?" she asked softly, touching Squire's arm lightly.

"Aye." His eyes were focused hard. He could see no reason to wait. It would not be dark for another couple of hours, but Squire was too eager to be able to just sit here. It had been more than a dozen years since he had seen the boy, he did not want to wait even another couple of hours. He rose and began making his way back across the face of the tree-covered mountain. The others followed.

"Is Black Bull dere?" Gravant asked when they began to mount.

Squire only nodded and pulled *Noir Astre* around. Once again, the others followed silently. Squire led them straight into the Blackfoot camp. He rode arrogantly at their head, the butt of his Hawken rifle resting on his right thigh, the barrel skyward.

Warriors watched him in surprise, as he stopped. He spit some tobacco juice on the ground to his side. "I be *L'on Farouche!*" he bellowed. "And I be lookin' for my son who be took from me a heap of years ago."

"There no one like that here," one warrior said. He stood with arms crossed across his burly chest. His hooked nose lent a patrician arrogance to the man.

Squire lowered the rifle and shot the man. He slid the rifle away and dismounted. The others did the same. "Ledoux, *gardez-vous les chevals*—watch the horses."

Ledoux nodded and took all the horses. He moved them back a little way, giving his companions room to maneuver.

"Either be givin' up my son, or come against me, lads," he challenged.

The Blackfoot warriors stared at him for a few moments, wondering if they were seeing an apparition. Then most of them charged, the rest headed for the cover of the trees.

Gravant and Train slid out tomahawks; Hannah and Li'l Jim would rely on their Green River knives. There was no time to think, just react. Each unconsciously picked out a warrior as his or her target and headed for the charging Blackfoot.

A warrior named Walks In Thunder, carrying a war club of pointed bone lashed to a hickory staff, rushed at Train. He swung the war club at Train's head, fierceness stamped on his face.

Train fell, rolled, and sprang up. Walks In Thunder turned and charged again, the war club whistling as it headed for Train's skull. Once more, Train dropped and rolled. But when he came up this time, he slipped his tomahawk away. He would concentrate on getting Walks In Thunder's weapon away from him.

Walks In Thunder grunted something in Blackfoot. Train could not understand him, but he caught the warrior's meaning when he saw the man's smirk.

"Eat shit, ol' hoss," Train muttered, "You don't scare me none, goddamnit." He wasn't sure he believed it, and he knew the Blackfoot could not understand him anyway. He just hoped he presented the right picture of fearlessness to the warrior.

Walks In Thunder moved fast and with certainty, swinging the war club in wicked little arcs, weaving a pattern in the air as the weapon sought out Train's head.

Train ducked and bobbed, fell and rolled, ran, whatever it took. He presented no target to the well-muscled Blackfoot. Walks In Thunder began to slow a little, and Train suddenly rushed up and in, grabbing the arm holding the weapon with both hands.

They stood nose to nose, sweat forming rivulets on their faces, breathing hard. Train squeezed with all his might, feeling the muscles in Walks In Thunder's bulging forearm, trying to get his foe to drop the club.

Suddenly Walks In Thunder lashed out and punched Train on the cheek with his left hand, making Train's head ring. But Train did not let go. Walks In Thunder hit him again and again. After the fourth blow, Train finally released his grip. He staggered back a few steps, shaking his head. He was open, vulnerable, and Walks In Thunder licked his meaty lips in anticipation of the kill. He brought the war club up in both hands, like an executioner with his ax.

Hannah suddenly leaped onto the Blackfoot's back, clamping her left arm around Walks In Thunder's throat and raking her short, ragged fingernails across his face, aiming for his eyes.

Walks In Thunder bellowed like a wounded bear, and his swing was a little off, nicking Train's shoulder. Hannah jammed a thumbnail into Walks In Thunder's one eye and ground it around. The man grunted and hissed. He grabbed Hannah's left arm and pried it from around his throat, then yanked hard, pulling her down and over his shoulder.

Hannah landed with a thump, her breath whooshing out. Walks In Thunder kicked her in the side. He lifted his foot to do it again, but Train slammed into him, tackling him. Walks In Thunder managed to hit Train in the side with the war club, but he had little leverage, and the blow was only a glancing one. Train pummeled him with his right hand, scrabbling for the war club with his other.

Walks In Thunder shoved Train off to the side, and they both staggered up. They faced each other warily, each man breathing heavily. Tears seeped from Walks In Thunder's damaged eye.

Hannah was up, too, and had run back to where she had started her battle. Tall Bow was a young, seemingly inexperienced warrior. He apparently had planned on impressing his elders. But Hannah fought as well as he, and it unnerved him.

Hannah danced away, always just out of reach of the Indian's two flickering blades. She darted in and out, her own knife glittering, drawing blood nearly each time she moved in.

Exasperated, he finally grabbed her in a bear hug when she came in on him once. He squeezed. His eyes opened wide in shock as he realized he had a woman—a white woman, no less—in his embrace.

Hannah spit on Tall Bow's face and bit his nose hard. Tall Bow howled and let her go, falling back a few steps. The warrior was stunned more by the realization that she was a woman than by the pain from his bleeding nose.

Hannah stood a moment, blowing heavily. She glanced around. "Oh, damn," she muttered, seeing Train in trouble. She did not hesitate. She kicked Tall Bow in the groin, spun and ran. Then she leaped on Walks In Thunder's back.

Now she had returned to finish the job.

Tall Bow had straightened. He was angry now, hateful. He no longer cared that she was a woman, not after she had kicked him in his manhood. He would show her now. Not only would he pound her into submission, he would take her forcefully, as a man should take a woman. He might even share her with his friends when he was finished with her.

But Hannah was angry, too. She had been unworried about fighting Tall Bow. But Train's being in danger had angered her no end. That and the fact that battles swirled around her. It was hot, noisy, and downright frightening. She wanted to kill this obnoxious young warrior and go help Train again.

Hannah feinted and jabbed, keeping Tall Bow off balance, not letting him bring his knives into play. But Hannah had a natural affinity with a knife, it seemed. A blade was almost an extension of her arm. Tall Bow had no chance. A few more feints and suddenly Hannah was face-to-face with Tall Bow, her knife buried deep in his gut and ripping upward.

The initial shock of it stopped him cold, and Tall Bow stood, silent. His eyes grew wide as the sharp blade tore through his vitals. He started to sag, but Hannah would not let him fall. She looked around, feeling strange at the streak of viciousness she felt. But this was a Blackfoot warrior, even if he was of a different band than the one who defiled her. The revenge was good.

Li'l Jim sliced off Bull Hump's scalp and yelled once in victory. His battle had been short. Bull Hump was not much bigger than Li'l Jim, but he was older and more weary. Still, the light of excitement was in his eyes as Li'l Jim dashed at him, knife held easily, prodding the air in Bull Hump's direction.

Bull Hump stood his ground, fending off the feints and jabs of Li'l Jim's knife with his tomahawk, the metal clanging dully. Li'l Jim caught a glimpse of Hannah flying past him, and risked a quick look to see her save Train.

Bull Hump also noted it, and he charged. Li'l Jim ducked and shoved forward, coming up inside Bull Hump's guard. The tomahawk hit off his back lightly after Bull Hump's arm struck his shoulder, knocking the 'hawk loose. Li'l Jim stabbed him three times in rapid succession, each bringing a grunt of pain from Bull Hump. It was only after Bull Hump had fallen onto his back, his blank eyes staring straight at the sun, did Li'l Jim realize how scared he had been. He pushed the fear away.

He moved in to quickly take Bull Hump's scalp. Then he glanced around, looking as to where he could be the most help to his friends. He had no concern for Squire.

The giant mountain man was his usual self in such a time and place. He seemed to be everywhere, ravaging through the camp like a madman, tomahawk and knife flashing in the dying afternoon sunlight. Most of the Blackfoot warriors were trying to avoid the whirling steel wielded by the giant, as they had been from the beginning. A few had tried at first to take the monster, hoping that it would break the medicine of these white invaders. They had learned quickly that such a thing was foolish.

Li'l Jim turned. Squire was in no danger. The young man turned to face another charging opponent when he saw that Hannah and Train also were faring all right.

Train had kicked Walks In Thunder in the face as both were trying to get up. Walks In Thunder fell back, his grip on the war club loosening. Train kicked the weapon away and drew out his tomahawk as Walks In Thunder managed to get up.

Walks In Thunder rushed Train, taking him a little by surprise. As he grabbed the younger man, he snatched his patch knife from a strap around his neck, ignoring the punches Train pelted him with.

Suddenly Train felt a sharp pain, then another. His arms exploded outward, breaking Walks In Thunder's grip. He moved back a few steps and touched his side. His hand came away with blood. "You bastard," he muttered as he looked at Walks In Thunder, bloody patch knife in hand grinning ruthlessly.

All sorts of threats and condemnation fluttered into Train's brain, but he shoved them aside as useless. He crouched a little, the tomahawk swinging lightly in front of him as he moved forward. "You're gonna be one unsightly niggur once this chil' gets done with ya," Train snarled.

"Come," Walks In Thunder said. His chest heaved.

Train moved fast, tomahawk swinging from both hands. Walks In Thunder tried weaving out of the way, but Train would have none of it; he just keep bearing down.

Walks In Thunder threw the patch knife, but it bounced harmlessly off Train's chest. The youth did not even slow.

Walks In Thunder ripped out his big knife, spitting out some blood. He came in with a thrust, and Train whipped the tomahawk around, slicing a large chunk of flesh from Walks In Thunder's arm. The Blackfoot dropped the knife.

"It's all over for you now, goddamnit," Train snapped.

Walks In Thunder spun and ran for the trees. Train threw the tomahawk, catching Walks In Thunder in the back, knocking him forward onto his face, where he lay, making a few feeble attempts to get up.

Train walked up, looking over at the rest of the fighting. Li'l Jim was rolling on the ground with another warrior, near a Blackfoot body. Hannah was face to face with Tall Bow, and Train thought to hurry over there to help her. But he could see the only connection was Hannah's knife, which was tearing a trail north from Tall Bow's stomach.

He saw another warrior heading for Hannah. Without thinking, but with his heart in his throat, he snatched out his pistol and fired. The warrior pirouetted and fell. When he landed, he was dead.

Finally Hannah could hold Tall Bow up no longer, and she let him fall, yanking her knife free as she did. She whirled, her face feral-looking, teeth bared. She spotted a warrior falling and noted Train with his smoking pistol in hand. She also saw that Li'l Jim seemed to be doing all right with his new foe. But Gravant looked like he could use some help.

The French-Canadian was being punished by a warrior named Shot in the Foot, who was pounding Gravant unmercifully with ham-sized fists. Nearly each blow split open flesh. Gravant had managed to get in a few licks early, and both men were covered in blood.

Gravant had blocked Shot in the Foot's first swing of his tomahawk with his own. He also parried half a dozen others. Then Gravant started to swing his own 'hawk. Shot in the Foot easily fended off the blow, and then slammed Gravant in the side of the head with the underside of his left fist. The blow shook Gravant, and he dropped his tomahawk.

Shot in the Foot kicked Gravant, who went rolling in the grass. As Gravant came to a halt and scrambled up, he pulled a knife. Shot in the Foot kicked him in the face, knocking him down again. Gravant lost the knife.

The warrior laughed and slid his tomahawk away.

Gravant scrabbled in the dirt and came up with the Green River. Then he rose unsteadily. Gravant thrust at Shot in the Foot, who spun easily sideways and sucked in his gut. The knife just missed, and he grabbed it, his hand half on the blade and half on the wooden hilt. His other hand grabbed Gravant's knife wrist and squeezed it until the fingers opened. Shot in the Foot flung the knife away into the dust.

"White-eyes die now," Shot in the Foot said gruffly.

"*Le merde,*" Gravant spit. "You 'ave no balls. Come and kill me den, you big, brave piece of shit." His voice dripped with scorn.

Shot in the Foot grinned and pulled his tomahawk again. As he swung it, Gravant tried feebly to ward off the blow. The metal blade nearly severed the arm just below the elbow. Gravant collapsed.

Shot in the Foot howled a war cry and lashed out with the tomahawk again and again. Gravant did his best to defend himself, but it was of little use. Gravant had resigned himself to a painful, bloody demise.

Gravant heard a loud, banshee shriek and waited for his end. But the rain of metal stopped. Through the haze of pain and blood, Gravant saw Hannah hanging like a leech on Shot in the Foot's back. The warrior was bellowing and jerking himself around, trying to fling the clutching demon from his back.

Hannah had seen Gravant's plight and ran for him. She saw Shot in the Foot hacking Gravant to bits. She screamed in rage and launched herself at the Blackfoot. When she landed, she locked her legs around his waist. Her left hand grabbed a shank of long greasy hair. With the knife in her right, she slashed at Shot in the Foot anywhere she could reach.

Shot in the Foot roared in anger. He finally flopped down onto his back, eliciting a muffled, painful grunt from Hannah. But she did not quit. Her knife flashed in and out. Shot in the Foot growled and tried to turn, to get at the raving beast slashing wildly at him. But Hannah was still locked onto him and moved where he did.

The Blackfoot's struggles began to weaken. Hannah kept stabbing Shot in the Foot until the warrior was still. She strained and struggled to get the Indian's heavy body off her. She finally did and lay there a moment trying to breathe.

It was strangely quiet, she realized. Then Train was looming over her on one side and Li'l Jim on the other. The two helped her up. She looked around, dazed. They had the battlefield to themselves.

"Mister Gravant," Hannah said. The three turned toward the bloody, prone figure.

Squire stood, breathing hard from his exertions. Three bodies lay within several feet of him. Others were more scattered. It took him a few moments to come back to his senses from the blood-soaked world in which he had been.

Slowly he straightened. He craned his head around, looking at the camp. "I be *L'on Farouche!*" he bellowed. "Where be my son?" The sound was eerie as it fought its way through the foliage and the sky.

-42-

Squire spun and ran for his horse. He leaped onto the great beast's back and kicked him into motion. He pounded through the camp and disappeared into the trees.

"Damn," Train muttered, worried about Squire and wondering what he should do. It took him all of two seconds to decide. "Li'l Jim," he ordered, "stay here with Marcel. Hannah, come on!" Without waiting for argument or discussion, he sprinted. A moment later he was in the saddle and racing after Squire. Hannah was right behind him.

Li'l Jim cursed a blue streak, wanting to go with Train and Hannah, but unwilling to leave Ledoux alone. He would do as he was told. That didn't mean he had to like it, though.

As soon as the quiet solitude of the trees enveloped him, Train realized the danger of his course of action. There were a passel of Blackfeet still alive, and many of them could be lurking behind the trees, ready to kill him and Hannah. It was too late now, though; he had to press ahead and hope for the best.

A few minutes later, Train saw movement ahead and jerked the reins hard. Right behind him, Hannah reacted instantly, but still almost ran her horse into Train's.

The two breathed in relief when they saw it was Squire. The huge man had a young, struggling Blackfoot across the saddle in front of him. Squire looked more uncomfortable than the dangling captive.

"That him?" Train asked. He felt funny, almost as if he had lost a father or something. He knew deep down that he saw Squire as something of a father, but he did not want to admit that.

"Aye, lad." Squire was tremendously ill at ease.

They rode back to the Blackfoot camp. Li'l Jim and Ledoux were herding Indian ponies into a pen made of ropes strung from tree to tree.

Squire stopped where the Blackfeet had started to build a fire. He shoved Blue Mountain off *Noir Astre*. The boy landed in a heap on the ground. Before the youth could rise, Squire was off the horse and grabbed Blue Mountain by the back of the buckskin war shirt and hauled him up.

Squire felt odd. On one hand, he wanted to, would normally, just thunk the Indian on the head to quiet him down. He had fought Blackfeet for too long not to feel that way. But this was his son, and he could not see him maltreating the boy that way. He finally settled for engulfing the youth in a bear hug. "Now stop your fussin', lad," he said gruffly. "It ain't gonner be doin' ye no good."

Blue Mountain continued to struggle, trying not to show the fear that had budded inside him.

"Ease up now, lad," Squire snapped, irritation growing, "Or I'll be trussin' ye up."

The young warrior began to realize the futility of resisting. He knew this giant could have easily killed him before. He did not know why this man, whom he assumed to be the fearsome creature his people called *L'on Farouche,* had not killed him. Perhaps it was to test his bravery with some torture. If so, he was determined to show his mettle. He quit struggling.

"Set, lad," Squire said, relieved that the youth was not fighting any longer. He released him. When the young man had sat cross-legged on the ground, Squire said, "Abner, ye and Hannah best be keepin' an eye on this here lad. He looks to be takin' off, ye do whate'er ye need to to stop him. Short of puttin' him under, of course."

Train and Hannah nodded solemnly, understanding the importance of their duty. Squire walked off to where Li'l Jim and Ledoux were just finishing the circle of rope, completing the corral for the Blackfoot ponies.

"Gravant?" Squire asked.

"*Il est mort,*" Ledoux said with a catch in his voice.

Squire nodded. He had assumed so. He wasn't sure if he was bothered by it. He and Etienne Gravant had been through some hellacious times together, but of late, he had found himself disgusted with what he saw as Gravant's lack of courage.

"I'm sorry, Nathaniel," Li'l Jim said.

Squire nodded. "Go on o'er with the others," he said. "Mayhap ye can get a fire goin' and see if'n ye can find some meat or somethin'."

"Damn, why me?" Li'l Jim grumbled only half-seriously. "Why's it always me got to do such work. Hell, that's woman's work."

"Ye find yourself a woman 'round here to take o'er such doin's, have at it, lad," Squire said without humor. He had too many things on his mind to worry about Li'l Jim's hurt feelings, real or not.

"There's Hannah," Li'l Jim said. He was not serious at all now.

"Ye got the balls to tell her she's got to be doin' such things, ye be a better man than most, lad," Squire said, nearly grinning.

"I expect she needs her rest anyway," Li'l Jim said with bravado. He smiled and headed off.

"Get some shovels, *mon ami,*" Squire said, turning to look at Ledoux.

The French-Canadian nodded and walked toward their horses. When he returned, Squire had moved off a little and found an appropriate spot. He was waiting. The two began digging. About the time they had a proper-size hole dug, Li'l Jim walked up with a Hudson Bay blanket in hand. He handed it silently to Ledoux, who took it with a nod of thanks. Li'l Jim glanced at Squire, who smiled fractionally, letting the young man know he had done the right thing. Li'l Jim, feeling good and sad at the same time, went back to tend the fire.

Squire and Ledoux wrapped Gravant's body in the blanket and placed their old friend in the grave. Ledoux gently placed Gravant's rifle and pistol on the body. Squire added a few pieces of jerky, a deck of cards, and two traps—the only ones anyone had brought. Squire figured that with the items, plus what Gravant had in his possibles sack, the old man would be able to make his way to the afterworld comfortably.

Within minutes, Ledoux and Squire had covered over the grave. They trampled the dirt as flat as they could and they covered it over with some rocks. As Ledoux knelt and offered up some prayers in both French and Latin, Squire headed to the fire. He sat and gratefully took the cup of coffee Li'l Jim handed him.

Squire looked deep into the Indian boy's blue eyes. It was eerie seeing a young, duskier version of himself. "Do ye know who I be, lad?" he asked.

"You are *L'on Farouche*," he said uneasily in Blackfoot. "An enemy of the Blackfoot." His eyes looked distinctly uncomfortable and thoroughly mystified, though his face was serene.

"Aye, I be that, lad. But I also be your father."

The youth showed horror at the very thought.

"Aye, lad. Ye be no Blackfoot. Ye be half-white and the other half Nez Perce. Ye and your ma was took from me whilst ye was but a babe. Abel Carney and his lads did it." His face darkened with the years of anger that still were not expunged with the vengeance he had exacted.

He battled the fury and relaxed. "I tried to get ye back, lad," he finally said. "Aye, for many a year I sought ye out. But I never was able to find ye nor those depredatin' sons a bitches. Till now."

"You lie." The youth was angry and scared. "I am Blackfoot. I am called Light Eyes. I am the son of Black Bull."

Squire's next comment was interrupted by a wild screech. As Squire stood and half turned toward the sound, Black Bull flew out of the trees.

Black Bull slammed into Squire, who grabbed the Blackfoot and flung him aside. Squire whirled and took two steps toward the sprawling Black Bull. Then Light Eyes leaped on his back.

Blood lust swept over Squire, and he entered another world, one in which he reverted to complete savagery. He grabbed his son by the hair and jerked him off, flinging him to the ground. Then he went for Black Bull. He smashed the warrior

back down, yanked out his knife, and moved in to finish the
Blackfoot off.

As Squire knelt on Black Bull's chest and brought his knife
up, Hannah screamed, "Nathaniel, no!"

At the same time, Train bolted up and tackled Light Eyes,
who had been ready to launch himself at Squire again.

Squire froze with his knife an inch from the pulsing carotid
in Black Bull's neck. He rose, grabbing Black Bull's shirt in
his left hand and hauled the warrior up. He turned and shoved
Black Bull toward the fire. "Set your ass down, lad," Squire
growled. His blood was still hot with the desire to kill, and he
was having a difficult time controlling it.

Train and Li'l Jim were sitting on Light Eyes, who was
struggling, though with little effort.

"Best be lettin' him up, lads," Squire said, regaining most
of his composure. When Li'l Jim and Train moved, Light Eyes
rose slowly. "Set next to Black Bull, lad, and don't be causin'
me no more goddamn trouble," Squire said evenly.

Light Eyes sat sullenly, and Squire turned to Ledoux, who
had hurried up during the brief fight. "Take a look around,
Marcel. Check and see if there be any other of these fractious
assholes lurkin' about ready to cause us grief."

"*Oui.*" Ledoux moved off.

"Best be helpin' him, Li'l Jim," Squire added.

The young man nodded and left, going in a different direction
than Ledoux had.

Squire sat. He cut off some meat and tossed it to Black Bull.
He did the same with Light Eyes. Then he sliced some for
himself. Train and Hannah got their own. Everyone but Light
Eyes tore into the meat. Finally, even the youth began to eat.

Finally Squire wiped his hands. "Ye heard what I told the
lad before, Black Bull?" he asked.

The warrior grunted acknowledgement.

"Then mayhap ye'd be tellin' him the truth of it." It was an
order, not a suggestion.

Black Bull shrugged. He could see no reason not to. He
was frightened in the presence of the Blackfoot's long-time
enemy, though one could not tell it on his face. "What *L'on
Farouche* says is true," Black Bull said harshly. "You will go
with him now."

"No," Light Eyes said adamantly. "I am Blackfoot. He is *L'on Farouche*. Enemy of my people."

"Aye, lad, I be that. I've fought the Blackfoot for many a year, over many a mile, lad." He spoke almost dreamily.

Black Bull felt a touch of pride. *L'on Farouche* was a mighty warrior and the Blackfoot by being his enemy became greater for it. "He speaks the truth, Light Eyes," Black Bull said.

The young, new warrior shook his head, not wanting to believe.

Squire nodded. "Your ma be a Nez Perce named Sings Pretty, lad," he said quietly. "We named you Ezekiel after my own pa, as well as your Nez Perce name, Blue Mountain. Ye was borned . . ."

Squire began telling the youth of his mother, of how the boy was taken, how his mother was defiled, and how she died, of Squire's hate for Carney and all the Blackfoot.

While Squire did that, Ledoux and Li'l Jim returned and sat quietly. "All is clear, *mon ami*," Ledoux said.

The youth sat and listened, dim memories dredged up on occasion. He and Squire were oblivious to the others, who sat or stood or dozed, waiting for them to finish. Light Eyes did not want to believe, resisted believing, but slowly he found he could do nothing else, especially after Black Bull added a note of confirmation now and again.

As Squire spoke, Light Eyes looked at his father with growing fear, admiration, and respect. Still, the youth said nothing.

Finally Squire stopped. "I've plumb talked myself out, lad," he concluded. Though Light Eyes still had not said anything, Squire somehow knew the youth accepted the truth of his parentage. "I ain't said so many words in the last ten year all together. But now that ye be knowin' of me and your ma, I'd like ye to be comin' with me to the settlements. And then to the mountains when the new beaver season be comin' on us."

"No. My place is here," Light Eyes said. There was no arrogance or defiance in his voice, only a note of reality. "These are my people now. The Blackfoot have raised me, cared for me, taught me. I have gone on the hunt with the men and now I have faced others in battle. I can sit in their councils. What can you give me that they can't?"

"Not a heap, I reckon." Squire looked pained. "I'd still be likin' it, though."

Light Eyes nodded, accepting that. It did not change his mind however. He could see no other life for himself. He had all he could need in the mountainous home of the Blood bands of the Blackfoot people. There he could find plenty of buffalo, elk, and mountain sheep. The water was cold and good. He had his eye on a young maiden named White Flower. A few raids against the American trappers and against the Crows and Nez Perce, and he would have enough horses to get himself a wife.

No, he was certain that this *L'on Farouche,* his father, could give him nothing.

Squire sat thinking. The meeting with his son hadn't quite been what he had expected or hoped for. He had sought it for so many years, had fixed it in his mind how it should be, that the reality was a disappointment. Perhaps, he thought, he should leave well enough alone. Ride out and forget he ever had a son. With Star Path pregnant, maybe another son would come along.

The thoughts jumbled around in his mind. First, a picture of an innocent babe, swaddled in a woolen trade blanket, then a picture of a huge, burgeoning Blackfoot warrior, face painted, one who might one day try to kill him as an enemy. Which was real, if either? he wondered.

While Squire had talked, Train, Hannah, and Ledoux unsaddled the horses, then returned. All sat with their own thoughts, nibbling meat or sipping coffee. None had had food since dawn, and they were ravenous.

Full dark had fallen over them. Hannah and Train, tired from their long day and the battle, wandered a few feet away from the fire and stretched out their bedrolls. Li'l Jim soon followed.

Ledoux lasted a while longer, before asking Squire, "You t'ink it's safe to leave de 'orses with no one watching dem?"

"Aye." Squire glared at Black Bull. "I'll be settin' up a spell."

Ledoux nodded. He moved off and crawled into his blankets.

Squire spent the night talking with Light Eyes, regaling the youth with stories of his fights with the Blackfoot and other Indians. He explained about old Marchand and LeGrande and more.

Black Bull got into the discussion from time to time, occasionally dozing off in between.

Just before dawn, Light Eyes stood and stretched. He wandered into the bushes to relieve himself. When he came back, he rummaged in the scattered supplies, came up with meat and put it to cook.

The sizzling meat woke the others, and they were soon huddled around the fire in various stages of wakefulness. After they had eaten and polished off more coffee, Li'l Jim said, "Well, what's it gonna be, Nathaniel?"

Squire glared at him. The giant seemed none the worse for not having slept in two full days. Then he looked at Black Bull and Light Eyes. He could sense an expectancy in the two Blackfeet.

He nodded. "Ye lads best be goin'," he said to Light Eyes and Black Bull. "Ye hurry, ye can be catchin' up to your *amis* afore long." He paused. "But I don't expect ye to be comin' after us, eh?"

The two stood and turned. They moved off, still half expecting to get shot in the back. Black Bull disappeared in the trees and foliage. Light Eyes was about to follow, but he stopped and turned to look at Squire, who was watching him. He nodded once and made a sign of friendship and respect. Then he, too, was gone.

Squire stood and began saddling *Noir Astre*. His face betrayed no emotion. The others silently began preparing to leave. Finally, Squire mounted. With a wave of his hand, he indicated that Ledoux should lead off. The others followed quietly, seeming afraid to say anything. Squire brought up the rear.

Ledoux hesitated near Gravant's grave for a moment and murmured a prayer in French. Then he rode on.

As they moved onto the trail between the trees, heading up the hill, Squire stopped and looked back. There was no sign of Light Eyes.

Finding his son had been anticlimactic. There had been an acknowledgement of mutual respect, but no great profession of love on either side—indeed, they were still enemies. Squire realized finally that his searching all these years was for something he never had—and never could have. He had only known that something had been taken from him, and he had to get that thing back, not for the boy, but for himself.

With a sigh, he decided he could live with his son as a Blackfoot, but he was not sure he could face his son in battle if it ever came to that, which it very well might. Still, something had touched him when he saw the big, strapping youth.

Hannah had stopped and watched Squire silently from a few feet away. As the big man turned back to the trail, she was sure she saw a look of infinite sadness on his face. He scowled for a moment, angry at having someone intrude on his private moment.

Then he half-smiled. "Best be movin' your ass, girl," he muttered.

She smiled back, but she did not move. "You gonna be all right, Nathaniel?" she asked quietly.

"Aye, girl." He flashed his biggest smile. With friends like Hannah and Li'l Jim and Train, he would indeed be all right.